Old Soul

'A sweeping work of literary horror . . . Eerie and suspenseful . . . The slow-burning tension and lush, atmospheric prose build a creeping sense of dread that lingers long after the final page. Fans of both the deeply personal speculative horror of Carmen Maria Machado and the subtle, character-driven mystery of Haruki Murakami will be enthralled' *Publishers Weekly*, starred review

'A perfect novel, one that is so compelling and criminally well written that you can't put it down . . . I can't stop thinking about it' Book Riot

'*The Ministry of Time* meets *The Leviathan* in this deeply imaginative, beautifully written hunt across centuries and continents' *Bookseller*, Editor's Choice

'*Old Soul* is an utterly addictive and completely immersive novel. Beautifully written and filled with engrossing characters and unforgettable landscapes, it is the most propulsive thing I have read all year' Lara Williams, author of *Supper Club*

'An extraordinary achievement. A brutal interrogation of art, connection and the meaning of and impulse toward life itself. I couldn't put it down' Beth Underdown, author of *The Witchfinder's Sister*

'A twisting, expansive epic of menacing wonder. This is a novel of expertly restrained power: a wild cat in a bejewelled cage' Kirsty Logan, author of *Now She is Witch*

'*Old Soul* enticed me in with a chance meeting between mysterious strangers with one thing in common: a nameless horror that haunts them. The novel that follows is expansive, twisty, gripping and intelligent; I loved it' Jenn Ashworth, author of *Ghosted*

'Beautifully written and at times terrifying . . . I was completely swept up in the atmosphere of the book and the plot continues to haunt and unsettle me, in the very best of ways' Emily Midorikawa, author of *Out of the Shadows*

'Susan Barker's diabolically haunting novel begs to be read over and over, its intertwined stories a feat of literary prestidigitation. Darkly magical and irresistible, *Old Soul* feels like it reveals a truth that's been long buried in our collective unconscious' Alma Katsu, author of *The Hunger*

'An enthralling, gritty fever dream of a novel and a fable for the modern age' Lucy Rose, author of *The Lamb*

'Elegant and eerie, mesmerizing and compelling, *Old Soul* is like a glorious and terrible nightmare that you never want to wake up from' Sam Mills, author of *The Watermark*

'Brilliantly thought-provoking, disturbing and highly complex, with the pace of a thriller and the heart of a tragic love story' Caroline Lea, author of *Prize Women*

'Sinister, mysterious and gorgeously realized, *Old Soul* is as good on the horror and subliminity of love (and its shadow, loneliness) as it is on nerve-flaying visions of the vicious supernatural' Kaliane Bradley, author of *The Ministry of Time*

'*Old Soul* is a mesmerizing story brilliantly told. The way the novel slowly reveals its dark secrets as it moves with ease and elegance across continents and eras is hugely impressive' Ian McGuire, author of *The North Water*

'*Old Soul* is like nothing else I've ever read . . . More than anything, though, I loved how it made me feel: like I'd woken up after a long sleep to see for the first time how terrifying and strange the contemporary world has become. This the kind of story you tell around a campfire as the lights of civilization begin flicker out around you; a global, intelligent and ambitious archetypal nightmare' Kristen Roupenian, author of *Cat Person*

'*Old Soul* snags the reader in its claw and mesmerizes from page one. I often wondered if I was devouring the story or vice versa, I was so engrossed. It is not an option to put this book down' Monique Roffey, author of *The Mermaid of Black Conch*

'Beguiles, terrifies and utterly seduces you as swiftly and slyly as the mysterious woman at its centre. It's at once a thriller, a postmodern mystery and an existential horror tale, but perhaps most deeply it speaks to our current moment: the drift and terrors of loneliness, the risks of intimacy and a piercing nostalgia that never lets us go' Megan Abbott, author of *El Dorado Drive*

'Sinister, unnerving and nightmarish. *Old Soul* will sneak into your dreams and haunt you' Claire Fuller, author of *Unsettled Ground*

'*Old Soul* is the perfect read for the chilly depths of winter: a clever, spooky metaphysical mystery that spans continents – and even planets. Susan Barker's novel kept me guessing until the end. You'll never look at Venus quite the same way again' Chloe Benjamin, author of *The Immortalists*

Old Soul

SUSAN BARKER

FIG TREE
an imprint of
PENGUIN BOOKS

FIG TREE

UK | USA | Canada | Ireland | Australia
India | New Zealand | South Africa

Fig Tree is part of the Penguin Random House group of companies
whose addresses can be found at global.penguinrandomhouse.com

Penguin Random House UK,
One Embassy Gardens, 8 Viaduct Gardens, London SW11 7BW

penguin.co.uk

Penguin
Random House
UK

First published 2025

001

Copyright © Susan Barker, 2025

Set in 12/14.75pt Dante MT Std
Typeset by Jouve (UK), Milton Keynes
Printed and bound in Great Britain by Clays Ltd, Elcograf S.p.A.

The authorized representative in the EEA is Penguin Random House Ireland,
Morrison Chambers, 32 Nassau Street, Dublin D02 YH68

A CIP catalogue record for this book is available from the British Library

HARDBACK ISBN: 978-0-241-68238-8
TRADE PAPERBACK ISBN: 978-0-241-68239-5

For Glen

Contents

Taos County, 1982

August 1st

I woke before dawn to an empty mattress. Wrapped myself in a bedsheet & went outside to find E on the bench in the clearing, staring out across the drought-stripped plains to the Sangre de Cristo Mountains; a jagged line against the shadowy blue sky. She was naked, near luminescent in the half-dark. Hearing my footsteps, she spoke without turning.

I couldn't sleep.

The wooden bench creaked as I sat besides her. I could sense she didn't want to be touched, & chilly though it was, I suppressed the urge to wrap her up with me in the bedsheet, or reach for her face or dark waves of hair. E still didn't turn to me. She remained gazing at the low peaks, beneath the constellations fading in the end of night sky.

T: What are you looking at?

E: I'm waiting for Venus.

T: O Venus, beauty of the skies. To whom a thousand temples rise . . .

I faltered, embarrassed. I couldn't remember the rest.

E: The beauty's a mask. Venus was once like Earth, but now it's an inferno. Its oceans boiled away and the continents are just black volcanic rock and rivers of lava. The atmosphere is crushing, vaporizing – sulfuric acid & carbon dioxide. Can you imagine it?

T: Not really.

Lately my imagination's limited to the block of Oaxaca granite I'm pounding away at w/ mallet & chisel for 10 hours a day in the studio.

E: Venus spins backwards, opposite to the spin of Earth or any other planet. And it spins slowly, at the pace of a walking man. A day on Venus is longer than a year. There.

I

I followed the end of her pointing finger. A tiny sphere of celestial light was appearing in the dip between two low summits. Eerie. Haunted. Pale. We watched silently for a while.

E: I dream I'm there sometimes. Walking toward the sunset at the speed that Venus slowly turns, so the sun never disappears. It just continues to set, forever.

I shivered, pulled the sheet tighter around me.

T: Sounds lonely.

Venus shone at the lower edge of the dusky, purple-streaked sky.

E: No. It's not.

Testimony 1 – Mariko

It begins at Kansai International Airport, by the gate for flight KL378 to Amsterdam. I'd sprinted there through Terminal One, after realizing at security the departure time I'd thought was 19:05 was actually 17:05. Sweaty, breathless and frantic from the repeated 'last call' of my name over the tannoy, I reached the empty lounge and ran over to the Dutch agent at the gate desk, pleadingly holding out my passport and misread boarding pass. She told me Gate 27 had just closed.

But the plane hasn't detached from the skybridge, a voice called out behind me.

A woman with a small wheeled suitcase was clipping towards us in low heels, her sleek black hair shimmering in the light streaming through the high Terminal One ceiling of glass and curvilinear steel. Her grey trouser suit, silk blouse and leather shoulder bag all exuded the wealth of business class.

The luggage is still being loaded on, she added.

Glancing through the glass wall at the Boeing 787, I saw she was right. The jet bridge was still connected and cargo containers were being lifted into the underbelly of the plane. The portholes showed passengers shuffling up the aisle or reaching up to stow bags overhead. Tapping at her computer, the blonde-chignoned agent frowned at the monitor and shook her head.

The gate's definitely closed, she repeated, and your checked baggage has just been removed. I can book you on the next flight to Amsterdam tomorrow. Change your connecting flights too if they're with us.

By now my heart rate and anxiety levels were returning to normal and I was resigned to the change in travel itinerary – it was my own fault for misreading the boarding pass after all. The other passenger, however, small though she was, looked ready to throw some weight around. Though her demeanour was poised, her eyes flashed entitlement.

I fly business class with your airline several times a year. I have over four hundred thousand frequent-flyer miles and an important meeting in Paris tomorrow. The skybridge is still attached and I see no reason why you can't let us on.

The gate's closed, the agent repeated evenly, her professional veneer showing no signs of cracking. The rebooking fee's 20,000 yen, but I'll waive it this time.

Informing us where to collect our suitcases, she scanned our passports and printed out new tickets for the following morning. Sighing, the woman accepted her ticket and cast a disdainful eye over her new itinerary. Then she left without a word, pulling her wheeled cabin bag over the vast and shining marble floors to navigate her way out of the terminal.

I took the express train one stop back to Rinku Town, checked into a budget hotel and WhatsApp-called my partner to tell him what an idiot I'd been. Then I headed out towards the seafront and ended up on the white pebble beach across the water from the man-made airport island, three kilometres out in the Seto Inland Sea. The orange sun was setting in the polluted sky, turning the cirrostratus clouds pink and gilding the waves so they scintillated towards the shore. I sat on the desolate stretch of pebbles and watched the blinking trajectories of planes taking off with a weird sense of being split in two – that a more functional version of me had made the 17:05 flight and was now crammed into economy, soaring over China or Inner Mongolia at an altitude of 35,000 feet, leaving the foggier, more hapless version behind.

The tide was coming in and I inched up the beach to keep the water from my Converse. It was chilly and dusk was falling, but something about the place exerted a pull on me, keeping me watching the half-sun vanishing beneath the dark gleaming waves as my backside numbed through my jeans. The giant Ferris wheel in the nearby Rinku Park lit up a lurid green, and as the wheel and its many passenger cars turned in slow revolutions, I remembered the time me and Lena got stuck on the Big Wheel in Southend-on-Sea. We were fifty feet up when it broke down – just the two of us shivering in one of those barred cages, Lena's long black hair whipping about in the freezing wind coming off the gull-shrieking North Sea. All she had on was a denim jacket over a vintage dress, so I lent her my jumper and we swigged Lambrini, smoked roll-ups and danced about to The Cramps on my Discman, listening through one earbud each, the cage creaking and groaning as we tried to stay warm. It wasn't long before Lena was half bent over, crossing her legs because she needed to pee.

Please, Lena, I said. Can't you hold it in?

I can't . . . she laughed. I'm bursting.

She squatted on the floor of the cage, dress gathered up in her lap, knickers around her knees, sighing in relief as a stream appeared between her ballet flats. And I climbed up on the seat as the stream trickled over to me, cracking up at Lena's panicked cry of *fuck* as the Big Wheel suddenly jolted and we started moving down.

That grey and drizzly day on Southend Pier had been back in February '05, and seventeen years later on the beach in Osaka, watching the last orange beams on the sea, I thought about how sad and strange it was that everything still reminded me of Lena. But perhaps it was important too. She'd been so alone in her thirty-two years, I doubted anyone ever thought of Lena any more, other than me.

Around seven or eight, I went to buy dinner in the FamilyMart in Rinku Town Station and bumped into the other late passenger who'd been refused entry at Gate 27. She'd changed out of her trouser suit into a black cashmere sweater dress and had a shiny red apple and a bottle of Evian in her basket. Our eyes met, recognition clicked, and without any greeting or remark on the coincidence of us meeting again, she said, I emailed the airline HQ in Amsterdam about that gate attendant. If you do likewise, we could have a stronger case. That attendant should be retrained and we deserve a refund.

Under the bright convenience-store lights, she looked airbrushed, of an indeterminate age between thirty-five and forty-five, her luminous face reminding me of the commercials for skin-whitening lotions ubiquitous in Japan. An auburn tint shone in her black hair as she looked up at me, intent on recruiting me to her cause.

D'you think so? I said. I mean, we were *really* late. And she was only doing her job.

She wanted to avoid the paperwork, that's all. And her laziness has caused me a lot of inconvenience. I just spent two hours rescheduling a week of meetings.

The woman looked stressed, and I supposed being flexible and grudgeless was easy when I had nothing important to rush back to London for.

OK. I'll send an email too then. If you think it'll help.

And though her expression didn't change, I could feel her warm to me – an ally. She extended a hand.

I'm Mariko.

I was holding a bento from the chiller cabinet, which I transferred awkwardly from right hand to left before shaking hers.

Jake.

Mariko glanced at the katsu curry in my hand – sweating beneath the plastic lid of the bento container. An appalled look twisted her face.

You aren't seriously going to eat that, are you?

I laughed. Either this or one of the corn dogs at the counter.

Mariko hesitated. I could sense her contemplating me – assessing my character, debating whether an intervention should be staged.

I'm staying at the Star Gate Hotel just next door. The restaurant there seems to have decent reviews. You can join me for dinner, if you want.

The restaurant was on the fifty-somethingth floor of Rinku Town's main skyscraper, from which Osaka Bay at night was a dazzling curve of illumination against the black void of the Inland Sea. The Sky Gate Bridge began directly beneath us, lines of traffic flashing and streaming over the kilometres of empty darkness between Osaka and KIX. The only diners, we sat by the window and pored over the menu together. After the waiter took our orders, Mariko asked, You travelled to Japan alone?

I nodded.

I taught English in Kyoto in the early 2000s. I've been staying with old friends from back then.

And what do you do in London?

I'm a primary schoolteacher.

Mariko was a Senior International Client Relations Manager for a Tokyo bank. A job title I'd learnt in the elevator up, when she'd showed me the email she'd sent the airline HQ on her iPhone (presumably to inform the tone and wording of my own). She nodded with polite disinterest.

Fun. Kids are so cute.

Yeah, it's fun. But hard work. I'm taking a year off actually.

Like a sabbatical?

I smiled.

Primary schoolteachers don't get sabbaticals. I've just been teaching for eighteen years straight and was feeling burnt out. And my father died last year and I had some money after selling his flat.

Mariko expressed her condolences about my father. Then she asked, What have you been doing in your year off? Travelling?

Not really, other than this Japan trip. Mostly, I'm just pottering around.

Pottering around?

Mariko's head tilted inquisitively. The wide collar of her cashmere dress sat on her pale shoulders, exposing her slender clavicles and throat. She was graceful and straight-backed as a dancer, and I found myself attempting to keep my elbows off the table, to pull myself out of my habitual slouch.

It means doing nothing really. Gardening. Reading books.

Pottering around, Mariko repeated quietly, almost to herself. I would go mad doing that for a year. Even a week.

She frowned then, perhaps thinking of the abyss of meaning or purpose she would fall into without her role as Senior International Client Relations Manager at her bank. The waiter put down our drinks – a beer for me, a pot of chrysanthemum tea for Mariko – and our conversation turned to London. Mariko had been on secondment in the City in the 90s (which put her in her mid-to-late forties – older than I'd thought) and had lived in Spitalfields. Every year since then she returned to shop in various Knightsbridge boutiques and dine in Michelin-starred restaurants with her London clients, from the sounds of it never venturing beyond zones 1 and 2. We then moved on to other European cities Mariko visited yearly – Paris, Rome, Madrid, her recommendations for where to shop and stay in each one straight out of *Condé Nast Traveller*. When I attempted to steer the conversation to what I remembered of the history or politics of a place, she glazed over, uninterested in the social realities beyond the bubble of five-star tourism. She showed me photos on her iPhone of a luxury eco-resort in Langkawi where she'd attended a yoga and wellness retreat earlier in the year, guiding me through the interiors and tropical gardens like an emissary from a world of refinement and taste.

We didn't exactly click, but I wasn't bored or drained the way I am when conversing with someone I haven't much in common with. There was something compelling about Mariko's poise and anodyne prettiness, which reminded me of a newsreader or an AI robot. As she spoke, I wondered at the time and expense that went into keeping her hair shimmeringly cut, her skin ageless and plumped, and her nails French manicured to perfection, so when she held up her cup of chrysanthemum tea there wasn't a single defect or chip. So uncanny was the effect of her flawlessness, when the waiter brought our meals over on lacquered trays and Mariko said itadakimasu and dug chopsticks into her buckwheat noodles, I was reassured by the messy human way she slurped.

Halfway through our set meals Mariko put down her chopsticks as though to give me her full attention and asked, What does your partner do?

I was chewing some prawn tempura. I swallowed too quickly and said, He's a social worker. That's how we met actually. We had a meeting about a pupil at my school.

He didn't want to come to Japan with you?

He has to work. We do our own thing from time to time.

Mariko nodded approvingly. You haven't sacrificed your independence.

I glanced at her hand. No wedding ring. She caught my glance and said, I'm single. I'm looked down on for being unmarried, for not having children. But I see how my male colleagues treat their wives and know I made the right choice.

Mariko spoke matter-of-factly, but not without a trace of bitterness. She glanced at the night view, the western edge of Osaka stretched out like a semiconductor with thousands of tiny diodes, emitting light. A passenger ferry moved through the nocturnal waters and aeroplanes blinked in the dark immensity of sky. In the glass, I watched her reflection speak.

My male colleagues cheat on their wives with hostesses. Some make clumsy passes at me, thinking I must be desperate for whatever attention I can get. They are wrong of course.

You can't report them for sexual harassment?

Mariko smiled at my well-meaning naivety, then changed the subject to a trip she was planning that summer to a horse-riding ranch in Patagonia. I finished my meal, and when a passing waiter came to clear away my tray, Mariko gestured he take hers away too, though half of her noodles, tofu and vegetables remained.

You aren't hungry? I asked.

I stop when I'm seventy per cent full.

Wow. That's very disciplined.

I *have* to be disciplined, she said. No meat. Eight hours sleep and Pilates every morning.

You don't ever slack off?

No.

Mariko mock-shuddered, but I could see in her eyes a genuine horror of letting go – of abandoning the virtuous rituals and routines that ordered her life. Which is why, when we split the bill, I was surprised by her suggestion that we go up to the hotel bar.

After some hesitation, Mariko ordered a whisky on ice – her first alcoholic drink, she said, for nine years. When I asked what the occasion was, she said she wasn't sure.

I haven't been feeling myself today, she admitted. I'm never so disorganized that I'm late for a flight . . .

I sipped my beer, unsure what to make of this confession. I was in a strange mood too. The more time I spent with Mariko, the more I felt the fleeting bond of strangers was intensifying, as though we were inexorably moving towards something, like two people who were going to have sex (which was more than unlikely in the case of she and I).

The whisky flushed Mariko's porcelain complexion and brought out a sheen on her forehead. Her composure slackened and her elbows, like mine, found their way on to the tabletop. We were on another subject entirely, when she abruptly said, Do I seem cold to you? Because I don't want a relationship?

No. Choosing to be single doesn't mean you're cold.

To be honest I find men mendokusai – troublesome.

Live your life as you like, Mariko. I'm sure you have a lot of friends.

Not really, she said.

The barman unobtrusively replaced our empty glasses with another whisky and beer.

But it's not that I'm cold or don't have feelings, she continued. I'm passionate about many things.

She began to talk about the house she'd bought in the Bunkyo-ku district of Tokyo and spent six months renovating – removing part of the first floor to create a living space with a double-height ceiling and installing glass walls around the central courtyard. She described how she sourced thousand-year-old Yakusugi cedar for the floors and shoji screen doors made by twelfth-generation Kyoto crafts-men. Mariko had then landscaped the courtyard into a Zen rock garden, with gravel raked into swirling patterns and centuries-old temple stones auspiciously arranged. Bonsai trees surrounded a fountain trickling into a lotus pond and every night Mariko illumin-ated stone lanterns, activated by an indoor switch, and sat in quiet contemplation of it all. She asked me if I had heard of Jun'ichirō Tanizaki's *In Praise of Shadows* (I hadn't). The Japanese aesthetics in Tanizaki's book – of simplicity, austerity, harmony and restrained elegance – had been the guiding spirit of her interior design. Every object in her home – every antique vase or ukiyo-e print – had been painstakingly considered in terms of shape and surface and shadowy interplay with its surroundings.

Every day after commuting home, she said, I soak for half an hour by candlelight in my cypress tub. Then I prepare and eat a simple vegan meal, and read a book or gaze out at my Zen garden and empty my mind until bed. I need this purification ritual. Otherwise I feel contaminated. Too crawling with filth to sleep.

Crawling with filth? I asked. From where?

Mariko shrugged. Tokyo. The subway. The bank and the men I work with there.

Do you feel that way now? In Osaka? With me?

Mariko shook her head. Osaka wasn't as bad as Tokyo. And she could tell I was a 'decent man'. Some of her co-workers disgusted her. When I asked why, Mariko hesitated, then said she had accidentally walked in on her boss watching something on his laptop. A naked woman cowering on her hands and knees. A Rottweiler clawing at her back. Mariko had apologized, as though she was the one at fault, and backed out of the conference room.

People can be monstrous, she said.

Then she closed her eyes. But I go to my beautiful home, shut the front door, and forget that they exist.

On her third whisky Mariko began to slur her words and repeat herself. Cashmere dress sliding over one shoulder to show her bra-strap, she lowered her head in her hands and rubbed her temples.

I feel lightheaded, she said. I should go to bed.

We settled the bill, then Mariko stumbled down from the bar stool. As I took her arm to support her wobbly steps out of the bar, there was panic in Mariko's eyes, as well as shame that something as simple as walking had slid out of her control. She kept apologizing, and saying how mortified she was, but inebriated guests not an uncommon sight, the bar staff barely spared us a second glance.

Mariko's room was on the forty-fourth floor. She slumped against the elevator wall on the way down, and outside room 411 practically turned her leather Balenciaga bag inside out in search of her keycard, dropping the apple and Evian she'd bought in FamilyMart on to the hallway carpet, as well as Chanel lipsticks and compact. She let herself into the room, and I gathered everything up from the carpet and followed her inside. She flopped on the bed, her dress up around her thighs and slender calves bulging against the bedcovers. She hadn't taken her shoes off, and the scuffed heels dug into the pristine white sheets.

Ugh. The room is spinning.

She laid the back of her hand over her eyes as though to shield them, and I angled the bedside lamp away from her and turned out the main light.

Maybe you should roll over on to your side? I suggested.

She did so, clinging to the mattress like a raft on a choppy sea.

Water, Mariko croaked.

When I turned to go to the bathroom, she added,

Not tap.

I filled the empty glass on the nightstand with the Evian, then placed the wastepaper basket by the bedside, hoping Mariko wouldn't be offended. She regarded me through her tousled hair.

I feel so undignified.

Don't worry about it. We all drink too much from time to time.

I glanced towards the door. The appropriate thing to do was to go, to leave Mariko to sleep it off. But she asked, Can you keep me company for a while?

I nodded and lowered myself into the easy chair at the end of the bed. Her hotel room was very tidy. Blackout curtains drawn, wheeled suitcase stowed away and grey trouser suit probably hanging in the wardrobe. Mariko rolled on to her back again and pushed herself up against the pillow. She gazed up at the ceiling. The hollows above her collarbones seemed excavated by shadow and her ribcage moved up and down under her black dress.

I lied to you earlier, she said.

Really? About what?

I *am* a cold person.

Awkwardly, and not entirely sincerely, I replied, I don't find you cold.

12

My parents died when I was in my twenties. I barely went to see them when they were dying. I was too busy with work. I abandoned my brother too, and now he's dead and I have no family left.

I stared at her, unsure how to respond.

You're being too harsh on yourself. It's just the whisky talking . . .

Alcohol makes the truth harder to avoid. When I'm sober, I make excuses for myself.

I'm sure you aren't as bad as you think you are, Mariko.

Her gaze slid from the ceiling on to me. The shadows stripped her of her lustre, emphasizing the lines around her mouth, ageing her. Clumsily, she brought the glass of water to her lips, spilt some down her chin, then wiped it with the back of her hand.

Do you have any family, Jake?

I'm an only child. My mother left when I was three, and it was just my father and me.

I see.

But my childhood was fine.

My brother was my twin, Mariko said. We were close as children, but when we were teenagers we stopped speaking. By the time we were adults we were estranged. When Hiroji died in 2011, over two hundred people came to his memorial service. He'd been so loved. But I'd found it so hard.

It's complicated with family, I said. There's so much history. So many psychic wounds that never completely heal.

I winced at how trite I sounded, but my words seemed to resonate with Mariko.

Yes, she murmured. Psychic wounds.

Less drunk now, as though her remorse about her late parents and brother had sobered her, she began to talk about the connection she'd had with Hiroji, back when he was alive. How she'd always felt the psychic tug of him, even when they were thousands of miles apart and hadn't spoken for years. In the weeks before he died, Mariko said, she'd had insomnia, and when she did sleep she'd wake panicked from dreams she was running through a bamboo forest, pursued by something evil and unseen. Her doctor diagnosed work-related stress and prescribed pills. But Mariko knew Hiroji was the cause – even though he was in Kyoto and she in Tokyo and they were completely out of touch. Something bad was happening to him. But she didn't reach out.

Eleven years ago, on the night he died, Hiroji called at three a.m., Mariko said. I didn't want to pick up. But then I did and he said he'd entered the mind of a higher-dimensional god . . .

A *what*?

That's what he said – a higher-dimensional god. He said he'd seen every moment of his life from conception to death. He'd seen us sharing our mother's womb as foetuses. I asked him if he was on drugs and he started to weep. He said, *I'm sorry, Mariko, for what I did. It's the reason you can't love anyone.*

Sounds like he was having a psychotic break, I said.

Mariko didn't seem to see or hear me. One of her heels had slipped off and she looked not at me but at scenes of the past reconstructed in her mind.

Hiroji told me this god had marked him out. That it had moved all his insides about so they weren't his any more. Then he said that I was marked out too . . . because we were twins and his flesh was my flesh and my flesh his flesh . . . So long as he was living and we were connected, it would come for me.

At the familiarity of Mariko's words my stomach plummeted as though a trapdoor had opened beneath me. Stunned, but not wanting to interrupt, I rose from my chair and began pacing between the end of the bed and the flat-screen TV.

Mariko didn't seem to notice as she went on, Hiroji said he was going to our bamboo forest to make another sacrifice. I asked what he meant by 'another sacrifice' and he only said if the sacrifice didn't work he'd be dead by morning. I told him he was scaring me, that he wasn't making any sense. And Hiroji said, *Don't let her in. She'll leave you alone when I'm gone.* Then he hung up.

Mariko described how she stood alone in her service apartment in the Asakusa district of Tokyo, confused. She dialled Hiroji's closest friend in Kyoto – an old childhood friend of hers too – but suddenly had no reception. She opened up Skype, but her laptop couldn't connect to the Wi-Fi. The lights on her modem were flashing, so she unplugged it from the wall socket and plugged it back in. Waiting for the internet to reconnect, she walked around her living room, waving her phone about, searching for a signal. She was frightened for her brother. And she was scared for herself, feeling whatever strangeness or malign influence Hiroji was under had seeped into her home.

The internet blinked out. As Mariko pulled her coat on over her pyjamas to go and try her cell phone out in the hallway or first-floor lobby, the intercom buzzed. The high-rise building had a video-call entry system, and a gaijin woman appeared on the LED screen on Mariko's wall. Late thirties, with dark, medium-length hair and an appearance Mariko could only describe as 'average', the Caucasian stared into the camera twenty-three storeys below. Mariko lifted the receiver to her ear and though the video was one-way, the woman seemed to be staring right at her as she spoke in barely accented Japanese.

Takahara-san, I've come to talk to you about Hiroji. May I come in?

Her voice was calm and reasonable, but remembering her brother's warning, Mariko hung up.

In the hallway outside her apartment, she finally found some reception. She got through to the voicemail of Hiroji's friend and was leaving a message when she heard the mechanical sound of the elevator rising in the shaft. Mariko lowered the phone. From where she was standing, she could see the numbers going up: 19 . . . 20 . . . 21 . . . 22. The elevator halted on the twenty-third floor and Mariko didn't wait to see who would emerge. As the sliding doors pinged open she flew back into her apartment and double-locked the door. Slow footsteps approached.

Mariko switched on the TV to some Korean rom-com, turned the volume up high. Then she sat on a floor cushion, hugging her knees to her chest. As the romantic comedy blared, she could hear knocking, a voice calling *Takahara-san* . . . *Takahara-san*. And she wondered if she was overreacting. What harm could possibly come from hearing what this woman had to say? But Hiroji's *don't let her in* replaying in her head, Mariko didn't even go and look through the peephole. Instead she remained in a state of vigilance for long after the woman appeared to have left, and eventually she passed out.

In the morning my phone rang, Mariko said. It was my brother's friend Kenji, calling to tell me that Hiroji was dead.

I stopped pacing and turned to face Mariko. Our eyes met for the first time since she'd started talking about her brother's call.

How did he die?

Some heart defect.

Did the post-mortem find anything strange?

In the shadows cloaking Mariko's face I discerned her jaw tightening in resistance. But I pushed on.

Were his internal organs the wrong way round? Reversed?

Mariko glared at me. How do you know about my brother?

I didn't know he existed until you began to speak about him twenty minutes ago. Did you tell anyone about this woman?

I made a statement to the police. But she wasn't on the building's CCTV.

The double bed creaked as I sat and angled my body towards her.

Mariko, I said. The things your brother said the last time you spoke to him . . . that something was moving his insides about . . . that they weren't his any more . . . I've heard it before. My friend Lena died in 2011 too, and she was saying similar things in the weeks before. And there was a woman, like the one who came to your door . . .

Grimacing, Mariko swung her heels to the carpet, knocking over the wastepaper basket as she stumbled to the bathroom. The lock turned behind her, and the toilet seat banged up against the cistern. Seconds later, the tiles echoed with retching and splatterings into the toilet bowl. As she vomited, I paced. For eleven years, the circumstances around Lena's death had haunted and confounded me. And now, six thousand miles from London, I'd crossed paths with a woman who seemed to have lost someone in the same way. Who seemed to have encountered, however briefly, the same unfathomable strangeness I had too.

Eventually the cistern thundered and the bathroom door unlocked. Mariko was clammy, smelling of puke, the look of suffering in her dark extinguished eyes as though her purging had only exacerbated her nausea. She lay face down on the bedcovers in her dress and only one heel, burying her head in the pillow as though willing everything to disappear.

Are you OK? I asked.

Please leave. I want to sleep now.

Mariko, I need to know more about what happened to your brother . . .

I don't want anything to do with this.

Do you have any contact details for Hiroji's friends? Anyone who knew him in Kyoto around the time he died?

No.

What about the friend you called that night?

Leave me alone.

Mariko . . .

Leave me alone. Leave my dead brother alone. Please just go away.

Our flight to Amsterdam left Kansai International Airport at 10:15 the next morning. At the departure gate I waited around until I was last in the queue to board the plane, expecting Mariko to emerge from the first-class lounge at any moment, nervously rehearsing what I would say to her. When I handed my passport to the gate agent – the same blonde-chignoned woman who'd refused us entry to the flight the day before – she reached under the desk.

This is for you.

The envelope had my name and flight number written on it.

Who's it from?

I don't know. The system's just flagged that I should pass it on to you. Someone from check-in or our airline desk sent it over.

As I walked along the jet bridge to the aeroplane, I opened the envelope. Inside was a slip of Star Gate Hotel memo paper with a name and telephone number scribbled on it. The name was Sigrid and the ten-digit number had an international dialling code. I found my seat and sat in a daze through the safety announcements and rumbling, seatbelt-harnessed take-off. After the fasten-seatbelt light went off, I went to business class to look for Mariko. But as I suspected, she wasn't on the flight.

Badlands – I

The dark-haired woman emerges from the gas station, brown-paper-bagged groceries hugged to her chest, the sun dazzling her eyes. She approaches the second-hand Toyota by the gas pump and sees the girl leaning out the passenger-side window, fretting in the side-view mirror, twisting her curls around a finger and tweaking them just so. The woman walks round to the trunk and dumps in the bags of hot dogs and marshmallows, bug spray and painkillers and Tampax and other overnight supplies. She digs out a cold diet soda and Juul pods for the girl, before slamming the trunk and pausing to take in the emptiness surrounding the highway. The brilliant blue sky and ferocity of sun over the miles of drought-stricken plains. She gets in the driver's seat and the girl turns from her reflection and laments, My hair's all fucked up. Today of all days.

Your hair's perfect, the woman assures her. There are women who'd crawl through broken glass for your natural curl.

The girl smiles, radiant with gratitude. Under her curls she has a round, uncommon face. Cherubic with a small pointed chin. Earlier, in her hotel room, the woman had watched the girl grooming herself for the trip. Making her skin 'dewy' and 'glowy' with cheap drugstore serums, smudging pink on her lips and thickening her eyebrows with a tiny brush dabbed in a palette of browns. The woman now passes the girl the chilled soda and Juul pods.

Oh my God, thanks. How much do I owe you?

That radiant smile again. Her wide-set smoke-grey eyes have a darker limbal ring. She knows, of course, she doesn't owe the woman a cent.

Rosa is the girl's name. *Rosa. Rosy. Rosy-lee.* A name apt for her plumpness and bouncy curls. The blue cotton of her sundress is tight across the swell of her chest, the straps digging into her shoulder flesh. She would be considered dumpy were it not for the sheer physical confidence she exudes. The woman's camera lens, when pointed at her, triggers an exhibitionist reflex – a coquettish pose no doubt perfected through years of digital self-portraiture. The girl pouts, angles her head and gazes seductively. And behind the camera, the woman is seduced. Finds her compelling to the point of infuriating lust (though long experience has taught her to keep this in check).

The woman buckles her seatbelt and asks, Ready?

The girl practically bounces in her seat. Her enthusiasm is part of her charm.

I'm so excited for this trip. I've been *nowhere* since I got here.

Your sister hasn't taken you sightseeing? To the Shiprock volcano? The Aztec ruins?

You kidding me? The only place Lissy's ever taken me was the grocery store when I first got here, so I could buy my own food and not steal hers. She won't even give me a ride when I'm late for work.

The woman half-winces, half-smiles in sympathy.

We'll more than make up for it today.

They drive away from the gas station down the lonely stretch of Highway 371. Down the eastern edge of Navajo land, surrounded by high desert of withered grasses, sagebrush and creosote dry enough to burst into flame. As they drive the girl vapes mango-scented fumes into the car, synthetic and nauseatingly sweet. She sips from the cold Dr Pepper wedged between her bare knees and chatters about astrology and Tarot and psychometric tests. She tells the woman how being a Scorpio with a Libra ascendant and moon in Aries has influenced the course of her seventeen years. She tells the woman about that morning's three-card spread and the significance of the High Priestess and the Hierophant and the Ten of Swords, *reversed*. How several online multiple-choice tests have confirmed she's an empath and explorer and an ENFP. (You're INFJ, she says to the woman, I can just tell.) And the woman veers between affection, bemusement and irritation as she nods and exclaims at the girl, smiling in the driver's seat through her growing discomfort (the fever in her blood from the E. coli in her urinary tract, and the Candida albicans deep in her vagina, causing a savage itch).

Vaping furiously, Rosa changes the subject to her latest obsession: the Law of Attraction. Does the woman know how it works? Like, on a quantum level? The woman admits she does not, so like a guru in a cloud of mango-scented incense, the girl points her Juul at the dashboard and explains.

See this dashboard?

I do.

Well, it's not really here.

It's not?

Because there's no such thing as solid matter, right? Just electromagnetic forces holding together teeny tiny quantum particles. And quantum particles don't exist unless you look for them. Like, our observing them makes them appear.

The observer makes them . . . manifest?

Exactly. And that's how the Law of Attraction works. But mac-ro-scopically. Our thoughts are waves of electromagnetic energy we transmit out to the universe. And those signals attract things back of that same frequency. So when you look at the world in a positive or negative way, you attract that positive or negative reality.

Like attracts like?

The girl nods and grins.

I *knew* you'd get it. Total INFJ. Our minds attract our reality. So if you worry about catching Covid, you'll probably catch it, right? It's all quantum physics.

The woman smiles. She has some intelligence, this girl. But like many she's been sucked into some online vortex of pseudoscience and emerged an acolyte.

Wow. It's so mind-bendingly complicated.

The girl's smoke-grey eyes are kind and encouraging.

Yeah, it's difficult to understand. But once you do, it's incredible. It's changed my life.

Then, smiling shyly, the girl makes a confession: she used the Law of Attraction to manifest the woman. Not three days ago the girl was despairing over the chasm between her dream of starting her own YouTube channel and her humiliating reality. Because how could she become 'Aurora Rose', a spiritual influencer enlightening others about the Law of Attraction, when she was just a seventeen-year-old high-school dropout, sleeping on her sister's couch? How could she record videos with the 'broke-ass' camera on her iPhone? But then the girl had snapped at herself, *don't be a fucking victim*, and began to repeat a mantra: *I am not a victim. The universe will protect me and I will overcome this situation. I am not a victim. The universe will protect me and I will overcome this situation.* A mantra that, like a lullaby, eventually sent her to sleep. And then the very next day she was cleaning a hotel room, billowing a sheet over a stripped-bare mattress, when a glamorous dark-haired woman emerged from the bathroom in a towelling robe – a woman towards whom Rosa felt an instant affinity or magnetic pull.

I felt the attraction too, the woman says. I could see straight away how special you are. That you had a unique look.

I thought you were messing with me, Rosa laughs. A photographer from Berlin, asking to photograph *me*, sweaty and gross in my housekeeping uniform.

Not at all. And the photographs only confirmed how gorgeous you are. I just *knew* that we were meant to collaborate, which is why I asked you out to lunch. And when you told me about your psychic YouTube channel—

Spiritual, the girl corrects.

—your *spiritual* YouTube channel, I knew I was *meant* to be your videographer. Now I know I was responding to the message you sent to the universe, to help you achieve your dreams.

Rosa beams her gratitude at the woman and they drive on through the hot and thirsty landscape, the wind bending and swaying the sun-scorched grasses and fluttering the leaves of the desert shrubs, parchment dry and crying out for rain. Hands on the steering wheel, glancing sideways, the woman says, Bet you're glad to escape Lissy's trailer for the night.

The girl swallows the last of her Diet Dr Pepper. Turns her pretty face and profusion of curls to the woman.

You have *no idea*. Lissy's a hot fucking mess. She's so stuck in that victim mentality, blaming the past for everything wrong in her life. She just can't get over all that stuff with our mom and piece-of-shit stepdad, and uses it as an excuse to, like, do drugs and cam-girl stuff and fuck random guys from bars.

The girl emits a sigh of despair.

And I wanna say to her, *Y'know all that shit happened to me too. But do you see me acting like a victim? Do I let it hold me back?*

You're the least victim-like person I've ever met, the woman agrees.

Rosa stares at the highway ahead, thrusting her chin in her grit and determination to be victor not victim, to not be diminished by her past.

This is gonna sound crazy, she says, but I'm manifesting a hundred thousand subs to the Aurora Rose channel by the end of the year. A million subs the year after that. I want a number-one podcast, then my own Netflix show.

That doesn't sound crazy at all, the woman gushes. I can feel the waves of electromagnetic energy emanating from you right now. I'm sure the quantum gods will fall at your feet with manifestations of everything you want and more . . .

Rosa shoots her the side-eye from the passenger seat and the woman realizes her mistake. She's gone too far.

What I mean is, she adds, the first Aurora Rose video we shoot tomorrow will be the first step to that success.

They turn off Highway 371 on to the gravel road descending into the badlands: the plains of grasses and tawny sand receding into the barrenness of crumbling, disintegrating sedimentary rock. As the Toyota rattles and rumbles over the loose dirt and stones, there's a gradual change of mood in the car. Gazing out the passenger-side window at the changing scenery, the girl is quieter. Subdued, the woman suspects, by the gathering of dark energies around them; a shifting turbulence just beyond grasp of the senses that can instigate unease in the more sensitive of psyches. Now the highway's far behind them, the girl's excitement is giving way to an apprehension about spending the night in the wilderness with this woman – this near stranger – miles from civilization and any other human soul.

They pull up in the dusty, windswept parking lot. From where they're parked, the Bisti Wilderness isn't much to look at: a flat, wide expanse of sun-baked mud and deep iron-oxide red mesas in the distance. But to hike beyond the hills is to enter a primordial landscape of stone; Cretaceous-era boulders and arches and ridges and eerie spires of hoodoos, all stark and terrifying and tens of millions of years old. The Sculptor had first told the woman about the badlands back in '82. About walking among the surreal rock formations when her work was stalled. They'd once planned to travel here together. But, of course, never got the chance.

In the passenger seat Rosa stares through the windshield at the empty parking lot. Demerara curls against the headrest, tote bag of make-up and Aurora Rose outfits clutched on her lap. The woman wonders again at the source of Rosa's unease. There are people who detect her malignancy straight away, like a dog sniffing out a tumour. Others can take hours or days. But most people she encounters detect nothing unordinary at all. The woman had the girl in the latter category, but perhaps she is wrong.

There's no one here, the girl remarks.

Don't worry, the woman reassures her. This is one of several access points to the badlands. We'll meet plenty of other hikers once we get on the trails.

Rosa turns to the woman. The Toyota's air conditioner cuts out with the engine and perspiration shines through the tinted serums on her plump face. A delicate blue forked vein pulses in her temple and iridescent powder shimmers on her eyelids. Seeming to look properly at the woman for the first time since the gas station, Rosa frowns and says, You gonna be OK hiking, Therese? I don't mean to offend, but you look kinda . . . *peaky* right now.

I had food poisoning last night, the woman explains. From the chilli at TJ's Diner, I think.

Really? That sucks.

I was shaky this morning, but I'm mostly over it now.

Rosa doesn't seem entirely convinced, and sensing her reluctance to get out of the car, the woman suggests, Why don't we send some positive thoughts out to the universe? Visualize the stunning videos we're going to make and the millions of subscribers you'll attract.

The girl half-smiles, but the crease between her eyebrows remains. The woman persists.

Let's visualize how your star's going to rise and rise, Rosa. And how everyone who was ever mean to you or wrote you off will fade into insignificance. How when you're stratospheric, you won't even remember their names . . .

This seems to do the trick. Rosa shines at the woman's prophecy, at the prospect of ascension and vengeance through monetized clicks and a prominent digital brand. Because for Rosa, as for most, fame is one of life's most glittering prizes. A consequence of mortality, the woman supposes. To want to shine like a star against the night sky of anonymous masses. To leave an afterglow when you die.

Rosa closes her eyes for a few seconds, takes a few deep breaths. Opens her eyes again and smiles at the woman. Positive thoughts, *sent*.

The woman claps her hands. Great. Let's get this influencer show on the road.

The girl unlatches the passenger-side door, shading her eyes as she exits the car for the blazing sun. The blue cotton of her sundress is creased and stuck to her thighs as she stands, and she reaches behind her to tug it loose, slinging tote-bag straps over her shoulder, stumbling a few steps towards the boundary fence and the miles and miles of desolate wilderness.

Alone in the Toyota, the woman glances in the rear-view. The rectangle of mirror reflects the car's shadowy interior, the worn and shabby upholstery of the empty back seat. For a moment all is still back there, then the edge of the reflection warps. And though she shivers and aches, the woman unlatches the driver's-side door and gets out. She glances up at the high desert sky, but in spite of her predicament, her body's mutiny, she sends no positive thoughts or SOS to the universe. Only slams the Toyota's door and walks round to the trunk to get her backpack and supplies.

Testimony 2 – Sigrid

She was waiting outside the S-Bahn. Tall, with cropped blonde hair, and wearing a grey hoodie and loose jeans. For a moment her striking appearance – her model's bone structure and intense blue eyes – intimidated me. But Sigrid's direct manner as she shook my hand gave the impression she didn't care for performing femininity or measuring the effect of her looks.

Welcome to Marzahn-Hellersdorf, Jake.

We stood at the exit to the station, making small talk about my flight from London, Sigrid's German accent staccato with harsh consonants. When I said it was my first time in the suburb of Marzahn, she smiled wryly.

Then we'll take the scenic route.

On the fifteen-minute walk through the dusty, polluted streets to the estate of Plattenbauten tower blocks where she lived, Sigrid pointed out the refuge for women fleeing domestic violence where she worked, her son Tomo's skateboarding park, her favourite Vietnamese café, and grimaced at some neo-Nazi graffiti under a bridge. As we rounded the corner of a GDR-era low-rise, I asked Sigrid why she had settled in an area of Berlin my guidebook described as *known for social deprivation and crime.*

I was broke, why else? When we left Japan in 2011, I had nothing. It was meant to be temporary, until we could afford the rent in Treptow or Neukölln. But then I got the job at the shelter, and Tomo liked his school.

She glanced at the concrete landscape around us. Pleasant enough on a late April evening, but I could see how colder, greyer weather could turn it oppressive and bleak.

I understand why you ask, Sigrid said. My friends in East Kreuzberg came to visit me more when I lived in Japan.

*

When we got to Sigrid's flat, I put my backpack down in her son's bedroom where I would sleep (Tomo was at university in Munich), then sat on his single bed, staring at his posters of German football teams and pro-skateboarders. I was disorientated. Jet-lagged still from Japan. I'd dialled the number on the Star Gate Hotel memo paper when I got back to London three days earlier, and when I explained to Sigrid why I was calling, she was shocked. Angry, even. Suspicious of this English stranger, rambling about her Japanese sister-in-law, and then the circumstances of her late husband's death. I didn't blame her for threatening to hang up.

Then I started to speak of Lena. As far back as I can remember, I told Sigrid, Lena was there. She'd lived in the block of flats down the road, and as two only children we'd latched on to each other. Knocked for one another every day, to play outside or walk to school together. Lena was always round mine watching cartoons, joining us for tea (Lena's mother Corina frequently dropped her off with my dad before she went 'shopping' or to 'visit a friend', returning hours later to pick her daughter up, steaming drunk). When Lena became estranged from her family in her teens, I became her emergency contact and next of kin; the one who supported her through all her struggles, in her twenties, with addiction and mental health. Sigrid listened quietly as I recounted the nightmarish things that had happened to Lena before she died. How she'd come to me, confided in me, and I'd dismissed what she was trying to tell me. Disregarded what I'd seen with my own eyes. How the guilt had been eating away at me ever since.

I glanced at the clock. An hour had gone by, during which Sigrid had been mostly quiet. What was she thinking? That I was delusional? Nuts?

Sigrid . . . ?

In the silence that followed, I feared she'd already hung up. Then she said, Can you come to Berlin?

Dinner was Thai takeaway, eaten on the yellow L-shaped sofa in Sigrid's living room, drinking wine and comparing memories of Kyoto, where I'd lived for two years, and Sigrid eight. During our conversation, however, I became distracted by a photograph on the wall of a Japanese man with a shaven head and a wide crooked smile.

Is that Hiroji?

I could see the resemblance to Mariko (though unlike his twin, there was a genuine spark of joy in his smile). Sigrid looked in the direction I was looking.

That was taken three years before he died.

He looks charismatic.

Oh, Hiroji was a *force* – so energetic and upbeat. He was the fun parent, and I was the imposer of bedtimes and healthy snacks. He was Tomo's favourite, for sure.

Sigrid tilted up her glass, swallowed wine.

How old was Tomo when Hiroji died?

Seven. When we came to Germany he needed months of therapy and had nightmares for years. I only hope what happened hasn't overshadowed what his father was really like.

I'm sure it hasn't, I said.

Sigrid responded with a tight smile.

After dinner she dug out several Kodak and Fuji envelopes stuffed with photos from her years in Japan. She and Hiroji had been dancers in a Kyoto butō troupe and there were stunning photographs of them onstage; ghoulish with chalk-white body paint, contorting their lean, muscular bodies into surreal shapes, faces expressing what could be terror or madness or joy. All the butō dancers looked not of the human species or world, but of another phantasmagoric reality entirely.

I can barely recognize you, I said of a photograph in which a buzz-cut Sigrid was dragging herself across a darkened stage; her eyes horror-stricken, her mouth a howl, all vanity sacrificed at the altar of experimental dance.

Butō was my escape, Sigrid said. When I was performing, I became someone else. All the negative, self-critical voices in my head shut up.

She paused. At least, at first.

How did you get into it?

I was in Tokyo, working as a model. Going to castings or shoots day in day out, where I'd get told to my face that my nose was too big or I was too fat. I had an eating disorder, was subsisting on sashimi and Diet Coke. And I was clinically depressed – though I don't think I knew it at the time.

I'm sorry. That sounds awful.

Butō saved me. One night, just by chance, I went to see a troupe from Kyoto when they were touring Tokyo and they were *electrifying*. Watching them reminded me of what it was like to get swept up by something incredible, you know? To feel *alive*. I went backstage after the show and asked the troupe leader – Hiroji as it turned out – if they ran workshops, and if I could take part, though I'd had no background in dance or performance art.

That was very gutsy of you.

It was very desperate. How much longer I could have gone on like I was, I don't know. I was half-dead and butō brought me back like a . . . defibrillator? Is that the right word?

Defibrillator, yes.

I was nervous, but met Hiroji at the rehearsal space the next day. He said I had potential and if I moved to Kyoto he would train me himself. So later that day, I packed up my room in Shibuya and ended my modelling career by shaving my head. My room-mates thought I'd joined a cult.

I worked backwards through the sets of photographs to the day Hiroji and Sigrid were married in 2003. The wedding party was in a reggae bar in Hiroji's hometown of Nagaokakyō; the bride and groom laughing with friends, making the peace sign and holding up bottles of Asahi beer.

You look so young, I said.

I was twenty-three. There should be laws against marrying so young. Hiroji was thirty. Older, but more immature.

You both look love-drunk too.

We were. But everything changed a year later when Tomo was born. It's hard to keep the romance alive when you're barely functioning on three hours sleep, changing diapers, cleaning up baby sick . . . And your husband's too busy leading all-day rehearsals to help.

Sigrid smiled and a floor lamp on timer flickered on. Dusk was deepening beyond the venetian blinds, shadows devouring the edges of the room.

That must've been frustrating.

It was. And Hiroji was never there. He'd stumble in at two a.m. after drinks with 'the troupe' that I'd later find out was just drinks with Aiko, or Hana, or some other pretty nineteen-year-old he'd singled out because of her 'potential'.

He was cheating on you? I asked.

Sigrid nodded. By the summer of 2011 I'd had enough. I'd spoken to a lawyer and picked up divorce papers. But I couldn't bring myself to serve them. Mostly because my depression was back and it took everything I had just to get out of bed, get Tomo ready for school and get myself through the day. Hiroji didn't abuse me in the way the women in the refuge where I work have been abused. But I understand how bad behaviour becomes normalized – why it can take so long to leave. If it wasn't for Damaris, perhaps I'd still be in Kyoto now.

The photographer from London?

Yes, Damaris from London. And the woman Lena met . . . ?

Marion from Berlin.

Damaris, Marion. Marion, Damaris . . . Sigrid said. The night Hiroji and I met her my instincts warned me something was wrong. But I didn't want to be the jealous wife, making a scene. That's what Hiroji always accused me of.

I held up my phone, asked if I could record her. She consented with a nod. The living room had become colder, warmth and light receding as though retreating from what was to come. Sigrid's arms were bare in her black vest, but she didn't look goosebumped or chilled. She sat up straighter, her eyes focused on the past, hardening in judgement of herself.

I regret it every day, she said. I knew what she was.

★

July, 2011. Under the high rafters of a darkened loft space of an old building near Imadegawa-dōri, an audience of thirty or so were seated on cushions on the creaky, splintery floor. They fanned shining faces with programmes in the humid Kyoto night, staring expectantly at the low wooden stage.

On to that stage Hiroji and Sigrid ascended to the percussion of drums and bamboo clappers and the eerie twanging of a shamisen. Hiroji bare-chested in shorts and Sigrid in a sapphire bodysuit, already darkening with sweat. Masks of blue iridescence painted around their eyes, they circled each other with slow exaggerated movements, drawing together and pulling apart as though attracted and repelled. It was a dance they'd choreographed together, in the performance of which Sigrid had once lost herself. But up on the stage that night she shrank beneath the gaze of the audience, excruciatingly self-conscious. As the drumming quickened, Sigrid's heart hammered and a familiar pressure began building in her chest and skull. All she wanted was to bolt, but she forced herself to dance the ten-minute-long death spiral with Hiroji until the very end, when they broke loose from each other to sink to their knees at the opposite sides of the stage. Only during the applause did Sigrid flee.

She didn't watch the other performances. She went straight to the shower room backstage, stripped in a stall and stood under the lukewarm spray. Dr Heinrich said it was important for her to keep on performing butō – to keep doing what she'd once loved. But now it was over she just wanted to disappear with the water spiralling into the drain. She was being selfish of course. Who would look after Tomo if she ceased to exist?

Sigrid lost track of time. When she heard another dancer enter the showers, she knew the show was over. She towelled herself dry and changed into a T-shirt, jeans and flip-flops, and slung her bag over her shoulder, planning to sneak out of the loft without speaking to anyone – to slip unseen past the other dancers mingling with friends and drinking cold Sapporo beers. But Nils from the German language school saw her emerging from backstage and grinned and waved enthusiastically, so Sigrid reluctantly went over to him and her other colleagues to thank them for coming. Half-jokingly they asked her why she hadn't mentioned the show (they'd spotted the listing in the *Japan Times*), and as Sigrid apologized, trying to appear friendly and relaxed, someone tapped her arm and said in British-accented English, You were phenomenal.

Sigrid turned to the dark-haired Caucasian woman in a black strappy dress, smiling admiringly at her.

It's Sigrid, right? the woman said. I saw your name in the programme. I'm Damaris.

Though the woman was slight and plain in appearance, she was commanding in presence and Sigrid's colleagues seemed to fade away as she was drawn into conversation with her. Damaris had a digital camera and she showed Sigrid, in the image viewer, the photos she'd taken of her and Hiroji during their performance.

What made your dance so extraordinary, Damaris said, was the intensity of the bond you had with the man you were dancing with.

Sigrid wasn't sure she believed her. Up onstage she and Hiroji had been going through the motions, barely making eye contact with each other. But she heard herself saying, He's my husband.

Married long?

Too long.

Sigrid had meant this to sound humorous, but it had come out pained. Embarrassed, she asked, You're a photographer?

Damaris smiled. Yes. From London, originally. Now based in Tokyo and here on assignment. I'm shooting maiko and geisha in Gion for a travel magazine.

Sounds glamorous, Sigrid said.

Though everything seemed glamorous compared to teaching German to Japanese housewives and translating manuals for Hitachi TVs.

Damaris smiled again. Last week I was in a Nissan factory, shooting car batteries for an auto parts catalogue. It's not all glossy magazines.

Hiroji joined them and Damaris introduced herself. Though Damaris's Japanese was clumsy and faltering, she began conversing with him in earnest, showing him the photographs she'd taken and describing how his performance had moved her. Sigrid could sense the British woman's attraction to her husband; handsome and thuggish with his shaven head, bare-chested still in his shorts. And though understated, late-thirties Damaris lacked the youth and explicit prettiness of Hiroji's 'type', Sigrid sensed the interest reciprocated. But it was something other than her husband's flirting that caused the sudden coursing of dread – that made her want to drag him away.

The aftershow party was at an izakaya on Kiyamachi-dōri and everyone gradually made their way out of the building and towards the subway. As she said goodbye to her German colleagues, Sigrid noticed that Hiroji, now in his shirt and jeans, had broken away from the main group and was with Damaris, who was flagging down a cab. Sigrid strode over, not caring how she looked as she caught her husband by the elbow.

Where are you going?

Hiroji turned, surprised by her urgent tone. Gion. Damaris is taking me to a bar there. She wants to discuss doing a photo series about the troupe. She says she knows an editor in London who'd love it.

You're not coming to Kiyamachi? Sigrid asked.

They'll be there getting wasted until six a.m. We'll catch them up later.

And seeing his wife's concern, Hiroji laughed. Everything OK, Siggi-chan? Would you like to come too? I just didn't think you'd want to talk business.

Sigrid glanced into the taxi and Damaris smiled magnanimously at her from the back seat.

Please do come, Sigrid. The taxi and drinks are on me.

The bar was on the second floor of a building on Pontochō-dōri and they sat by a window overlooking the narrow alley of traditional wooden kyō-machiya, where two teenage girls dressed up in summer kimonos for the Gion Festival tottered under the hanging paper lanterns in their wooden sandals. Other than the girls, the alley was empty, Kyoto's Saturday night drinkers in the rowdier streets of the neon-lit clubs and karaoke parlours. As soon as the barman brought over their drinks, Hiroji's phone buzzed. He went to take the call, and as Sigrid looked about at the minimalist decor of the bar Damaris sipped her whisky and said, I expect people tell you how beautiful you are all the time. But you don't care much for your looks, do you?

Sigrid shrugged. I don't like the status that comes with being a Westerner in Japan. Especially if you're white.

You don't like attention much, do you?

Not for how I look.

Damaris leaned forwards over the table, dark strands falling over her eyes, the strap of her black cotton dress sliding over a shoulder. She was more sensual in the shadowy bar. More alluring than the earnest Englishwoman she'd presented as back in the loft.

I admired the way you danced tonight. I could see how agonizing it was for you to be up onstage with all those eyes on you. But you held it together really well.

Sigrid could feel her blood drain. Dr Heinrich had reassured her that no one could see her internal struggle while performing.

Don't worry, Damaris said, responding to Sigrid's dismay. I doubt anyone else noticed. I recognize melancholia in others. I suffered from it once myself.

And in spite of her growing aversion to the woman, Sigrid couldn't help but ask, How did you get better?

Autotomy, Damaris said.

Au*to*tomy?

When an animal chews off its own limb to escape the trap it's caught in. So painful at first you think you won't survive. But you do. And then you are free.

I don't understand the metaphor.

Damaris smiled again, leant towards her again, into the low candle, burning in its glass holder.

You remind me of a girl I once photographed in Wales. You have the same blue eyes and pale face. You'd have the same hair too, if you grew yours out. She lived in a hamlet called Angels Singing and was more angel than girl herself. Crippled though. In a wheelchair.

Damaris looked wistful at the memory of this 'crippled' girl, and Sigrid asked, Why did you photograph her?

But Hiroji returned, a Mild Seven smouldering between his fingers as he announced to Sigrid in Japanese, That was Tetsuo about the ticket sales. We broke even last night, and tonight made a profit of fifteen thousand yen. Enough to buy everyone in the troupe a drink.

He raised his tumbler of whisky. This calls for a toast. *Kampai.*

They all clinked glasses as Hiroji sat back down next to Sigrid.

But butō's not about the money for you, is it? Damaris said.

Hiroji grinned at her. Unlike Sigrid, he hadn't showered. His face was smeared with blue paint left behind by make-up removal wipes, and he smelt, not unpleasantly, of sweat.

My sister works in finance, he laughed. She thinks I'm out of my fucking mind.

Out in the alley, rain began to fall. On the other side of the room, the lone barman smoked and gazed out the window overlooking the Kamo-gawa flowing ceaselessly in the dark towards the Inland Sea. At their candle-flickering table, Damaris spoke for a while in broken Japanese – with Sigrid translating when needed – about the series of photographs she was planning of the butō troupe. She wanted to interview some dancers too – to understand, for example, what had drawn them to the 'dance of darkness and decay' which often involved contorting the body into shapes considered ugly, crude or grotesque. Though Damaris seemed to direct this question at Hiroji, Sigrid responded in English with the same practised answer she'd given for years.

Butō's also called the dance of metamorphosis. And that's what performing butō is for me. Breaking out of the chrysalis of the ego. Becoming something dreamlike and strange, but meaningful and true . . .

Sigrid stopped herself there. Damaris was smiling sympathetically at her. Because the photographer knew, as Sigrid did herself, that butō no longer brought her transcendence or joy. She'd been rotting in her chrysalis for years. Oblivious to his wife's pain, Hiroji joked in Japanese, Man, that's deep, Siggi-chan.

He grinned at Damaris. I just got into butō cos it's really fucking cool.

Out in Pontochō-dōri the rain came down harder and the lanterns swayed in the wind. Damaris ordered some sake, which the bartender brought over on a tray and poured from a tokkuri flask into small ceramic cups. Smiling, Damaris proposed a toast: *to the dance of metamorphosis.* They clinked again and Sigrid took a wincing sip. Looking at Hiroji, Damaris said, You're being modest. When I watch you perform I know I'm watching someone channelling from the depths.

The depths? Hiroji asked.

Of unconsciousness, Damaris said. Where the darkest truths are repressed.

Hiroji laughed. *Wild.*

Sigrid wondered how the photographer's Japanese, broken only minutes earlier, had suddenly become fluent. She asked as much, and Damaris tapped her ceramic sake cup.

This loosens the tongue.

Then, looking contemplatively at Hiroji, she asked, What inspires your choreography?

Hiroji shrugged. Art. Music. Sometimes dreams.

Damaris's dark eyes shone as though intrigued. Any recurring ones?

He frowned as he reflected on this. Sometimes of my mom and dad. They died when I was in my twenties, but in my dreams they're alive and we're drinking tea and talking in our old house in Nagaokakyō . . . And I wake up with just the *saddest* feeling.

Listening to him, Sigrid had a pang of sadness too. She hadn't known her husband dreamt of his late parents, both of whom she'd never met.

You're a child in these dreams? Damaris asked.

I don't know. But in other dreams I'm definitely a kid. Like, running around the bamboo forest with my sister, behind our old house. There was an abandoned shrine where we used to play. Creepy as fuck, but I always felt safe there. Like, protected, you know? My dad said it was sacred. I dream of that shrine a lot.

And your sister . . . Damaris said. Are you close to her?

We're sort of estranged.

Hiroji never spoke much about Mariko. Sigrid had assumed they'd drifted apart because they had nothing in common; one twin an introverted banker, the other an extroverted artist. But the way he looked at Damaris suggested otherwise.

35

Is she younger? Older?

We're twins.

Twins, Damaris murmured, fascinated. And you had a falling out?

You don't have to talk about her, Sigrid cut in.

But Hiroji gazed at Damaris, under the sway of something in her eyes – something understanding and reassuring, gently coaxing him to expose more of himself.

We were close as kids. Inseparable. Like the same person, sometimes. But over the years, since she left home, she . . . became distant.

He knocked back his sake and replenished his cup from the tokkuri flask. And with compassion and a terrifying perceptiveness, Damaris said, You were *too* close?

Hiroji glanced out the window at the rain. What do you mean? Sigrid wanted to ask, incredulous.

It didn't seem so bad at the time, he said. The boundaries . . . were blurred.

The sudden understanding made Sigrid reel. She'd only met Mariko once, when the troupe performed in Tokyo three summers before. A quiet, elegantly dressed woman, she'd exchanged a few polite words with her twin brother and sister-in-law before leaving, turning down their invitation to join them for drinks, saying she had an early flight the next morning.

Gently, Damaris said, You mustn't blame yourself.

Hiroji laughed then. The distressing laugh of someone in pain. He turned from the window to Damaris's solicitude, which Sigrid sensed to be a trap.

How can it be your fault? Damaris continued. Your closeness was mutual, no? Not coerced . . .

Sigrid said sharply, *Enough*.

Damaris halted her sake-loosened tongue. Then spoke as though in contrition.

I apologize. I didn't mean to cause upset.

We need a change of scene, Sigrid said to Hiroji. Let's take a taxi home and talk about this there.

I got a message from Aii, he replied. They're waiting for us at ING. I'd rather go and hang out.

OK, ING then.

They rose from the table, Damaris peeling 10,000-yen notes from her wallet to pay the bill, and Hiroji stumbling into the toilets, much drunker than Sigrid had realized. Taller than Damaris, Sigrid looked down at her as she said, The party's just for members of the troupe.

Sure.

Damaris smiled at Sigrid, then added in the fluent German of a native speaker, But before I go, be honest with yourself. What are you really protecting? Hiroji? Or the version of him you prefer?

Then she went to the bar, put the money down, nodded at the barman and left.

The rain was torrential on the ten-minute dash from Pontochō-dōri to Kiyamachi. Outside ING, Hiroji stopped at a vending machine to buy another pack of cigarettes, and rather than waiting in the pouring rain Sigrid ran into the bar and the drunken embraces of their friends. She looked back at the door, expecting Hiroji to make an appearance, but he didn't come. Ten minutes later she took out her phone to call him and saw his text: *Not done talking to D. We're getting another drink somewhere. Be there soon.*

She called him and called him, but it went straight to voicemail each time.

Sunday morning the alarm woke Sigrid. Her relief to see her husband sprawled beside her on the futon became disquiet as she remembered the night before. But she was late to pick Tomo up from his friend's, so quickly dressed, and choked down her antidepressant with canned Boss coffee before rushing out.

That Sunday was the parade for the Gion Festival, so Sigrid took Tomo and his friend Eiji to watch the procession of tall Shinto floats at Karasuma-Oike, where the crowds, thirty-three-degree heat, taiko drums, gongs and flutes all conspired to worsen her hangover. The children irritated her too, with Tomo pestering her for change for vending-machine sodas and to be hoisted up on to her shoulders, and Eiji whining every half-hour he needed to pee. Sigrid was glad when the parade ended and they could go to an air-conditioned MOS Burger for lunch. As Tomo and Eiji squabbled over the Angry Birds app on her phone, Sigrid drank an iced coffee and let her thoughts churn. About Hiroji and his estranged twin. About Damaris and the tendrils she'd unfurled to probe about in her husband's psyche.

When they returned home around four, Hiroji was out. Sigrid distractedly watched cartoons with Tomo for an hour, then microwaved convenience-store bentos for dinner, before making Tomo take a bath and putting him in bed. As she kissed him goodnight, he said, Eiji says his mom feels sorry for me.

Why?

Cos our family's not normal.

Sigrid sat on the bed and looked at her son in the blue glow of his Doraemon light. She swept some strands of light brown hair out of his eyes – Eurasian eyes that kids at his elementary school had begun to tease him about. She didn't need to ask why Eiji's mom thought they weren't 'normal'. Mrs Takahara was a gaijin and Mr Takahara wasn't a salaryman but a Suzuki-riding bartender. Both could be seen on YouTube performing semi-naked, orgiastic dances.

We should try not to care what other people think, Tomo, she said. Besides, who's to say what normal is?

She thought of Keiko Kobayashi in her apron, carving apple slices into bunny ears for Eiji's bentos and mopping her immaculate floors. She added, Those who judge others tend to be unhappy in their own lives.

Though she'd spoken in German – a private language between mother and son – Tomo responded in Japanese.

But *you're* unhappy.

Sigrid was startled by her seven-year-old's observation. What makes you say that?

You just are. That's why Dad doesn't come home.

Sigrid sighed. I'm sorry, Tomo. I don't mean to be . . . I mean, I'm not . . . And your dad's not here cos he's working at the bar tonight, remember?

38

Tomo didn't look convinced, but Sigrid was too tired to persuade him. Just ignore Eiji's mom. Try to go to sleep.

She kissed him again and backed out of the room.

When Hiroji came back after midnight, Sigrid put down the Shūsaku Endō novel she was failing to concentrate on and went to the darkened kitchen where she could hear him moving about. The fridge door was open, Hiroji standing in the yellow glare as he reached inside. And in the second before the fridge door swung closed, Sigrid had the dizzying sense he was someone else. Someone whose illuminated profile was identical to her husband's, but that of a stranger who'd entered their home. The door suctioned shut and cloaked in darkness again, Hiroji unscrewed the bottle of green tea he'd taken from the fridge. When Sigrid reached to turn on the kitchen light, he said, Don't. I have a headache.

She left it off. Voice and dark silhouette were both irrefutably Hiroji's, but the sense he was an imposter wouldn't leave. Leaning against the kitchen counter, he gulped down the tea, watching Sigrid watching him before lowering the bottle.

What is it? he asked.

Are you OK?

I'm fine. Other than the headache.

Hiroji rasped a hand over his stubbled skull – an unconscious habit of his, though this time something about the gesture (the angle?) struck Sigrid as odd.

Where did you go with that woman last night? she asked.

A jazz bar. Then we drank some convenience-store beers by the Kamogawa before I got the first train home.

I was calling you . . . but it went straight to voicemail.

My battery was dead.

She stared into his dark, illegible face. Why was she so disoriented? His smell was the same at least – the musk of his sweat mixed with the beer and smoke of Daisuke's bar.

Listen, she began. About Mariko . . . what you said . . .

I made that up.

Why . . . ?

At his wife's look of aghast, Hiroji shrugged. Damaris wanted to hear something shocking, so I said something to shock her.

But why that? It's a fucked-up thing to say.

He swigged some more tea. I was drunk.

The same dread Damaris had induced in her the night before was surfacing again.

Did you see her today? Sigrid asked.

No. She's gone back to Tokyo.

Will you see her again?

Hiroji sighed. I thought you were going to work on this jealousy stuff.

I'm not jealous. Something's *off* about her.

Look, save it for Dr Whatever-his-name-is . . .

He drank the last of the tea, put the bottle on the counter.

I'm wiped and going to bed.

He walked out of the kitchen, his shadowed face passing her as he went down the hall into their bedroom. She hesitated, then followed him in. He was already on his side of the futon, under a sheet and out within seconds, while Sigrid lay tense and awake beside him for the rest of the night.

. . . I can't stop thinking about his face in the fridge light. Hiroji but *not* Hiroji . . . I can't get the idea he's some doppelgänger out of my mind . . .

On Sigrid's laptop screen, Dr Heinrich nodded along with her as he'd done between nine and nine fifty every Wednesday night for the past three years. His leather chair creaked as he leant forward to jot down another note in the daylight streaming through the windows of his Schöneberg office, Germany being seven hours behind. Sigrid shifted her cramped legs on the floor cushion, her laptop positioned on the low table in her Minami-ku apartment. Dr Heinrich looked up from his notebook.

And since Sunday night? This fridge incident?

He's been avoiding me, Sigrid said. It's summer holidays and he looks after Tomo and his friend in the afternoons. As soon as I get home from work he'll rush off for his bar shift. He wears sunglasses, barely says a word. I can't push the issue, because Tomo's there. And when Hiroji gets in late after his shift, he doesn't come to our bed. He passes out in the living room.

Do you wake him in the morning? Attempt to talk to him?

Tomo's there. I let him sleep.

Dr Heinrich *hmmm*-ed to himself. Do you think the avoidance could be mutual?

Sigrid flushed and Dr Heinrich went on, Has anyone been in touch with you about his changed appearance? From the bar where he works? From the dance troupe?

No.

Behind his wire-rimmed spectacles, Dr Heinrich frowned and made some more notes. He looked up again, his expression sympathetic.

Sigrid, have you heard of Capgras syndrome?

Capgras syndrome?

It's the delusion that someone close to you has been replaced by a replica.

But something *has* happened to Hiroji.

Please hear me out, Sigrid, Dr Heinrich continued. Capgras delusions are caused by a disconnect between the part of the brain that recognizes faces, and the part of the brain that produces the usual emotional response to a familiar face. This sense that your husband is a 'bad' imposter replacing the 'good' man you married may have been growing in you for years. Throughout his repeated infidelities. Throughout his lack of concern about your depression . . .

But it's just been since Sunday night.

Your inability to integrate this shocking revelation about his twin into your understanding of who Hiroji is may have brought it to a head. Now when you see Hiroji's face, your limbic system doesn't respond in the usual way. The unfamiliar response to his familiar face has led to a splitting. The conviction Hiroji's a stranger.

Sigrid hoped Dr Heinrich didn't notice the tears blurring her eyes. So I'm *mad*?

No, and it's just a hypothesis. And in your case it could be more to do with unconscious denial and suppression than something more serious, like neurological damage or schizo-affective disorder.

She took a deep, shaky breath. How do I get rid of this?

I'm a psychotherapist, Dr Heinrich said, tapping at his keyboard. You need to speak to a psychiatrist. I've just looked up the details for an American specialist – Dr Franklin – at an international clinic in Kyoto. Your English is fluent?

Sigrid pressed the heels of her hands into her eye sockets, her vision a blizzard of black and white. This wasn't happening. What if she *was* mad? She'd be put on antipsychotics. They could take Tomo away.

The first step to overcoming this, Dr Heinrich said, is to acknowledge this is a delusion. So, whenever the delusion arises you must remind yourself of the underlying cause. The problem is not with your husband, but your *perception* of him.

Right, she said despondently.

I'll send you Dr Franklin's details after the session. I recommend you call and make an appointment as soon as possible. His office opens tomorrow at nine.

But when the fifty-minute Skype therapy session ended, Sigrid didn't look up the American psychiatrist's Kyoto clinic. Instead, she blocked Dr Heinrich, then called the receptionist in his Schöneberg office and cancelled their regular Wednesday nights.

Saturday afternoon, Sigrid's upstairs neighbour Mrs Kimura was hula-hooping in the car park outside their six-storey building. Swivelling her hips in pink leisurewear, her small white terrier Umeboshi sitting and watching obediently. Sigrid was on her way out to pick Tomo up from his friend's. She was running late when Mrs Kimura called, Takahara-san. Can I have a word?

Sigrid smiled at her neighbour and propped her sunglasses up on her head. Is something the matter?

Mrs Kimura grabbed the hula hoop and stilled her hips. She was out of breath and sweat trickled from the hairline of her tight, black-dyed perm. She cast her eyes reproachfully over Sigrid.

What's your husband doing up on the roof?

On the roof?

Yes, in the early mornings. Mrs Oyagi went up to do her callisthenics but had to rush back down. He was naked. Being peculiar.

The sensation of unheimlich that swept over Sigrid then reminded her of Sunday night, of the stranger with Hiroji's face illuminated by the open fridge. Umeboshi started yapping as though hurrying Sigrid to reply, and she heard herself say in a flat monotone, He must've been trying out some new choreography.

Sigrid's upstairs neighbour didn't seem appeased. She bristled – most likely at the lack of grovelling apology.

Mr Takahara must keep his clothes on. I know nudism is popular in Germany, but this is Japan. Your landlord, Mr Saito, is a friend of mine, remember? I don't want to have to call him to make a complaint.

Sigrid nodded. He won't disturb you again.

That night when Hiroji got back at two a.m., Sigrid was waiting for him in the living room. Candles were lit on the low table and the sliding doors to the balcony were open, the chirruping of cicada and the citronella scent of incense drifting in through the mosquito screen. *This is a Capgras delusion caused by a disconnect between the part of my brain that recognizes Hiroji's face, and the part of the brain that produces the usual emotional response*, she thought as he entered the room. She gestured to a floor cushion on the tatami mats.

Please, she said. We need to talk.

Hiroji sat opposite his wife, his expression blank, several days of stubble beneath the darkness concentrated in his eyes. He lit a cigarette, exhaled a plume towards the mosquito screen.

What have you been doing up on the roof? Sigrid asked.

Dancing. Trying out some ideas.

Naked? At five a.m.?

I can't sleep. And there's space up there.

You'll get us kicked out. Mrs Kimura'll call our landlord if anyone sees you again.

Hiroji turned to the balcony and exhaled. *This is a Capgras delusion*, Sigrid thought, gazing at his profile in the candlelight. *This is a Capgras delusion.* He turned back to her and she said,

What's going on with you, Hiroji? You've been acting weird since we met Damaris last week.

At the mention of the English photographer she detected a tensing, but he said, What do you care, Sigrid?

What do I care? You're my husband.

For now.

What?

I saw the papers. In your bedside drawer.

Sigrid was startled. She hadn't thought he was interested enough in her to go through her things.

If you want a divorce, he said, then I'm filing for sole custody. I'll get it too. You know how the laws here work.

She stared at her husband. Though she'd been putting it off, she'd taken it for granted Hiroji would acquiesce. Their marriage hadn't been working for years – he knew that as much as she did.

Why are you being unreasonable? she asked.

You're not taking my son to Germany.

I wasn't planning to.

But was that true? Though incapable of 'planning' anything in her depressed state, in her more optimistic moments, yes, she'd had vague daydreams of starting over with Tomo in Berlin. And Hiroji – or this stranger with Hiroji's face – knew it. His voice chillingly flat, he said, I'll tell the courts about your depression. All the pills you take, the days you spend lying in bed. I'll tell them about that night. If I hadn't come home early and called the ambulance, Tomo wouldn't have a mother right now.

Sigrid had to focus on keeping her voice and breathing steady – on hiding how his threats destabilized her.

That was *an accident*. I took too many because I wanted to sleep. And Tomo was at Eiji's house.

That makes you a responsible mother? Waiting until your son's at his friend's before your suicide attempt?

You *know* it wasn't a suicide attempt, Hiroji. You can't just—

Can't what? I have the hospital receipts. One stomach pump. One IV drip. One psychiatric evaluation . . .

Sigrid was trembling. Never had Hiroji been this malicious

before. Neglectful and selfish, yes, but never cruel. This man impersonating her husband and staring at her with his strange black eyes – who was he? He reached for his Mild Seven and rose to his feet, and Sigrid realized she didn't know what he was capable of. And she was afraid.

Where are you going? she asked.

Out.

In the doorway, he glanced back.

But don't worry. I won't go far.

Four nights later Sigrid was in the bathtub, staring at a pink disposable razor on the side and trying to muster the energy to drag the blade over her stubbled legs, when the phone on which she'd been numbly scrolling Facebook minutes earlier started buzzing on the toilet seat. She reached for it with slippery hands and saw it was Keiko Kobayashi – Eiji's mom. Tomo's elementary school was on summer vacation and they had a childcare arrangement where Keiko looked after Tomo and Eiji in the mornings, and Hiroji took the boys out in the afternoons, usually to Umekōji Park, where he coached them in baseball. Sigrid expected the call was about some change in this weekday schedule, but Keiko's refined Kyoto accent wavered between anger and apology as she said, My husband and I have decided we cannot let Mr Takahara look after Eiji-chan any more.

Oh. Water splashed as Sigrid sat up straighter. Why?

And it's better that Tomo-chan stops coming to us too. I know it's short notice, but I hope you understand.

I *don't* understand.

Mr Takahara . . . is unwell.

What did he do?

But Keiko wouldn't explain. Tremulously, she said goodbye and hung up.

Tomo was awake when she went into his room. Sitting up in bed and shining his flashlight around the walls, which were covered in posters of the Hanshin Tigers and various anime characters with exaggerated eyes and wide exclamatory mouths.

Tomo-chan, Sigrid said. What are you doing?

Can't sleep, he said.

Sigrid sat on the end of the bed, and Tomo turned off the torch. In German, she told him about the phone call. Did Tomo know what his dad had done to upset Eiji's mother? Her son shrugged and broke eye contact with her. Sigrid kept on. Where had his dad taken them that afternoon? To the park? Pachinko? Had he let them ride on his motorbike? In the blue glow of the Doraemon night light, Tomo shook his head.

Where, Tomo?

Dodging her gaze still, he said, Bamboo forest.

Dad took you and Eiji to the bamboo forest? Which one? Arashiyama?

He shrugged again. Dunno.

Tomo-chan . . . If Dad did something bad, you can tell me. You can tell me anything, you know.

We were playing a game.

What game?

Shinigami.

Sigrid remembered the word from a volume of Japanese folklore she'd once read.

Shinigami? The death god?

In faltering German, Tomo went on, He was butō dancing. Pretending Shinigami was inside him. He made his belly wriggle like snakes and Eiji got scared.

So he stopped?

Tomo frowned, searched for the words in German and coming up short switched to Japanese.

He said we had to *kill* something . . . to get rid of Shinigami.

Sigrid's heart quickened. Your dad didn't *kill* anything in the forest, did he?

Just pretend. Eiji started crying because he's a *baby* . . . So we went home.

What did he *pretend* to kill?

But Tomo shut down – guiltily, as though he'd done something wrong, making Sigrid suspect Hiroji had sworn him to secrecy.

Troubled, she pushed him for more details, but Tomo started to cry, and Sigrid realized Eiji wasn't the only one who'd been scared.

She rang Hiroji several times. Left voice messages and texts, each a reiteration of the same thing: *Eiji's mom called. Stay at Daisuke's tonight. Tomorrow we need to talk.* She looked for her and Tomo's passports, to check the expiration dates. Both were missing from her bedside drawer.

At midnight she slotted the security chain on the apartment door, went to bed and had a dream in which Hiroji woke her in the dark – naked under the bedsheets, his mouth hungry and insistent on hers. Sigrid had kissed him back, pulled him over her, inside of her, and they'd moved together, his hips rising and falling between her thighs. But as Sigrid had gazed up at her husband in the darkness, she realized the man staring back down at her wasn't Hiroji but the intruder with her husband's face. And her arousal turned to terror as she lay still beneath him, willing it to be over, willing herself not to scream, repeating in her head: *Capgras delusion, Capgras delusion, Capgras delusion . . .*

Just before dawn, the door buzzer. Persistent and loud. Sigrid lurched up and sleep-staggered to the intercom. Mrs Oyagi was furious. Mr Takahara was up on the roof again. Would Mrs Takahara get him down from there? Sigrid hung up and stumbled back to the bedroom. She pulled a loose cotton robe on over her vest and knew she'd no choice but to leave Tomo for five minutes. She would lock the door on the way out.

Up on the roof the light was spectral and blue-tinged over Minami-ku, the residential blocks and industrial warehouses stretching to the confluence of the Katsura and Kamo rivers in the south. Hiroji was standing to the east, towards the first glimmer of sunrise on the horizon. He was naked, clothes on the asphalt, and the rear of his butō-trained body completely still. It was cool up on the roof, the atmosphere charged and seared as though lightning had recently struck, ionizing the hairs on the back of Sigrid's neck.

Hiroji?

He began to dance, the blue-hued light seeming to bend and warp around him as he moved, shoulders and hips near-dislocating as he twisted into contortionist shapes Sigrid had never seen before – from Hiroji, or any other dancer – his body quivering from an exertion that seemed to demand every fibre of muscle, every firing nerve. Sigrid was mesmerized. Hiroji's double-jointed movements seemed impossible, as did the distortions they sent through the air. The dance was terrifying, as though he was compelled by forces outside of himself.

It was then she saw it, by Hiroji's bare feet. Limp, perhaps lifeless. White fur matted with blood. Sigrid's heart reverberated in her chest.

Hiroji.

He straightened up, turned to her. Even at a distance of ten or twenty paces Sigrid could see the dark turbulence in the centres of his unfocused eyes. He was Hiroji but not Hiroji. Her husband, but some other man. His genitals dangled in their dark thatch and his smooth white chest and pale nipples were marked by finger-smears of blood.

What happened to Umeboshi?

He stood still. Or not still. Something was moving under his taut and muscular stomach, under the skin and subcutaneous fat. It was as though Hiroji's intestines had come to life in the abdominal cavity, and were wriggling about, searching for a way out. *Like snakes.*

Sigrid didn't ask again about Mrs Kimura's dog. She turned and fled.

'A family emergency,' Sigrid told her boss when she called to request the day off. She couldn't tell him the emergency's exact nature, just as she couldn't answer Tomo's questions (Why was Mrs Kimura screaming? Why did the policemen come?). Instead she let Tomo play computer games in his bedroom while a locksmith changed the lock on the front door and she called round Hiroji's closest friends – all deeply concerned, all determined to find him (though Hiroji's phone was off and he hadn't shown up at Daisuke's bar since the previous Sunday night). At lunchtime, Sigrid got a phone call from a solicitor. Mrs Kimura was demanding four million yen to cover Umeboshi's funeral expenses and the cost of a new pedigree terrier, or she was taking them to court. Sigrid then got a phone call from their landlord, giving the Takaharas twenty-eight days' notice of their eviction next month.

When Kenji, Hiroji's oldest friend, drove over from Higashimukō around five, Sigrid could have wept with relief. Tomo had been in a subdued mood all day, and the appearance of Uncle Kenji with take-out boxes of pizza and a yo-yo he'd made specially for Tomo in his carpentry workshop was like the storm clouds parting. They ate the pizza in the living room then played karuta, Tomo cheering up enough to shout and slap the cards. Tomo then showed off his yo-yoing to Uncle Kenji, then his Hanshin Tigers and Astro Boy sticker collections until Sigrid had to drag him away to get ready for bed.

When Tomo had settled down to sleep, the grown-ups sat in the living room with cans of beer, the electric fan blowing the smoke of Kenji's American Spirit on to the balcony through the mosquito screen.

Tomo told me Hiroji was pretending to be Shinigami in the bamboo forest yesterday, Sigrid said. Do you know anything about Shinigami?

Cigarette between fingers, Kenji pushed some long black hair out of his eyes, his arms inked with sleeves of Shinto gods and mythological beasts.

Sounds like a game me, Hiroji and Mariko-chan used to play when we were kids. One of us would pretend to be Shinigami and chase the other two. When you were caught, you had to pretend to be possessed. Like, writhe about with eyeballs rolling back. It was just a silly game, to creep ourselves out.

Tomo said he saw Hiroji's stomach wriggling during the game, Sigrid said. Like there were snakes inside him. And up on the rooftop this morning, I saw it too. It was horrifying. I don't know what it was, but I know what I saw.

Cross-legged on the tatami, Kenji didn't suggest she'd imagined it.

49

As soon as Hiroji comes back we'll take him to a doctor, find out what's wrong.

I don't *want* him to come back. I don't want him near us right now . . .

Then I'll take care of him. Help him get the help he needs.

Kenji tapped ash from his cigarette. He wasn't charismatic in the same way Hiroji was, his presence unassuming and quiet, his narrow face too commonplace to hold a stranger's interest or attention. But his eyes were deeper, calmer and more reflective, giving Sigrid the impression, when she spoke, that Kenji was not only listening but trying to inhabit her point of view. So she told him about the night with Damaris, the change in Hiroji and the dread that had been with her ever since. She told him about Dr Heinrich's Capgras delusion theory.

I noticed Hiroji had changed too, Kenji said. I dropped by Daisuke's bar last Sunday and it was like . . . You know when an actor's had plastic surgery and you know something's different? But you can't say exactly what? I put it down to not seeing him in a while.

Sigrid nodded, first relieved, then dismayed. So it wasn't all in her head.

This photographer, Damaris. You been in touch with her again? Kenji asked.

I've googled her but can't find her. She must've lied about her name.

Sigrid knocked back some more beer. In all the strangeness they'd been discussing, the thing she wanted to ask next was the hardest to bring up.

Listen, Kenji. That night in the bar, Hiroji said that he and Mariko were estranged because they had been 'too close' as adolescents. He took it back the next day – said he'd made it up. But did you know anything about that, when they were younger?

Too close? Kenji frowned.

For an uncomfortable moment Sigrid thought she would have to explain, then Kenji seemed to understand.

I never picked up on that. But then I wasn't the most observant kid. I *do* remember when we were fourteen or fifteen, Mariko-chan changed. She'd always been a tomboy, riding bikes and running around the bamboo forest with me and Hiroji. But in the last year of junior high school she mostly stayed in her room, studying.

Did she fall out with Hiroji?

All I noticed was that she went from being our friend to not wanting anything to do with us. Then she got a scholarship to a private all girls' high school, and stayed in the dormitories there, because it was far away. I wrote her a couple of letters, but she didn't write back. Mariko-chan just, like, disappeared.

Hiroji must've hurt her in some way, for her to cut off all contact. I know how . . . *selfish* he can be. I wonder, *if* they were 'too close' . . . was it mutual?

I don't know, Sigrid. I really don't know . . . Actually, I sent her a message today, asking if he'd been in touch with her.

And?

Kenji took out his phone, then held up Mariko's reply for Sigrid to read.

Haven't seen or heard from him in years.

The next morning, after dropping Tomo off at Jeong Hoon's house (the only classmate whose Korean mother wasn't part of Keiko Kobayashi's gossipy network), Sigrid went to the German language school and taught six classes back to back. Then, at four p.m. – her 'lunch break' – she shut herself in an empty classroom and lay down on the tatami mats for the hour before her final class. She closed her eyes, not expecting to sleep, but she did and she dreamt she was in a bamboo forest at shadowy dusk or dawn, where she saw two naked men in the distance, amongst the slender trunks of bamboo. Approaching, weaving through the trees, Sigrid saw that one man was squatting on the torso of the other, who lay on the mulchy decomposing matter of the forest floor. The squatting man was using a knife to carve flesh from the other man's mutilated chest. A cry escaped Sigrid and both men turned their heads, the one with the knife grinning with blood on his teeth. Seeing that both were Hiroji, she screamed.

★

Halfway through the last German lesson on her timetable, her cell phone rang. The caller was Jeong Hoon's mother, so she stepped out of class to answer.

Everything OK? Sigrid asked.

Min-Ji couldn't speak at first – struggling to form the words. Then she stammered, I . . . I wouldn't let him in . . . But he shoved me out of the way. He just barged straight into my home.

Where's Tomo?

He took him. I don't know where.

The police said they'd radio all the on-duty officers in Kyoto to let them know about her husband and missing son. They said they'd check the surveillance footage of the CCTV cameras surrounding Jeong Hoon's street and in the nearest train stations. Kenji drove over from Higashimukō within half an hour, sawdust in his long black hair, clothes stained with linseed oil, and together they called everyone Hiroji knew. Kenji put a message on Facebook saying Hiroji and Tomo were missing, and Sigrid's phone rang and buzzed dozens of times with messages of support and offers to help. Some of the troupe even drove around Kyoto searching games arcades, Mister Donuts and KFCs and other places where a father and seven-year-old son might hang out. Sigrid called her husband over and over, but his phone remained off.

In this way, the night passed; Sigrid pacing back and forth in her soon-to-be-evicted-from apartment, smoking Kenji's American Spirits, making and answering calls, and ignoring Kenji's suggestions she eat or get some sleep. Around three a.m., feeling her lungs were congested with wet cement, she stepped out on to the balcony into the night, gasping for air. Kenji came out after her and Sigrid turned to him.

I can't stop thinking about that murdered dog, she said. I can't stop thinking that he might . . .

The sentence was left unfinished as Kenji's phone buzzed in his pocket. He took it out.

Mariko-chan. Missed call.

Mariko?

They exchanged glances.

She's left a message. Must've called while I was speaking to some-body else.

Kenji dialled voicemail and brought the phone to his ear.

She's saying Hiroji called her tonight.

The sky was lightening on the drive to the outskirts of Nagaokakyō. They turned off the Meishin Expressway near the Suntory factory and sped through paddy fields and residential streets, up the hills in the west. Hiroji's parents had died, and the residence sold years before Sigrid met him. So when Kenji pulled up at the end of a bamboo-shrouded lane, she was encountering Hiroji's one-storey childhood home for the first time.

When she'd called the Minami-ku precinct, they said they would dispatch an officer to meet them at the address. But Sigrid couldn't wait. Mariko's voice message was on a loop in her head (. . . *he said he's in our shrine, to make another sacrifice . . .*) and she sprang out of Kenji's car and towards the trail leading behind the house.

The temperature was a few degrees lower in the forest – a cold, damp, mosquito-infested place – and staring into the tall, slender bamboo that extended for many kilometres into Kyoto Prefec-ture, Sigrid was confounded as to which way to go. Kenji caught her up.

If I remember, the shrine's upstream, he said. Fifteen minutes away, I think. It's been over twenty years . . .

He led the way into the grove, weaving in and out of the maze of trees creaking all around them, the leaves swaying and crashing in the breeze, vertiginously high above. Though the first crepuscular light was filtering through the canopy, it wasn't long before Sigrid had lost all sense of which direction they were heading in, or the way back to the car. Stumbling after Kenji in her sandals, under-growth scratching her bare calves, Sigrid had the feeling of sentience all around them, of the forest watching them moving through it, the trees speaking to each other in a language of eerie fluting and groaning and percussive knocks as they bent in the wind, spreading word of human trespassers.

She chased Kenji until they reached a narrow ankle-deep stream which he pursued further into the grove. On and on they went, for longer than fifteen minutes, and Sigrid began to fear Kenji'd made a mistake, that the shrine was in another part of the bamboo grove entirely. Then he cried, *There.* Up ahead in a small clearing was the gate of an old Shinto shrine, the vermilion paint flaking from the rotting wooden pillars. They ran under the gate's double lintel and Sigrid could feel the strange dark energies that resonated throughout the forest becoming stronger there, unbearably so. A few crumbling steps led up to a derelict hall for worship, the entrance guarded on either side by eroded stone lion-dogs. Inside, under the half-missing roof, a low buzzing filled Sigrid's ears, and through the gloom she saw a sleeping bag, the charred remnants of a fire, empty Pocari Sweat bottles and Tomo's Hanshin Tigers baseball cap. By the altar, heaped before the statue of some Shinto god, carcasses droned with flies. Two dogs. Blood pounding in her temples, she spun around, screaming through the forest.

Tomo-chan . . . Tomo-chan . . .

Kenji took off, zigzagging through the trees. She went after him, confused, until she saw what he was running towards.

Through the segmented limbs of bamboo: Hiroji. Naked. Kneeling with forehead on the forest floor. Spine rounded and his arms stretched out in front of him, palms turned up. Buttocks on dirty-soled feet.

Kenji sank down beside his friend. Shook his shoulder, turned his glassy-eyed head to the side.

He's not breathing, he shouted. I'm calling an ambulance . . .

The roar in Sigrid's skull drowned out the rest. Her heart imploding, she strained her eyes through the trees and shouted for Tomo. Then, twenty or so metres away: a flash of colour amongst the slender trunks. The yellow of the shorts Tomo had worn the previous afternoon. The blue of his T-shirt stripes. Sigrid began to run over, darting through trees towards her son. But he did not run towards her. He ran the other way.

Tomo-chan. Stop. It's me.

He fell over with a cry. But when she reached Tomo he was up again and limping away, wrist clutched to chest. Sigrid caught him by his arm and Tomo flailed against her.

Let me go. Shinigami's coming!

There's no Shinigami, Tomo.

And Tomo cried, It killed him. I saw it.

Tomo-chan. Come with me. *Please!*

Sigrid pulled her son into her embrace. But Tomo fought her as though fighting for his life. Screaming, he lashed out, hitting her with his injured wrist, kicking her shins, Sigrid unable to restrain him as he yelled, *No. It will kill me. Let me go.*

★

We sat on the yellow L-shaped sofa in the early hours of Saturday morning, the darkness thinning beyond the venetian blinds at the approach of day. Sigrid had a patterned throw over her shoulders, her legs tucked beneath her, and I could almost see the fissures in her calm, steady exterior – the deep fault lines formed by the events of that summer eleven years ago.

We flew to my mother's in Düsseldorf as soon as I was cleared of any involvement in Hiroji's death, Sigrid said. I was just desperate to get Tomo out of Japan . . . Kenji took over the death admin. Let me know when the post-mortem discovered situs inversus, that Hiroji's internal organs were reversed from left to right, and determined heart failure to be the cause of death. Same as Lena.

I nodded. We'd been over it already.

Before I left Japan I made a statement to the police about Damaris, Sigrid said. Stupid of me to think I'd be taken seriously – a gaijin woman, raving about Shinigami and snakes . . .

I told the Coroner's Liaison Officer about Marion, I said. That I suspected she had something to do with Lena's death. He was sympathetic, but told me situs inversus is caused by a one-in-ten-thousand mutation in the gene for left to right asymmetry. It couldn't just happen at the age of thirty-two. Astonishing there'd been no adverse effects – at least, not until her death. But Lena'd developed that way in the womb.

Sigrid reached for the cardboard box of photographs we'd sifted through earlier in the evening.

I found something cleaning out our apartment after Hiroji died. At the time it struck me as creepy, nothing more significant than that. Now I'm having second thoughts.

She passed me the black and white photograph. In it, Hiroji was standing naked on a riverbank, shoulders back and arms out by his sides like da Vinci's *Vitruvian Man*. He stared at the camera lens with a flat and empty gaze. Tabula rasa, void of character or thought. The image was chilling. Fascinating. I recognized the aesthetic.

Damaris took this?

Sigrid wrapped the patterned throw tighter around her shoulders. I don't know. He's by the Kamogawa, and he said he and Damaris drank beer there together. You said Damaris – Marion, that is – took a photo of Lena?

Yes. Lena asked me to destroy it. But it was similar to this one. Exploitative somehow, though she wasn't naked. She just didn't look human any more.

My flight back to London was late on Sunday evening and shortly before I left for the airport the front door opened and Tomo walked in carrying a backpack, home from college for a few days. Like his mother, he was obscenely beautiful and moved with the languid ease of someone habituated to the admiring gazes of others, his confidence far removed from any teenaged awkwardness. Sigrid introduced us and Tomo politely said hello, apologizing that his English 'wasn't great', before having an exchange in German with Sigrid about (as far as I could translate) his train journey from Munich. After speaking to his mother, Tomo hovered at the table and said in English, You know my Aunt Mariko?

I nodded.

She put me back in touch with your mother.

This was Sigrid's explanation for my being there; we'd been friends in Kyoto and lost touch.

I've never met my aunt.

Nihon kaerimasu ka?

I don't speak Japanese.

Surprised, I repeated my question in English. Any plans to go back to Japan?

Tomo shrugged. I'm going to Barcelona to study Spanish this summer. And then I'm doing a year abroad in Mexico, and backpacking around South America, so . . .

His phone then vibrated in his pocket, reminding him of the more immediate and exciting world of his friends. He excused himself.

Nice to meet you, Jake. Hope you have a good flight back to London.

He disappeared into the bedroom where I'd slept over the weekend. Moments later loud techno came through the door.

He doesn't speak Japanese? I asked.

Never. And if I speak it, he claims not to understand.

Sigrid pushed her chair back and began gathering up our dinner plates. It was nearly time for us to set off for the S-Bahn. Leaning over the table for my water glass, she glanced at his bedroom door and said, Whatever happened to him that night, no child psychiatrist could get it out . . . And what kills me is I just don't know. When Hiroji called his sister to say he was making another sacrifice, did he mean our son?

Badlands – II

It's so fucking hot, says the girl. I'm, like, *vapourizing*.

The woman smiles as she waits patiently for Rosa to catch up, but behind her sunglasses regards her coldly. She's not much of a hiker, this girl. She struggles in the heat, pink-cheeked under the wide-brimmed sun hat the woman's lent her, stumbling over the clinkers metamorphosed by ancient coal-seam fires, now scattered across the Bisti Wilderness like the shards of a hundred thousand broken terracotta pots. The woman has more to complain about, her T-shirt soaked and muscles aching under her heavy backpack, DSLR camera and other equipment. She's feverish, lightheaded, the fluid in the labyrinth of her ears gently spiralling. But as Rosa reaches her she says sympathetically, Not long until the shale hills. There's more shade there, so we can stop and rest.

Footfalls crunching over crumbling rocks, they continue east across the wide arroyo-crossed valley floor, trudging slowly under the relentless sun and blue sky, clear of any wisp of cloud or soaring bird. The barrenlands appear near-lifeless. There's snakeweed, yellow tufts of grass and hardy desiccated shrubs, but nothing with a beating heart save themselves.

The blue cotton of Rosa's sundress billows out in a gust of wind and she holds her hat with one hand to prevent it being snatched from her curly head.

It's like we've gone back to biblical times, she says. Like we're gonna be out here for forty days and forty nights with Satan tempting our asses.

The woman backhands sweat from her brow. The Old Testament was two seconds ago as far as these badlands are concerned, she says. The ground under our feet is tens of millions of years old.

Rosa glances at the sun-baked mud beneath her cheap sneakers, her shadow bobbing out in front of her.

All of this was once dark dripping rainforest, the woman continues. Two-hundred-foot-high trees. Prehistoric creatures. And swamps and rivers flowing to the sea that once divided America.

Under her sun hat, Rosa gazes around with the sceptical look of a creationist. But then she says, I read somewhere this place is a graveyard of dinosaur bones. From that asteroid that wiped everything out. The one with the weird name . . .

Chicxulub.

Yeah, that one. Crazy how everything can be gone in just one second.

Much longer than a second, the woman says. Chicxulub was just the beginning. Many species died from the chain of earthquakes, volcanoes and tsunamis it triggered. From the ash clouds suffocating the Earth and all the burning debris falling from the sky. But the dinosaurs spent thousands more years on a planet sick from climate disruption before dying out for good.

Like global warming, says the girl.

Yes, and it's happening again now. Droughts, extreme weather, wildfires and floods. In a hundred or two hundred years, much of America might be like this wilderness . . .

The girl wrinkles her nose slightly, as though a song she dislikes has come on the radio, or she's been served a portion of something unpalatable.

This is why I need to be a spiritual influencer, she says. People can use my videos to learn about the Law of Attraction to empower themselves, and then use that self-empowerment to bring positive change to the world. Like, manifest a better future, for humanity.

The woman smiles at the girl.

Your positivity movement will undo all the catastrophic damage we've done to the environment, I'm sure.

Exactly. *Fuck* doom and gloom.

They leave the wide flat wash and enter an undulating area of sandstone hills: pale and gleaming yellow, striated with layers of volcanic ash from ancient eruptions, glittering purple and black. The sun beats down and the landscape beats back with the immensity of deep time; long-vanished worlds contained in each sandstone mound, millions of years compressed into geological layers inches thin. Looking around, the girl doesn't remark on the topographical strangeness. Instead she says, I gotta pee. Where can I go around here?

The woman pulls a pack of Kleenex out of her shorts.

This whole place needs watering.

The girl flings off her hat and tote bag and takes the tissues, her cotton dress strikingly blue against the yellows and browns as she rounds the corner of a hill. Watching her disappear, the woman thinks of the myth of progress. In the near future, when scarcity is rife and civilization's on the brink, will her reverence for life be defeated? Or will she thrive in the chaos, her will to survive intact? Part of her wants to stick around out of sheer voyeurism, to see how far the conquering species will fall.

The dizziness sweeping over the woman brings her back to her reality. If she wants to bear witness to the future she must first get through the night ahead.

The girl reappears, but instead of gathering up her tote bag to resume their hike to the hoodoos, she ascends a low sandstone mound. Shading her eyes with a hand she stares from her vantage point across the stark, erosional landscape, back the way they came. The hot dry wind presses blue cotton against Rosa's thighs and sends her brown curls into disarray.

You said we'd see other hikers, she says.

It's a weekday, the woman replies. People are at work. Or they hike early in the morning, before it gets too hot. We're here for the sunset.

Rosa turns her back against the sun and gazes down at the woman. In her pensiveness her smoke-grey eyes appear to darken and eddy, tenebrous as thunderhead clouds gathering before a storm. Keen to avoid the apprehension of the parking lot, the woman reassures her, Nothing bad's going to happen, Rosa. What are you afraid of?

The girl hesitates. I don't know, Therese . . . Sometimes I feel like you're mad at me or something.

The woman removes her sunglasses, her brow furrowed with bafflement and a hint of hurt.

Why would I be mad?

Up on the sandstone mound, Rosa is flustered. She glances at the woman's grazed knees and bruised forearm (a tumble down some stairs, the woman had said, though the haematoma's wrapped around her wrist like blackened fingers). Her distrustful gaze moves up to the tubercular paleness of the woman's face and dark eyes, unshaded now, both sharp and febrile. She appears to notice once more, with pity and distaste, her state of deterioration, and the woman flashes with impatience for their situations to be reversed.

You sure I haven't pissed you off or anything? Rosa asks.

The woman smiles reassuringly. Don't be silly. I just frown a lot in photographer mode . . . Speaking of which, how about I take some test shots of you? Here?

What about getting to the hoodoos?

We've time for a quick shoot.

The backpack's on the ground but the DSLR camera's around the woman's neck. She unscrews the lens cap and holds the view-finder up to her eye as the girl descends the sandstone formation. Rosa takes a compact out of her tote and holds it to her face.

Ugh. I'm so puffy and red. And the sun hat's flattened my hair.

You look gorgeous, the woman says.

But the girl takes out some dry shampoo, tips her head upside down and begins spraying her roots. She tosses her head the right way up again and begins to wind each spiral around her finger, frowning intently in her compact to arrange them just so. Sensing the woman watching her, Rosa says, I just need a couple of minutes. That OK?

The woman shivers. Her mouth tastes of blood and she can feel the pathogens moving through her, inflaming her body as her immune system recedes. She wants to get to the hoodoos before the agents of decomposition reach her organs, before she's more dead than alive. But it was her idea, stopping for photographs.

No problem, she says.

The girl needs twelve minutes, it turns out, to dab the pink of her complexion with concealer and re-create the glossy, thick-browed look of TikTok make-up tutorials. But when she's ready she gets straight to work against the backdrop of primordial stone and sky. The woman expects her to pose like she did in the hotel room: hand on hip, throwing over-the-shoulder glances at the camera like an influencer flaunting the plump and curvy body at the centre of her lucrative brand. But instead of pouting, Rosa smiles serenely and places her hands together in a namaste. Behind the camera the woman hides her smile, and as she clicks and clicks is struck anew by Rosa's seventeen-year-old loveliness. The smooth skin, supple with collagen, endearingly pimpled here and there. The shimmering limbs, chubby and delectable in the heat. Gazing upon Rosa brings all the pleasures of objectification, but at the centre of the woman's admiration is a covetousness. A yearning to shed her own weakened corporeal form and inhabit the girl's instead; every succulent cell of her, every inch of juvenescent flesh.

As Rosa poses in the sunlight refracted from the pale fossiliferous rock, the woman realizes she's far from calm. The warmth, compassion and spiritual enlightenment she's trying to project are undermined by the clench of her jaw, the skittishness of her eyes like a horse about to bolt. The woman lowers her camera and says, Everything OK, Rosa?

Just kinda tense . . .

The girl walks around, shaking her arms and rolling her shoulders as though shrugging off her nerves, and the woman thinks of how rare it is for one of her subjects to not remain under her sway. But then it's rare for so many months to lapse after one of her offerings and for her disintegration to begin (her mortuary smell no doubt why her hold's diminished in power).

The woman wonders: does the Sculptor feel this wretched in the terminal stages of her cancer? Despite everything that happened between them, in her excruciating state of inside-out rot, she feels connected to her. But while the woman will recover, if all goes to plan, the Sculptor will soon be in the ground. (And then, will she let her go?)

She lifts her camera. Ready to try again? she asks Rosa.

Sure.

But the girl's smile is forced, and the woman knows when darkness falls she'll have her work cut out assuaging her fears. Because she can't have a repeat of what happened with the man two weeks earlier. She *won't* have a repeat of it. Not at any cost.

The moment she saw him in the Albuquerque dive bar she knew he was the reason she'd driven down the old Route 66 and into the district of boarded-up shopfronts instead of back to her hotel. Blond, mid-to-late thirties, boyish face flushed by one a.m. blood alcohol levels, the man was unremarkable in himself. But it had attached itself to him, the swarming of dark energy around him telling the woman that he was the one. She sipped a glass of red wine at the bar and watched him playing pool with his friend. Watched his ex-military posture as he leant over the table with his cue or stood waiting his turn. There were a dozen or so other drinkers in the bar – throwing darts, sharing pitchers of beer. Gradually she entered the man's awareness. The lone woman on the bar stool, shining in his periphery until he couldn't help but glance over, flattered, intrigued.

By two a.m. his friend had gone and they were drinking together at a table cluttered with tequila shot glasses and half-sucked segments of lime. They'd played a round of darts, but now were talking, leaning into each other in the sweaty woozy closeness of the bar, the night shifting into a more intimate gear. There was no secret to it. She let the man's presence stir up the want in her. Let sex be the subtext as she twisted her long-stemmed wine glass, twisted herself towards him on her stool, her dark eyes devouring him as he spoke about his job at the power plant, the three kids he had visitation rights to every other weekend and their trip to the Rattlesnake Museum that afternoon. He spoke about his tour of Iraq in 2004 and the heat and monotony of the desert, the day-to-day protecting of supply routes, and insurgent bullets pinging from armoured trucks. He spoke of an ambush with explosives and comrades maimed and dead, his words detached but circling something frozen and speechless at the centre of him. Then he laughed, awkwardly, inappropriately, and the woman reached for his hand and pressed it against her bare thigh. And he laughed once more in surprise, but began to stroke her with roughened fingers, his light blue eyes rippling with relief. Because here was some reprieve from it, at least for one night; in this woman, offering herself up to him in her thin black dress.

They drove out of the city, heading down a backcountry road in the south. They walked out into the barrenlands together, the woman looking up at the explosion of stars in the night sky until he blocked her view; tongue in her mouth, erection pushing through his jeans, hands everywhere. She went down on her knees on the stony ground and he clutched her hair in his fist as she moved over his cock, looking up through the darkness at him as he grimaced in pleasure, or sneered, or both. Then he dragged her up again by the wrist and over to the hood of the car. Yanked up her dress and splayed her there beneath him; moaning and gasping as he fucked her, shuddering and wet.

Darkness was fading when it was over. Buckling his belt, looking around at the desolate landscape emerging in the gloom before dawn, the man murmured, Where the fuck are we?

The fog of precoital excitement had cleared and, sober now, he looked strangely at the woman as though seeing her properly for the first time. Noticing the German tourist wasn't as attractive as in the bar, perhaps. Older. Not slender but scrawny. Her lustre gone, her skin anaemic, her hair lank and thin. He frowned at their desert surroundings again, as though they were somewhere not of this world. And though the woman hadn't taken him for a perceptive man, he seemed aware of the cast of unreality around them. The perturbation of something beyond the reach of the senses, watching them with multitudinous eyes.

He checked his iPhone. How the fuck's it nearly five? I gotta get back. Kaitlyn gets back from night shift at the hospital soon.

The woman unpeeled herself from the hood of the car and stood on shaky legs; inner thighs bruised, semen dripping out of her. Bending over, she brushed gravel from her shins and grazed knees, wondering if they would scab.

Sure, she said. No problem.

But she stumbled round to the driver's seat, checked the ignition, then her bag and called, D'you remember where I put my keys?

He reeled around. You're fucking kidding me?

Twenty minutes later the man – Brandon, his name was Brandon – was still walking in frustrated, desperate circles around the Toyota, sweeping the bare ground with the flashlight on his phone as the woman turned out every compartment of her bag and crawled around in the car, groping under the front seats. Every so often she glanced to the east, where the sun was still beneath the vast and empty desert horizon. They were still in the terminator – the shadowy line that divides the Earth between night and day. Stars were vanishing as the dark dissolved in the sky. Another quarter hour and Venus would rise.

The Polaroid camera was in the glove compartment, loaded with colour film. The woman placed it on the roof of the Toyota in its black leather case, then went and sat on the hood again. On hands and knees by the passenger-side door, Brandon shone his phone under the chassis.

I'll call someone, the woman said. There's probably a twenty-four-hour service in Albuquerque that can tow us back. We'll be out of here in an hour or so.

Brandon jumped up, the prospect of spending another hour out there apparently heightening his instinct that things weren't right. It was almost extrasensory, his perception of it. It reminded the woman of the way snakes and small mammals detect stirrings in the depths of earth, days before a quake. Must be Iraq, she thought, the sharpening of his vigilance and preternatural sense.

That's no good. I gotta be back by six thirty. I'm walking to the highway. I'll hitch.

The I-25's twelve miles down that track.

Twelve miles?

Brandon looked rattled. How'd they end up so far from Albuquerque? How come he hadn't noticed her driving him so many miles to get laid?

Plus there's zero traffic on a Sunday morning, the woman added. It'll be quicker to wait to get towed.

Brandon glared at her. He could sense her deception, just as he could sense the disintegration around them; the shifting of time and space around the rupturing to come. He leant in closer, his breathing jagged, his gaze accusing and fierce.

You're fucking with me. Those keys can't just have disappeared. Where are they?

He loomed over her as she sat on the hood. Threatening violence with his six feet of height, his 220 pounds of muscle and flesh. And she could see in his blood-splintered eyes how he despised her. The alluring spell she'd cast in the bar had lifted and he could now detect the whiff of putrescence about her, the trillions of seething microbes rising up beneath her feverish skin. But she knew her decay and weakened state aroused him too. He was stiffening again, in fact.

She reached to stroke his cock again through the crotch of his jeans and, glaring, he grabbed her wrist. Twisted and squeezed. And feeling the haemorrhaging of tiny vessels under his grip, the blossoming of a bruise, she smiled.

I wouldn't, Brandon.

Fear sharpened in his eyes at the agitation around them. The trembling of the web of reality; the invisible threads he and the woman were entangled in, quivering at the spider's approach. He released the woman's wrist and stepped back. Then noticed the Polaroid camera on the Toyota's roof.

What's with the camera?

I was going to take a photograph.

Of what?

The sunrise.

The reminder of daybreak seemed to give him another jolt. Afraid, he looked at the scrubland stretching for miles in every direction, over to the low hills. The woman said, I'm calling roadside assistance. We've got reception, *just*.

With a scowl of resignation, Brandon said, Fine. I'm gonna take a leak.

Her phone was on the dashboard and she sat in the driver's seat pretending to google a tow service as, fifteen yards away, Brandon relieved himself of the night's draught beer, pissing in a wide arc into the dirt. He fastened his jeans again, and only when he looked furtively back at her did she realize what he meant to do. She leapt out of the car as he started running in the opposite direction, arms and legs pumping wildly as he sprinted hard and fast through the scrub. She started after him, but a stabbing in her side stopped her. He fled towards the low hills in the west, leaping over arroyos, so she couldn't pursue him on four wheels or catch him up on foot.

When the pain subsided, the woman took her camera from the roof and got back into the driver's seat. She dug her fingers into the incision Swiss Army-knifed into the headrest foam, retrieved her keys and started the ignition. Coughing, she turned the Toyota around and drove down the dirt track, alarmed by the rattle in her lungs. As she coughed into her hand, Venus appeared on the shadowed horizon, and removing hand from mouth she saw the blood splattering her palm; as good as any warning that Brandon had been her last chance to fuck up.

The Bisti sun scorches down on the badlands and around the fifty-photo mark Rosa breaks out of the calm, spiritually centred persona she's trying to project.

Maybe coming out here was a bad idea, she says. Maybe we should go back.

Why d'you say that?

I'm just not getting it right. Not getting *her* right.

Her?

Aurora Rose.

Rosa brushes some curls out of her eyes, her cherub's face creased with consternation. The woman lowers her camera and says, What are you talking about? Come take a look.

The girl bows her head over the digital camera's viewing pane as the woman moves through the images. In every photo the prettier, left side of Rosa's face dominates and the sun's luminosity hides any blemishes or flaws. She's exuding just the right amount of confidence and spirituality, smiling at the camera like the girl who knows all the secrets to bending the universe to her will, to manifesting what she wants. Secrets for those who watch, like and subscribe.

The woman knows she's captured the girl as she wants to be seen – that she's photographed the Aurora Rose fantasy the girl has in her head.

Oh my God. I love these. *Thank you.*

She beams up at the woman, delight at the first steps of her dream's actualization eclipsing her fears.

And the woman beams back. Don't thank *me*, Rosa. This is all *you*. You manifested these photos. Just like you manifested *me*.

Testimony 3 – Bedwyr

Angels Singing. A remote settlement of stone cottages in moorlands studded with sheep and craggy rocks, drizzle-grey and miles from any main road. Bedwyr's house was set apart from the hamlet, further up a hill, and I leant into blustery winds as I went up the trail. Thrashing through weeds and nettles to his front door, I could detect the movement in the cottage's stone walls; the subsidence and slow buckling towards collapse.

They'd warned me Bedwyr was a recluse who spoke to no one, so I slotted my letter through the stiff-hinged letter box before turning to hike back to the youth hostel for the night. I'd no idea if Bedwyr's daughter was the same 'crippled girl' Damaris had mentioned to Sigrid in the Pontochō-dōri bar, but after hours in the nearest farmer's café where a hush fell when I spoke English, then on surrounding country lanes, accosting strangers who gaped uncomprehendingly at my questions, Ceridwen, daughter of Bedwyr, was the only 'girl in a wheelchair' who'd lived in Angels Singing that the locals could recall.

The next morning I returned to Bedwyr's cottage. Breathless, soaked by fine mizzle, I knocked and waited. Knocked and waited again. After twenty minutes, just as I was about to leave and commence the long journey back to London, the door unlatched. The stooped occupant was in his seventies, with straggly white hair and a haggard expression half-obscured by beard, his Aran jumper and corduroy trousers hanging from his shepherd's-crook frame. I began to introduce myself and he said, She's dead.

I'm sorry?

My daughter. Dead nearly thirty-five years.

I'm sorry to hear that, I said.

The locals hadn't known Ceridwen was deceased. She'd moved away to Swansea, they'd heard.

They tell you I'm a murderer? Bedwyr asked.

His tone was flat. Only vaguely curious about what the dozen or so souls who lived nearest to him had said.

I hesitated. They mentioned that you went to jail.

HMP Usk. Twenty-five years.

Right.

Bedwyr stared at me then, long and hard. Confrontational, I assumed at the time. In retrospect, however, I think he was deliberating whether to break his years of silence. Whether to invite me in or shut the door in my face.

I read your letter, he said. There *was* a woman who came and took Ceridwen's photo. But she wasn't Marion or Damaris. She was Liesl. From Leipzig. She took my daughter's photo before my daughter went strange. That was in 1988.

How old was Liesl? The woman in my letter was in her late thirties in 2011.

So was Liesl in '88.

They can't be the same person then.

Bedwyr continued his long, hard stare.

She wasn't natural, Liesl. She had a peculiar smell.

He pulled the door wider. Stepped back so I could enter. The village shopkeeper had told me that after Bedwyr's arrest a gang of teenagers had attempted to burn the cottage down but only succeeded in setting themselves on fire, the ringleader dying in Bedwyr's garden. The cottage had since had the reputation of being cursed. No one had attempted to break in or vandalize it during his twenty-five years in jail, and there'd been no attempts at vigilantism since his release in 2013.

I remembered this as I crossed the threshold, following Bedwyr inside.

I kept this place spick and span when Ceridwen was here. Now it's just me, there's no point.

I nodded as though I understood, but I understood not at all how anyone could live as Bedwyr did, in a room of peeling fleur-de-lis wallpaper, mottled black by spore-exhaling mould, with a trail through the junk to the armchair where he spent his days, doing what I don't know, for there was no television or radio or books. I sat on a hard wooden stool by a fireplace that remained unlit, despite the dampness of my hair and clothes. When I began to speak about Lena, Bedwyr cut me off.

I've no interest in your friend.

There were faded photographs of Ceridwen on the mantelpiece. She was ethereal, with flaxen hair and melancholy eyes. Half-girl, half-faerie-queen illustration from a Victorian children's book, the wheelchair handles rising behind her like the curved back of a throne. The photo frames were the only objects in the room not thick with grime or dust – the glass recently polished. When he caught me staring at her, Bedwyr said, Ceridwen was born ablebodied. Walking at one, running and hop-skip-jumping at two. Alys, her mother, and I couldn't keep up with her. Then, when she was five, she curled up into a ball and did a rollover off the top of the stairs of our house in Swansea. I was in the kitchen when I heard the thumping and the screams. Alys and I found her at a funny angle on the hall carpet. I still remember the chill that came over me when she said, *Daddy, I can't feel my legs.*

I can't imagine. Such tragic luck.

Bedwyr shrugged.

After Ceridwen's accident, one of us had to care for her full time. Because I worked at the factory and was on a lower wage, it was me. I left my job and Alys stayed at hers at Littlewoods . . . Kept her busy, Littlewoods. Always home late from overtime that wasn't on her payslip, Alys was. When I found out about the affair she was having, I gave her a choice: end it, or never see me and Ceridwen again. Alys walked out on us, went to live with the other man. She was pregnant within the year. Divorced me, married him. As I said to Ceridwen, it was as though she wanted to start a new family with an able-bodied child.

Above his beard, Bedwyr's eyes were stony and castigating at the decades-old betrayal. I gave the faintest of nods, beginning to understand why Ceridwen looked so unhappy in all the photographs.

Money was tight when Alys left. But then my great-uncle died.

Left me this cottage and enough inheritance to get by on. So we moved here in '82. Ceridwen was upset to leave the special school she went to, but I was glad to get out of Swansea. I thought it would be better for her to grow up in a place where there's no crime, no litter, no factory smoke . . .

Bedwyr stared through me, reflecting on his mistake.

You met Liesl here? I asked. In Angels Singing?

That's right.

*

Liesl. She appeared in church one Sunday. Reverend Parry mentioned her at the start of the service: 'And a warm welcome to Liesl, who joins us from East Germany.' The congregation of forty or so had all turned to look at her, and Liesl had timidly dipped her head: a peaky-looking woman, in a dowdy cardigan, blouse and ankle-length skirt. Throughout the service Bedwyr noticed Ceridwen stealing inquisitive glances at her. She'd never met a German before. All she knew of Germany came from Bedwyr's lessons of the Second World War.

After the service, Bedwyr was pushing his daughter in her wheelchair out of the chapel, when Liesl approached. Beaming, she told Ceridwen what a beauty she was, like a 'Dresden doll', and Ceridwen turned pink to the collar of her Sunday dress. Bedwyr wasn't one for standing around and chattering meaningless inanities after Sunday service, but he was curious about the East German.

I thought citizens of the GDR aren't allowed to travel to the West. How did you get out?

Liesl said she'd been smuggled over the border in a butcher's van, buried under the carcasses of slaughtered pigs.

To this day I can't stomach a pork chop. But for my freedom it's a small price to pay.

She then told Bedwyr she'd spent the summer in Wales, hiking around Snowdonia, the Cambrian Mountains, and now the Brecon Beacons. Though she looked close to forty she didn't mention any family, and Bedwyr thought it unseemly that this woman was drifting around on her own. When Liesl said she was a photographer and gushed about how wonderful Ceridwen would look photographed in the late summer light, he was further ill at ease.

Perhaps we could do a photoshoot in the garden of your home? Liesl suggested. In exchange for a German lesson?

Before Bedwyr could say no, Ceridwen squealed with excitement. Oh, *please*, Father. Can I do a photoshoot? And learn how to speak German too?

Bedwyr sighed. In her thirteenth year (she was two weeks from fourteen) his daughter had become difficult – complaining that she wanted to go to the comprehensive school where her friend from the village Tanya Matthews went, and that the RE and history lessons he taught her weren't enough. So hoping to appease her, he invited Liesl to join them for Sunday lunch, before which she could photograph his daughter and teach her some basic German. Only when they were driving the miles from the village back to Angels Singing, Ceridwen's wheelchair folded up in the boot and Liesl chattering from the back seat, did Bedwyr begin to feel he'd made a grave mistake. But now he'd invited the East German, he couldn't uninvite her. He couldn't very well put her out of the car and on to the moors.

Bedwyr had seasoned the leg of lamb and peeled the spuds before leaving for church. All he had to do was mix the Yorkshire pudding batter and arrange the meat, vegetables and lard in baking trays. Once Sunday dinner was in the oven, he went to usher Liesl and Ceridwen out into the garden, to get the photoshoot over with, but walked into the living room to an unexpected sight: Liesl lying with eyes closed on the sofa as Ceridwen leant over her in her wheelchair, pressing a damp flannel to her forehead. His daughter looked at him in distress.

She has a migraine. I gave her some aspirin, but she's in so much pain. She can't move.

She ought to go back to her bed and breakfast, Bedwyr said. I'll take her now.

But Ceridwen begged him to let Liesl, who was clearly not up to the car journey, stay until she had recovered. So Bedwyr grudgingly made up the bed in the spare room, then roused Liesl to help her to shuffle, piteously hunched and wincing, up the stairs. Supporting the East German, his arm around her shoulders, Bedwyr found himself nauseated by her smell. Not that of the perfume that she'd recently dabbed or spritzed, but the foulness emanating from beneath, as though the stink of pig carcasses in the butcher's van had permanently rubbed off on her. He deposited her on the narrow bed, drew the curtains against the sunlight, then shut the door.

Several times he knocked on the spare room to check if Liesl had recuperated enough to go back to the village. But she remained in agony, and when the B&B's nine p.m. curfew passed, Bedwyr knew, in spite of all his misgivings, Liesl was now an overnight guest.

Though Ceridwen had her own pink-walled room, every night she slept with her father in his double bed. There were reasons for this, one being the closeness between them, and another if Ceridwen needed the toilet, Bedwyr could carry her there. It maddened Bedwyr that most people would think this sleeping arrangement wrong. That most people had suspicious, perverted minds and could not believe that a father and daughter sharing a bed could be innocent, loving and chaste. So he and Ceridwen kept it from other people and that night they kept it from Liesl as well. At ten o'clock he carried Ceridwen up the stairs to her seldom-used bedroom and helped her into her white cotton nightdress. He led their prayers, then tucked her in and kissed her goodnight. Alone in the master bedroom, Bedwyr was keenly aware of his daughter's absence beside him, and sure that Ceridwen was equally bereft.

The next morning he woke earlier than usual, around four or five, with a nameless dread. He went straight to Ceridwen's room and was thrown into a panic by her empty bed. Ceridwen couldn't move around without her father's assistance. Her paralysis was such that she couldn't even crawl. *Liesl*, he thought. *Liesl has taken her.* He burst into the spare room; the narrow guest bed was empty too, the quilted bedspread thrown back. He was about to rush downstairs when some noise outside sent him to the window. He yanked aside the curtain and was astounded to see, in the weak light, Ceridwen and Liesl at the back of the garden, under the crab apple tree. Astounded, because his daughter was standing in front of her wheelchair as Liesl held up a camera, taking her photograph.

Bedwyr stared. The last time he'd seen Ceridwen on her feet by herself was before the accident eight years earlier, yet there she was, standing five feet two. She looked weightless, as though levitating, and more beautiful than Bedwyr had ever known her to be. Long pale hair shimmering down her back. Cotton nightgown hanging loosely over the pubescent swell of her breasts and hips to graze her ankles. Even from the upstairs window, Bedwyr could discern a dangerous sensuality about her – her lips parted, as though in some lustful state. It snapped Bedwyr out of his trance. He hurtled down the stairs, two at a time, and out into the garden to the innocuous sight of Liesl pushing Ceridwen in her wheelchair across the grass towards the back door.

What is this? he shouted, charging at them.

Liesl looked perplexed. Her church-going clothes were rumpled and her camera hung from a strap around her neck. Some dark strands had come loose from her long plait.

I woke early and heard Ceridwen cry out. She needed help to get to the bathroom. Then she said she was having trouble sleeping, so we came out here to take some photographs.

She wasn't in her wheelchair, Bedwyr cried. She was standing up.

Liesl frowned and shook her head. No, Bedwyr. You're mistaken.

He looked at his daughter. I *saw you*. Out of your chair. Standing up.

I . . .

Ceridwen was dazed, as though she had forgotten how to speak, and Bedwyr was disturbed because it reminded him of when he'd found her after the accident, concussed and at an unnatural angle at the bottom of the stairs. Liesl moved aside as Bedwyr seized the wheelchair handles from her and pushed his daughter into the house. He parked her in the living room, closing the door on her before confronting Liesl again in the hall.

Give me that film, he said, pointing at the camera around her neck. You didn't have my permission to photograph my daughter.

Liesl put her hand over the camera. I had *Ceridwen's* permission, she said.

Infuriated, Bedwyr swiped at Liesl, reaching to snatch the camera. Liesl laughed and took a step back. A change had come over her. She was no longer contrite, but bemused.

Are you going to fight me, Bedwyr? Do you want to try?

Liesl's smell wafted over to him then: the reek of abattoir and butchered swine. Stomach turning with nausea, Bedwyr shook his head at her in disgust.

I want you to gather your things and leave. Now.

Liesl nodded, camera still clutched to her chest. Then she smiled with such disarming sweetness that it seemed proof of what Bedwyr suspected all along. That she was unnatural. That she could manipulate her face to any affect. That her entire being was a perfidious mask of surging life, behind which lurked something not-living and predatory.

Thank you for your hospitality, Bedwyr, she smiled. You and your daughter have been so kind.

After Liesl was gone, Bedwyr made porridge and tea for breakfast, then got Ceridwen washed and ready for her lessons. As she read aloud from her textbook on the Industrial Revolution, Ceridwen stumbled over the words and had some difficulty answering the questions at the end of the chapter. But to Bedwyr's relief, his daughter was back to normal by elevenses, and he put her slowness down to her extremely early start. Several times that day and over the days that followed, Bedwyr interrogated his daughter over what had occurred with Liesl in the garden. Had she regained use of her legs? Each time Ceridwen insisted she had no memory of standing up, and Bedwyr began to wonder if the 'miracle' he saw was just a blunder of his recently woken mind.

On the Thursday evening after Liesl's visit, they were playing Scrabble when the telephone rang, surprising them both. Bedwyr answered it, and to his dismay it was Tanya Matthews from the village. He wheeled his daughter out to the hall, then returned to the living room to listen to Ceridwen's side of the call. Bedwyr disliked Tanya Matthews immensely. She'd been a tolerable friend for Ceridwen when they were primary-school age, but at fourteen Tanya was grubby, make-up smeared, and stank of cigarettes and the mousse with which she aggressively scrunched her permed hair. Tanya's mother (her father's whereabouts were unknown) was a barmaid at the village pub, and let Tanya run wild with an older boyfriend called Darren, whom Bedwyr had once seen as he drove through the village, French-kissing Tanya in that sloppy barely-coming-up-for-air way of teenagers. Whenever Ceridwen spoke to Tanya, hearing of youth clubs and *Top of the Pops*, she would be disconsolate afterwards. And tonight would be no exception, because Tanya had called to invite her to a party at her house on Saturday night. After hanging up, Ceridwen wheeled herself back into the living room, hopefulness glittering in her eyes.

No, Bedwyr said.

What if you pick me up early? Ten? Or nine thirty?

No. You'll be the only handicapped child there. They'll tease you.

But Tanya says they're all dead nice. Her best mates from school. And there's only going to be ten of them.

Bedwyr laughed.

Ten? You know what Stacey Matthews is like. She'll be pulling pints at the Nag's Head and won't be there to supervise. There will be alcohol. Gatecrashers. You can't go. Now come and play Scrabble. It's your turn.

Dejected, Ceridwen wheeled herself over to the coffee table. The sight of it hurt Bedwyr's heart – he hated to make his daughter sad.

You're upset, but it's for your own good. Really, Tanya's to blame for inviting you without any thought of your disabilities. She's inconsiderate.

No, Ceridwen protested. She's *not*. She's my best friend and puts herself out for me more than anyone.

Bedwyr didn't like the way his daughter contradicted him. He didn't like how she held Tanya in such high esteem.

Really? More than anyone? What do you think *I've* been doing for you all these years? Caring for you day in day out, wheeling and lugging you around because you're handicapped and can't walk? Don't you think I have *put myself out*?

Ceridwen looked at her father, fraught.

I didn't mean it like that.

Perhaps I ought to leave you like Alys did. Perhaps then you will appreciate all I do for you.

Ceridwen broke down then. She cried in her wheelchair and Bedwyr watched with conflicting emotions. What he said was cruel, but she needed that short, sharp shock from time to time. She needed to be reminded of how much she needed him. He went and knelt in front of her, bowed his head and apologized. He would never ever leave her. Caring for her was his life's purpose and joy. Ceridwen wept with relief and threw her arms around him.

Lift me up, Father. Carry me.

He scooped her up and carried her over to the armchair where he sat with her, rocking her to and fro on his lap. The game of Scrabble was unfinished as they clung to each other until it was time for bed.

Bedwyr slept through the night and woke to the stillness that shrouded their cottage when there was no wind or rain. As usual Ceridwen was his waking thought, and the mattress springs groaned as he rolled over to watch over his daughter's sleep. But she wasn't there. He leapt up, his mind blank with terror as he flew along the upstairs landing, checking all the rooms before hurling himself down the stairs. Bedwyr found her in the kitchen, in her wheelchair by the wide-open back door, the chill of the night's end seeping in. Bewildered, Bedwyr was about to cry her name when Ceridwen's murmuring stopped him. She was speaking sotto voce as though to an imaginary friend, pausing every so often to listen and laughing melodiously. Bedwyr crept nearer to hear what she was saying, but it was indecipherable.

It was then Bedwyr became aware of the strangeness in the garden. Birds were singing possessedly in the trees and the flowers and plants were shining, though the sun had yet to rise over the

Beacons. All of the Lord's creation seemed ecstatic, singing in rising crescendo, but it was *ungodly* – that much Bedwyr knew. He moved to the side of Ceridwen's wheelchair and recognized that same wantonness from under the crab apple tree with Liesl: her eyes bright with pleasure, her lips parted seductively. She was exposing herself. Pulling her nightdress above her waist as though to show herself to some imaginary lover on the lawn. Bedwyr spun her wheelchair round to face him.

Ceridwen!

His shout broke her out of her strange trance. Ceridwen looked around, stunned to find herself in the kitchen.

How did you get downstairs by yourself?

I . . .

She gaped down at her cotton knickers and threw her nightgown back over them, mortified. The cottage walls shook as Bedwyr slammed the back door and pushed his daughter into the living room. He brought the New Testament down from the bookshelf, the crucifix down from the mantel and pulled a chair up opposite his daughter.

I don't know what devilry this is, Ceridwen, but in times of doubt and uncertainty, we turn to our Lord for guidance. *1 Corinthians 13:12* . . .

Ceridwen clasped her hands together, fearfully bowed her head, and Bedwyr led them in Bible readings and prayer, all the while thinking of the East German woman and her smile before he had thrown her out. Her smirk of foreknowledge of what was to come.

Bedwyr took Ceridwen to Dr Edwards, the village GP, explaining that he'd found Ceridwen downstairs with no recollection of how she got there. Dr Edwards tested her reflexes with a small hammer and concluded the motor functioning of her legs was deadened as ever. He said he'd refer Ceridwen to a specialist at the hospital to have more tests done, but the waiting list would be several weeks.

That evening, Bedwyr locked Ceridwen's folded-up wheelchair in the cupboard under the stairs. He locked the cottage's doors and windows and when they went to bed he hung the keys from a string around his neck, before using a length of rope to secure Ceridwen's ankle to the bedpost. The night passed without incident.

On Saturday afternoon, Bedwyr came in from gardening and heard Ceridwen's tinkling laughter in the dining room. Avoiding certain floorboards, he crept up the hall to the door, which was ajar. Ceridwen was in her wheelchair at the dining table, upon which her needlework and bobbins of thread were arrayed. Her embroidery hoop was neglected, however, as she smiled and murmured at something in her hands. Bedwyr strode into the room, determined to know what Ceridwen, having seen her father, was now shoving under her leg.

What's that? Show me. *Now.*

Reluctantly, Ceridwen handed her father a faded black and white photograph of a woman with a port-wine birthmark on half her face. A woman whose beak-nosed appearance would be odd even without her disfigurement. On the back of the photograph, someone had written in black ink: *Ursula, Künstlermodell, Hochschule für Grafik und Buchkunst, 1968.*

Where did you get this?

Liesl's bag, Ceridwen said, shamefacedly. When she had her migraine. She had an envelope of photographs.

Bedwyr scowled.

Why steal *this*? It's such an ugly photo.

I just wanted it.

Ceridwen's eyes were downcast, her plaits dangling either side of her pretty head, full of the secrets she kept from her father.

What were you saying just now? he asked. Before I came in?

I don't remember, she whispered.

Bedwyr didn't believe her. I'm keeping this, he said, pocketing the photo.

Turning to leave, he saw Ceridwen's pain to be separated from it, and he wondered if this Ursula in the photograph had something to do with his daughter's odd behaviour of late.

All the more reason to keep it from her, he thought as he locked it in his nightstand drawer.

Sunday morning, Bedwyr woke at daybreak to the steady drumming of rain, weak light through the curtains, and Ceridwen gone from the bed. The bedcovers were thrown back on her side, and the rope that had secured her ankle to the bedpost was torn and frayed as though gnawed through by a sharp-toothed animal. Downstairs, the back door was still locked, but a damp chill rushed in through the hole smashed into the window above the sink. Through the shattered pane, Bedwyr could see Ceridwen lying on the muddy ground underneath the crab apple tree, drenched by the lashing rain. Her soaked nightgown was up around her waist, and her head thrown back as she writhed, rubbing herself between the legs. Near-howling in fury, Bedwyr fumbled with the back-door bolts and struggled to fit the correct key in the lock. By the time he was outside, Ceridwen had stopped moving. She lay under the tree amongst the windfallen apples, completely still as the sky unleashed yet more rain.

Oh my Ceridwen. What is happening to you?

As Bedwyr crashed to his knees beside her, Ceridwen didn't look at him. The faintest of smiles twitched on her lips, and Bedwyr knew she wasn't in her right mind. Bleeding cuts on her legs from the broken window glass needed urgent attention and he put his arms under her to carry her indoors. But he struggled to stand bearing her weight, and they both splattered back into the mud. Upon landing, Ceridwen shrieked with laughter and cried, Leave me be, Bedwyr. I'm not yours. I belong now to him.

It had stopped raining when Reverend Nigel Parry arrived at quarter past nine. Over a pot of Earl Grey and custard creams, Bedwyr explained the situation (taking care to censor the more immodest parts) and the reverend gazed contemplatively at Ceridwen, who was in a cable-knit jumper and jeans, having had a long hot bath and her cuts (none so deep as to need stitches, mercifully) tended to by Bedwyr. Ceridwen had come out of her hysterical state when Bedwyr brought her indoors, but since Reverend Parry's arrival her pretty face had assumed a sly look. Bedwyr supposed she was smirking at the reverend's rosacea and the dandruff on the shoulders of his tweed jacket, and later he would have to correct her misassumption of superiority. After all, who was a handicapped thirteen-year-old girl to look down upon a hard-working vicar who had served his parishioners for over twenty years? Who had come to help them in their darkest hour?

Well, it *does* sound as though there's been some restlessness in your cottage lately, Reverend Parry said. And I *do* sense an energy here. Perhaps this Liesl invited something into your home.

Bedwyr palled and the reverend smiled reassuringly. Nothing to be concerned about, I'm sure. These energies are rarely malevolent. A house blessing will heighten the presence of the Holy Spirit in your home and discourage anything that's not meant to be here.

Bedwyr pushed Ceridwen in her wheelchair, following Reverend Parry from room to room as he liberally sprinkled holy water on the furnishings and rugs and intoned, *May the God of peace bring peace to this house. May the Son of peace bring peace to this house.*

They went out into the garden, to the crab apple tree, which Bedwyr had mentioned as the area of some 'activity'. Under the grey overcast sky, Reverend Parry repeated his blessing, sprinkling holy water on the trunk and apple-strewn ground. Then, unexpectedly, he stepped back, reaching for the silver cross around his neck. He smiled at Bedwyr, shaky and insincere.

Shall we go back indoors?

The reverend then began to stride towards the cottage as though restraining himself from breaking into a run.

In order to speak privately to the priest, Bedwyr left Ceridwen in the cottage and accompanied him out to his car.

All is not well, is it? Bedwyr said.

Reverend Parry's smile lacked the spiritual fortitude of when he first arrived.

I'm going to consult with a former colleague, Clare Daniels, who's vicar of a church in Pontypool. Clare has trained at the Ministry of Deliverance.

Bedwyr was aghast. The Ministry of Deliverance? You think Ceridwen is *possessed*?

Reverend Parry laughed nervously. Oh no, nothing like that. It's just that I sensed a presence under that tree. Reverend Daniels should be able to assess the situation with her expertise. I myself lack the requisite . . . experience. She may have to charge a fee but—

I will pay any fee necessary, Bedwyr said.

The reverend opened the driver's-side door. I will pray for you and your daughter. My feeling is the disturbance in your home will only be temporary. It may be connected to Ceridwen's adolescence. I have heard that puberty . . . well, I'm no expert on such things.

He paused and then said, May I ask, Bedwyr, does Ceridwen have any friends her own age? I know she is home-schooled and, well, she seems a very isolated child. Her solitariness may have something to do with the cultivation of these strange energies.

She's not solitary, Bedwyr corrected. She's in the company of her father every day.

Reverend Parry nodded, but Bedwyr saw the judgement behind the politeness of his eyes.

Well, I'll be in touch once I have spoken to Reverend Daniels.

Bedwyr watched him drive away, irritated that Reverend Parry, like most people, saw fit to opine on what he didn't understand.

Bedwyr hoped against hope that Reverend Parry's house blessing had worked, though Ceridwen remained unlike herself, continuing in her remoteness and odd trances of daydreaming. Then, on Wednesday afternoon, Bedwyr entered the dining room and saw that Ceridwen, instead of completing her schoolwork as instructed, had turned her wheelchair to the sash window overlooking the garden, dreary now the summer blooms had withered away. The sky was darkening and he could see her smiling reflection in the glass.

What are you smiling at?

In the warped glass, her reflection stared at him with unwavering pale blue eyes.

Nothing, Father.

Her deceitful look made him want to shake her, but instead he said, Do you think I don't see you smirking at me? Or at Reverend Daniels when she made time in her busy schedule to speak to you on the telephone? I've had enough of your supercilious attitude, Ceridwen. How you can be so ungrateful to people who are trying to help you, I don't know.

Slowly, she manoeuvred her chair around to face him. I never asked for your help. I don't *need* your help.

Such was Bedwyr's shock he couldn't for a moment speak. Then he laughed. If you really have no need of me, I ought to send you off to your mother's in Swansea and be done with it.

The threat of sending her away to Alys never failed to reduce Ceridwen to tears, but this time she looked at her father with dry eyes.

Very well then. Send me to live with my mother. I know in my heart she loves and misses me and would welcome me with open arms. And I would also like to know the half-brother and -sister I've never been allowed to meet.

She didn't mean it. She was calling his bluff. Nonetheless, fury consumed Bedwyr like flames leaping hellishly up from beneath his feet.

Alys cares *nothing* for you, he spat. She abandoned our family to be with that other man. That's the kind of selfish, irresponsible woman she is.

You threw her out, Ceridwen countered. You shoved all her clothes into bin liners and threw them into the street in front of the neighbours. Then you told vicious lies about her in court and moved us far away from her.

Bedwyr couldn't breathe. The tachycardia he'd suffered when he found out about Alys's affair returned: a fast and arrhythmic pounding in his chest. How dare she speak to him that way?

You have no idea what you're talking about. *No idea*. You were *seven years old* back then.

As Ceridwen stared with cynical eyes, Bedwyr went on, Reverend Daniels will be here Saturday. The reverend will know how to cast the Devil out of you. She'll know how to bring me my daughter back.

Or she'll run from this cottage like Reverend Parry, Ceridwen said. Jump in her car and break the speed limit driving back to Pontypool.

Then she rotated her wheelchair back to the window

84

overlooking the garden, which had darkened considerably during their appalling exchange, as though in preparation for some early autumn storm.

Later, over dinner, Bedwyr watched Ceridwen push her vegetable stew about with her fork, lost in the privacy of her thoughts. How did she know about the row in the street when Alys left? Or the custody battle? Had one of Alys's letters somehow reached her? *Vicious lies in court*, indeed. If only Ceridwen had heard how her mother had *slandered* him. Fortunately for Bedwyr, the judge had seen through her abused-wife act. Had seen Alys for the lying adulteress she was.

Not for the first time Bedwyr reflected on what Reverend Parry had said by his Volvo. That the 'strange energies' he detected could be connected to Ceridwen's 'solitariness'. It was testament to Bedwyr's desperation that evening that he cleared his throat and said, How about you invite Tanya over for your birthday on Friday? I can prepare a tea party for you both.

Ceridwen looked up uncertainly from her stew. Really? Tanya can come round?

Bedwyr winced at the thought of common-as-muck Tanya Matthews at their dining table. Just for an hour or so, for your birthday tea.

For the first time since Liesl had entered their lives, Ceridwen beamed at her father. Oh, thank you! Can I phone her?

Once you've finished your dinner.

Ceridwen bowed her head over her vegetable stew and began to eat with a haste Bedwyr knew not to mistake for appetite.

Bedwyr always made a fuss of his daughter's birthday and her fourteenth was no exception. He made her a breakfast of pancakes, over which Ceridwen unwrapped all of her father's lovingly chosen gifts and politely thanked him. As usual Alys had sent a long letter, but Bedwyr had judiciously thrown it away the day before, seeing no point in upsetting Ceridwen on her special day. He was glad the storm late on Wednesday night had blown down the telegraph poles in Angels Singing so he didn't have to be vigilant of an attempted call.

In the afternoon, Bedwyr prepared the sandwiches and decorated the dining room for the tea party – blowing up colourful balloons and hanging the *Happy Birthday* bunting across the chimney breast. The door knocker banged at twenty past four and when Bedwyr answered it Tanya was waving goodbye to Stacey Matthews, who'd dropped her off in her rusty old banger of a Ford Cortina.

Hello, Bedwyr, Tanya chirruped. Where's the birthday girl?

What a fright Tanya looked, with her tight corkscrew perm, electric-blue eyeliner and the waistband of her school skirt rolled up to show her pudgy thighs. Reluctantly, he replied, Dining room.

Tanya grinned and ran past him to Ceridwen with much shrieking and ado. Bedwyr then watched in annoyance as Ceridwen opened Tanya's presents: a cassette of rap music, a *Just Seventeen* magazine and a purple nail varnish that he would later have to confiscate until Ceridwen was an appropriate age.

During the tea party, Bedwyr sat in silence as the girls chattered, Tanya Matthews somehow able to stuff herself with sandwiches, crisps and fizzy drinks while jabbering non-stop. She mostly told stories about the comprehensive she went to; horror stories of a supply teacher locked in a cupboard by students and a boy setting fire to his blazer with a Bunsen burner. Tanya also boasted of her Saturday job. Though barely fourteen, she was working at the village hairdresser's, washing hair and sweeping up cuttings.

I'm learning perms, she said, running her grubby fingers through Ceridwen's pale tresses. I can do one on you if you like. You're so gorgeous, Cerys, I reckon you'd look like Kim Wilde.

Though Bedwyr was thoroughly irritated by Tanya, he appreciated her enthusiasm when he brought out the chocolate cake he'd baked, flickering with fourteen candles. They sang 'Happy Birthday' and Tanya shouted, *Make a wish* and clapped and whooped as Ceridwen blew the candles out. The delight on his daughter's face made the hour enduring Tanya Matthews almost worthwhile.

Once they'd eaten some cake, Bedwyr turned to Tanya and said, Time for you to go back to the village. I'll give you a lift.

Am I not staying over? Tanya asked, nodding at her backpack. Brought my sleeping bag and jim-jams and *everything*.

Bedwyr scowled at Ceridwen, sorely regretting not supervising her phone call to Tanya on Wednesday evening. His daughter stared back innocently in her red velvet dress.

You can't stay over, Bedwyr said. We have a very important visitor coming all the way from Pontypool tomorrow morning.

Tanya's blue-rimmed eyes widened. But my mum's at her mate Karen's hen do in Cardiff tonight and I don't have a key to get in the house 'cos I lost mine at the swimming baths on Tuesday.

Bedwyr glared at her. Tanya wasn't allowed to sleep over at the best of times, never mind with all that had been happening in the cottage of late.

You're just going to have to phone your friends until you find somewhere else to stay.

And Ceridwen looked at her father and said, But aren't the telephone lines down from that storm? Why can't she just stay here, Father? It's my birthday after all, and it's just one night.

That evening Bedwyr struggled to read in the living room, distracted by all the music and thumping and Ceridwen's wheelchair rolling over the floorboards above. At ten o'clock, Bedwyr looked in on them and was enraged to see Tanya had made Ceridwen up like a teenage streetwalker, her hair backcombed into a bouffant. Ceridwen's eyes were suspiciously bright, her cheeks suspiciously pink, and Bedwyr was sure he could smell Bacardi, masked by hairspray. Glowering at them both, he checked his temper and said, *Ceridwen*. Scrub that filth off your face, brush your teeth, say your prayers and get into bed. You too, Tanya. I want you in your sleeping bag. Lights out by ten thirty and no talking. Understood?

He left the room and they dissolved into giggles. It would take Ceridwen twice as long to change into her nightgown and get into bed without her father's help, but he vengefully left her to it, instead going downstairs to lock all the windows and doors.

Later, he lay in bed, kept awake by the girls ignoring his orders and giggling. Every half-hour he banged on the wall and shouted, *Go to sleep*, which only sent them into pillow-smothered hysterics. Bedwyr drifted off around two, grinding his back teeth at their disobedience and consoling himself that he would soon forbid Ceridwen from ever seeing Tanya again.

Daybreak. A screaming wrenched him out of sleep and Bedwyr was up and running before he could process what was happening. Ceridwen's bedroom door was open. Tanya was gone from her sleeping bag but his daughter was there, sitting up in bed.

What's going on? he asked.

Ceridwen only stared blankly in response, so he continued towards the source of the commotion downstairs. Tanya was banging and kicking the front door in her desperation to open it, yanking on the latch.

Tanya. What in God's name?

She spun around, her face unrecognizably twisted with fear.

Open the fucking door, she yelled.

Mind your language, Tanya Matthews. Now, what's going on? Did you and Ceridwen have a fight?

Tanya flew at Bedwyr, dragged him doorwards with all her strength. Just to rid himself of the encumbrance he took out the key and unlocked the door. He watched her run out into the chilly mid-September dawn in her pyjamas and nothing, not even socks, on her feet.

Wait, for goodness' sake, he called. You'll catch your death.

But she ran out of the front gate – presumably to Angels Singing, or her village four miles away.

Bedwyr was as irritated as he was disturbed. What choice did he have but to drive after her and make sure she got home safely? He ran upstairs to get Ceridwen and found her still sitting up in bed and ravenously gnawing on something in her hands. It was a crab apple. Her bedspread was covered in rotting vinegary apples, in fact. Had Tanya brought them with her?

Stop that, he ordered. Now, what's Tanya screaming about?

Ceridwen spat rotting apple and laughed. Something about his daughter truly terrified him, but leaving her alone in the cottage wasn't an option, so Bedwyr lifted her from the bed, his lower back spasming dangerously as he brought her down the stairs and out to the car.

They set off, the speedometer needle wavering between thirty-five and forty miles per hour as they drove through Angels Singing and up the winding, stone-walled country lane to Tanya's village. The sun glinted orange and pink on the eastern horizon and the misty moorlands stretched for miles around them, craggy and wild. The empty road meandered into the distance with no sign of any adolescent girl in pyjamas, and Bedwyr was mystified as to her whereabouts. In the passenger seat beside him, his daughter stared through the windscreen at the road ahead. If she was worried for her friend, she gave no outward sign of it.

We should have seen her by now, Bedwyr muttered crossly.

For the first time that morning, Ceridwen spoke. Tanya's dead.

Clutching the steering wheel, Bedwyr looked incredulously at her. *What?*

She's dead. They're sending me to Swansea after this.

What are you talking about?

And I have Liesl to thank, for Liesl came here to save me.

Save you? From your father who has loved and taken care of you all these years?

Staring ahead, Ceridwen said, They're sending me to Alys, and I'll be free of you.

Bedwyr turned to his daughter. Through gritted teeth, he said, Not if I *strangle* you first.

Bedwyr. Watch the road.

He glanced through the windscreen. Tanya stood frozen as they drove towards her. Large, shocked eyes and mouth crying *no* under spiral curls, her hands rising up as though to ward off a blow. Bedwyr slammed on the brakes, but they shot forward at speed because he'd pressed the accelerator instead and Tanya smashed into the wind-screen and flew upwards. Seconds too late, his slippered foot found the correct pedal, and father and daughter were thrown into their seatbelts as they lurched to a halt some distance in front of Tanya, who was slumped where she'd landed, against a low stone wall.

Bedwyr gripped the steering wheel. He had to get out and check the damage he'd done to his daughter's best friend. But he couldn't move.

In the passenger seat beside him, Ceridwen began to laugh.

*

Dusk was gathering as Bedwyr and I stood by the dead stump of the crab apple tree he'd chopped down, doused in petrol and burnt when he was released from HMP Usk.

The coroner believed Tanya had been interfered with, Bedwyr said, and I was arrested and detained in custody. Ceridwen couldn't make any statement to the police in my defence because she wasn't right in the head. Post-traumatic stress, apparently. They sent her to Alys in Swansea, and three weeks later she was found dead in her wheelchair from heart failure. They let me go to her funeral under police escort, and I sat handcuffed at the back. After the service Alys attacked me. In her third trimester with her fourth child she was, but that didn't stop her from trying to kill me with her bare hands.

Bedwyr shook his head glumly.

Alys's been dead fifteen years now. Cervical cancer. I try not to bear a grudge.

I asked Bedwyr what the twenty-five years spent in prison were like. How he had got through the long sentence to come out unbroken (a word regretted as soon as spoken; Bedwyr was indisputably a broken man). He laughed hollowly, as though he too was only too aware of this.

My first years in HMP Usk I was persecuted by some other inmates. Some of humanity's dregs who took a disliking to me. They broke my fingers, slamming them in a door. Poured a boiling kettle down my trousers. Thing was, I was so numb with grief over Ceridwen, I didn't care . . . How did I get through the twenty-five years? I read the Bible. I prayed every day. I wrote letters to Ceridwen too. Thousands of letters, pages and pages long. I am sure she's read them all, up in Heaven.

Bedwyr pointed up to the sky with such heartbreaking certainty that I could only nod. We turned and trampled through the weeds to the cottage and re-entered the kitchen where the rancid sink was crowded with filthy crockery, and the countertop with opened tins with serrated rusty lids.

Do you ever think of selling up and moving away? I asked.

Bedwyr bristled at the suggestion. Ceridwen's presence is still in this cottage. I feel very close to her here. If she hadn't died, she'd be forty-seven today, and we'd still be here together. Living as peacefully and lovingly as we were before Liesl came along.

I nodded faintly. Bedwyr bitterly went on, Liesl was the Devil. And I have *proof*.

He reached into his trouser pocket, withdrew a black and white photograph, five by seven inches in size. Ceridwen stood in her long nightdress under the crab apple tree, silken hair spilling over her shoulders, gazing into the camera lens as though mesmerized. The wheelchair was abandoned behind her and though her feet were on the ground she appeared weightless, floating up in the photographer's trap.

I found it in her trinket box after I was released. How Liesl got it to her is a mystery. Only *I* brought the post in from the mailbox every day, in case Alys sent one of her letters.

Though I was studying the photograph still, Bedwyr shoved it back in his pocket.

Evil, I suppose, has its ways and means.

When the taxi from the village pulled up at eight p.m., Bedwyr saw me out. Elderly and frail beneath his crooked back, he stood in his front doorway and said, A fool's errand, hunting Liesl down. What will you do when you find her?

Though I'd spent ten hours in his cottage, this was the first question Bedwyr had asked about my motives. What I'd witnessed back in 2011, what Lena and his daughter had experienced in common, Bedwyr hadn't been interested to know.

I'm not hunting her down, I said. I just want to get closer to the truth of what happened to my friend. I just need some answers.

When my Ceridwen and I are reunited in the Kingdom of Heaven, Bedwyr said, I shall get my answers then. But you're not a Christian, are you?

No, I said. Neither was Lena.

Well then, Bedwyr replied. Your answers will *have* to come from the Devil, because you're never seeing your friend again.

Then he shut his cottage door.

Badlands – III

Hoodoos jut into the vast blue sky. Some wide and volcano-shaped, others eerie spires casting spindle shadows on the ground. In the west the sun descends, gilding each and every protrusion of stone down one side. The dark-haired woman scans the landscape through her DSLR camera lens before coming to rest on the foreground and the girl, who brushes a stray curl from her eyes and smooths the floral dress stolen from a hanger in her sister's room. Her cheek tics nervously but she returns the camera's gaze with her determination to captivate the thousands – if not *millions* – who'll doubtlessly soon be watching through their screens.

Behind the camera tripod, the woman counts down. Three, two, one. *Action.*

Rosa stands taller, smiles cryptically as she sweeps her hand at the surreal pillars of stone behind her and, deepening her voice with documentary-narrator gravitas, begins.

Some Native American tribes believe hoodoos are the spirits of ancient people turned to stone by a Coyote god. I cannot say if this is true, but what I *can* tell you is that this place has an intense spiritual energy. These hoodoos called to me – they called to me in a dream, which is why I've come to shoot my first video here, in the Bisti Badlands of New Mexico.

Joining hands together in prayer, she dips her head. Namaste. I'm Aurora Rose and welcome to my channel . . . Today we're gonna be talking about some super-spiritual stuff: the Law of Attraction and manifesting your best life.

Her monologue goes on. Half an hour of recording and Rosa has assumed the persona of Aurora Rose with ease, convincing the woman that she has the hustle and confidence to persuade others she's a guiding spiritual light, illuminating the confounding darkness of human existence with inspirational quotes. It's a shame that no one will ever see the videos, the woman thinks. She's sure the channel would be a success.

Besides Rosa is a low pyramid of rocks she'd carefully arranged before the shoot. She crouches and pushes the rock at the apex so it tumbles down, toppling others with it.

Life ever feel like that to you? she asks. All your problems sliding out of your control? But what if I told you your life's all just a manifestation of your thoughts? And by turning negative thoughts into positive ones you can *stop the avalanche*?

Rosa stands, begins to speak about the transformative power of mantra, and behind the camera tripod the woman's scalp burns through her thinning hair. More had come out under the hotel shower's scalding spray that morning, the dark strands swirling around her toes and clogging the plughole. Her tongue prods teeth loosening as bacteria work under the gums – microbial timebombs ticking deep in periodontal sockets. How badly does she smell? Later, she will slather on more citronella insect repellent to mask any sulphurous odour, to keep the blowflies from buzzing around her in the night, looking for an orifice in which to lay their eggs.

Follow your bliss, Rosa is now saying, and the universe will open doors for you. The universe will hear your mantras and make them *actualize*. Because all the universe is just a manifestation of your thoughts . . .

She has it the wrong way round of course, the woman thinks. Our thoughts are a manifestation of the universe, along with all matter and physical laws. Along with all living things and Aurora Rose herself – a fleeting instant in the cosmos, senselessly, mindlessly manifested. Then gone.

The woman's pulled out of her reveries by Rosa striding towards her and reaching for the DSLR camera, which she swivels around on the tripod. The woman steps backs as Rosa points the lens at her.

This is Therese, she says. Exhibit A. The videographer I manifested for myself with the Law of Attraction. Say *hi*, Therese.

In front of the camera, the woman reluctantly smiles. *Hi.*

I asked the universe for help, and the universe sent me Therese. The moment I saw her I was like, wow, who is this glamorous

European woman? And we start talking and, I swear, I could feel this, like, *cosmic connection* between us. Did you feel it too, Therese?

The woman winces at the sharp, shooting pain in her back molar. The timebomb's just detonated, her nerves flaring. She's going to need ibuprofen and amoxicillin to keep the inflammation down.

Rosa, she says. Can you please stop filming? I'm not exactly camera-ready.

Are you kidding me? Therese, you're so sophisticated, even without any make-up on. Like a French film actress or something.

Rosa's smile takes it for granted her flattery's done the trick. And the woman could indulge her, she supposes. The recording will be deleted later on. But part of her resists, conscious of how wretched she must look as the forces that sustain her recede. Like she's three hundred years old. Like she's just been dug up.

Keeping the DSLR lens focused on the woman, the girl speaks to the imaginary audience. Guys, Therese didn't know about the Law of Attraction before we met. But now she's a total convert. *Like me.*

Rosa smiles, oblivious to her subject's discomfort. So, Therese, what's *your* bliss? What dreams do *you* want to manifest?

For this fucking toothache to quit, the woman thinks. For you to turn off the fucking camera and shut up. She eyes one of the late-Cretaceous-era rocks strewn on the ground. She could bludgeon the girl with it. Shatter her skull, so she doesn't have to endure another word on the transformative power of positive thought. But she says, To live is my bliss.

Rosa laughs, confused. But, Therese, you're, like, *already alive?*

The toothache centres consciousness around it. The pain pulsates to her jawbone, inner ear and cranium – exacerbating anger, impatience. But the woman attempts a smile, mouth closed in case there's blood.

And I want to keep on living.

But the Law of Attraction can make anything possible. What about your career? You could become a famous photographer that people are still talking about in a hundred years' time? Like, win a Pulitzer or something?

The best way to be immortal, the woman says, is not to die.

The girl laughs. Well, she replies. Good luck with *that*.

An hour later, the woman and girl are sitting on a barren shale hill, drinking warm Coronas and watching the sunset colour the sky with lurid reds and turn luminescent the clouds that have rolled in from the Chuska mountain range. The girl vapes menthol fumes and stretches out her legs, having tugged the sneakers off her swollen feet. The woman's feet ache too, but she keeps her weeping mess of blisters and blackened toenails in her hiking boots. She hugs her bruised shins and grazed knees (squirming with maggot larvae in last night's dream) to her chest. The drugs are taking effect at least, lessening her toothache so she can cast her mind outwards again, to the girl and the 'cosmic connection' between them both.

Psychedelic, right? the woman says. Who needs acid when you have this sunset?

The girl nods absently at the sun in its death throes, quieter than before. She's had a long day of course. Seven hours of vacuuming hotel rooms and changing bedsheets, then the long hike through the desert and the performance of Aurora Rose. But the woman knows the coming nightfall has subdued her too. What terrors, human or inhuman, could surface from the badlands at night? The woman intends to make a campfire and hopes the girl will feel as protected by the blaze as their ancestors did. And if toasting marshmallows doesn't lift her spirits, there's mezcal.

Up on the hill, the woman notices a man heading west across the valley floor, about two hundred metres distant. He's near-silhouetted against the sun and dark phosphorescence of sky, but the woman can make out he's masked like a bandit, with a trucker's cap over his Jesus of Nazareth hair. She's about to point him out to Rosa – *look*, another hiker – then stops herself. He's more vagrant than hiker, could unsettle more than reassure.

The girl looks where the woman is looking. Vapes and remarks, Masks are kinda overkill out here.

The woman murmurs agreement as they watch the solitary figure move across the wide valley floor. He looks around, appearing to spot them up on the hill, before quickly turning away again. Odd. The woman raises her DSLR camera, points it at his back and clicks.

Meth head, says the girl. Probably has a trailer out in the De-Na-Zin.

Probably, the woman says.

I went to school with a guy like that. Now he's in a correctional facility in Grants.

If he harasses us, he'll regret it.

Leaning back on her hand in her floral dress, the girl looks curiously at the woman. You got a gun, Therese?

I don't need one.

The girl doesn't laugh or ask how the woman can protect them without a weapon. She watches the man in the trucker cap disappearing into the gloaming, her silence seeming to take the woman at her word. He vanishes from sight, and the woman says, You hungry?

Starving.

Hot dogs, OK?

Sure. I could eat, like, a thousand.

They turn their backs on the last orange ebbs of sunset and descend the hill to where the woman has pitched up the blue canvas tent. The girl opens another Corona, sits and clicks through the day's photoshoot on the DSLR, searching for the most flattering shots. The woman uses a rock to dig a hole for the Duraflame logs, which should burn for three or four hours, taking them into the depths of the night. Then she looks across the landscape fading in the dusk, over at the horizon where, in nine hours' time, the Morning Star will rise.

Flames leap up from the shallow pit and she goes into the tent to get the frankfurters and hot-dog buns. Unzipping a pocket on her backpack to get her can-opener out, pain stabs her in the side, a scalpel incision from within. For a moment she's incapacitated. Holding her side, holding in her screams until the pain recedes and she can think. She needs something stronger than ibuprofen. Tramadol or OxyContin, resisted so far because of their sedative effects. But perhaps sedation's what she needs, because at the thought of colonies of bacteria rupturing her intestinal walls and invading her bloodstream, her heart pounds. She unscrews prescription vials. Grinds the bitter pills between her back teeth, swallowing the powder down.

She returns to the campfire. The girl's sprawled out, vaping and leaning back on her hand again, having wrenched herself from the digital gallery of Aurora Roses to gaze up at the first stars. The woman drops to her knees, vacuum packs of Oscar Mayer Classic Wieners and a bag of hot-dog buns spilling from her arms. When she sees the woman Rosa straightens up.

Therese . . . you *OK*?

It's vertigo. Comes and goes.

Vertigo?

Dizziness. It'll pass.

The woman can no longer fake a reassuring smile. She shuts her eyes and wills the opioids to rush through her blood, to block every pain receptor in her body, to stop the shriek of agony. She hears the girl say, Maybe we should go back to Farmington? Like, to the ER?

Unnecessary.

Hesitating in her scepticism, Rosa says, Um . . . well, can I get you anything?

The woman wants to laugh. *What can you possibly get me, you fucking imbecile? We're out in the fucking desert and I'm falling apart.*

Some water. Flask's by my backpack.

Rosa nods and goes to the two-man tent. Watching her disappear through the canvas flaps the woman feels a deep envy of the girl's painlessness. Of her health and youth and years left to live. She recognizes the vengefulness of her envy – how it wants to strip Rosa of what she possesses as though taking back what's rightfully hers. To leave what remains for the scavengers and carrion birds.

But then there'd be nothing left for *it*.

The woman reminds herself she has just this night to get through. Just nine hours. She closes her eyes and deep in her sockets the man trudges across the blood-red landscape of her mind. She remembers, of course, where she's seen that Jesus of Nazareth hair before.

She opens her eyes and gropes for the camera. Opens the image viewer and scrolls through dozens of Rosas to the most recent photo. Zooms in.

Four weeks ago the woman had landed in Albuquerque Sunport, then bought a used Toyota in cash and driven up the I-25 – past Santa Fe, past Taos, and into the northernmost parts of New Mexico. Night had fallen by the time she reached State Road 522, leaving behind the fluorescent-lit gas stations and budget motels of Questa to drive into the rural emptiness; the only lights for miles around her headlamps shining on the cracked asphalt speeding beneath her and the stars glittering above in the vast extraterrestrial sky. The woman drove through plains of withered grasses, with broad mesas in the west and the Sangre de Cristo Range in the east; the peaks black against the indigo night, the rugged mountainsides embedded with the spiral fossils of shells that had once been at the bottom of the ancient sea. She sped up the lonely highway, its median line rushing by like Morse code, and encountered not a single other vehicle before she reached a turn-off without any sign-post. She nosed her Toyota down the rutted road, her headlights now out as she bumped and shuddered over the rocky hardpan, heading east. Two or three miles later, she parked off to the side and turned off the engine, waiting in darkness, listening to the pings and ticks as the metal cooled. Then, when she was ready, she got out and stretched, looking up at all the stars in the black vacuum of space, then all around her at the nowhereness of the land, before setting off, pursuing a trail cutting through the scrubby desert plains. The woman walked by the shimmer of the quarter-moon, the warm and breezeless night scented by sagebrush and shaggy-barked juniper trees, creatures rustling away at her approach. She walked to the trilling of insects, as though she was under a spell. One foot in front of the other, obedient to something other than conscious will.

When the woman reached the clearing in the trees she saw that not much had changed. The secluded house and adobe studio were as she remembered them from thirty-four years ago, and the old steel bathtub was still at the side of the house, though filled with well-tended cacti and succulents now, indoor plumbing having long since been installed. Lights were on in the studio and, barely breathing, the woman left the concealment of the trees and crept to the window in the studio's far wall, out of sight of the house. And lo, there she was: the Sculptor, now seventy-two years old. Chemotherapy-bald head shining under the overhead light. Clay-streaked smock hanging from her frail frame. Living and breathing, *just*. What did the woman feel, seeing her again? Sadness? Revulsion? Shock? She was struck then by a memory of the Sculptor in that same studio at the age of thirty-two: hawkish eyes determined behind her visor, muscled arms pounding at Oaxaca granite in her vest and dungarees; her body artistic intent made flesh. The woman remembered kneading the knots out of the Sculptor's aching shoulders and back when she finally, after hours of toil, put down her tools. The Sculptor whispering in the woman's ear, *Are you even real?*

Now the dying Sculptor was working on a block of granite, yet to assume her imagination's shape. Trembling from the mallet's weight, she raised her hand above her mastectomy-flattened chest, struck the chisel with a fraction of the strength she'd once possessed. Why? the woman wondered. The Sculptor had abandoned stone carving decades ago – had installed a kiln and potter's wheel in her studio instead. Why return to such a brutal medium at this late stage, in the imminence of death? Did she think she could make up for lost time in her last enervated weeks? For abandoning her calling, for half a life's regret?

But perhaps the woman has regrets too. Why else had she looked the Sculptor up and discovered the JustGiving page to raise funds for her medical bills? Why else had she packed a bag and booked those flights? Bought a car and driven for hours to walk through the Taos County wilds to stand outside her window in the night? The woman was suddenly angry at herself. Why conflict herself with this longing? With this pathetic craving? The woman's never sad – at least, not like this. Not for the past, because nostalgia only ever lies. And not for another person, because people only ever die.

The door to the studio opened. A fortyish man entered; long

black hair to his shoulders, in flannel shirt and jeans. The woman recognized him, though the last time she saw him he'd been seven years old – a solemn, preternaturally watchful child. The stepson – Eddy – went over to his stepmother and put his hand on her shoulder. Told her to stop, to come inside the house, that it was late, she needed to get some bed rest, etcetera. But composed and dignified (always so fucking *regal*, even near death), the Sculptor shook her head. *No.* She wanted to keep chiselling, *to work.* Two headstrong wills, clashing, but the woman couldn't stick around to see who'd win. Because Eddy glanced to the window where she stood, and immediately she shrank back, turned and disappeared into the trees.

Night descends in the Bisti. The crater-marked half-moon shines in the dark sky, surrounded by a bright multitude of stars. Duraflame logs burn in the shallow pit and the woman and girl turn frankfurters on skewers over the flames. Rosa is talking about her ex – a manager at the Shop 'n Save and a 'digital soldier' against the deep state, who spends his after-work hours decoding cryptic messages posted on online forums. Rosa talks about child-trafficking rings who keep stolen babies in cages underground. About how each dose of the vaccine contains lab-engineered parasites that hijack the brain to bring you under government control.

And you believe that? the woman asks.

Rosa chews her hot dog thoughtfully. Why're they trying so hard to censor it if some of it weren't true?

The woman can't muster the energy to answer the girl. She is suffused with a wonderful weightlessness as though she's been released from gravity and all her earthly concerns. Not only have the opioids diminished the pain in her guts, they've made her problems diffuse too. Not good, the woman thinks, when she needs to be on edge, her nerves stretched tripwire taut.

The girl tears open a packet of mustard with her teeth. She squeezes it on to the hot dog on her lap but squirts it on to her dress.

Oh, shit. Lissy's gonna kill me.

The woman hands the girl some napkins, which only smear the

mustard more, and Rosa rushes over to the tent to remove the dress and rinse the yellow stain with bottled water.

By the fire in her opioid trance, the woman holds her skewered frankfurter over the Duraflame logs. She's not hungry, but the flames are – their ravenous tongues licking the meat, turning it to smoke and blackened carcinogenic remains. Staring into the blaze of incineration, the woman thinks of her own death – how the longer she lives the less she can countenance it. What an outrage to be cast out of consciousness and interred to rot in darkness or cremated to seven pounds of inorganic dust. An injustice she will make any sacrifice to avoid.

Though there's no wind, the flames turn strange. They flatten as though compressed, then leap like solar flares, bending from the sun's gravity. The woman knows it is near and she reminds herself there's just the night to get through. Fewer than nine hours now of Rosa's jitteriness, and Eddy, somewhere out there in the wilderness of primordial rocks, staking them out, unaware he's staking out his own death.

Just one night. And the woman has lived through many, many nights before. What's one more really, in the span of things?

Testimony 4 – Jürgen

At first, he appeared Mephistophelian in the dark recesses of the Gohlis bar – his eyes glinting in the shadows, lustrous grey hair falling to the shoulders of his leather coat as he swilled a glass of red wine. Yet his smile as I approached was nervous, his defeated slump shattering any illusion of sinister powers or intent. The decades had carved character into his craggy face and as we spoke I noticed his prosthetic left eye – the pupil rigid and unnerving in the fixity of its gaze compared with the dilated one on the right. Though unseeing, it somehow appeared the keener and more perceptive of the two; as though operating separately from Herr Unterbrink, making sharper judgements than the mind cogitating behind it ever could.

Jürgen said, When Ursula Pohl disappeared in '68, no one bothered looking for her. The Stasi had evidence she'd defected to the West. Everyone has forgotten her over the years. Except me.

In the near-empty bar, he kept his voice low, as though we were still living in the paranoid era of listening devices under bar stools. But I knew in 2022 it wasn't Stasi informants that he was skittish about.

None of the lecturers I spoke to at the Academy knew her, I said. But none of them had taught or studied there before 1980. Only Bernard Schilling recognized her from the photograph. He said, *That's Jürgen Unterbrink's muse.*

I'm flattered Professor Schilling still remembers me. He must have taught thousands of students over the years, and I was a mediocre painter at best. What is he now? Ninety? Ninety-two? How is he?

Not well. His wife told me he has stage 4 colon cancer. But he was in his studio in Spinnerei, where the lecturers at the Academy said I'd find him, standing at his easel.

Jürgen nodded with respect and a certain amount of awe. He'll drop dead at that easel, paintbrush in hand . . . Discipline. Work ethic. Draughtsmanship. He practically beat that into us as undergraduates.

He was very helpful. He found your contact details for me.

Jürgen bared tobacco-stained teeth in what could've been a grimace or a grin. Out of the five days I'd been in Leipzig, I'd spent three convincing him to talk. First by email (no reply). Then a call to his mobile (Sorry, I don't want to know, Jürgen had said before hanging up). Then a longer email all about Lena (no reply). Another call to his mobile (no answer – I left a voicemail, pleading my case). Then, finally, a call to the office of the German language school he owned. (I think you *do* want to know about the others who went through what Ursula did, I'd insisted, because if that woman took Ursula's photograph, I know she went through hell.) I'd expected Jürgen to hang up again, but he responded with a long and weary sigh. So, you're in Leipzig then?

In the wood-panelled corner of his local, he said, Can I see the photograph?

I dug the faded black and white image out of my backpack and looked away to give Jürgen some privacy with the port-wine-stained woman and whatever fifty-four-year-old memories she stirred up. Bedwyr hadn't been reluctant to part with the 'ghastly thing' and much of my journey back to London had been spent studying it. *Ursula, Künstlermodell, Hochschule für Grafik und Buchkunst, 1968.* The deathly look in Ursula's eyes reminded me of those Victorian daguerreotypes of someone propped up in their rigor mortis for posterity's sake. The birthmark obscuring half of her face and neck and creeping beneath her blouse had probably overshadowed every other aspect of her identity wherever she went.

I've seen this before, Jürgen said. Back in '68. Romy left it as a calling card after spending the night at Ursula's apartment.

How long was that before Ursula disappeared?

A week or two. You say it was stolen from a German photographer travelling around Wales?

Yes, in 1988. She took similar photographs of the Welsh girl, and Lena and Hiroji. All dead within weeks.

As Jürgen held the five-by-seven-inch photo in his large hands, he stroked a thumb across Ursula's monochrome face, as though tenderly smoothing back some strands of her mousy hair.

How old was this German woman, he asked, when you met her in 2011? Romy was in her mid-thirties in '68.

I hesitated. Mid-thirties. Forty at the most.

Jürgen frowned. He took a long and thoughtful swallow of his wine, lowered the glass and mused, She must have excellent genes.

Two grizzled old men entered the tavern then. Working-class Leipzigers of Jürgen's generation, who called out greetings as they went to the bar. Jürgen raised his hand in a half-salute, then glanced back at me. His comment about the genes had brought about a shift in the understanding between us. Recognition of the unspeakable conviction we shared.

Did you spend much time with Romy? I asked.

Jürgen shook his head. I met her on only two occasions. The first at a party in '68, and the second time by chance two years after Ursula's disappearance. I confronted her. I demanded to know what she had done to Ursula and . . . well.

He tapped a finger against the hard and shiny prosthesis in his left eye socket before sliding the photograph back across the wooden table to me. He continued, She said if I ever mentioned Ursula to anyone again, she'd be back for the other eye.

That was over half a century ago, I said. I'm sure you're safe now.

But in truth, I wasn't convinced. Neither was Jürgen.

I hope so, Jake. I'm too old to start learning Braille . . .

At seventy-five, Jürgen was a formidable drinker. Though he matched every pilsner I (pacing myself) finished with two or three glasses of red wine, he showed no signs of drunkenness, not even later in the evening when my words slurred and trains of thought frequently derailed. When I listened back to the recording of our conversation, Jürgen only becomes steadier and more controlled, his recall of fifty-four years ago sharper with every unit of alcohol consumed.

My friend Stefan Hellewege spotted Ursula on a crowded tram in '66, Jürgen said. He jumped off at her stop and pursued her through the streets to the library of Karl Marx University where she worked. Propositioned her as she pushed a trolley of books around the shelves. Stefan was in his second year at the Academy then, into symbolic paintings. He wanted to paint Ursula – for her birthmark to represent the glaring flaws in the SED or something. An extra-curricular project, of course.

Ursula didn't mind being exploited like that?

Not at first. She shared his political leanings. She wanted to help a dissident artist.

Where's Stefan Hellewege now? In Leipzig still?

He hanged himself in 1989, on the Lower East Side in New York. He'd defected to the West in 1968. Around the same time Ursula vanished, which is why everyone assumed she went with him.

They were together?

Not officially. Ursula's father worked for some SED ministry and pulled strings to get her a large apartment where she let Stefan live and paint rent-free. He hosted meetings of his underground artist collective in her living room, threw parties. She cooked for him, washed his clothes, lent him money, tolerated his indiscretions . . .

Why?

Perhaps she didn't think she deserved better, because of how she looked. She was older than he was. Twenty-nine. Had never had a relationship before. When Stefan was arrested late in '66 for organizing a secret exhibition of 'state-hostile' art and sentenced to a year in jail, she was devastated. All the artwork for the exhibition, including Stefan's portraits of Ursula, was confiscated. Likely destroyed.

Did you paint Ursula for the exhibition too? Professor Schilling said Ursula was *your* muse . . .

Ursula only sat for me after Stefan was sent away.

Your paintings of her were symbolic? Political? Like Stefan's?

Jürgen seemed to take offence at this. No. I painted her because she was beautiful.

He pronounced this wistfully, though in the photograph Ursula Pohl wasn't attractive in any conventional sense.

You were romantically involved?

Jürgen was rolling a cigarette. In his distractedness he seemed to have forgotten what he was doing and shreds of tobacco were spilling out of the ends.

We were close for a while. But when Stefan was released from prison and returned to Leipzig, Ursula refused to have anything to do with me.

Because she felt guilty about your affair?

No.

Unterbrink's half-rolled cigarette had fallen apart. He dropped the unsmokable remains on to the table, then looked up with a tortured expression.

If only that was the worst thing I did.

*

Why are you so full of hate?

Behind her round wire-rimmed glasses, Cornelia blazed at him and Jürgen could feel his chances of getting laid slipping away. It was pretty much the only reason he'd dragged himself to the party on Holsteinstrasse, into the room crowded with young drunken bodies in black turtlenecks and jeans, and spent the last hour – a whole hour! – cross-legged with earnest Cornelia of the frizzy red hair and aspirations of being a Great Poet. His prospects had seemed promising at first. But the more he drank the more her idealism rubbed him up the wrong way, until he'd had to set her straight: Dubček won't succeed. Moscow will gun down the uprising in Wenceslas Square. And there was no chance of a Prague Spring happening in Leipzig. Not when the citizens couldn't even stand up to the dynamiting of their seven-hundred-year-old church. Perhaps it had all come out a touch rancorous and spittle-flecked, but he certainly wasn't full of hate.

Truth, he corrected. I can't stand hypocrisy.

Cornelia creased her freckle-smattered brow. So I'm a hypocrite? Is that what you're saying?

Well, I read your poem in the *Leipzig Review*.

And?

Such lovely stanzas about your two weeks helping the farmers in Mecklenburg with the potato harvest. The rosy-cheeked peasants!

The dirt of an honest day's labour under your fingernails! The sweet aroma of cattle dung! The complete and utter lack of political truth!

Cornelia coloured. You know I can't write about that.

Right. You're only establishing yourself as a poet because you're censoring the truth, which, in my opinion, makes you a lousy poet. If you have any integrity, you should just quit.

Is that why you quit being a painter? Integrity?

Jürgen shrugged and swigged from his bottle of schnapps.

How convenient, she went on, that you can hide your lack of talent behind such moral righteousness.

Then, with an actual shudder, Cornelia got up and went over to her friends – most likely to tell them what a shit he'd been.

Jürgen drank more schnapps. What did it matter, anyway, whether he got laid or not? It had been three months since Stefan's release and return to Leipzig. Three months since Ursula had left to be with him, and far from getting over her, Jürgen was only feeling worse – despite his attempts to convince himself he was better off without her, a woman most would consider ugly, freakish even. A woman whose Sturge-Weber syndrome caused seizures she needed medication to control. In the privacy of their love, she'd accepted and understood him like no one else and reminding himself of Ursula's physical afflictions never cured his obsession. Even on the rare occasion he managed to charm or persuade an Anna or Margaret or Cornelia back to his attic room, they couldn't distract him. All he wanted was Ursula. Grinding coffee beans in her dressing gown, or posing on a stool in front of his easel, or lying in his bed, the irregular edge of her port-wine stain like the border of a territory he once could enter, but was now exiled from.

The Holsteinstrasse party went on around Jürgen, and after half an hour of everyone instinctively shunning his gloomy presence, he decided he might as well go home, jerk off, then pass out from the last of the schnapps. He went upstairs, along the landing, and opened the door to the room where the coats were piled. Except he had the wrong room. In the semi-dark, three naked bodies writhed like a single creature on the bed – all shuddering flesh and moans and the clumsy rhythm of three-way coition. Jürgen stood in the doorway, stunned. The dark-haired woman faced the door as she sat impaled on the groin of the (unidentifiable) man on his back beneath her, as another man (one of the party hosts, Harald Schultz) sodomized her, presumably, from behind. Gasping, the woman met his gaze from under her dark tangle of hair and for all her carnal abandon had a sharp gleam of intelligence in her eyes, as though she knew exactly who Jürgen was as he stood entranced by the explicit scene. He backed out of the doorway and shut the door.

Jacket forgotten, Jürgen wandered downstairs and into the kitchen. Shaken up. Aroused. Confused. It wasn't the first time he'd walked in on people having sex at a party, so why was he so rattled? Perhaps it was the way the woman had locked eyes with him, but both men had remained unaware of the door opening, though the landing light was bright and Jürgen had stood there for several seconds. It didn't make sense.

Jürgen lit a cheap filterless cigarette from the ring of flames on the stove. Günter, another of the party's hosts, had begun strumming a guitar in the living room, and Jürgen had the kitchen to himself as people drifted towards the Wolf Biermann singalong. It was then that the woman from the threesome appeared, modestly dressed now in shirt and wool skirt; buttoned up, tucked in. Her dark hair was combed straight and there was no sweat or flush of exertion on her sloe-eyed face, which was attractive in a subtle and unobvious way, and polite in expression as though meeting Jürgen for the first time. She introduced herself as Romy, an acquaintance of Günter's visiting from Dresden, and was so sober and composed that Jürgen began to doubt she was the same woman in the darkened room (because how could a woman who wasn't mindlessly drunk let herself go like that?). But then she said, It was you earlier, wasn't it?

I was looking for my jacket.

Heat rushed unexpectedly to his cheeks, annoying Jürgen. Why should *he* be the one to feel embarrassed? Romy's lips twitched, amused, and Jürgen wondered if the unlocked bedroom door wasn't so much oversight as exhibitionism.

Well, it's serendipitous you didn't find your jacket and leave.

Oh?

You're Jürgen the painter, aren't you?

I'm Jürgen the postal worker.

Romy frowned. But I saw your painting in Harald's room. The one of the woman with the port-wine stain. I asked Harald who painted it, and he said it was you. That you gave it to him. It's mesmerizing.

It's the last one I did before I quit, Jürgen said. And it's mesmerizingly bad.

Cornelia hadn't been exaggerating about his 'lack of talent'. Despite years of rigorous training at the Academy, he lagged well behind his peers. Deficient, for instance, in the technical flair and brilliance of Stefan Hellewege, who painted Ursula with the verisimilitude of the old masters.

I disagree, Romy said. You've captured something about her I bet she doesn't reveal to other artists. Some radiance and ease with herself that she'd perhaps possessed as an infant, before any awareness of her birthmark. You were in love with her, weren't you? In every brushstroke, it's there.

For a moment Jürgen couldn't speak. Unnerved that his feelings were so apparent in his art.

I hope you have a change of heart about quitting, Romy continued. You have something *unique*.

She smiled at Jürgen and he wondered then at his chances of sleeping with her, this slight and perceptive woman of middle age (thirty-five? thirty-six?) whose anodyne looks were interrupted by occasional flashes of some beauty or power that he sensed she was somehow suppressing from the eye of the beholder, lest it startle or terrify. It made Jürgen wary, but the memory of Romy writhing deviantly between two men was enough for him to cast his wariness aside.

If you would pose for me, perhaps I'd be inspired to paint again.

Romy sparkled at his attempt at flirtation. Perhaps I will. Or you could pose for me? I'm a photographer, looking for a model here in Leipzig – the more idiosyncratic the better. I was thinking of that woman in your painting, actually. Who is she?

Jürgen's cigarette hissed as he stubbed it in the sink. He really didn't want to speak of Ursula, but if it meant a fuck, so be it.

Ursula Pohl. But she's not an artist's model any more.

Oh. Why?

Apparently she's had enough of egotistical male artists fetishizing her birthmark.

That's a pity. Do you think an egotistical female artist could persuade her?

Romy touched his wrist above the hand that had extinguished the cigarette and the flesh tingled erogenously. She gazed intensely at him and Jürgen swallowed, his throat suddenly constricted and dry.

You can try. She's usually in the main library of Karl Marx University during the week. Works there nine to five.

Romy smiled. She removed her slender fingers from his tingling wrist.

Thank you, Jürgen.

Jürgen swigged his schnapps for courage. All the indications were there, but still he was unsure.

Look, d'you want to get out of here? I have cognac and more cigarettes back at my place on Oststrasse. It's only a ten-minute walk.

Romy laughed. How can I refuse? Go and fetch your jacket then, Jürgen. I'll wait here.

Turning to conceal his excitement, Jürgen left the kitchen, ran upstairs to Günter's room and dug through the pile of coats on the bed. He refrained from putting his Bohemian leather jacket on as he went back downstairs, intending to drape it chivalrously over Romy's shoulders as they left the party instead. But when he re-entered the kitchen Romy wasn't there, nor in any other room of the tenement house.

A week later Jürgen was in his attic room, hunched over a bowl of solyanka and bread, lining his stomach for a Friday night of drinking at Auerbach's with whichever acquaintances or strangers he might bump into there. The transistor radio was tuned to a West Berlin station playing psychedelic rock, but Jürgen was undistracted from his thoughts about a letter he'd opened at work that day, sent from a 'Leipzig schoolboy, aged 16' to a BBC radio programme that read anonymous letters from 'behind the Iron Curtain' out on air. In looping cursive with a distinctive sixty-degree slant, the teenager had written down his grievances with his 'education of lies'. 'Why do my teachers pretend that we live in a country where everyone is equal and free and cared for, when we're in a 108,000-square-kilometre prison of propaganda and poverty?' Jürgen had placed the letter on the pile for his supervisor, but now regretted not repairing the envelope with a *Damaged in Transit* sticker and throwing it in the sack to be sent overseas. The letter writer was anonymous, but they could take fingerprints from the paper and saliva from the reverse of the fifteen-pfennig stamp. They could analyse handwriting samples from every sixteen-year-old boy at every school in Leipzig and source the ink. Jürgen usually did his job without much conscience, yet that evening he couldn't stop thinking about the machinery of oppression he'd set in motion, clanking and grinding towards the teenage boy.

If the Leipzig schoolboy ended up in prison, he wouldn't be the first Jürgen had put there – and this, he knew, was what his conscience really wrestled with. When he'd informed on Stefan's 'state-hostile' exhibition the Stasi agent had assured him that they'd only cancel the show and confiscate all the paintings. But the agent had lied – something Jürgen had desperately tried to explain to Ursula after she'd overheard him talking again to that same agent (who'd wanted him to 'continue surveillance' of Stefan after his release) and confronted him. Ursula had only been disgusted by the excuse.

You knew they were lying. How could you not? Deep down you wanted to punish Stefan for being more talented than you.

She'd ended the affair, and though she'd kept his secret, he behaved like a persona non grata anyway. Dropped out of the Academy, quit painting, got the job at Deutsche Post. Every time he thought of how he'd got his best friend locked up for a year, Jürgen grabbed his coat and went to end all further thought at the nearest bar.

As Jürgen finished his solyanka he was dimly aware of the

doorbell ringing down below. Then his landlady, Frau Heinz, called up the stairs.

Herr Unterbrink. You have a visitor. A *lady* visitor.

Jürgen jumped up, banging his head on the low sloped ceiling. Had Romy got his address from somewhere? Had she come to apologize for the other night? He opened the door and called down.

Send her up.

He snapped off the radio and was shoving clothes in the laundry basket when Ursula Pohl entered in a beige trench coat, a headscarf covering her mouth and nose so only her eyes were visible. Conflicting emotions surged through Jürgen, the foremost of which was joy. She had sworn she would never speak to him again.

Ursula. What are you doing here?

Have I been followed?

Above the scarf her eyes were frantic. Something was different about her, but Jürgen couldn't put his finger on what. He went to his tiny attic window. The dusky street of tenement houses down below was deserted and the Wartburg and Trabi parked along the broken kerbstones were empty. The coffee shop opposite Frau Heinz's house had several signs in the window: *No coffee. No hot lunches. Closed until Monday for burst pipe. Closed until Friday for electrical issues.* The windows were dark.

I can't see anyone. What's going on?

She tugged the headscarf from her head, exposing her light brown hair and the port-wine stain that split her face and neck into lightness and dark. The deep-red nevus began on Ursula's scalp, spilling like paint from under her hairline down the side of her face, dividing her into halves: one plum-coloured, like darkening blood; the other blanched pale. Jürgen had gazed upon this Sturge-Weber pigmentation thousands of times and knew its periphery and variegation of shades contained within. Something wasn't right, but what? Why such terror in her eyes? Then he realized. The birthmark had flipped from the left of her face to the right. As though the reflection Ursula avoided for days and weeks at a time had stepped out of the mirror and taken her place.

★

At the small round table, she drank the cognac Jürgen had poured. Staring at her, he began to see it wasn't just the birthmark that had flipped. Ursula's crooked widow's peak and the bump on her nose both slanted the wrong way. The odd freckle had leapt to the opposite side. The left-to-right reversal fascinated him. It frightened and appalled.

She held up the backs of her trembling hands. See my grandmother's amethyst ring? This morning I noticed it was on my right hand instead of where it usually is on the left. I thought I'd put it on the wrong hand by accident . . . Then queuing at the Konsum this afternoon a neighbour kept staring at me, asking if I had changed my hairstyle, or had a makeover. I looked at my reflection in the window and nearly fainted. I dropped my basket and ran out.

She reached for the tumbler. Gulped some more cognac down. When I got home, I found this on the doormat.

She removed an envelope from her trench-coat pocket and passed it to Jürgen. Inside was a black and white photograph of Ursula in her living room, with her port-wine stain on the wrong side. But what disturbed Jürgen even more about the image was the sense of soullessness, of departed life, as though he was staring at Ursula's corpse. He couldn't bear the sight of it. He handed it back.

Who took this?

A woman I was with last night. She was searching for a book in the library yesterday – an old monograph that was out of circulation and lost somewhere in the basement stacks. I found it for her and she insisted on taking me out to dinner to thank me. We got on so well we ended up at my place afterwards, drinking schnapps and talking. I drank so much I can't remember the photograph being taken, or her leaving and my going to bed. Only waking on the divan when Stefan got back from his night shift at the factory.

Dread hammered in Jürgen's chest. He'd a knack, it seemed, for setting the machinery of destruction in motion towards others.

Her name was Romy, wasn't it?

Ursula flinched in surprise. You know her?

Jürgen told her about the Holsteinstrasse party. Had Romy

mentioned him? Had she asked to photograph her? Ursula shook her head.

She gave the impression she'd come to the library to search for a book . . .

Do you think Romy could have caused all this?

The words to describe what *all this* was evaded Jürgen.

How? Ursula said. It's beyond science. Paranormal.

But Jürgen wondered then if it *was* science. If Romy had drugged Ursula into unconsciousness and subjected her to some Mengele-like experiments. He had heard gruesome stories of Nazi scientists amputating the hands and feet and even the limbs of concentration-camp prisoners and transplanting them to the opposite sides. But Ursula's transformation was flawless, without any stitches or evidence of surgery. SED politicians often boasted that science was advancing exponentially under Communism. Had it advanced enough to reverse a human being?

You need to see a doctor, he said. Get a full medical check-up. And we should report Romy to the police. Tell them what's happened and that we think she caused it. They can investigate this for you . . .

Ursula flattened her hands against the table, pushing herself back as though ready to bolt.

No. They'll lock me up in some research facility. They'll cut me up and experiment on me. I'll never see daylight again.

Jürgen realized she was right. But if they couldn't go to the authorities, what *could* they do?

I'll find Romy, he decided. Ask her what happened last night. Günter should know where she's staying in Leipzig, or her Dresden address. I'll go tonight. Maybe she can change you back.

He paused. What he said was preposterous. But no more preposterous than what had happened in the first place. At the prospect of Jürgen leaving, Ursula looked afraid.

Can I stay here while you're gone?

Yes. But what about Stefan? Won't he wonder where you are?

I left a note saying I had to go to Zwickau because my mother's ill. I told the library the same. Stefan won't be able to handle this.

He didn't notice when he saw you this morning?

No.

How could Stefan not notice?

Ursula glared at him. You *know* why.

He did. He'd heard from some friends that prison had reduced Stefan to a near-catatonic depressive who, on his days off from his job at the chemical factory, wanted only to sleep.

I'm so scared, Ursula said. Can I stay here for a few days? Just to keep out of sight?

Jürgen reached across the table for her hand – the right hand that had been her left the day before – and squeezed her fingers and her grandmother's amethyst ring. He gazed into Ursula's face, both familiar and unspeakably strange, and it was as though he was staring directly into a fissure ripped into the fabric of reality – an absurd and leering gash that defied all meaning and comprehension. But it didn't make him love her less. She needed his protection. She needed *him*. It was a nightmare. It was a dream come true.

You can stay for as long as you like, he said.

So she stayed.

Throughout his workday Jürgen worried about her. He'd rush back to Oststrasse as soon as his shift at the sorting office was over, cursing the traffic that held up his tram, stopping by the Konsum to buy potatoes, sauerkraut, wurst and a cheap bottle of wine. In the attic room of Frau Heinz's boarding house, Ursula would be seated at the small round table, her wrong-sided birthmark striking in the gloom, her trench coat on over her sweater and pleated skirt for warmth. Cigarette suspended between lips, she'd strike a match as he entered and smoking no longer risked betraying her presence to the landlady.

How was your day? Jürgen would ask.

Uneventful, Ursula would shrug, exhaling a plume.

What did you do? Jürgen would persist.

Nothing much.

Looking around, he would see this was the case. Despite having ten or more hours at her disposal, Ursula never bothered to make the rumpled bed or clear away the coffee pot or his breakfast plates from that morning. She didn't touch the contraband *Der Spiegel*s, Solzhenitsyn and Bulgakov (usually hidden under a loose floorboard) that Jürgen left out for her to read, nor the dark bread and goat's cheese he'd left for her lunch. As the sink was still full of dishes, she obviously hadn't sponge-bathed (as Jürgen had suggested) or washed her lank hair. The only evidence of activity was the malodour of the *Neues Deutschland*-covered bucket and some notepaper on the table, upon which Ursula had written only two lines: *Dearest Stefan, I'm sorry* . . . The screwed-up balls of paper around her chair legs made it clear it wasn't her first attempt.

It's not good to sit around staring into space, Jürgen once said disapprovingly. You need some mental stimulation.

Exhaling towards the sink and Jürgen's shaving mirror, which she'd turned to the wall, Ursula replied, I heard your landlady cleaning the stairs and I spent an hour with the dead spiders and mouse droppings under your bed. It was fairly stimulating trying not to sneeze from all the dust.

Then she paused and said, But how was *your* day, Unterbrink? Censor many letters?

In the evenings they had dinner, drinking wine and listening to the radio or the children playing in the street below, taking turns to be machine-gunning border guards and defectors running for their lives. But Jürgen's small pleasure in their domesticity was marred by Ursula's obvious unhappiness. He had hoped, once her shock had subsided, that their love affair might resume, but she pulled away from attempts to draw her into a deeper intimacy; flinching when he tucked a loose strand of hair behind her ear, sliding her hand back when he affectionately covered it with his own. When they'd been lovers, Ursula had always listened attentively to Jürgen's every word – passionately siding with him as he described run-ins with professors, other students and Hilda in the canteen; admiring his intellect and lack of sentimentality as he diagnosed the ills of society and the political system that controlled it. Now, however, her disinterest in Jürgen was clear. She seemed altogether detached, consumed by a despair that one evening compelled her to leap up in her trench coat and pace beneath the low sloped ceiling.

What if I'm stuck like this? What if I never change back?

Jürgen winced at her loudness, hoping the other tenants wouldn't hear.

Then we'll leave the GDR, he said. We'll go to the West where no one knows us.

What about my mother and sisters? What about Stefan? I can't leave them.

What *about* Stefan? Jürgen thought bitterly.

But Ursula appeared not to notice his hurt feelings as she looked at him and pleaded, You *have* to search for Romy again.

We've been through this. I searched all over Leipzig. Harald hasn't heard from her since screwing her at the party. And Günter doesn't know any Romy from Dresden; she lied about being his friend. I knocked on the doors of *everyone* who'd been at Holstein-strasse that night. I searched cafés, concert halls, bars . . .

Search *again*.

What's the point? She's gone.

You could go to Dresden.

Right. I'm sure I'll bump into her on the street. Perhaps on the platform when I get off the train.

Scowling, Ursula muttered, Stefan would've found Romy by now. If he wasn't so—

At the second mention of Hellewege, something curdled in Jürgen. Stefan who didn't even notice you'd changed?

And whose fault is that?

She turned her back on him and went over to his narrow single bed (that Jürgen had offered up to her on her first night, mistakenly thinking he wouldn't be sleeping on the floor for long). Without bothering to remove her trench coat, Ursula crawled under the bed-spread and turned to the wall. Sighing, Jürgen said, OK, OK. I'll go to Dresden.

But Ursula didn't respond – perhaps she knew it was hopeless too. Later, after drinking what wine was left and brushing his teeth, Jürgen lay down on the bedside rug and pulled the scratchy blanket over him for warmth, resentful about the aches and stiffness in his limbs from the wooden floor, resentful about the *Neues Deutschland*-covered bucket that *he* had to empty in the second-floor toilet every night. Resentful that Ursula never lifted a finger to clean or tidy up though she was home all day. Such was his resentment, it took him half the night to fall asleep. Ursula now depended on him for everything: food, water, shelter, company. She wasn't nearly grateful enough.

The next morning Jürgen woke at first light to the sight of Ursula convulsing. She stood in the centre of the room in her chemise, twitching and shaking as though in the grasp of an epileptic fit. Jürgen rushed to her, grabbed her shoulders and called her name as she shook in myoclonic jerks. Then she slackened and Jürgen caught her before she slumped to the floor.

He brought her over to the bed and laid her down. When she returned fully to consciousness she was strangely composed. Tranquil, even. She apologized to Jürgen for scaring him. The anticonvulsant pills she took for the seizures caused by her Sturge-Weber syndrome had run out and she didn't have a new prescription.

You should see a doctor, Jürgen said. Get your prescription renewed.

No. Swear to me you won't call a doctor, Jürgen.

But what if you have a seizure when I'm not here? It's too dangerous.

It didn't feel dangerous.

As she lay with her head on the pillow, a dreamy look entered Ursula's eyes. Do you believe in angels, Jürgen?

No, I don't.

Just now I saw one. It was incredible. It had wings as large as this attic and was made of shimmering particles of God. It sang to me that I was blessed. Chosen. I wanted to weep with joy.

Jürgen was unnerved. The grand mal had left her paler and weaker, though her nevus flammeus seemed vivified, as though the capillaries beneath had expanded and were pulsating, leeching Ursula of blood and vitality from elsewhere.

Do they usually cause these visions? Your epileptic fits? he asked. Ursula only closed her eyes and smiled.

That evening when Jürgen returned from the post office, Ursula didn't touch the bread and liverwurst he'd brought for supper. Instead, uncharacteristically for one usually so keen to deflect attention from herself, she began speaking of her twenty-nine years of being Ursula Pohl. Trench-coated, her birthmark livid under the solitary attic bulb, she spoke as though onstage, performing a monologue for some unseen audience beyond Jürgen in his chair. She spoke of her childhood: how her father would ask Ursula's mother to keep her out of sight when important guests were visiting, how her mother had once caught Ursula scrubbing her face with bleach in order to look like her sisters, Clara and Inge. At school she had been nicknamed Sanitary Napkin, and teachers often reminded her to count her blessings she lived in the GDR and not the Capitalist West, where the fascist regimes locked people like Ursula up. She had been dissuaded from studying for her Abitur and sent to secretarial college instead. In her first clerical post, certain men had been attracted to the birthmark, or to what it had made her: meek and timorous and unable to stand up to their transgressions. And then there was Stefan, who'd exploited her first for artistic gain, and then for emotional and material support. Who'd only made love to her with the lights turned out or flipped over on to her stomach.

What about me? Jürgen protested. I'm not as bad as Stefan or those other men.

Ursula glanced at him then returned to narrating her autobiography, of which Jürgen was not a part. For as long as she could remember her port-wine stain had been a curse. Only now was she discovering that her Sturge-Weber syndrome was a blessing.

Romy told me that in some ancient civilizations a birthmark like mine meant you were 'chosen'. Marked for a divinity to come and show you the higher realm. What I experienced this morning . . . was so much like that.

Jürgen stared at Ursula, incredulous. Romy deceived you. She's a liar.

Ursula smiled. Or she's the servant of angels, and her lies reveal the greater truth.

Daybreak and Jürgen was woken by Ursula having another seizure. On her back on the floor, shuddering as though a high voltage was passing through her. She foamed at the mouth and Jürgen, scared she would choke, leapt up from the bedside rug to roll her on to her side. Helplessly he watched, until the force went out of her, leaving her limp.

As she recovered on the bed, slower this time, blood trickled from the corner of her mouth on to the pillow. Alarmed, Jürgen wiped it away with his sleeve, wondering how badly she'd bitten her tongue.

Are you in pain? he asked, and Ursula shook her head, looking to Jürgen like someone in a state of morphine bliss. Jürgen knew she needed a doctor – to check her tongue, to administer some medication for her epilepsy. But he knew better than to make that recommendation again.

Was the angel there? he asked instead.

Ursula nodded and closed her eyes. Blood on her teeth, she smiled.

Jürgen ran to Rosa-Luxemburg-Strasse. Stefan worked the night shift at the chemical factory and would be home by six or seven. Jürgen wasn't sure how the reunion would go, but he couldn't keep what was happening to Ursula to himself any longer, and had to get her chequebook. If he was to bribe a doctor to visit her in Oststrasse, he needed more money than was stashed under the floorboards of his room.

The April day was cold. He shivered in his leather jacket on the steps of the building, ringing the bell to Ursula's apartment, and a middle-aged man with a trimmed moustache came out of the main entrance.

Looking for Fräulein Pohl and her boyfriend? They've defected to the West.

Jürgen vaguely recognized the man as the upstairs neighbour

who had banged on Ursula's door and threatened to call the Volk-spolizei during Stefan's wilder parties.

That's not true.

Isn't it? This building was crawling with Stasi yesterday. They went into Fräulein Pohl's apartment and I could hear them turning the place upside down. They came up to interview me. It was brief. What do I know about those hippies on the third floor?

What makes them think Ursula's defected?

The man looked around, then whispered, Think? They *know*. They say Fräulein Pohl wrote cheques to a man in an organization that helps people escape. And her boyfriend had been broadcasting their plans to leave. It got to the Stasi through informants. It's a miracle they got away.

Jürgen rang the bell again. It was impossible to tally what the man said with what he knew. Ursula was in his attic, not the West. The man zipped his anorak up over his petit bureaucrat's shirt and tie.

Waste your time then, he said, walking down the steps. The building manager says a family are being allocated the apartment now. About time. It wasn't fair that an ugly immoral spinster like Fräulein Pohl got so many rooms.

Could there be two Ursulas? One Ursula, the right way round, who'd fled the GDR with Stefan? And another Ursula, mentally and physically disintegrating in his room? The absurd possibility crossed Jürgen's mind on the way back to Oststrasse but he dismissed it. Stefan must have accessed Ursula's bank account, stolen hundreds of Ostmarks from her and fled on his own. Jürgen thought of Stefan's lost year in prison and wasn't sure if he wished him ill, or well, or nothing at all.

He went up the boarding-house stairs, daunted by the task ahead of persuading Ursula that a check-up from Dr Koenig (who'd said on the telephone he'd 'attend for a fee' after his surgery closed at five p.m.) wouldn't result in her being experimented on in a Soviet research facility. But when he got to the attic room there was no Ursula to persuade. Her trench coat was gone from the door hook and her shoes from the mat. Heart knocking violently in his chest, Jürgen checked the bathrooms on the second and first floors, and banged on the doors of the six other tenants, two of whom were home and hadn't seen a woman with a port-wine stain. Frau Heinz, in her curlers and pink quilted housecoat, was listening to GDR1 in the sitting room. Her exaggeratedly arched eyebrows arched higher at Jürgen's question.

Was she here last night, Herr Unterbrink? This boarding house does not permit lady visitors past ten p.m. I trust you haven't been breaking the rules.

The street outside the tenement was deserted, but the coffee shop over the road was open that day, and a server with long hair and a goatee leant over the counter. The bell above the door tinkled as Jürgen charged in and the server glanced up from the breasts of the *Das Magazin* centrefold with a nonchalance typical of customer service in the GDR. He gave the impression of having had his eyes glued to the centrefold all morning, but to Jürgen's surprise he said he *had* noticed a woman in the street about an hour earlier. Tall, in a long coat, with a scarf around her head 'like an Arab'. She'd been waving at passing cars, trying to flag one down, until a Trabi stopped and she'd jumped in. The server couldn't remember the Trabi's driver, or number plate or even the colour. The headscarf woman, however, stuck in his mind.

She gave me the creeps, he said. Like something evil was hiding under that scarf.

Ursula I (oil on plywood, 65 cm by 40 cm, 1968). Ursula stands in a trench coat, reversed from left to right. Painted in chiaroscuro, in shades of rose madder and vermilion, in shades of anaemic white, the disintegrating horror of her expression is rendered in near-impasto brushstrokes, vigorous and coarse. *Ursula II* (oil on canvas, 50 cm by 70 cm, 1968). The subject lies post-seizure on Jürgen's single bed, pale as exsanguination except for the nevus flammeus blazing on her face and the blood vessels flaring in her rapturous gaze. *Ursula III* (oil on canvas, 100 cm by 70 cm, 1968). The subject screams in the mottled shaving mirror on the attic wall and her reflection screams back; their hands dragging down their cheeks, exposing the pink flesh inside their lower lids, their mouths dark tormented caves.

Ursula IV . . .
Ursula V . . .
Ursula VI . . .

She proliferated on canvas as he worked at the easel in his attic, dripping paint on the sheets of *Neues Deutschland* spread over the floor, ignoring Frau Heinz's complaints about the white spirit fumes leaking on to the stairs. He painted as though the ceaseless repetition could solve the mystery of what had happened to her. Jürgen had already sought out the answers in life, had spent weeks searching all over Leipzig, had taken the train to Zwickau (only to discover the Stasi had got there first, and the Pohls had disowned their GDR-fleeing daughter). But reality had yielded not a single answer. So he painted into the void.

In 1969 Jürgen returned to the Leipzig Academy – ostensibly to finish his degree, but mainly to quit his job and paint round the clock in the high-ceilinged studios. By day he produced scenes of peasants and factory workers in the style of Werner Tübke for his portfolio. By night, however, after everyone had left, Ursula continued to multiply on his canvases. Singly or doubly now, as mirror-image twins, floating or flying or tumbling out of the sky. Dual Ursulas side by side, foreheads touching so that the port-wine stains came together like the symmetry of Rorschach blotches (the crimson wings of a butterfly perhaps? Or the aftermath of carnage, of splattered blood?).

Jürgen's monomaniacal painting of Ursula was soon ridiculed in the department. More than one professor warned that his lazy and indulgent surrealism, deficient in Marxist ideology and class consciousness, could get him expelled. But in spite of the mockery and disciplinary threats, Jürgen could not stop painting her – the compulsion intensifying as he began to feel something other than his own imagination guiding his hand, communicating with him through his brushstrokes and dark palette of oils. But what? Each night he entered into the fever dream of painting, determined to find out.

February 1970, Jürgen went to Budapest on an exchange programme organized between art schools of the Freundesländer, replacing, at the last minute, a more accomplished student taken ill with appendicitis. Though he'd anticipated the change of scene from Leipzig, he found Budapest to be just another shade of Eastern Bloc grey; the bridge-crossed Danube and streets of Austro-Hungarian architecture merely another stage set for Soviet hegemony, and the Hungarian Royal Drawing School, where students were trained in the same paint-by-numbers Socialist Realism as at the Academy, just as uninspiring. Russian was the common tongue between Jürgen and his Magyar classmates – but as it was a language they all resented and didn't speak well, Jürgen's conversations with the Lászlós and Zsuzsannas tended to be brief. This, paired with Jürgen's depressed air, meant he spent most of his time after class roaming the streets of Budapest and drinking cheap pálinka on his own.

Halfway through the exchange he surfaced from an eight-hour session to a painting of Ursula holding hands with her doppelgänger in reverse, both of them floating in some dark interstellar space. But it was the third figure that made Jürgen stumble back from his finished canvas, confused. Lurking in the background. A pair of sloe-eyes. A barely-there smirk. Jürgen had no recollection of painting her. She'd just appeared. Disturbed, he painted over her, black over black over black, then took the canvas from the easel and dumped it in some bins over the road from the Hungarian Royal Drawing School. When he returned the next day, it was gone.

One restless Sunday night Jürgen wandered from his student dormitory in South Pest to Erzsébetváros, where passing a backstreet kávéház he saw a familiar-looking woman seated at a candle-glimmering table with a man. She reminded him of Romy, but with a short gamine crop and an extravagant mink coat draped over her shoulders to compensate for the inadequacy of a slinky black dress. She was immersed in conversation with her older, grey-headed companion, who exuded the quiet authority of a professor or member of the intelligentsia, and though they weren't touching or seated too closely together, Jürgen sensed the atmosphere of restrained sexual intimacy. He stood at the window and his conviction grew. She didn't just resemble Romy, she *was* Romy. More glamorous than the night he'd first met her, her pixieish cut making her cheekbones more pronounced and smoky make-up emphasizing her eyes, which, even as they gazed seductively at the man, possessed the same acuity as at Günter's party, sharp enough to puncture the soul of whoever she had in her sights. Smiling, her male companion made some witticism and Romy laughed and touched the back of his hand – fleetingly, discreetly, but with an erotic charge that lingered between them, palpable even to Jürgen standing outside. The pleasure radiating through her struck Jürgen as obscene – sickened him in fact. It was an outrage that Romy was flirting and drinking a carafe of wine when Jürgen was uncertain if Ursula was living or dead.

He entered the kávéház, a wobble in his step from the pálinkas he'd already had.

Romy.

She glanced up, her eyes innocent of who he was. In polite Hungarian with a Russian accent, she said, Excuse me?

Jürgen continued in German. Romy. We met in Leipzig two years ago.

She responded in the Russian of a native speaker, Forgive me. I don't speak German.

Jürgen stared angrily at her. Now only a metre or two from her, he was in no doubt she was Romy. That behind her pretence of confusion she knew exactly who he was. In Russian, for the benefit of the man, Jürgen said, What did you do to Ursula?

I beg your pardon?

Romy's eyes signalled her distress to her handsome companion, and he intervened in Russian with a Hungarian accent.

My friend doesn't know who you are. I suggest you leave us alone.

Jürgen pointed an accusing finger at Romy. In broken Russian – deteriorated further by the alcohol in his veins – he said, Two years ago. In Leipzig. She changed Ursula, my friend. Ursula had this purple on her face . . . Jürgen pointed at his left cheek . . . and *she* moved it to the wrong side. Then Ursula . . . *gone.*

Romy turned to the man. Exasperated laughter punctuated her exasperated speech and Jürgen didn't need a Hungarian translator to understand what she was saying: *I've never been to Leipzig. I've never met this Ursula. I've never seen this man before in my life.* He stood with anger gathering force within him. He leant over the table, smashing the wine carafe to the floor as he pushed his face towards Romy's. He hissed in German, *Liar.* I know it's you. What happened to Ursula? What did you do to her?

Alarmed, Romy swerved back in her seat and the older, five-o'clock-shadowed intellectual raised his hand and beckoned to someone over Jürgen's shoulder. Within moments Jürgen's arms were being seized. Waiters were cursing him in Hungarian and brusquely scuffling him to the door, where he was ejected into the street.

It was another three hours before Romy emerged from the kávéház. She and her Hungarian lover stood outside together, bickering in the cold; the man perhaps insisting he walk her home and Romy insisting she would be fine, her German accuser out of sight, most likely harassing other women in other bars. Eventually they kissed goodnight and to Jürgen's relief the man set off in the direction of People's Republic Street, no doubt to catch a tram or taxi to his wife and children in the Buda Hills. Though impatient to chase after her, Jürgen counted to ten in the corner of the bar across the road, then stumbled drunkenly from his stool and over to the door.

Romy's heavy coat of mink and taut calves in dagger-like heels were disappearing round the street corner when Jürgen got out-side. He dashed after her and reached the corner as Romy was turning yet another, this time on to Király Utca, where Jürgen trailed her at a distance of twenty metres, his coat collar turned up and head angled down from the halogen street lamps, though Romy didn't once look behind her, striding quickly as though in a hurry to get home. She slipped into an alley leading towards the Jewish Quarter, and Jürgen reached the passageway just as she pushed through a tall wooden gate, presumably into the back yard of her residence.

Jürgen approached the gate. He hesitated. Should he enter? On the other side, Romy ended his deliberation for him, speaking in the German she'd claimed not to know.

Why don't you come in? We can talk privately in here.

With a queasy lurch he understood he hadn't shadowed her undetected; he'd been lured. Yet he entered the yard where Romy stood in the three-quarter darkness, her coat of Siberian mink silvery in the moonlight, her heels inches tall. She looked unreal to Jürgen, like an apparition, and as she breathed white vapours into the cold he couldn't quite believe she was sustained by lungs and respiratory system and not some other metaphysical means. The yard was at the back of a restaurant kitchen, closed for the night, and crowded with wooden crates and overflowing bins. Not where Romy was staying. She looked at Jürgen with a recognition she had earlier suppressed, then down into her leather clutch bag. Groping around inside, she spoke again in German.

I remember your painting, but not your name.

Jürgen. And you? Do you go by a Russian name now? Olga? Masha?

Romy sighed. Snapped her bag shut. I left my cigarettes at the bar. Do you have one?

Jürgen reached into his leather jacket for his cheap, filterless Karos. Only as Romy's face shone in the flame he extended to her did Jürgen balk at his obedience. Why hadn't he said no? When the cigarette was lit he slammed the lighter's hinged lid.

What happened to Ursula?

Fräulein Pohl? She exhaled her name with the smoke. Didn't she defect to the West with her factory-worker boyfriend?

You know that's not what happened. Ursula showed me the photo you took.

A diaphanous veil of cigarette smoke shifted over her face. Beneath her dark urchin's cut, she frowned.

Photo?

Of her reversal.

Romy let out a small, incredulous laugh.

Her *reversal*. What a strange and ludicrous flight of fantasy.

I know what I saw. And I know you were responsible.

Are you accusing me of witchcraft, Jürgen? I thought such backwards superstition had been wiped out in the GDR.

Jürgen glared at her.

You deformed her. You ruined her life.

With a glint of antagonism in her eyes, Romy said, Wasn't Ursula born into the ranks of the defective of our species? The only thing she was useful for was keeping library shelves in order. What life was there to ruin?

She smiled and Jürgen wondered what she was. All he could see was dissemblance. Smoke and mirrors masquerading as some kind of femme fatale, when the truth was far more monstrous. Her mink coat had fallen open, exposing her black dress and subtle cleavage, but it was her throat, pale and slender above her clavicles, that tempted Jürgen's hands.

You sound like a Nazi, he said.

Do I? I mostly disagree with Nazism. It's a flawed ideology.

He stepped closer. Anger cracked his voice. What happened to Ursula?

Romy only shook her head as though in pity and sadness. One thing Nazi ideology got right was the need to purify the gene pool. Fräulein Pohl's elimination only benefits our species.

Elimination. The word winded him like a punch in the guts. She's dead? Jürgen rasped.

Romy smiled and stepped towards him. She reached for both of his hands with her own. Pressed them over her black silk dress and breasts.

I left you at that party, she said. But you can have me now. If you're ready to move on from Ursula, that is . . .

She parted her lips suggestively and caressed his stubbled cheek. Enraged, Jürgen's hands found their way to her throat. Wrapped around her windpipe gently enough to measure her pulse. But far from being threatened, Romy only gazed as though intoxicated and Jürgen sensed the gathering of some unknown force in the freezing night around them. The same quickening, perhaps, that Ursula had been convinced was an 'angel' visiting her in his attic room.

Come on then, Romy whispered. Come on.

Ursula. He thought of what she'd done to Ursula, and in the same moment he began to throttle her, he flew backwards into the yard's brick wall with bone-slamming, rib-cracking force. Stunned, wheezing in pain, he looked around. No one was there. Only Romy, gloating through the darkness.

Can't move on from that freak of nature, I see.

Had *she* pushed him? He staggered up, lunged for her again, but a blinding white flash of agony stopped him. It was a gouging, deep in his left eye socket. A dagger behind the eye. Jürgen screamed. His hands flew to his face, but found only a cavity, the warm gush of rupture and blood. He dropped to his knees, clutching the wound. The pain obliterated everything except the flashes of colour and light in the eye that remained – like the fireworks of an ocular migraine. Kneeling, hand clamped to mutilated socket, some sight returned to Jürgen's remaining eye. Romy was walking towards him; determined, not yet through with him. But it was the buckling and warping of the night behind her, reality parting like the Red Sea to make way for some unknown entity, that made Jürgen certain he was about to die.

A yellow light flooded the yard. Above the restaurant kitchen a window opened and a man leant out and shouted in Hungarian. Through his debilitating pain, Jürgen understood one word: *Police*.

Romy looked up at the window in annoyance. Standing over Jürgen now, she peered down with a faint wrinkling of disgust.

Count your blessings, Herr Unterbrink. But ever mention Fräulein Pohl again, we'll be back for the other eye.

She turned on her heels. The gate swung, open and shut, and she was gone.

At Szent Rókus Hospital two policemen took a statement. In his hospital bed, woozy with morphine, surgical dressing over his throbbing left socket, Jürgen described how he'd been jumped in the alley and dragged into the yard. It had been too dark and too violent a blur for him to get a proper look at his attackers, but they were both male and at least 1.8 metres tall. When the policemen said the restaurant manager – the one who'd heard Jürgen scream – had seen a woman with him, Jürgen shook his head. A woman? There'd been no woman there, he insisted, ignoring his interviewers' exchange of looks.

Jürgen didn't complete his remaining three weeks at the Hungarian Royal Drawing School. When he was discharged from the hospital he returned to Leipzig, where the first thing he did was get rid of his Ursula paintings, burning all forty-seven of them in a bonfire. Later that year, Jürgen graduated from his degree with a portfolio of proud and noble workers, heroically toiling in the coal mines and steel-manufacturing plants. Then he returned to Deutsche Post where he remained for another eighteen years until the collapse of the GDR.

For a long time Jürgen's disfigurement was a reminder of his brush with evil. Of the sinister forces that had stolen his left eye and devoured Ursula entirely. Every time the glass prosthesis stared back at him in the mirror, or he took it out and regarded the lid, sunken over the eyeless cavity, scenes came unbidden to his mind. Ursula being shaken by 'angels'. Romy in furs and heels, smirking at him through the darkness. But the years passed, and the memories lost some of their power as Jürgen's present-day life became more demanding: his marriage to Marlene and their passionate fights and reconciliations; his unruly stepsons, Werner and Hedwig, both incapable of staying out of trouble for long. Ursula became a ghost who sometimes haunted his dreams, and Romy a tormentor in his nightmares, menacing him with sharp tools for the gouging of his other eye.

In 1991, Jürgen received a letter from Budapest. The letter writer, a woman called Zsófia Szénes, apologized (in German, translated by a friend) for contacting him out of the blue; she'd tracked him down through the Hungarian Royal Drawing School, then the Leipzig Academy and Professor Bernard Schilling, who Jürgen still drank with occasionally at Auerbach's. Back in the winter of 1971, browsing in a junk shop in South Pest, she'd spotted an oil painting. Irresistibly drawn to it, she asked the shopkeeper who J. *Unterbrink* (as signed on the canvas) was. The shopkeeper had shrugged. He'd found it by the Hungarian Royal Drawing School the year before and it was hers for five forints. She'd purchased it and taken it home. Zsófia had enclosed a photograph with her letter. Did Jürgen recognize it? He did. The only painting of Ursula he'd made during the Budapest exchange. The one he'd dumped in the bins.

Since finding out his identity in '71, Zsófia Szénes had thought many times of writing to him. But only now, after twenty years, had she worked up the nerve. The mirror-image women had a power over her, she confessed. Were they based on anyone he knew? The more Zsófia stared at the painting the more it seemed connected, in her mind, to a tragedy that had befallen her family in '57 – a tragedy she couldn't go into in the letter. She wanted to ask him about the third presence in the painting, obscured beneath thick slashes of black paint. A presence she'd encountered before in a photograph of her late Aunt Klára, taken before she died.

After reading the letter, Jürgen poured a shot of whisky. Then another and another. He'd just been issued a fiancé visa from the Canadian Embassy and was soon leaving for Vancouver with a Canadian national called Patricia, who was six months pregnant with their first child. They were planning a shotgun wedding. They were setting up a German language school. After thirteen years of Marlene, his mid-forties happiness with Patty was a blessed miracle he didn't want to jeopardize. So he burnt the photograph of his Ursula painting and didn't reply. But he hung on to the letter and return address for reasons he could not explain.

*

After midnight in the Gohlis tavern the barman yawned as he collected glasses from the tables, an unlit cigarette wedged behind his ear. The place was closed but he'd yet to throw me and Jürgen out, perhaps out of respect for the hundred-odd euros we'd spent on wine, pilsners, bar snacks and meals. I was drunk and, swaying on my bar stool, I could see in Jürgen's seventy-five-year-old face traces of his younger selves. Jürgen aged twenty-one at the tenement party on Holsteinstrasse. Jürgen aged twenty-three, wandering the streets of Erzsébetváros. Angry young men. Heartbroken. Afraid.

After I emigrated to Vancouver, I rarely thought of Ursula, Jürgen said. Patty and I were so busy, raising our two daughters and running our German school. But since returning to Leipzig, I'm reminded of Ursula everywhere I look. I can't say that Ursula was the love of my life – that dubious honour belongs to Patty, even though we're long divorced. But Ursula is the biggest mystery. She comes to me sometimes in dreams.

I glanced down at my phone. In my drunken state I was unsure it was still recording, so I touched the display. Twelve hours forty-one minutes and counting.

Can you describe the dreams?

Sure. They're the same every time. I wake at daybreak to Ursula standing at the end of my bed, looking as she did in 1968. Port-wine stain on the wrong side, bare-legged in one of my shirts. She stares with curiosity at my wrinkly old-man's face, and I ask, Where have you been, Fräulein Pohl? West Berlin, she says, with Stefan Helle-wege. We both laugh, because we know it's a lie.

Upturned glasses rattled as a barman loaded a plastic crate into the dishwasher. The main lights came on and I winced, flushed and bleary-eyed.

Do you ever dream of Lena? Jürgen asked.

I nodded.

All the time.

Badlands – IV

On her back on the loom-woven Navajo blanket, the woman gazes up at the night-time desert sky. The stars are staggering; so many other suns in the darkness, so many light years apart. Her mind light with OxyContin, the woman begins to float up from the Bisti Badlands, up from the barren strata of rock. Leaving flesh and bones and beating heart behind, she rises out of her tormented body, up into the cosmological past of the sky.

Besides her, the girl exhales into the dark. A cloud of menthol vape fumes drifts across all the distant shining gods. Alpha Centauri. Ursa Major. Orion and Betelgeuse.

Man, she says, the Oxy's really kicking in.

An hour earlier, when the fire had gone out and the darkness consumed them, the girl had become apprehensive. Scared. Asking to go back. The woman told her that she had some painkillers for her endometriosis (*Oh, that sucks. My mom's friend has that. That why you don't have kids?*) and gave a couple to Rosa to swallow with mezcal to help her relax. Reckless perhaps, with the Sculptor's son nearby. But preferable to talking her down for the rest of the night.

The temperature's dropped but the woman's feverish blood runs hot. Despite the opiates she can still feel the dull pain in her guts, the colonies of bacteria eating her from the inside out. A tingling itch – ringworm? herpes zoster? – crawls like fire ants all over her skin and the woman wants to scratch until she's bleeding and raw. But she's in the presence of the girl, so she curls her fingers into fists, stares up.

All these fucking stars, Rosa says. They make me feel like a teeny-weeny sneeze particle or something.

The woman murmurs her agreement, but in truth the spiralling cosmos never shifts her from her pre-Copernican sense of being the centre of all things. Never makes her feel insignificant or small. The girl props herself up on her elbow and reaches for the mezcal. The bottle sloshes as she swigs, and the woman feels the inquisition of her eyes under her tumbling curls.

Can I ask you something personal, Therese? the girl says. Are you ill? I mean, like cancer-ill or something?

The woman replies, Nothing serious. Just the food poisoning from last night.

Her gaze flits to the girl. Her pretty face is dark but the woman can discern her expression in the light of the crescent moon and stars. Rosa's pout is unconvinced. Citronella insect repellent scents the breeze between them. The woman slathered it on earlier. Can the girl detect the putrescence beneath?

You're so different to anyone I've ever met, Rosa says. D'you ever get lonely, travelling around on your own?

No, the woman says. I never get lonely. Everywhere I go I make new friends.

The girl sprawls back down on the zigzag-patterned blanket. Picks up her Juul, exhales a cloud and makes her confession: she has no friends and is the loneliest she's ever been. Sometimes she misses her ex, Tyler the Shop 'n Save manager, though he pressured her into stealing phones out of her high school's gym lockers (which got her expelled in junior year) and into making videos for him (illegal videos, because she was sixteen). When he dumped her she took the bus to Farmington and was heartbroken for a while. Now she's just lonely. Lissy's trailer is just about the loneliest place on Earth, with Lissy camming or tending bar all night, then bringing home disgusting men and sex screaming through the particleboard. Soon as her YouTube channel starts making money, Rosa's moving out.

I'm gonna be single for a while. Focus on my career, before I manifest myself a husband and some kids. Ideally, I'd like to be married by twenty-five, and have two babies by thirty.

Lost in her stargazing, the woman's only half-following. Rosa's disembodied voice drifts over.

You want to meet someone? Fall in love, start a family?

No.

You don't want to get married?

I was, once.

So, you're divorced?

He shot himself.

Oh my God. Like, suicide? That's *horrible.* I'm so sorry, Therese.

Don't be.

The woman still dreams of him. Dreams of flashes of temper and eruptions of rage, of fists and spit and the cold metal barrel of a hunting rifle forced in her mouth, breaking a tooth. She wakes from these dreams humiliated as though she's soiled the bed, though she's long free of him, and of her sons, who grew into his likeness. Long ago she went to their graves and walked over the bones interred in the same plot. And nothing is what she felt. Which is why the dreams anger her. They drag her back against her will to the time she was weak. Now she is powerful. She has triumphed over him and yet he remains in her unconscious, like a splinter she can't prise out.

Rosa's curiosity is palpable in the dark.

You really weren't sad when he died?

Not really.

You didn't love him?

No.

Because she can sense her coldness has unnerved Rosa, because the opiates have dissolved the filter between mind and mouth, she says, There was somebody once, though. A sculptor.

Who you were in love with?

The woman doesn't get to answer. Out of the darkness comes the rumbling of falling rocks, some distance away. The girl looks to her with fear-widened eyes. *What's that?*

The disturbance hangs in the night, changing the character of the terrestrial darkness to one of menace and shadowy threat, lurking just beyond the peripheries of sight.

Gravity, the woman says. The badlands are disintegrating. Rock formations are crumbling here all the time.

She'd like for it to be the Sculptor's son. For him to charge out from behind the shale hill in a confronting rage and for the Tyrant to lay waste to him. But she only senses the oscillations of ground and rock and sky. And the entropic principle of the universe, slowly eroding the barrenlands to dust and, in time, nothing at all.

Why aren't you scared?

I've lived too long and seen too much to be scared.

You're what? Thirty-five?

Three hundred, give or take. I'm an old soul.

The girl laughs, reaches for the bottle. Wow. You must've seen *a lot* in three hundred years.

Oh, you know . . . Wars, famine, genocide. The banal, unending spectacle of everyday human cruelty and avarice.

The girl knocks back some mezcal. She wipes her mouth then holds the bottle neck out to the woman, like a local news reporter with a microphone.

Must've been tough living through all that. Can you tell the folks at home how you survived?

The first hundred years were a struggle, actually. Hand to mouth. But I grew resourceful. I learnt how to invest, how to die and inherit my own wealth. And it's become easier for a woman to move through the world on her own.

D'you ever get bored, living so long?

Never. That's why I don't want it to end.

So you can't ever die?

It's harder for me than most people.

The girl's arm a dark silhouette, she waves the bottle over at some rocks. Say I smashed this bottle and stabbed you in the chest, like, a dozen times. Will that kill you?

You can try. But people have attempted to stab or shoot me before. It never ends well for them.

The girl laughs, but uncertainly now. You're freaking me out.

I'm just messing with you, the woman says. I'm high.

The girl falls back on to the blanket and they lapse into a silence, drifting into the separateness of their thoughts. The rocks breathe out around them; the fissures and cracks contracting after the day's expanding heat, the fossilized bones, claws and teeth shifting in their entombed slumber of seventy-five million years. The woman can feel the sentience of the desert at night. She senses the sharp instincts of creatures both reptilian and mammalian darting across the nocturnal landscape, evading predators, stalking prey. She can feel Rosa besides her, the slow tempo of her blood, the oxycodone and ethanol depressing her central nervous system, suppressing the clamour of her fears. She watches the girl distract herself, reaching for her phone and illuminating its fractured screen. A reflex because there isn't any signal for miles.

Oh, fuck, exclaims the girl. My battery's on zero per cent.

The screen goes black and she sighs. She looks around and shivers, the night chill seeping into her flesh, and the woman suggests they get into the sleeping bags. So they zip themselves up inside and lie back down under the vault of the northern celestial hemisphere, staring backwards in time to the shining of suns millennia in the past. The woman hopes that the stars will pull Rosa into sleep, but she detects only a sharpening of her companion's fears. Fears of something evil circling their campsite. Fears that, far from being irrational, intuit some truth.

The OxyContin has passed its half-life in the woman's blood and pain begins its resurgence in the roots of her molars, in her putrefying insides. She would like some more opiates, to enter into her astral projection again, but she gave the last pill to the girl and has no other choice but to endure until her stay of execution in several hours' time.

The girl wriggles about in her sleeping bag and speaks into the dark. You ever get anxious, Therese?

About what?

Just, like, being alive and in the world and shit.

Only when 'being alive' and 'in the world' are under threat does the woman's blood pressure rise. But she says, Sometimes.

Me too. I mean, I *did*. But my spiritual practice of chanting mantras and manifestation helped me get it under control . . . Positive visualization is, like, my . . . *centring tool*.

The girl's confident Aurora Rose voice falters. As they both know, far from 'centred', she's been on-and-off anxious since the Bisti parking lot.

What's yours?

The woman closes her eyes.

I imagine myself in a deep dark cave.

Sounds creepy.

A specific cave, in South America, beneath a mountain range called the House of the Gods. It's deep in a twenty-two-kilometre labyrinth of passages and streams – most of them uncharted. The darkness is absolute. But shine a flashlight and the cave's glittering quartzite, full of mineral formations surreal as any Bisti hoodoo.

Yeah, that would freak me the fuck out. What's centring about *that*?

Well, it's about as far as you can get from the human world.

You like to be alone, huh?

Perhaps it's the drugs, but the woman's slow to answer. Rosa asks another question. Do you miss the Sculptor?

For a moment the woman is confused. Then she remembers her confession. *There was somebody once.* Somebody she'd recently boarded two planes, bought a car and walked all the way through the Taos County night to see. Somebody who'd been a presence in her mind ever since.

Sometimes.

Did you love her?

Startled, the woman turns to the girl. She's zipped up in her sleeping bag, her curly head peering out the top. How guileless she looks. Innocent and younger than her seventeen years.

The connection we had was deeper than with anyone I've ever known.

You were, like, soulmates?

But the woman doesn't have time to consider whether they were soulmates or not. More rocks are falling in the darkness around them. Louder. Closer. The girl lurches up in the sleeping bag. Glancing around, she whispers, Shit. That sounded nearer.

It did.

It sounded like it was on purpose.

Maybe it was.

Not funny, Therese.

Why don't we go up on the shale hill? Take a flashlight? It's nothing, you'll see.

The girl nervously agrees and they pull on hiking boots and sneakers and walk on legs stiff and strange from the hours of lying down, up to the low plateau where they'd watched the sunset hours earlier. Under the blaze of stars and crescent of moon they gaze across the dark valley floor stretching to the horizon. The woman shines her flashlight beam into the blackness. The battery-operated light flickers, blinks, then fails.

Don't be afraid, says the woman. We can see more without.

She's right. The lunarscape of rocks and boulders and hoodoos emerges as their sight adjusts. Though the woman's in pain, the shadow of death moving through her, necrotizing her cell by cell, she feels more alive up on the shale hill. She can sense the dark energy pervading the space around them and she closes her eyes, surrendering to its hypnotic sway. The girl senses the strangeness too.

It's like a dream up here, she says.

She shivers in her T-shirt and wraps her arms around her shoulders. The sinuous curve of her profile's so lovely the woman can't resist reaching for a stray curl and tucking it behind her small ear. The girl flinches and the woman smiles affectionately. Oh Rosy-Lee, the woman would like to say, how skilled you are at walking the tightrope of deception. But I never said the Sculptor's a she. You slipped up.

But the woman only smiles instead.

Testimony 5 – Jake

My own testimony should be the easiest. But unlike with Sigrid's or Jürgen's or even Bedwyr's, every time I sit down to write what happened to Lena, I freeze. I can't construct a narrative. Is it because I'm too close to things? Or simply that I'm scared? Since she died, all I have left of Lena is a box of items I cleared out of her room. I've carried this box around with me from place to place, stowing it in attics and wardrobes for the past eleven years. Unable to throw it away or look inside. Today, after staring at a blank screen for hours, I've opened it up. A jumble of stuff, covered in desiccated strands of Lena's rolling tobacco. Random possessions that will have to say what I cannot.

'Marion's' pencil sketch of Lena

I found this folded-up A2-sized portrait under the mattress when I stripped Lena's bed after she left. A sketch of Lena side-on, naked on a stool, upstairs in a pub in Stoke Newington. Heels on horizontal footrest, straight-backed with hands on lap. Long black hair over her shoulder blades.

In April 2011, Lena had been earning twenty-five pounds every Wednesday night as a life drawing model. She was unselfconscious about being naked, didn't have the same hang-ups as most people. When I asked her what posing for the class was like she told me how the close attention of the room, the gazes sliding over her, the scratchings of pencils and the murmurings of the instructor, commenting on a nipple or knee, would sometimes come together in an erotic tingling over her skin. But mostly, she said, she was bored and uncomfortable during the ninety-minute sessions. Fighting the urge to scratch an itch, fixated on the Marlboro Light she would smoke the moment she stepped out of the pub.

Marion first approached her after an evening class. Lena had noticed her standing behind one of the easels – an attractive woman in her late thirties, in a black mohair sweater, silver jewellery and jeans. In her deep and charismatic German accent, Marion said, You're a wonderful model. Look.

Marion handed her a piece of A2 paper. Most sketches of Lena were amateurish – comically misshapen and inert, or superimposed over cylinders and spheres. But the German's portrait was skilful and profoundly alive, with some spark of vitality in the eyes that the living, suffering Lena immediately coveted.

Keep it, Marion said.

Lena thanked her. She rolled the paper up and put it in her backpack before Marion could change her mind. Then they clumped down the narrow pub stairs together, the German asking Lena how long she'd been a life drawing model for, and if she was an artist herself, offering to buy her a drink (which Lena declined – after collecting her twenty-five quid she usually fled the pub as she would a burning building).

Will I see you next week then? Marion asked.

Yeah, I'm modelling next week.

They shook hands by way of goodbye, Marion's grip as though she didn't want to let her go. Then Lena hurried to catch her bus.

When I found the sketch, following Lena's death, I was surprised that she had hung on to it after what happened. Yet at the same time I could see why. In a few masterful strokes Marion had not only captured the essence of Lena, but enhanced it, drawing Lena as she wanted to be: strong, confident and at peace with herself. I realized the portrait was a seduction attempt. That even before they'd spoken, Marion had been plotting to reel her in.

Miscellaneous leaflets

- NHS pamphlet on quitting smoking
- NHS leaflet about cervical screenings
- Alcoholics Anonymous booklet on the Twelve Steps

Lena was four months sober and attending AA when she moved in with me and Simon at the end of 2010. Almost at once, it put a massive strain on my relationship with Si, who beneath his irritation at Lena leaving damp laundry in the machine, eating his vegan ice cream and other acts of inconsiderateness, bore deeper grudges dating back to Lena's pre-sobriety days. The incident Simon brought up the most was New Year's Eve 2009, when a vomit-splattered falling-down-drunk Lena had lashed out at him at a party in Seven Sisters, yelling that he was a 'pompous, pretentious, subtitle-loving prick'. Before moving into the spare room in Simon's maisonette she'd written him a letter, apologizing for all her sins against him. (I got one too – it ran to thirty-two pages.) But Simon neither forgave nor trusted her and was only waiting for the cataclysmic breakdown in her sobriety that would justify his throwing her out.

I'd told Si about Lena's childhood, of course. About what I'd seen twenty years earlier in that damp council flat on the Becontree Estate. Lena's mother Corina screaming at her daughter in Cantonese, fury disfiguring her face. Shaking her daughter about by a fistful of her hair, pinching bruises into her arm, or banging her into the wall.

Look, I get it, Simon said. Lena's upbringing was like some misery memoir or *Nil by Mouth*. But that doesn't excuse the fact that she's toxic. You need to cut her out of your life.

But I could no more cut her out than I could amputate an arm or a leg. And when she started AA and had to move out of her flatshare of twenty-somethings, I spent hours and hours persuading Simon that Lena needed our help. I'd lost my mother to addiction and I couldn't lose my best friend too. And, grudgingly, Si listened until I wore him down.

Cassette tape: Lena and Jake's Craaazy Hits 1989!!!

The title's biroed on the cardboard insert, over a Pritt Stick collage of pop stars cut out of *Smash Hits* magazine (Kylie, NKOTB, Milli Vanilli). The cassette's one of the many chaotic 'radio shows' we recorded – pretending to be DJs announcing each song, before singing over our favourite tracks from a *Now That's What I Call Music!* compilation (played on another stereo in the background). *Lena and Jake's Craaazy Hits 1989!!!* was probably taped after school or during one of the many weekends Lena stayed at ours. I was astonished to find it – that she'd been sentimental enough to keep it for over twenty years.

As far back as I can remember, we were together. Watching cartoons and drinking warm Ribena on the sofa. Playing out in the street on Fisher-Price roller skates, dragging an old vacuum cleaner about and pretending it was Boris (our imaginary dog), or dressing up in net curtains for our 'wedding day'. I think the childcare arrangement between Corina and my father was reciprocal at first – two single parents who'd met at the nursery gates, helping each other out. But as Corina's drinking got worse, only my dad took care of us – no longer trusting Lena's mum with me for even five minutes.

Most Saturday mornings, Corina would drop Lena off at ours then disappear. Late afternoon, Lena would wait by the window for her, and my dad would silently put extra fish fingers under the grill so she could join us for tea. We kept a spare toothbrush, flannel and pyjamas for Lena, and when darkness fell she'd top and tail with me in my bed. Corina wouldn't show up until the ten o'clock news – slurring and bumping into the hallway walls. Often, my dad wouldn't let her take Lena home with her – and after spitting something vicious, Corina would lurch off.

Why didn't my dad call social services? He'd had schoolfriends who'd been in children's homes in the 70s – had seen what had become of them as adults. And perhaps he saw how close Lena and I were. I was 'shy' and had 'difficulty mixing' and Lena was like a sibling to me. My dad and I were no substitute for Lena's family though – only a sticking plaster over her deep wound of maternal abandonment. I remember one night Lena whispering in bed, Where d'you think your mum is?

Dunno.

D'you think she loves you?

No. I . . .

Least you've got your dad. *He* loves you, 'cos he stayed.

Yeah.

Lena didn't speak again until I was drifting off, her ferocity waking me in the dark.

I wish my mum would fuck off like yours. I wish she was *dead*.

My current partner Liam's mum had a ghetto blaster in her attic. I brought it home yesterday, inserted *Lena and Jake's Craaazy Hits 1989!!!* and pressed play. The tape must've been recorded during our first term of comprehensive school – the beginning of five long years of unpopularity, occasional bullying and chronic low-grade misery for us both. But listening to Side A for the first time in thirty-three years, I was struck by how giddy and joyful we sounded. Two eleven-year-olds in their squeaky, high-pitched bubble of excitement. 'MC Lena' introduces the show in a zany, transatlantic, Kid Jensen-like drawl, and then we sing along to 'She Drives Me Crazy' – giggling, out of tune, getting the lyrics wrong. I'm quiet at first, but Lena yells, *Louder, Jake!* until I'm as noisy as she is. After Fine Young Cannibals there's a 'weather report'.

Lena: Today it's gonna RAIN, and tomorrow it's gonna RAIN and after that I DON'T KNOW . . . ARRGH GET OFF MY BACK!

Jake: Yeah, just look out the window, ya dummy. It's RAINING. It's England! Take an umbrella!

We squabble over what song comes next, then there's the clunking of us fast-forwarding and rewinding a tape. 'Eternal Flame' – a Lena solo – comes on. She sings over Susanna Hoffs, her voice sweet and sad and wise beyond her eleven years.

I hit stop. Someday I'll listen to the rest, but not today.

Photograph of me and Lena in 1983

Taken at my fifth birthday party. I don't have a memory of the party itself – only the photograph of Lena with bowl-cut black hair in a blue chequered dress, and me in Spiderman pyjamas (that I'd apparently refused to change out of) as we sat together on the brown settee in my living room, unsmiling in front of a large hundreds-and-thousands sprinkled trifle on the coffee table.

My dad gave us each a copy of this photograph. Mine was stuck to the fridge in Si's kitchen in 2011 and Marion noticed it when she came to our dinner party. Lena invited her the week after they met – encouraged by Si (whose eyes had lit up when he heard Marion was a curator from Berlin, as though from the tiniest bump of cocaine).

You grew up together, right? Marion said. Like brother and sister.

She smiled at us, her dark hair piled into an elegantly messy bun, her shirt crisp and white. As the rest of the table – Si's film academic friends – glugged through bottles of wine, Marion sipped on sparkling water with a lemon slice. Out of solidarity with Lena's sobriety, I guessed.

Yeah, Lena said. On the same estate in Dagenham. Like siblings. Jake's the only family I've got left.

Lena looked gorgeous that night, her lips a slash of bright red, her eyes kohled, her long hair straight out of a shampoo advert. But it was Marion's fascination with her that really made Lena *glow*. I should've been happy for my friend, basking in the attention of this glamorous German curator. Instead I was uneasy. I didn't know why.

Si's dinner parties were usually hard for Lena. She struggled around all the booze and, like me, was often too intimidated by Si's posh and articulate friends to say very much. That evening, however, I remember Marion's presence emboldened Lena as alcohol once had. Neither was drinking, but they both seemed giggly and intoxicated. They spoke to each other in low conspiratorial tones and smiled together – smirked even – at Si's friends' bitchy dissections of films, books and academic papers. Somehow they turned the atmosphere strange, so it wasn't Lena but everyone else who was self-conscious of what they said.

Near the end of the evening, Hugh (formerly of 8os synthpop band Oceanic Absences, now a leading expert on Haneke) pushed his thick-framed glasses up his nose and began complaining about a film he'd seen about a sex worker in Birmingham. Apparently all the male characters had been 'nasty and exploitative' and the women 'unlikeable'. There had been a 'gruelling' sexual assault scene with a bottle.

Why do these films have to be so harrowing? Hugh lamented. So overwrought and one-note?

Lena grabbed a bottle of Glenfiddich. A dangerous gleam in her eyes, she leant across the table and stabbed it at Hugh.

Perhaps we ought to rape you with this, she said. Then you'll get why that film was so harrowing. *Overwrought.*

Hugh laughed nervously. He couldn't tell if Lena was joking. Neither could I.

By midnight, the film academics had left, and Si gone up to bed. Only Marion was still there, having a quiet and intense conversation with Lena in the living room. I lingered in the kitchen, doing the post-dinner clean-up, for some reason not wanting to leave Lena alone with her downstairs.

It made no sense. During the worst of her alcoholism, Lena had had an addiction to one-night stands with 'dominant' men from Craigslist ads. Encounters that sometimes left her with bruises and strangulation marks. Marion was objectively much less of a threat than any of these sadistic men. So why was I so on edge? Lena was thirty-two, I reminded myself as I loaded the dishwasher, and acting as custodian of my friend's sex life was just plain weird. So I said good-night to them and went up to bed, leaving Lena and Marion alone.

A Happy Gilmore DVD case containing the missing Blu-ray from Si's Criterion Collection Complete Rainer Werner Fassbinder (!)

The Bitter Tears of Petra von Kant. Si's favourite. Maybe I should post it to him? As far as I know, he's still at the same address. He went mad looking for it, back in 2011. Turning sofa cushions upside down, checking in all his other DVD cases (no mean feat – he had a collection of over five hundred on custom-built shelves). And the whole time Lena had taken it, to wind him up.

Lena wasn't particularly keen on Si's art-house films. Even less keen on Si's explaining them to her on the rare occasions she joined us for a Jarman or Greenaway screening on the projector. But I suspect the main reason she committed this act of petty larceny was because she knew Si looked down on her for dropping out of Camberwell and only working for temp agencies in the decade since. Because she was always breaking stuff (cafetières, the wooden pepper mill, the Hydroluxe showerhead) and losing things (house keys, mobile phones) and if no one cooked her dinner, she'd have a Pot Noodle or toast. Because she was a depressed alcoholic on SSRIs.

To be fair to Si, Lena was scornful of him too. Of his Le Creuset casserole dishes, of his cats, Kubrick and Fellini, his crank-handle pasta maker, his framed vintage Tarkovsky *Stalker* poster, his stacks of barely read academic film-studies journals and *LRBs* . . .

But what Lena disliked most about Simon was the way he treated me.

Can't you *see* how uninterested in you he is, Jake? she once said. Uninterested in what you think or say or even what you want to watch. Your favourite film's *The Thing*, for fuck's sake.

Back then, I couldn't see it. But now I can. We would've broken up sooner or later, I'm sure. What happened with Lena just brought it all to a head.

A silver hair fork, three-pronged, with Bohemian garnet jewels

I found it vacuuming under the armchair a week after Si's dinner party. It was heavier than I expected it to be when I picked it up, and expensive-looking – silver, or silver plated, in an elaborate filigree design studded with russet gems. Not from Claire's

Accessories, that was clear. I put it on the sideboard, and when Lena walked in minutes later, I turned off the vacuum cleaner and handed it to her.

Is this Marion's?

Lena nodded and turned the silver hair fork over in her hands. There were a few strands of white hair wound around the long teeth (though I hadn't noticed any grey in Marion's hair the previous Friday). Frowning, holding the hairpin in one hand, Lena pulled at the hairs with the other. The white gossamer strands were stretchy and disintegrated in her fingers like cobwebs.

Gross, I said. Is that actual *hair*?

Repulsed, Lena wiped her hand on her dressing gown. She held the silver hairpin away from her, but at the same time seemed mesmerized by it. Lena had quit modelling for the life drawing class that week (saying the thought of being naked in a roomful of people now made her feel sick) so I asked if she had plans to meet Marion again.

No, she said.

But she took the silver hair ornament back to her room.

I'd heard Marion leaving around six a.m. after Si's dinner party, but Lena hadn't mentioned if anything had happened, romantic or otherwise. Sensing that she didn't want to talk about it, I didn't ask. I was only relieved that Lena's acquaintance with Marion had ended after that one night. Again, I couldn't say why.

Yesterday, I took the silver hair fork to an antiques dealer in Chancery Lane. He examined it under his jeweller's loupe, astonished.

Where did you get this? he asked. Last time I saw one of these was in an auction house in Vienna.

He said it was Hapsburg-era Austrian, nineteenth century. A hundred and fifty, possibly two hundred years old. He offered to give it a 'proper valuation' and to buy it from me for a 'fair price'. I said I'd think about it and took the silver hair fork back.

Please, give my offer some serious consideration, the antiques dealer said. That could fetch you upwards of ten thousand pounds. You've no idea how rare it is.

A lanyard with Lena's ID card for Pinsent Martin Cooper

The *Temp Staff* ID card has a smeary, faded photo of Lena above a barcode. She had the lanyard on the evening I went up to her room with a bowl of Si's dahl, about a fortnight after Marion. She was under the duvet in her work clothes, and when I asked what was wrong she said she'd had a panic attack that morning during a meeting with the boss and some 'very important clients' from Copenhagen. Later, HR had called her in and informed her that due to 'unforeseen restructuring' they were going to have to 'let her go'. She made me promise not to tell Simon. She had enough for that month's rent and would find another job soon. She'd just been having a rough week.

There's this crushing feeling in my chest, Lena said. Like, all the fucking time. Even as I'm sat here talking to you. It's like I've just had some terminal diagnosis or something . . . And I know the only thing that can take the edge off's a drink.

But self-medicating never works, does it? I said, carefully. Drinking only suppresses the anxiety for a while and you have to—

And you have to keep *drinking* and before you know it you're back in that *destructive cycle* again, Lena said, parroting my AA tone. I know the script, Jake. I've been to a hundred meetings.

Even so, I gave Lena the usual advice. Maybe ask your GP for some new medication? Start seeing a therapist again – private this time, I could help pay. Get in touch with your sponsor, Jez, let him know you're struggling. Lena was barely listening. She scratched distractedly at a flare-up of eczema on her wrist, before blurting out, I know how this is going to sound . . . but in the mornings there's something on me. In this bed. Heavy. Suffocating. There's this blackness in front of me, so I can't see it. But I feel it reaching inside me . . . groping in my organs and guts. I can hear squelching. I can't scream or move and I know I'm going to die.

Lena's breathing had become shallow and quick. At the fear and conviction in her eyes, my stomach dropped. I told her it sounded like sleep paralysis. A bad dream.

But it's not in my head, Lena protested. I can *feel* it.

You need to see a therapist again, I said. It's probably some child-hood trauma that's resurfacing in your sleep. Or maybe it's the time of year. Y'know, the anniversary of her death.

Lena frowned at me, genuinely surprised.

You think I'm sad about that?

Green fuzzy frog toy from Southend-on-Sea

I'd won it for Lena in February 2005 from one of those claw-grabber games. I probably spent three quid's worth of tickets manoeuvring that claw about trying to pick it up.

We'd gone to Southend that day to visit Lena's mother Corina in hospital there. I remember the stink of disinfectant, boiled vege-tables and incontinence. I remember the Saturday morning cookery show blaring on the fourteen-inch TV in Corina's room. When she set eyes on me she hissed at Lena, Why's he here?

Corina's stage 4 liver cirrhosis had turned her bilious yellow. She was fifty-four but looked about seventy; denture-less and shrunken in her hospital bed. Lena had hoped she'd be too far gone to speak, but Corina had enough bitterness left in her to vent about her daughter's neglect. Lena sat in a hard orange plastic chair, scowl-ing and eating a bag of salt and vinegar crisps, as a jaundiced death-gasping Corina cursed and rattled abuse in Cantonese. Dis-loyal daughter this. Traitor that.

Afterwards Lena and I walked along the pier with our fish and chips. It was cold and drizzly and Lena only had on a denim jacket and vintage dress that the wind whipped around her legs. I asked her if she was feeling OK after seeing Corina, and she had only screamed with the seagulls – a lung-bursting scream at the vast choppy grey of the ocean. Then she dragged me to the amusement park and on to all the fastest, most dizzying rides. I still have some photos of Lena from that day, laughing and swigging from a bottle of Lambrini as she went round on a carousel horse.

Corina died two and a half months later, but her daughter was far from free.

The Hammer. Official Match Day Programme: West Ham Utd v. Coventry City, December 11th 1993

My dad was a Hammers fan. So from the age I knew what football was, I was too. We could only afford to go to Upton Park every month or so, but followed every game on Radio Five, with mugs of tea in the potting shed in Parsloes Park (where my dad worked for the council as a gardener) or on deckchairs in our yard on sunny days, my dad allowing me a sip or two of his Carlsberg. Even when I realized that I wasn't particularly into football, I kept up the pretence – wanting us to have a common interest, a hobby we could bond over. I know I troubled my father when I reached my teens. I wasn't sporty and didn't knock about with the other lads on our estate. I mostly hung out with Lena, listening to strange, angsty bands with male singers who wore eyeliner. That I seemed as passionate about West Ham as he was reassured him slightly.

By the time I was fifteen, I dreaded the Upton Park matches and the stadium of thirty thousand chanting, swearing, jeering, aggressive men. Men constantly yelling homophobic slurs, making me tense and prickly in my own skin. One Saturday, we had tickets for the match with Coventry, but Great-Aunty Viv had had a fall, so my dad couldn't come. He suggested I take 'a mate' instead. Of course, I got the Tube to Upton Park with Lena, who suggested we scalp the tickets outside then splurge at Tower Records. But my dad had saved up for them, and guilt and obligation had me tugging her inside.

In the stalls, Lena was bemused, sticking out with her pierced nose, dyed neon-red hair, Pearl Jam T-shirt and sarcastic cheering. When the bubble machine started up and thousands of men in Dagenham Motors strips raised their arms and began bellowing, 'I'm Forever Blowing Bubbles', she cracked up. We scored a goal early in the first half and the stadium roared. As the players leapt on each other, Lena said, Fucking hell. They're practically *snogging* each other.

Shut up, I hissed.

But Lena laughed. Not sure why your dad thinks bringing you here will make you straight. This is the gayest place I've ever been.

Later, in the kitchen, I was shaking frozen oven chips out on a baking tray for tea and Lena was perched on the countertop, reading out the starting line from *The Hammer* (picked up off the Boleyn Ground on the way out).

Lee Chapman's pretty fit, isn't he? Lena said.

I s'pose.

But Steve Potts is the sexiest.

I shut the oven door and set the timer for the chips.

What about you? Lena asked. Who d'you like?

No one.

C'mon. You watch these guys week in week out. You must fancy *one* of them.

I don't.

I always tell you who *I* like.

It's not the same.

Lena lowered *The Hammer* and gave me a look. How is it not?

Fine, I said. Trevor Morley.

Ha, I knew it! I know your type—

Good game? my dad asked.

We turned to the kitchen doorway, where my father stood in his woolly West Ham beanie and bomber jacket, flushed with cold. We hadn't heard him come in.

Yeah, it was really fun, Lena said chirpily. I *sort of* get what all the fuss is about.

Sad I missed the penalty . . . er, Morley's penalty, my dad said. Caught it on the radio though. Sounded top-flight.

Yeah, I said, it was brilliant.

My dad smiled and nodded, but from the expression in his eyes I knew he'd overheard my conversation with Lena. And though I wouldn't come out to him for another six years, he knew.

A blister pack of ten zopiclone 7.5 mg (expiry date: 08/2012).
Mostly empty.

On a rainy night in early May, 2011, I stumbled to the toilet around four a.m. and out of the bathroom window saw that the kitchen light was on, spilling into the dark garden. Peering through the single-paned glass, I could just about make out the shadowy figure of Lena on the patio. The rain was coming down hard and, concerned, I went downstairs to check she was OK. But when I got to the kitchen, the sliding patio doors were wide open, and she wasn't there.

The shed door was ajar at the bottom of the garden. It was usually closed. Had she gone inside?

Lena, I called.

No reply. I stood by the patio doors as the rain pelted the lawn and hydrangea bushes, certain Lena was in the shed and I should go to her. But suddenly I was too disorientated to move. Si's back garden wasn't the same. The shed appeared disjointed, as though the wooden slats and window and door had all skewed into some strange non-Euclidean geometry I couldn't make sense of. I stood there bewildered, as though reality itself had gone slanted and malign.

A sharp cry from the shed jolted me out of my trance. I walked through the rain to the end of the garden as though in a dream, and when I got to the shed, I reached for the torch hanging from the hook inside by the door. The batteries were old and I shone the feeble beam around the usual clutter of boxes and gardening tools, plastic-sheet-covered lawn mower and barbecue. No Lena. As I began to back out of the shed I heard the cry again. Softer this time. Her bare muddy feet were under the workbench. Confused, I knelt down. She was lying on her back in the narrow gap, in her rain-soaked Pixies T-shirt and shorts. She rolled her head towards mine, unblinking in the weak torchlight.

What are you doing? I asked.

Wet strands of black hair were draped over her eyes. Pupils blown wide, she stared right through me.

Lena . . . ?

Look, she whispered.

She pulled her T-shirt up above her navel. She hadn't been eating much and below her ribs her flesh was sunken and concave. I wasn't sure what she wanted to show me. Then I saw a sudden bulge moving under her skin. Like a rat, tunnelling about in the stomach of a corpse.

I dropped the torch. I fumbled with it again, hands shaking, but couldn't get the light to turn back on. In the dark Lena wasn't visible under the workbench, but I could hear her. The faint gurgling in her throat, and something else, coming from inside her. A squelching sound.

Heart thumping, I dragged Lena out by the arm. I hauled her to her feet in the shed and marched her back through the rainy garden to the house. As soon as we were inside, she pulled away from me. Went straight up to her room, leaving muddy footprints on the carpeted stairs. She climbed into her bed in her soaking-wet clothes and turned to the wall. I stood in the doorway, watching.

Lena, I said. You OK?

Her back turned against me, she spoke.

My insides aren't mine any more. They're his.

What do you mean?

Silence. I went over to the bed and she was in a deep sleep.

By the next morning I'd convinced myself that my half-sleeping mind had imagined the bulge in Lena's abdomen. When I called her during my first break at school, I didn't even mention it. Instead I asked what she'd been doing in the shed at four a.m. Lena said she had no memory of it.

My insomnia this week's been hell, she said. I knocked myself out with a couple of zopiclone.

A white envelope with Lena written in cursive, calligraphic script. Torn open. Empty.

Jake, can I show you something?

Lena had just got in from her Friday night AA meeting and I was doing some Year Five lesson prep on the sofa while Si was out at his colleague's leaving party.

Sure, I said.

Lena came and sat next to me, looking as rough as she'd done in her first week of alcohol withdrawal, with bruise-coloured shadows around her eyes and a cold sore weeping on her lip. She handed me an envelope with her name on it. Inside was a photograph of Lena stooped in our front room, blurry from the longer exposure in the dim light, the window's plantation shutters open wide. The photographed Lena stared blankly at the camera, her head, shoulders and arms drooping in such a way that she appeared suspended. Dangling like a carcass with a hook in its back, waiting on a butcher's rack for dismemberment. Beside her was a foggy darkness, like some murky atmospheric secretion captured on film. The photo was debasing. Dehumanizing.

Jesus, I said. What's this?

It came through the door the evening after Si's dinner party. The one Marion came to.

That was six weeks ago. Why didn't you tell me then?

I was scared.

Marion took this?

I don't remember. I think so.

I stared at the photograph. It was bizarre. Marion had developed it then delivered it by hand? Anonymously? The next day?

I asked Lena, What happened between you and Marion that night?

Lena shut her eyes. I couldn't tell if she was trying to remember or to push the memories away.

I don't know, Lena said. We kissed though. I remember . . . kissing her.

How can you not remember? I asked, incredulous. Do you think she Rohypnoled you?

I don't *know*.

She opened her eyes again, looked at me in desperation.

Get rid of the photo for me, Jake. Please . . . destroy it. It marked me out. Led something to me. And now it won't stop coming for me.

Lena, I said sharply. It's *not real*. You've just been having nightmares. Parasomnias or something.

Sure, she smiled sadly. Bad dreams.

I can't remember what I said after that. Probably some reassurances that Lena would get through this difficult period soon enough. Then she got up and left the room, taking the torn white envelope with her in her daze.

Later that night I put the photo through the shredder that Si used for our bank statements and bills. I hoped to God there'd be no more talk of 'something coming for her' after that.

Paper napkin from the Orford Bistro, very creased

One Friday at the end of May I came home late from work to my dinner on the back hob and Si's agitation; his grey hair sticking up, his burgundy pullover crackling with static over his Oxford shirt. He put a plate of butternut squash risotto on the table in front of me, poured us each a glass of wine, then sat opposite for 'the talk'. Lena had set the smoke detector off that morning. He'd rushed downstairs to a saucepan of beans burning on the hob and smoke pouring out from under the grill. Lena had been 'zonked out' on the sofa, and when he'd shaken her and confronted her, she'd groggily told him to 'fuck off' before slumping back to sleep. Her mess was everywhere. Junk-food wrappers and Rizlas in the kitchen, the garden littered with butts of the roll-ups she chain-smoked all night, pacing the patio with her hair over her face like 'that wraith girl from *Ringu*'. Si'd had enough of cleaning up after her. And he was sick of her 'violent temper'. He'd seen her, on her way up the front path to AA that evening, kick Fellini.

How dare she kick my cat? Fellini has more right to live here than she does.

I'm sorry, I said.

The worst thing's her *mood*. It's like this constant leak of toxic gas, poisoning everything. It's making *me* ill and depressed.

I'll speak to her.

No, Jake. When I say I've had enough, I mean I've had *enough*. It was only supposed to be temporary, her living here. It's time for her to move on.

The next day, a Saturday, I coaxed Lena out to Walthamstow Village for lunch. She slouched in the café in an old Adidas tracksuit; pale and exhausted-looking, her hair lank and unwashed. After the waitress brought over our paninis, Lena listened sullenly as I gave her the rundown of everything Simon was aggrieved about.

I forget how neurotic Si can be.

You nearly burnt his house down. You *kicked his cat.*

Lena stuck her leg out and pulled up her jeans to show me her shin, scored by angry red claw marks.

His cats have been attacking me. It was self-defence. But . . . I'll apologize. And I'll be more careful. It's just I haven't been sleeping and—

It's too late, I said. Si wants you to move out.

Beneath Lena's despondency, panic stirred. Where will I go?

What about your stepdad's in Chelmsford?

Kevin? I haven't seen him since Mum's funeral.

You could find a room. I can lend you enough to cover a deposit and your first month's rent. And you should be OK once you start your new job at Tesco.

Lena's voice became higher, tighter – pleading, almost. She was twisting a napkin in her fingers, as though wringing it out.

Can't I stay over the summer? I don't feel like I can—

It's not up to me, Lena. It's Simon's house.

She glared at me then – the glare of an angry, abandoned child. We both knew I *could* help her stay over the summer. I could persuade Simon, as I had before. But some part of me didn't want to. Since Lena'd moved in, me and Si hadn't had much privacy or time to ourselves and he was growing distant. If she left, we could reconnect. I could see the accusation in Lena's eyes: that I was selfish and choosing Simon over her . . . and maybe I was. But she was being selfish too. Lena knew how lonely I'd been.

Si's my first proper, long-term relationship, I said, and you've never even bothered trying to get on with him. For *my* sake.

Like Simon's ever bothered with *me*. He's so fucking *egotistical* . . .

I took a deep breath, pushed back my chair. Just popping to the loo, I said.

Sure.

When I got back, Lena was gone, but I didn't run out looking for her like I usually did. I finished my latte and panini, then asked for the bill. But Lena had already paid.

Jez's crystal

Quartz, I think. Glittery pink and white.

As Lena's AA sponsor, Jez really went above and beyond. When she was going through her 'bad patch' he not only met up with her on week nights, but cycled over at the weekends with his Tibetan singing bowl and chakras chart to give Lena lessons in breathwork and Transcendental Meditation. Jez also brought Lena various candles and 'healing crystals'. I suppose this is one of them.

The night Lena disappeared, Simon nudged me awake in the darkness. Around three a.m.

She agreed not to bring back random men, he hissed.

The sounds of fucking, of a man and woman moaning together, were coming up through the floorboards from the living room below. It was excruciating. Just when I thought it couldn't get any worse, Lena started crying, Hit me. C'mon, you pathetic cunt, slap me.

I can't take any more of this, Si said.

He grabbed a hardback from the nightstand and thumped the spine three times on the floor. Confusingly, the man let out a howl, as though Si's blows had landed on him directly. Lena's laughter rang out in the living room before the house reverberated with the slam of the front door. Looking out through the slats of the Venetian blinds I saw a man limping Quasimodo-like up the street. Shirtless. Barefoot. His belt flapping around his jeans. From the long blond dreadlocks, I could tell it was Jez.

She has to go, Si said.

I know, I said. *Please*, wait here. Let me go check on her.

Downstairs, Lena was in the shadowy living room, and to my utter dismay was stumbling drunkenly, struggling to button her dress up over her lacy black underwear. A lamp had been knocked over and a vodka bottle was smashed on the floor. As she flailed around, Lena stepped in the glass shards.

What happened to Jez? I asked.

Jez?

Lena creased up with laughter and I realized she was paralytic. Angry, I flipped on the main light and reeled. Blood was splattered up the white wall, like a hurled glass of wine. Lena had no visible injuries. It must've come from Jez.

She laughed again but directed it over my shoulder. Simon was staring open-mouthed between Lena and the bloody wall.

I want you to move out, I said. First thing tomorrow.

Feral eyes glaring through strands of black hair, dress hanging open over her bra and flushed chest, Lena spat, I'll go *tonight*.

Lena took a suitcase of clothes, her laptop and passport from the desk drawer, leaving behind some bloody footprints and the rest of her stuff. Though I asked her to explain what had happened with Jez – should I call the police? – she refused to talk to me before she went. I transferred a thousand pounds into her bank account, so she'd have enough for a deposit for a room, then sent her a text to tell her. She never replied.

Three weeks later, I waited outside Our Lady and St George's Church, hoping to catch Lena after her AA meeting. She still wasn't responding to my emails, her phone was turned off, and I wanted to check she was all right. Just like the Friday night before, Lena wasn't among the people shuffling out of the church hall. But Jez was, walking rigidly, a metal halo brace around his dreadlocked head, bolted to four vertical metal poles that extended down to a harness around his torso. Half his face was covered in surgical dressing and when he saw me he flinched.

Jez, I called. Can we talk? About what happened with Lena?

He grimaced, and I saw his teeth had been wired together to fix a broken jaw.

No, he said.

Blank-eyed, he walked away.

Lena's floral dress and second-hand suede jacket,
sealed in the mortuary's plastic bag

The size 10 tea dress, cornflower blue, was from Top Shop, bought in 2007 or 2008. The vintage 60s suede jacket is from a stall in Camden Market. Lena purchased it in 1996, with her wages from Kwik Save. I'd watched her trying it on, helped her decide. Both items of clothing are covered in stains.

The evening of June 28th, 2011, I got a missed call from an 0208 number and a voicemail. When I played it, it sounded as though Lena was drunk, and near some railway line, as trains kept rumbling past and drowning her out. She said she was sorry she hadn't been in touch for the past month, and for the trouble she'd caused at Simon's. She didn't blame me for kicking her out.

I want you to know: you were the best person in my life. I was so unhappy growing up and having you as my best friend saved me. I always had someone to talk to, somewhere to go. You're such a good person, Jake, and I hope you have a happy life.

Lena was silent for a moment, during which I could hear traffic and people shouting, in high spirits or anger, I couldn't tell.

It's watching me all the time now, she said. I can smell my own death. My insides are butchered meat. This time it's going to end me, but I won't let it. My death's my own—

Lena abruptly cut off. The payphone must've run out of money. I dialled the number and the random person who eventually picked up said they were outside Plaistow Station. I called 999 and told the operator about Lena's possible psychosis and suicide risk. But as I suspected there wasn't much they could do. I took a cab to Plaistow, but by the time I got there she was long gone.

Teenagers found her on the roof of a tower block in East Ham, the day after her phone call. I had to go and identify the body.

The coroner ordered a post-mortem. They opened her up from pubic bone to throat and found that Lena had situs inversus, her internal organs reversed from left to right. The reversal of her heart meant the left ventricle was malformed; a congenital defect that had gone undetected for thirty-two years. Her high blood alcohol levels had probably (the pathologist's report conjectured) exacerbated the strain on her heart, leading to the cardiac failure concluded to be the cause of death.

As I would later explain to Sigrid, the Coroner's Liaison Officer insisted she'd developed that way in the womb. When I asked them to look up Lena's dental records, they found an X-ray from her last visit to the dentist, aged thirteen. When the X-ray didn't match, they said it must be due to 'patient record confusion'. I told the Coroner's Liaison Officer about Marion, the photograph, and Lena's account of something 'reaching inside her' and 'groping in her organs'. He listened sympathetically, then gave me a contact number for bereavement counselling services. The post-mortem had found no evidence of external interference or 'foul play', and there was no possibility of opening an investigation into her death.

I can see Lena, up on that tower-block roof, the wind blowing through her suede jacket and tangling her long hair. I can see the sky lightening around her and the Canary Wharf skyscrapers on the far horizon, though Lena probably only had eyes for the paving slabs below. Because she intended to jump, I'm certain of that. She was about to climb up on the ledge and enter into the freedom of her descent. Because in her desperation her only escape route was smashing herself into the concrete. But something got there first.

You're such a good person, Jake, Lena had said, during that last phone call. But I don't think so. All I can ever think of is how badly I let her down.

Badlands – V

Wake up, Rosa. It's nearly sunrise. Time for your photograph.

She shakes the girl's shoulder until she opens her eyes and squints up at the woman, kneeling by her sleeping bag in yesterday's clothes, a camera on a strap around her neck. During the hours Rosa has slept the night has transitioned to its latter phases, stars and constellations exiting the sky as the strange energies on terra firma intensify. Not that the girl notices. Drowsy, she frowns as though she's woken from one dream into another.

Can't we do them later? she mumbles. It's still dark. I'm sleeping.

But this is why we camped out here, remember? To take your photograph at *sunrise*. When the light's most spectacular.

Rosa wriggles up in her sleeping bag. She peers through the half-darkness at the woman, who's pale and sweaty, fighting to keep the desperation out of her eyes.

You OK, Therese?

The woman's not OK. The OxyContin's worn off and the pain is shrieking now, a siren drowning everything else out. She can see herself through the girl's eyes, in the shadows long before dawn. The bones standing out in her face, blue veins protruding in her neck, her scalp visible through thinning hair. She's halfway between the living and the dead. She can practically feel the maggots in her mouth, burrowing through the rotting meat of her brain.

I'm hungover, the woman says. Too much mezcal.

Suppressing a shiver, she manages a rueful smile. I have *no* tolerance for alcohol.

No offence, Rosa says, but you look like you need to go to the ER.

She shrinks back as though from the woman's decomposition. As though from her gangrenous soul.

The ibuprofen will kick in soon enough, the woman says. In the meantime, why don't we get your photo taken? The sun's about to rise.

It's dark and chilly and five a.m. The sun will be beneath the horizon for another hour yet. The girl glances at the charred remains of the fire, the pitched-up tent, the mezcal and tortilla chips from the night before. But something other than the woman's deterioration disturbs her now, some presence she can sense, lurking beneath the appearance of things. She hastens out of the sleeping bag, pulls a sweater over her vest and shorts. She quickly laces her sneakers, and the woman knows Rosa's not preparing to have her photograph taken. Just like the Iraq War veteran she picked up in Albuquerque, she's preparing to bolt. To run to the Sculptor's son and tell him she can't go through with whatever they've planned. Rosa casts her gaze about the wilderness. It's obvious to the woman she doesn't know the way, but in her state of fight or flight, getting lost, dehydration and heatstroke are the less immediate threats.

Let's go up on the hill, the woman says. I can capture the landscape behind you, the sun coming up in the east.

Rosa flinches at her.

Your nose is bleeding.

The woman touches her fingers under her nose and they come away black. She feels the trickle over her lips and tastes septic blood – the contamination of her haemorrhaging guts. She gropes in her shorts pocket for a tissue to staunch the flow. Blood seeps backwards into her throat and she swallows, not wanting to alarm the girl by spitting it out.

I don't want any more photographs, Rosa says. I've changed my mind.

The girl retreats a step. The Polaroid camera's on a strap around the woman's neck. She has her hiking boots on but can't be sure her determination to survive will lend her enough strength to chase. To tackle the girl to the ground and hold her in place. So as Rosa backs away the woman changes tack. She lowers the tissue, hoping the nosebleed has stopped.

Last night, I wasn't being honest with you, she confesses. About being ill.

The girl tips her head to one side.

You *do* have cancer?

Pancreatic. Stage four and terminal. I'm in a bad way, as you can see. But even so, when you sent a call out to the universe, Rosa, I answered it. I summoned my remaining strength and brought you here. I planned everything out for you. I wanted everything to be perfect, at your video shoot yesterday and now your photograph. Dying has made me reflect on how I've lived a self-centred life. How I've taken what I wanted and not given back. Which is why I'm determined to do something for *you*, Rosa. To help you launch your Aurora Rose YouTube channel, if it's the last thing I do.

Shit, Therese, Rosa says. Why didn't you tell me? I mean, you really don't have to.

But I *do*, Rosa. You *manifested* me. I showed up for you, and now can you show up for me? Just one photograph up on the shale hill?

Rosa appears fraught. I . . .

The woman forces tears. She crumples up her face, puts a wobble in her voice.

This is the last time I'll ever come out here. The last time I'll ever see the sunrise over the Bisti Badlands.

Rosa sinks a tooth into her bottom lip, bites indecisively. One photo?

The woman nods. One photo.

Um . . . well . . . OK.

The woman wastes no time. She reaches for Rosa's wrist and drags her up on to the plateau where the badlands are a windswept vastness before them, the sun beneath the barren layers of long-extinct worlds. Rosa frowns at the woman's Polaroid camera.

You're not using your digital?

It's for a retro 70s aesthetic. You'll love it.

The girl's frown swerves to their surroundings. And then she senses it. The presence is much stronger up here. The tiny pores in the membrane between worlds are dilating so the dark tentacular energy can intrude, creating shimmering distortions of time and space. Terrified, Rosa spins on her heel. The woman lunges as she runs. Grabs the back of Rosa's head by her curls and yanks.

What the fuck, Rosa shrieks, jerking backwards, hands flying to the woman's hand clutching her hair, tearing it out of her scalp.

Get the fuck off me, you crazy fucking bitch!

Screaming in fury, a bent-over Rosa hits and claws at the woman's hand, scratching and breaking the sulphurous skin with her nails. On the eastern horizon, Venus appears. The Morning Star shines at the edge of the Earth and something surges forth from the unseen world. It spirals around Rosa, pulling her into its dark vortex, snapping her into a trance. The woman releases Rosa's curls. She steps forward as the girl straightens up, mute with the strangeness of it all. She cups Rosa's round cheeks with her mouldering hands and stares at her. Yesterday's make-up smudges her stunned eyes, foundation smears her shining brow and freckled nose. Leaning towards her, the woman tenderly presses her bloody lips against the girl's astonished Cupid's bow. She pulls away and the girl stares at the woman, her lips marked by her blood. Stepping back from the offering, the woman says, Blame the Sculptor's son. He set you up.

Rosa's smoke-grey eyes and mouth widen as the Tyrant enters her. Knowing some part of the girl still hears and comprehends, the woman goes on.

You're right about the Law of Attraction, Rosa. But your belief that you manifested me to serve your dreams is mistaken. I'm the servant of an entity far more powerful than you could ever imagine. This entity manifested you, Rosa. It manifested *you.*

Urine spills down the girl's legs, splashing on the ground. She convulses slightly as the Tyrant moves through her, seeping into every vessel of blood, every valve and chamber of beating heart, sliding into her cranial vault and the wrinkled hemispheres and lobes within which her innermost memories and thoughts are contained. The woman detects the Tyrant's libidinous energy, flickering like a tongue at the girl's viscera. Its caresses more intimate than any lover's, stimulating her every organ into erogenous zones, moving like peristalsis through the glistening coils of her insides. Rosa sways, her eyes bright with exquisite pain.

Rosa vanishes. A moment of glitch, then she's back. The woman knows she's been to the higher dimension the Tyrant comes from, where one is conscious of every moment on the continuum of one's life from beginning to end. The perspective of a god that no human mind can endure without falling into an oblivion from which scant few memories can be retained – splinters of truth, shards of Hell.

Her appearance has changed. Like many who go to that higher place, she's been reordered, molecule by molecule, from left to right. The asymmetry of her face – the steeper arch of eyebrow on the left, the wider nostril on the right, now reversed. The woman holds up her Polaroid camera and regards the girl and her changed physicality through the lens. Frames her. The Tyrant stares out at her through the girl's eyes: the pupils black and enormous, the centres tunnelling to the imposter within.

The eastern sky appears in turmoil behind the girl and her halo of curls, roiling darkly around the superterrestrial entity she contains. A wind gusts and scours across the desolate wastes.

Look at me, Rosy-Lee.

Responding to stimulus she's only dimly aware of, the girl looks.

Smile.

The instruction to smile falls on deaf ears. Unblinking, she stares and the woman captures the possessed and possessor both with a click. Keeping her promise, she takes only one photograph. It emerges with a whir from the slot at the bottom of the Polaroid camera and she pinches it by the corner, waves it to dry.

The Tyrant begins to depart. The woman's far from recovered, but her toothache and the lacerating pain in her guts are already diminishing. The tide of decomposition is turning within as her immune system fights back. She can feel the flow of blood returning to her cheeks. That death has been postponed.

Rosa, however, looks worse for wear. Empty, with absence of mind and unseeing eyes, black and viscous as oil. There's not a mark on her, but the woman detects the mutilation within, the shadow of the coming slaughter cast from another realm. The stain of the Tyrant's upon her, and when she later catches sight of what was captured in the Polaroid, the Tyrant will return.

The woman's nose had continued trickling as she took the photo and she wipes the blood, smearing her forearm beneath. Blood and phlegm splatter the ground as she spits. They should get a move on. They've yet to deal with the Sculptor's son.

You know what, Rosa? she says. You're right. Maybe we should go back to Farmington. But I think it's *you* who needs to see a doctor, not me.

Shorts damp with urine, the girl nods, compliant as a psychiatric patient recently electroconvulsed.

Sure, she says.

Testimony 6 – Zsófi

One Saturday afternoon in April 1967, Zsófia Szarka and her mother Ezster were leaving Kerepesi Cemetery by the west gate when Zsófi announced, I have thirteen hearts but no other organs.

Cheeks damp with tears wept over the graves of dead Szarkas and Szabós (relatives thirteen-year-old Zsófi had never met), Ezster appeared not to hear her daughter.

I have thirteen hearts but no other organs, Zsófi repeated. What am I?

Ezster glanced irritably at her.

Not now, Zsófi.

A *deck of playing cards.*

Zsófi smiled. Her class recently had a contest for who could solve the most brain-twisters and she had won.

Here's another. I only live where light is but shine a light on me and I die. What am I?

Zsófi, I have a headache, Ezster said. I was up at four this morning for a ten-hour shift at the laundry. I haven't patience for your riddles.

But it's so simple, Zsófi insisted. I only live where light is but shine a light on me and I die. What am I? *Guess.*

Ezster sighed. I don't know.

A *shadow.*

Zsófi smiled. *Another.* What question can a person *never ever* say 'yes' to?

Her mother ignored her. Zsófi repeated, What question can a person *never ever* say 'yes' to? In class, I got this one *straight away.*

Ezster continued to not reply.

Mrs Toth says I'm 'highly imaginative', which is why I'm so good at brain-twisters. But I suppose you're not, which is why you're only a laundress and not—

Enough, Ezster snapped.

They'd reached Keleti Station and their usual left turn on to Rákóczi Street. But, looking around, Ezster gestured that they turn right instead.

Very well, Clever Clogs. It's puzzles you want? So be it.

They walked along Thököly Street, north-east towards Budapest's City Park. It was a sunny day and Zsófi too warm in her woollen coat and long socks, perspiration gathering at her nape where her hair was pulled into two long plaits. They walked for ten minutes along the street of large houses for those with Socialist Workers' Party connections, before Ezster stopped outside a four-storey building.

That's Almásy House, she said. Where Cousin Mátyás lived before his mother died and he came to live with us.

Almásy House was a crumbling art nouveau fairy tale with a frieze of stone cherubs and flowers around the upper casement windows. Turquoise paintwork peeled from the arched main doorway and the stucco facade was still pockmarked by stray bullets from the Second World War and what Zsófi's father referred to as the 'Hungarian-Soviet Friendship Month of '56'. Nevertheless, it was much grander than the tenement where the Szarkas lived in South Pest.

Was Cousin Mátyás rich? Zsófi asked.

Ezster snorted.

His mother Klára was the kept woman of a Muscovite. That's how they came to live here.

Ezster then pointed up to a large casement window on the third floor. That's the parlour in which the Muscovite and Mátyás's half-brother József – the Muscovite's illegitimate son – were found dead.

Oh, Zsófi exclaimed. From the gas leak?

Ezster hesitated. Then she said decisively, There was never any gas leak. That's just what we told you back when Cousin Mátyás came to live with us. But you're thirteen now. Old enough to know the truth.

Zsófi widened her eyes at the ten-year-long deception and Ezster said, So Mrs Toth said you were 'highly imaginative', did she?

Zsófi nodded.

Well then. Imagine this. One morning in March '57 Cousin Mátyás is awoken by shouting in the parlour. He rushes to the parlour, but the door's locked from the inside. He can hear his mother and the Muscovite – Comrade Gyurkovics was his name – fighting in there, and his two-year-old half-brother, József, crying. He runs to the neighbours to get help, and they come and break down the locked parlour door. But they're too late. Mátyás's half-brother and the Muscovite are dead from strychnine poisoning. And Klára's dead on the pavement outside Almásy House, having tumbled from the third-floor window.

Ezster paused to let the tragedy's lurid particulars sink in. Then she asked her daughter, So, Miss Know-It-All. What happened?

Zsófi's mind raced with the possibilities.

The Muscovite locked them in the room. He poisoned them all and Klára jumped out of the window to escape.

The post-mortem found no strychnine in her blood, Ezster said. Only the key to the parlour door.

Zsófi frowned. In her hand?

In her *stomach*.

She *swallowed* the key?

Correct.

So *Klára* poisoned them then? Locked the door and swallowed the key so they couldn't get out. Then jumped in suicide.

You've cracked it, Ezster said.

Zsófi smiled, satisfied. Then her mother added, Except the third-floor window was locked behind Klára. Can you explain how she locked it after she jumped?

So the Muscovite threw her out? Because she poisoned him and his son? Then locked the window?

The amount of strychnine he had in him, he'd be lucky to move a finger, never mind all that bulk. Comrade Gyurkovics must've been a hundred and fifty kilos. Plus his right arm was broken and in a plaster cast. How could he have thrown her out?

Then perhaps someone else . . .

Who else? The parlour was locked from the inside, remember? Only the three of them in there.

Ezster seemed pleased to see her daughter stumped. Then her expression darkened as she looked back up at the third floor of Almásy House.

I warned György never to marry her.

Why?

Klára was too beautiful for my brother.

What's so bad about beauty?

She couldn't be loyal and wait for György after the war. Not when she could flutter those eyelashes and seduce some wealthy Communist cadre into supporting her. When he was conducting a tour of the shoe factory she worked in no less!

Zsófi held her tongue. Uncle György had been pulled off the streets of Erzsébetváros at the end of the Second World War and sent to a Soviet labour camp in a cattle truck. After a few years, it would've been obvious he wasn't coming back.

Ezster tutted, looked from Almásy House to her daughter and said, *Are you dead?*

Huh?

What question can a person never ever say 'yes' to? *Are you dead?*

Then she gestured to Zsófi that they begin the journey home.

The traumatic events at Almásy House were clearly the reason Cousin Mátyás was so odd, Zsófi realized. Ten years older than her, his blond matinee-idol looks were diminished not so much by his blindly staring eyes as the quality of not-thereness about him, as though he had one foot in another reality. He was reclusive, only leaving his tiny cupboard of a room to join Zsófi's family for evening meals, his silently chewing mouth contributing nothing to the Szarka family chatter. And he only left the apartment to tap his wooden cane through the streets of Ferencváros to the school for the blind where he taught Braille, or to attend Sunday service at his Orthodox church. Zsófi and her sister Zsuzsanna rarely spoke to their twenty-three-year-old cousin, but had a fondness for blindfolding themselves with their father's neck ties and tapping Mátyás's cane around their cramped apartment – a giggly game that stopped the day Ezster warned: Your cousin began to go blind at thirteen, Zsófia. Keep tempting fate and the same will happen to you.

Cousin Mátyás was so quiet Zsófi forgot he existed for weeks on end. But after hearing from her mother about the mysterious deaths of Aunt Klára and his brother, she became curious. Late one Saturday night, after all the Szarkas had gone to bed, Cousin Mátyás was playing chess against himself in the kitchen (his only hobby as far as Zsófi was aware). Pretending she wanted a glass of water, Zsófi went in. Loitering by the sink, she said, I saw the building where you used to live. Near City Park.

Mátyás didn't respond. He was hunched over the board, rubbing a knight between thumb and forefinger. His teakwood set was crafted for blind players, the darker squares raised, with pegs to hold each chess piece in place.

It's so tragic, the way your family died.

Again, her cousin ignored her. Slightly put out, Zsófi said, Doesn't it madden you, not knowing what happened in that room?

Finally, with a flicker of irritation, he spoke. I know what happened. The Tyrant got them.

Cousin Mátyás pushed his chair back and left the kitchen, abandoning his chessboard mid-game.

His cryptic response only made Zsófi more curious. One Sunday when her family were out and Cousin Mátyás at church, she sneaked into his room to snoop. Under the bed next to his teakwood chess set was a cardboard box, inside which Zsófi found a large silver crucifix, some Braille documents and a bundle of photographs of Mátyás when he was around her age, with his late mother Klára and half-brother József. Photos of them in a rowboat together (Lake Balaton?), seated at a white-clothed table in a fancy kávéház (the Gerbeaud?) and standing together by the rakparts of the Danube. The younger Mátyás astonished Zsófi – he was so unlike the strange and dour young man who lived with her family. He was smiling for one and looking at the camera with bright not-yet-blind eyes. Aunt Klára had blonde curls, wore dresses with pointy busts, nipped-in waists and flared skirts, and exuded the beauty that had made

Comrade Gyurkovics request she be taken off the factory production line and re-employed as his 'personal secretary'. Two-year-old József was chubby and cute, and resembled his large father, whose cadre's belly strained the buttons of his white shirt and waistcoat as Józsi sat on his knee.

The Szabó family photographs evoked in Zsófi sadness for her cousin's loss. Until the last photo in the bundle that is, which made her entire being leap in fright. It was a portrait of Mátyás's mother in an elegant room with a chandelier (the murder-suicide parlour of Almásy House?). Klára wore an evening-gown, with bitten-looking lips, cheeks smudged with rouge and curls disordered as though a small tornado had swept through them. She appeared stunned and wide-eyed, like the camera flash was a lightning strike, erasing the contents of her mind. But what disturbed Zsófi most about the decade-old photograph wasn't Mátyás's mother. It was the other presence *inside* Klára. She could feel the animus of it, staring out though Klára's eyes, and Zsófi knew – she just *knew* – that the entity in the photograph was, at that very moment, cognisant of her. Watching her. She remembered her cousin's words: *The Tyrant got them.*

Zsófi flung the photographs back in the box as though they were on fire. Then shoved it back under Mátyás's bed and fled.

Day after day she puzzled over the brain-twister of Almásy House. Had Klára murdered her lover and son, then jumped to her death? Had the Muscovite killed them all? Had Cousin Mátyás been involved somehow? Getting to the truth seemed impossible when she knew nothing of these people and her cousin wouldn't speak to her for more than a few seconds at a time. Then one day the solution came.

Zsófi approached her cousin after dinner on Sunday evening as he rinsed his plate in the sink.

Can we play chess together?

Why?

Because chess is a game for two. You always play alone.

Mátyás blinked, appearing for a moment flattered until blankness returned to his face. You don't know the rules.

You could teach me.

I haven't the patience.

But you teach Braille at the school for the blind.

Well, her cousin said. They pay me for that.

He left the kitchen and disappeared into his tiny room.

Peter Szénes was Zsófi's classmate. A shy and gangly boy who'd won a Budapest-wide junior chess tournament the previous year. Speaking to girls was such a rarity for Peter that his cheeks flamed when Zsófi approached, but he agreed to give her beginner lessons in a kávéház after school in exchange for a coffee and (she would later find out) Zsófi's company. She was frustrated with chess initially, but Peter Szenes was a wise and kind instructor, his bony wrists overshooting his shirt cuffs as he showed her how the pieces moved and how to strategize against one's opponent. Gradually Zsófi took to the game, battling valiantly across the chequered board with her foot soldiers, cavalry and monarchy. Sometimes she even got the better of the Budapest junior champion himself, with whom she eventually fell in love and married in 1974, and would remain married to until his death from bowel cancer in 2014. But we leap too far ahead.

In late June 1967, one month after she began her chess lessons with Peter, Cousin Mátyás marched into the kitchen on a Saturday evening and confronted Zsófi, who was seated at the table.

You've stolen my chess set.

Zsófi replied, It's right here. I've set the board up so we can play.

Cousin Mátyás stared at her – or the space above her head – uncertain whether to be cross or pleased.

What colour would you prefer? she asked. Black or white?

Zsófi then remembered he was blind. What did the colour matter to him? But he pulled out a chair.

White.

So began the cousins' first ever game of chess, beneath the watchful gazes of older generations of Szarkas and Szabós; all now dead and in wooden frames on the kitchen walls. They played for twenty minutes, Zsófi speaking her moves out loud for Mátyás, using the algebraic notation Peter Szénes had taught her. She started out strong – stronger than her cousin. After capturing his bishop, she plucked up the courage to say, I saw the photograph of your mother in her ballgown.

Mátyás scowled in Zsófi's direction. You're not to go through my private things. I'm telling Aunt Ezster.

I'm sorry. The only reason I bring it up is because . . . Zsófi hesitated.

Because? Mátyás said.

I saw something. In your mother's eyes. Watching me.

Visibly rattled, Mátyás didn't respond.

What was it I saw? The Tyrant?

Slowly, her cousin nodded. Yes.

He moved his pawn one square forward.

I started to see it after I went blind.

★

In February of 1957, not long after macular degeneration had ravaged Mátyás's central vision and the outer rings were mottled by some other unknown disease, two things happened. The first was that a Russian woman called Vera moved into Almásy House. The second was that Mátyás began to 'see' things in the blackness that had consumed much of his sight.

His mother Klára had no friends. Even if Comrade Gyurkovics had allowed them, the other tenants of Almásy House kept a polite distance from Klára because of her extramarital arrangement with the cadre. But one afternoon Mátyás came home from school (later than usual – a burst water main had led to his memorized route being closed off, and a stressful detour) and was surprised to hear his mother had company. Tapping his cane, he walked the nineteen steps to the parlour and Klára introduced him to Vera from Apartment 5. Turning his head sideways to use what remained of his peripheral sight, Mátyás made out parts of Vera. Short dark curls and Marlene Dietrich eyebrows. Bold red lipstick. Shirt and trousers in a masculine style. She spoke Hungarian with a Russian accent.

Pleasure to meet you, Mátyás. I've seen you around. You always look preoccupied by clever thoughts.

Mátyás nodded but stepped no closer. Losing his sight had sharpened his sense of smell and he was struck by Vera's musky perfume – too fancy and expensive-smelling to be manufactured in the Eastern Bloc – and the fainter odour beneath it, that reminded him of a rotting bouquet of flowers or spoilt meat.

Vera had brought some records over. Illicit American jazz played on the gramophone and Klára sounded so joyous in the company of the glamorous Russian (a photo correspondent for *Pravda*! she later gushed) that Mátyás did his best to suppress his misgivings, because the dark churning entity – the one he'd recently begun to 'see' in the black tunnel where he'd once had central vision – had appeared by his mother again.

Is something the matter, Mátyás? the Russian asked. You're looking at us very strangely indeed.

Are you having one of your imaginings? Klára asked.

Imaginings? Vera asked.

The dark energy pulsed, but Mátyás shook his head and turned to tap his way out of the room. In the hall, he heard his mother explain through the jazz, Recently, Mátyás has been 'seeing' this shadowy thing near me. In the part of his eyes where he's gone blind.

How peculiar, Vera murmured.

I took him to see his ophthalmologist and Dr Szirtes said, *The mind abhors the vacuum blindness creates, so projects its own imaginings into the dark.*

Or perhaps a second sight has come to replace the first? Vera suggested. What he sees is actually there?

Klára laughed. Goodness, I hope not . . .

Mátyás tapped his way into his room and went to his desk to continue his game of chess from the day before. But unsettled by his sense that the energy shifting around his mother was connected to Vera in some way, he sat by the board without moving a single piece.

Comrade Gyurkovics, it could be said, was a family man. Having no inclination for whores or tempestuous affairs, he was instead devoted to not one but two families: the first with Svetlana and his daughters in the Buda Hills, and the second with Klára and his young son on Thököly Street. Though work often kept him away, Comrade Gyurkovics took his responsibilities as patriarch seriously, wire-tapping Klára's apartment to make sure all was well, and hiring an ex-ÁVH man to trail Klára whenever she went out. Though he visited Almásy House only three evenings a week, it could not be said that Comrade Gyurkovics neglected Klára. Not when his surveillance of her extended to every minute of the night and day.

So Gyurkovics knew all about the Russian woman in Apartment 5. When he came for dinner that evening, he warned, You're not to associate with her again.

But why? Klára said, sounding pained. She's perfectly nice.

A perfectly nice *invert*, Gyurkovics scoffed.

But—

No buts, Klára. Not so much as a nod in the hall. Understood?

He resumed eating his lamb chop and the evening proceeded as usual: Klára attending to his needs with a tight and dutiful smile, and Mátyás getting Józsi ready for bed, so that Comrade Gyurkovics could spend time alone with his second wife, before his driver took him back to his villa in the Buda Hills and his first.

The next evening, Klára called her eldest son into her bedroom to zip up the back of her evening gown. Vera had stopped by earlier to say she had tickets for the State Opera House, and Mátyás stood in disquiet as his mother sprayed her curls with hair lacquer and painted her lips, quivering with excitement to be going out with her new friend.

When she was gone, Mátyás tucked Józsi up in bed, but after turning out the lights in the room they shared, he lay worrying in the dark. He'd never known his mother to behave so recklessly. What was so special about Vera that she would break Gyurkovics's rules for her, consequences be damned? Mátyás remained awake after midnight when Klára and Vera came home, chattering and giggling together as they played Vera's jazz records in the parlour. Mátyás could smell their cigarettes and hear the clink of pálinka glasses and the sound of dancing on the parquet floor. As his mother laughed with abandon, bumping drunkenly into the Hapsburg-era furniture, Mátyás knew the dark palpitating entity was in there too.

In the morning while Klára slept, Mátyás got Józsi up and fed with poppy-seed brioche and apricot jam before taking him up to his babysitter 'Aunt' Dorottya, in her tiny attic rooms on the fourth floor.

When Dr Szirtes had diagnosed that he was going blind, Aunt Dorottya had been an unexpected source of strength for thirteen-year-old Mátyás, assuring him that the light of God could counter the darkness consuming his vision. Aunt Dorottya had a second cousin in fact who had been *cured* of her blindness by His divine light. So she guided Mátyás on the path towards Him with regular Bible lessons and Sunday services at her Orthodox church, and every morning after he brought Józsi up, he and Aunt Dorottya would pray together, the ritual lending Mátyás courage to navigate yet another day of encroaching blindness and hopefully prove himself devout enough that God might restore his sight.

That day, however, prayer wasn't the foremost of Aunt Dorottya's concerns. She ushered the boys inside and whispered, That Russian woman in Apartment 5 has been leading your mother astray. The Soviet Lapdog won't like it, will he?

Though Mátyás had not intended to say anything, his fears came tumbling out. Beneath the headscarf worn over sparse white hair, Aunt Dorottya narrowed her eyes. She needed no persuading of Vera's sinister plans.

That Russian's cast a shadow over Almásy House since moving into Margit's, she said. The mark of the beast's upon her, I'm sure.

The mark of the beast? Mátyás asked.

Shawl over loose cotton house dress, hobbling from the bunions rubbing inside her slippers, Aunt Dorottya went to her linen cupboard and removed a leather-bound Bible from underneath her hand-embroidered tablecloths. After finding the relevant page, she read, *Revelation 14:9–10: And the third angel followed them, warning, If any man worships the beast and his image and bears his mark in his forehead or in his hand, they shall drink of the wine of the wrath of God . . . and be tormented with fire and brimstone . . .*

Vera worships the beast? What beast?

The beast that rose from the sea with seven heads and ten horns, Dorottya intoned. The beast of all mortal evil and sin. Mr Farkas, my late husband, bore the mark of the beast, though he bore it against his will. Many times he came to me helpless and weeping, and many times we prayed to the Lord to purify Mr Farkas, to make him holy and devout. For years we did this, but it wasn't enough to erase the mark.

Aunt Dorottya's voice hoarsened with pain. Mátyás knew from Comrade Gyurkovics that the late Istevan Farkas had been arrested for sodomy (which Mátyás knew was to do with kissing another man) and beaten to death by the other prisoners in his cell. *Deservedly so,* Gyurkovics had said.

And now Mr Farkas is in Hell. For eternity. Do you remember Father Szalai's sermon on Hell, Mátyás?

He did. Father Szalai had described infernos and screaming naked sinners impaled on stakes in the ground, grinning imps flaying their skin or carving them up with knives. Stomach lurching at the memory, he asked Aunt Dorottya, Can Vera put the mark of the beast on my mother?

I fear this is what the Russian intends, Aunt Dorottya replied. So we must pray. We must pray for God to intervene.

The old woman grasped Mátyás's hands and they prayed.

All day at his school for the blind, Mátyás struggled to concentrate. It was dusk and raining when he got back to Almásy House, and bumped into Vera coming out of the arched turquoise doors, recognizing her perfume and the whiff of malodorousness beneath it, before confirming it was her with his ragged edges of sight.

Hello Mátyás, she said. Our soirée didn't keep you awake last night, I hope.

Detecting the note of displeasure in her voice, Mátyás stammered no and Vera's large umbrella opened like a flock of birds taking flight. As she went on her way down Thököly Street, Mátyás rushed upstairs.

180

Apartment 9 was still, Klára not yet out of bed. Stamping his boots on the doormat he trod on something that had been pushed under the door. He felt it was a sealed envelope and, holding it up to the side of his head, Mátyás made out the addressee: 'Mrs Szabó'. Guessing it was from Vera, he put a kettle on to boil and steamed the seal. Inside was a photograph of Klára in her evening gown and out of his blindness Mátyás 'saw' the perturbation of dark energy straight away. Not lurking close to Klára like in previous days and weeks, but invading her entirely.

The mark of the beast. Mátyás saw it upon his mother and *knew* with something other than his rational mind that the image was harmful and had to be destroyed before Klára saw it too. He struck a match and burnt the photograph over the sink, but his relief was temporary. Vera probably had more photographs and negatives. Probably in the darkroom Klára mentioned the Russian had for developing her *Pravda* photos, down in Apartment 5.

Apartment 5 had been seized from Aunt Dorottya's friend Margit by the government in '54, and Margit expatriated to a farm in Southern Transdanubia for reasons unknown. Aunt Dorottya had kept a spare of her key, and more than once had joked to Mátyás that the Communists were probably too cheap and lazy to change the locks.

Tapping his way with his cane, Mátyás moved towards the front door. The loss of his sight had narrowed Almásy House to a few routes, memorized down to the last step. Margit's apartment was terra incognita as far as he was concerned and if he wanted to save his mother before Vera returned he hadn't a moment to waste.

That evening Comrade Gyurkovics came for dinner. As they ate their chicken paprikas, Mátyás was braced for the explosion to come, but Klára was only distracted. Mátyás could smell the rose-scented powder she usually used to cover dark circles under her eyes and, though she was subdued, he detected no fear or contrition in her voice for her outing to the State Opera House, or the parlour lights blazing until dawn. The mark of the beast wasn't upon her like in the photograph and out of the corners of Mátyás's sight her appearance seemed the same. So why did Klára seem wholly other to herself, as though the very substance of her being was pulsing with change?

Later, when the yelling and hitting began behind their mother's bedroom door, Józsi crawled into his big brother's bed and Mátyás hugged him as he sucked his thumb. As the beating went on, Mátyás prayed to God to stop Gyurkovics. He prayed a heart attack would fell him mid-thump.

When the Muscovite left, Mátyás went to Klára, who insisted she was fine through the locked bedroom door. As much as he pleaded, she refused to let him in, until he eventually returned to his room.

Some hours later, tendrils of smoke wound their way into Mátyás's dream and nudged him awake. An intruder sat at the end of the bed, and as he opened his mouth to scream, Vera said, Don't bother. She won't hear you. Nor your brother or Gyurkovics's spies. This bedroom isn't tapped.

Józsi was sleeping next to him. He did not stir. Mátyás heard the creak of a leather-gloved hand as Vera brought her cigarette to her mouth. Staring blindly through the darkness, Mátyás's second sight perceived her mask had slipped to reveal the void of humanity underneath.

You know why I'm here, she said.

Mátyás didn't speak. He'd panicked down in Apartment 5, scared that she'd return and catch him. In the darkroom he'd knocked over a tray of chemicals and torn down a washing line of photos – too rushed to sort through which were of Klára, which weren't – and shoved them in his coat. Then he'd grabbed all the strips of negatives he could find and fled.

I know you see the Tyrant, Vera said. It wants back what you stole.

Mátyás's heart was thundering. The Tyrant?

I . . . I didn't steal anything.

Vera dropped her cigarette on the rug, put it out under her shoe. Mátyás then heard her reach into her coat and withdraw something with a spring-coiled flick. He could smell it, the steel edge stained with death. She'd used it before.

If you don't return them, I'll slit her throat.

The darkness swarmed with her malignancy and though he knew it wasn't an empty threat, he croaked, I haven't got them.

Vera laughed.

And before I slit your mother's throat, I'll slit your brother's.

The cigarette smoke dispersed, Vera's rotting stench had become stronger, so strong Mátyás wanted to retch. He understood that Vera's composure was an act. She urgently needed the photos of Klára marked by the beast, and the urgency was to do with the gangrene taking over her flesh.

What will you do with the photographs?

Show one to your mother.

Why?

At the end of the bed, Vera flicked the switchblade in and out. Not threatening; fidgeting.

Because those are the rules.

What will happen to her afterwards?

Nothing. The Tyrant will move on.

It will leave her alone?

Yes, Vera said. So if you want your mother to live, return them to me now.

Mátyás knew she was lying. That his mother seeing herself with the mark of the beast would cause her harm.

Can't you put the mark of the beast on Comrade Gyurkovics? he asked. Then photograph *him* for the Tyrant.

He could hear Vera's half-smile in the dark. The Tyrant chooses, not me. And I doubt Gyurkovics is to his taste.

Then how about . . . ?

That's not how it works, Vera said. The photo's already been taken. Too late to choose another.

Too late? Mátyás wondered. Too late for who? For Vera, obviously. Her stench of decrepitude was worsening by the day.

If my mother doesn't see that photograph you'll die, won't you?

The mattress creaked as she stood up. The blade sprang out. Not fidgeting this time.

Thirty seconds, Mátyás.

Under his pillow were two large iron keys. One to Margit's apartment, one to the wooden trunk under the bedroom windowsill. He grasped one and counted its teeth under his thumb. On shaking legs he walked from the bed to the antique trunk where he kept his childhood keepsakes and old photos of his father, György. He unlocked the lid, then reached inside for what he'd taken from the darkroom. Given Klára had been awake when he'd got back to Apartment 9, he hadn't had the chance to burn them. He turned and walked in the direction of Vera, holding out the stolen photographs and negatives. She snatched them up.

Tell anyone I was here tonight and I will know. I will return to kill you. Understand?

Mátyás nodded.

On your nightstand is a glass of water. I want you to drink it all down in one go. Then get back into bed beside your brother.

Tears pinpricked Mátyás's eyes. Is it cyanide?

No.

The switchblade was still in her hand. She waved it towards the nightstand, and he went miserably over and found the glass. He swallowed the bitter liquid down, climbed into bed next to Józsi and within seconds it was as though a plug had been pulled, his consciousness sliding away like water into a drain. Before it was gone entirely, he managed weakly, Now will the Tyrant leave my mother alone?

But before an answer came he was out cold.

It was late afternoon when he surfaced from his drugged sleep. He stumbled to the parlour, scared of what he might find, and Klára cried, Ah, he's awake! Józsi and I were shaking and shaking you this morning, but you were sleeping like the dead. Do you feel unwell? Are you coming down with something?

No.

Mátyás turned his head sideways and saw the damage Gyurkovics's fist had inflicted the night before. One black swollen eye. Two grazed cheeks. His mother, however, didn't appear upset. She was smiling down at a large leather-bound photo album on the table, the pages creaking as she turned them.

What are you doing? he asked.

Vera came by, Klára said. Before dawn if you can believe it! But she had to rush to return to the *Pravda* offices in Moscow for a few days and wanted to drop off a photo she took of me the other night.

She turned the album a hundred and eighty degrees to her son who stepped forward to see. The photo was identical to the one he'd burnt over the sink, with the Tyrant in her eyes.

Lovely, isn't it?

Aberrantly cheerful, Klára breezed on, I was putting it in the album and got sidetracked by all these photographs of György. He's such a handsome man, your father.

Her carelessness threw Mátyás into panic. Did she want to goad the Communist into beating her again?

Mother, he whispered. Be careful what you say.

Oh, Klára laughed. I don't care. *Gyurkovics, I know you're listening. Mother.*

The Tyrant appeared in Mátyás's sightlessness. The dark maelstrom around Klára's head more forceful than before, as though it had gained in strength. Affectionately, Klára said, You have your father's eyes Mátyás. You take after him, you know.

That evening Comrade Gyurkovics came to Almásy House and all through dinner Mátyás could choke nothing down. Klára, however, was unintimidated. For once she hadn't bothered to cover up her injuries or pretty herself before the Muscovite's arrival, prompting him to drily remark, How rushed off your feet you must've been today, Klára, to come to the table looking so slatternly.

Slatternly? she murmured.

Your hair's a mess. Blouse untucked, petticoat showing.

When she didn't apologize, Gyurkovics growled, Don't let yourself go. If you think you have any appeal beyond your looks, you're wrong.

After dinner, Józsi toddled off to play and Mátyás took the crockery to the kitchen. Scraping plates into the dustbin, he heard Gyurkovics howl. Alarmed, he went to the hall and heard the Muscovite hurry past him and slam out of Apartment 9. Mátyás rushed to the parlour, where his blindness was confronted by the tene-brousness of the Tyrant, whirling over Klára at the table.

What happened to Gyurkovics?

György's sent a guardian angel to take care of me until he gets back, Klára said. It won't let him hurt me again.

What are you talking about? Mátyás blurted. He's *dead*.

Chair legs scraped as his mother stood up. Her footsteps approached and moments later there was a stinging slap across Mátyás's cheek. Voice trembling, she said, Don't ever speak that way about your father again.

It was the first time Klára had ever struck him and Mátyás turned and left the parlour, unsure what shocked him more, the slap or what she'd said. He stood for a long while over the sink of dishes, hot water gushing out of the tap like something had broken loose.

Every day that week Mátyás went to his Orthodox church and prayed. He prayed to God to rid his mother of the Tyrant. He prayed to God to save his mother's soul and to restore her to her rightness of mind.

His prayers went unanswered. The Tyrant had come to stay, its dark oppressive energy near his mother constantly now as she lounged about smoking and daydreaming and listening to Vera's jazz records. When the gramophone was off, she hummed to her-self like someone who'd recently fallen in love, sometimes dancing in the arms of an imaginary partner on the Persian rug. She no longer went out to the shops or hair salon, and instead of getting dressed spent all day in the white cotton chemise Mátyás knew his papa had bought her with wages he'd earnt as an apprentice tailor in Vörösmarty Square – a chemise previously kept folded away with naphthalene, unworn in the twelve years since György went miss-ing. The cooking and cleaning were neglected, but Klára didn't seem depressed. In fact, she was the most languorously content Mátyás had ever known her to be.

For seven days, Comrade Gyurkovics stayed away from Almásy House, then one evening he dropped by unannounced. Squinting through his dark-smudged vision, Mátyás discerned that the comrade's right arm was in a white plaster cast, in a sling beneath his open coat. Though he strode authoritatively into Apartment 9, his henchman was by his side.

Where is she? he barked.

Mátyás said she was in her room, and Gyurkovics nodded at the ex-ÁVH thug, who led the way to the parlour and stood in the corner as the cadre sat in an armchair with Józsi on his knee. Bouncing his son, Gyurkovics spoke in his baby-talk voice.

Your crazy mama attacked Papa last week. The vicious bitch broke his arm. Can you believe it?

Hunched over his chessboard at the dining table, Mátyás could not. Gyurkovics was much bigger and stronger than his mother. He'd beaten her with impunity for years. So why now had he brought a bodyguard with him? Why were his eyes darting nervously about?

Look at this pigsty, Józsi. How slovenly she's become since losing her mind. Once we've locked her up, you can come to live with Papa. Svetlana will be your mama and she'll do a much better job.

The darkness in Mátyás's head crashed like waves as Gyurkovics went on, And as for your blind and subnormal brother, we'll send him to rot in a Siberian labour camp. Like father, like son.

That night Józsi was fretful, and Mátyás hugged his little brother and sang him lullabies until he nodded off in his bed. But as Józsi slumbered, Mátyás's mind raced, and he was still awake before dawn when the telephone rang and his mother got out of bed to answer it. Comrade Gyurkovics was the only person who ever called, and with the Communist's recent threats in his ears, Mátyás crept to the parlour, feeling his way along the walls. The door was ajar and out of the peripheries remaining of his vision he saw Klára in her billowy silk robe, standing by the window in the grey before dawn. She murmured into the receiver, winding the telephone cord around her fingers as she gazed out into Thököly Street. Her affectionate tone made it clear to Mátyás it wasn't the Communist on the other end of the line. Shivering in the doorway, he sensed a strange energy about his mother, like the oscillations of a tuning fork, vibrating at a frequency that couldn't be heard by human ears. He caught some breathless words: György . . . yes . . . I will end it . . .

Mátyás understood then that the Tyrant was in the telephone. Turning his blindness towards his mother, he perceived it pouring out of the dark perforated holes of the receiver she cradled to her head. It seeped into Klára's mind and swarmed out into the room like a pestilence of black flies, buzzing into Mátyás's accursed second sight. But this wasn't some Old Testament plague sent from God. This was from Beelzebub himself. The mark of the beast.

What could Mátyás do? He went to his church, got down on his knees and prayed. That evening he unplugged the telephone, then hid it where his mother wouldn't be able to find it, and went to bed.

*

One o'clock in the tiny Ferencváros kitchen, Cousin Mátyás stared down at the chequered board with his sightless eyes.

Knight to f3?

Yes, Zsófi said. *Check.*

It's rare for a woman to play so well.

He sounded almost accusing, but Zsófi smiled. That's the nicest thing you've ever said to me, Cousin Mátyás.

I need to concentrate, he said irritably.

He frowned, fingers hovering above the board, touching various pieces as though to cement their positions in his mind. Afraid his attention would be diverted from recalling the events of March '57, Zsófi said, So you hid the telephone from your mother?

He ignored her for a minute, focused upon the board. Then he moved his bishop and to her relief said, Yes. But the Tyrant couldn't be stopped by a disconnected line.

*

A ferocious shaking woke him before dawn. Klára leant over his pillow in the darkness, her unwashed hair hanging in Mátyás's face and the sour rankness of her breath making him gag as Vera's rot had done.

Where is it? she snarled.

A shrill *ring* from the antique wooden chest under the windowsill answered her before Mátyás could, and his heart shrank in confusion and terror. Klára charged over in a billow of silk and impatiently rattled the lid of the chest.

Unlock this now, she demanded. Or I'll smash it apart.

He groped under his pillow for the key, then went and unlocked it. Klára lunged in the chest for the rotary phone before holding out her hand.

The key.

Józsi was out of bed now, tugging at Mátyás's pyjama bottoms as he handed the heavy iron key to his mother. Klára slipped it into the pocket of her silk gown, before hurrying with the disconnected telephone to the parlour, to speak there privately to her long-dead love.

That morning he took Józsi up to Aunt Dorottya's as usual, but as they got down on their knees to pray he said, Do you know of any stronger prayers? For protecting my mother?

Protect her from what? Aunt Dorottya asked, suspiciously. The Russian's gone back to Moscow, hasn't she? And you stole those photos of your mother from Margit's apartment.

When Mátyás lowered his eyes and did not reply, Aunt Dorottya said, What's been going on, Mátyás? Why haven't I seen Klára this week?

The burden too much to bear for a moment longer, Mátyás crumbled. He told Aunt Dorottya about Vera's visit in the night and the Tyrant's subsequent reign over his mother and Apartment 9. Aunt Dorottya crossed herself.

The Tyrant's possessing your mother's mind and soon it will possess her soul. Once it has her soul there'll be no judgement of God for her upon death. Only Hell. Where the late Mr Farkas ended up.

Can't Father Szalai help us? Mátyás cried. Perform an exorcism?

Father Szalai won't do exorcisms any more. No priest in the Hungarian People's Republic will – they don't want to end up in jail.

The babysitter then insisted he and his brother come and stay with her, since the Tyrant was too dangerous to be around. Mátyás, who often secretly pretended Dorottya was his grandmother, was moved. But how could this arthritic old woman protect them both?

Thank you, Aunt Dorottya. But we just can't abandon her.

It was a decision he'd regret for the rest of his life.

Very early the next morning, Mátyás was woken by the slam of the front door. He heard Comrade Gyurkovics stomping down the hall, yelling, *Klára . . . What the fuck are you playing at, calling my home?*

It was unheard of for the Muscovite to come to Almásy House so early, and Mátyás got up to find out what was going on. *Stay in bed*, he whispered to Józsi, but his little brother came waddling after him into the parlour where Mátyás could smell freshly brewed coffee on the table and pastries warmed up in the oven. He heard the swish of Klára's crimson silk dressing gown and could sense the mania about her, radiating from her in dangerous waves. Mátyás could perceive the Tyrant up by the ceiling, a dark metaphysical chaos near the crystal tiers of the chandelier.

After climbing the three flights of stairs, Comrade Gyurkovics was panting, and Mátyás knew he would be pink-faced and sweaty as a glazed ham. Squinting, he made out the coat draped on his shoulders, hanging open over his wrinkled shirt, the tails loose over his trousers. His right arm was still entombed in plaster cast, supported by its sling.

Who the fuck do you think you are calling my house at four a.m.? Speaking to my fucking *wife*? This *emergency* better be good, Klára.

Klára calmly poured Gyurkovics a demitasse of coffee. She handed it to him and said, Why don't you sit?

Furious, but not one for being on his feet if he could help it, Comrade Gyurkovics lowered himself into a dining chair and drank some coffee, holding the cup with his left hand. Mátyás stood near the door, and Józsi, scared by Papa's shouting, hugged his older brother's pyjama legs. Mátyás heard Klára unscrew the lid of a jar, then the clink of metal on glass as she spooned out apricot jam. Then she approached to give Józsi the spoon to suck like a lollipop.

Get on with it, Klára, Comrade Gyurkovics snapped. Before I wring your neck.

And radiant as a bride about to walk down the aisle, Klára said, My husband has come back to Budapest.

There was a pause, then Gyurkovics laughed. A bullet went into the back of György Szabó's head in Siberia in 1951. I saw the execution records myself.

Klára smiled pityingly at him. He's at Keleti Station now and will be here shortly. I've called you here, Gyurkovics, to break our arrangement off first.

Keleti Station? Gyurkovics sneered. He's rotting in a mass grave. And soon *you'll* be rotting too, in the asylum where I've—

Gyurkovics's contempt was stopped dead in its tracks. Black liquid splashed the tablecloth as the demitasse slipped from his grasp. The Muscovite's hands began to tremor and shake.

Klára? he said, panic in his voice.

Mátyás was frozen, unsure what was happening. Józsi whimpered, *Papa*, and for his brother's sake Mátyás turned for the door. But Klára was ahead of him. She slammed the door shut, locking the four of them in the parlour, and depositing the key in her robe's silk pocket. Knocking his chair over backwards, Gyurkovics lumbered towards her, twitching and jerking out of control.

Key . . . he gasped.

Through his deteriorated vision, Mátyás saw Klára extract the key again with a defiant look. She flung her head back, opened her mouth wide and dropped it down her throat, gagging it down. The Muscovite came at her, clumsily swinging his left fist, and the next thing Mátyás knew all hundred and fifty kilos of Gyurkovics had been slammed by the Tyrant into the wall across the room. Mátyás ran for the telephone. But as he dialled the operator, Klára wrestled it from him. He heard her open the casement window and hurl the jangling telephone down into Thököly Street. Out of the edge of his sight, Mátyás could see that Gyurkovics was unconscious, slumped against the wall.

Why are you doing this? Mátyás cried.

I promised György I would make everything like 1945 again, Klára replied. Just the three of us. You, me and Papa.

Józsi. Mátyás knew where to find him. His little brother would be curled up under the dining table – his usual hiding place when Gyurkovics lost his temper. Mátyás crawled underneath and felt for him. Józsi was limp and still. He shook his two-year-old brother and cried his name, but found no breath, no pulse. Mátyás ran to the locked parlour door again and desperately twisted and yanked at the handle. But the key was in his mother's stomach and there was no getting out.

Klára crouched on the ledge of the casement window, holding on to the stone masonry as she leant halfway out. She'd slipped off her crimson silk robe and wore the chemise György had bought her for her eighteenth birthday. She'd lost weight during the days she had lost her mind and the white cotton hung from her half-starved shoulders and back.

Your father's coming, she cried. Five minutes and he'll be here.

Mátyás saw the godless murmuration of the Tyrant in the far corner of the room, and with the same sense he knew the hour had come for it to drag her soul away for an eternity in Hell. Tears stinging his eyes, he approached Klára.

Mama . . . do you think Papa will recognize me? I was only a baby when he left.

Fearing the Tyrant could read his mind, he thought only of how much he loved his poor demented mother, and hoped this love would be enough to obscure his intentions, even from himself. He stood beside Klára as she balanced on her toes on the window ledge, like a bird on a perch. She turned to him.

Oh, *Mátyás*, please don't cry. Of course Papa will recognize you. You're his only son.

By the other curtain rail, the distortion of the Tyrant lurked, imperceptible to sighted eyes.

Mama, Mátyás said. I love you. I'm happy you'll be with Papa again.

Klára let go of the stone masonry to tenderly wipe tears from his cheek, and Mátyás placed his hand on the small of his mother's back, surprisingly warm through the cotton chemise. He closed his eyes.

I love you too, Klára said. And I'm sorry about your brother. I was just so worried György wouldn't want to live with another man's child.

As Mátyás shoved her over the ledge the Tyrant roared out of the casement window after her. He could sense it pursuing his mother as she fell heels over head and smashed on to the pavement below. Moments later the Tyrant rushed back to Mátyás, suspended in his blindness, metamorphosing the darkness into diabolical forms. And somehow Mátyás knew this meant his thirty-two-year-old mother had died in the empty street, that he'd dispossessed the Tyrant of her soul.

Mátyás waited for retribution. It couldn't possess him – the Russian hadn't taken any photograph – but it could tear him apart. Yet retribution didn't come. The Tyrant just disappeared, as though it had no further reason for being there now that Klára was dead. Mátyás crawled back under the table and gathered his brother, still warm in his flannel pyjamas, into his arms. He knew the Muscovite was now dead too and they'd put him on trial as Klára's accomplice. He would be executed for murder though he was only thirteen years old.

★

Checkmate, Mátyás said.

Quarter to two in the kitchen of the Szarka residence, Zsófi could barely breathe. Her cousin had just confessed to murdering his mother ten years earlier, for reasons most would consider delusional – symptoms of psychosis, in fact. She stared at Mátyás, who was preternaturally calm and intent on the game.

How . . . ?

Distraction. Your queen and bishop were guarding your king, but I pulled them away with my rooks and made you focus on the wrong thing.

No, Zsófi said. How did you get out of the locked room? My

mother told me you were outside the parlour. Your neighbours had to break down the door to get inside.

I'll say it again: distraction. You need to see past distractions to what's hiding in plain sight.

Hiding in plain sight?

Then it came to her, the revelation as sudden as the shrill ring in an antique chest.

Klára swallowed the wrong key.

Mátyás stared straight ahead, his expression hard to read. His thumb rubbed the crown of the captured king he was holding in his hand.

After Aunt Klára took back the telephone you unplugged, Zsófi said, she confiscated the key to your wooden chest, putting it in her robe pocket. The same pocket into which she put the key to the parlour door. She swallowed the wrong one by accident.

Mátyás put her king down in defeat.

You learn fast.

*

Under the table, Mátyás rocked his brother to and fro and sang him a lullaby. How long he hugged Józsi for he didn't know, but at some point, the edge of his vision rippled with red silk. On the parquet floor was his mother's robe, stripped off before her husband came home. The sight of it nudged Mátyás to the memory of Klára shaking him the morning before and all that had followed. Hardly daring to hope, he crawled over and turned the remaining key out of the silk pocket. Counting the teeth under his thumb, he identified the key for the parlour door. And Mátyás knew, in spite of his devastation, he wanted to live. Not to hang for Gyurkovics's death.

He went to the casement window and with the wreckage of his sight saw a street sweeper bent over his mother's shattered corpse. The street sweeper looked up and Mátyás darted back, slamming and locking the window, before using the velvet drape to wipe his fingerprints away. One last farewell to Józsi and he wiped his fingerprints from the parlour door handle, before locking it behind him and dropping the key into the kitchen drain. He stumbled out of Apartment 9, up to Aunt Dorottya's, readying himself to pretend ignorance of the murders that had just occurred.

*

Cousin Mátyás said to Zsófi, Sometimes I regret not drinking the rest of Gyurkovics's coffee and lying down next to Józsi.

Zsófi vehemently shook her head. She was only thirteen but recognized survivor's guilt. Had seen it in Ezster, who'd survived every last Szabó by the end of the war. But her cousin's guilt was complicated by matricide – something Zsófi, though she and Ezster had their disagreements, couldn't conceive of.

Don't speak like that, she said. You *saved* her. She's God's to judge once more.

She reached across the kitchen table and placed her hand over Mátyás's. He pulled away.

The Tyrant comes back to me sometimes.

Zsófi shivered. In this apartment?

Here and not here. In my second sight.

What does it want? Zsófi asked.

Her cousin shrugged. Nothing, I think. Once my mother died it went away. But it's left some residue of itself behind. Some smear of evil, that comes and goes, of which I'll never be cleansed.

He smiled bleakly to himself.

Marked.

After that Saturday night Mátyás never spoke to Zsófi again. Once more they were two strangers who happened to be blood relations living under the same roof. Then, in October 1967, Mátyás had a nervous breakdown. He stopped leaving his room and barely ate the meals her mother served him on a tray. And knowing the night of the chess game had brought the horror of her cousin's past surging back, Zsófi wrestled with her guilt.

In March of 1968, Mátyás left the apartment for the first time in six months and was knocked down and killed by a tram near Vörösmarty Square. Zsófi's twenty-four-year-old cousin had been tapping across the road with his wooden cane, and it was determined an accidental death. Zsófi suspected otherwise.

After Cousin Mátyás's funeral, Zsófi searched under his bed for the cardboard box. Because she now knew she had in common with Mátyás the gift of 'second sight', and she wanted to see the photograph of Klára possessed by the Tyrant again, to prove to herself she hadn't imagined it. But the bundle of black and white photographs was missing and whatever happened to it, Zsófi never found out.

In November 1971, seventeen-year-old Zsófi and her boyfriend Peter Szénes were browsing in a junk shop in South Pest when she came across an oil painting by a J. Unterbrink. The painting was of twins with port-wine-stained faces; each woman a mirror image of the other, luminous and soaring in some unearthly dark. But what Zsófi noticed first about the painting wasn't the twins. It was the Tyrant, lurking in the background under the aggressively and haphazardly slashed-on black paint. She could feel the dark palpitation of it in the beginnings of her second sight, and though Unterbrink's painting frightened Zsófi, she knew it was of too much significance to be left in the junk shop. Ignoring Peter's protests that it was ugly, she purchased the canvas. Brought it home, cloaked it in dust sheets and buried it in her wardrobe. Only twenty years later, after rediscovering the painting while moving house, did she send a letter to the painter, Jürgen Unterbrink, and only after another thirty-one years did Zsófia Szénes, née Szarka, receive a reply. But not from the artist, from me.

Forest Gate, June, 2022. Sixty-eight-year-old Zsófia Szenes was on my iPad screen, her twenty-six-year-old grandson Zoltán next to her on the sofa, translating his grandma's Hungarian into English. Zsófi had a silver-grey bob and, as well as the usual decades of wear and tear, deep laughter lines around her eyes. She wore a lilac shell suit and reading glasses dangling from a beaded chain, and though she'd lost her husband Peter in 2014, she struck me as a woman happy in her life. Throughout the hours we spoke, her phone buzzed with messages from children, grandchildren and church friends, and several cats and dogs she'd adopted from an animal rescue shelter made appearances on-screen (her tortoiseshell cat at one point getting its claws tangled up in some crocheting Zsófi had stuffed down the side of a sofa cushion – much to her hilarity). Zsófi waved her hands about as she spoke in Hungarian, animated by a brightness that seemed the exact opposite of what had driven her Cousin Mátyás to despair.

Zsófi became sombre, however, when she showed me Jürgen's painting. She tilted the 50-by-70-centimetre canvas up towards her laptop camera and I recognized the Ursulas from the photograph Bedwyr had shown me. Only just. Jürgen hadn't been falsely modest when he said that he was a below-average painter. The renderings of Ursula were so amateurish, I only knew it was her from the port-wine stains. Yet despite the lack of mimetic skill the painting had a phantasmagorical power about it. A mesmeric sway.

Zsófi spoke to her grandson in Hungarian and he translated. My grandmother wants to know if you can see *the Tyrant*.

Zoltán widened his eyes in mock-terror. A postdoctoral researcher in Computer Science at Imperial College, back visiting family in Budapest for the summer, he was bemused and cynical about all that his grandmother wanted him to translate. I squinted into the background of the painting. All I could see were brushstrokes of black; slapdash and impasto-thick.

No, I admitted. I guess I don't have second sight.

I then showed them the photograph of Ursula Pohl that Bedwyr had given me (Ceridwen's photo, Bedwyr, understandably, had not given up). Zsófi put her reading glasses on, and upon seeing the real-life Ursula in black and white, gasped. She spoke a few words in Hungarian to her grandson.

She says it's exactly like the one she saw of Klára.

She sees the Tyrant?

Zoltán didn't need to translate. Zsófia nodded and spoke some more to her grandson.

She's seen enough, he said. You can put it down now.

I obeyed, then I showed them Marion's sketch of Lena at the

life drawing class in Stoke Newington, holding it up to my iPad's camera. Zsófia murmured to her grandson in Hungarian. Zoltán translated.

My grandmother says your friend was very beautiful, but she can't see any Tyrant in the drawing . . . But *I* have a question for you, Jake. What are those numbers and letters underneath?

Back in 2011, before I'd packed Lena's portrait up in the box of her stuff, I'd noticed something at the bottom of the A2 paper. The indentation of something written on an overlying page by someone pressing too hard with a pencil or biro. Lena had left behind a tin of pastels and, without quite knowing why, I'd taken one out and rubbed it gently over the indentation, revealing a string of sixteen digits and characters, nonsensical to me.

I don't know, I said. Something written on the previous page. I'd forgotten about it.

Looks like a v2 onion address.

A *what*?

A URL for the dark web.

Oh.

Support for v2 domains is being phased out on network relays and servers, Zoltán said. And the site admin's probably migrated it to a fifty-six-character v3 address, which is more secure.

Right. So it's gone?

Or inaccessible. But I can check.

Um . . . sure.

I held Marion's sketch up to the iPad camera, and Zoltán explained to his grandmother what he was doing as he took a photograph with his phone.

Two days later, I was out walking on Wanstead Flats when I got a WhatsApp call.

I found it! Wow, it wasn't easy. I had to download an older Tor Browser version and use a wiped-clean laptop. But *somehow* I could access the site.

The London day was sunny and bright, with low scudding clouds in a blue sky. I came to a standstill on grass worn thin by five-a-side football matches. With an apprehension verging on dread, I asked, So what's on it?

Zoltán hesitated. Nine hundred miles away in Budapest, on the other end of the call, his swallow was loud enough for me to hear.

I'll send you a file of screenshots, Jake. It'll take a while – there's a lot on there. But I think you need to see for yourself . . .

Badlands – VI

The girl won't stop throwing up. Keeled over in yesterday's blue cotton sundress, she retches with hands on knees, splattering mezcal and stomach bile on to the dry and cracked valley floor. The woman's seen this reaction before and knows the girl can't purge herself of what she really wants out of her. The Tyrant's desecration clings to her insides.

Oh, Rosa, the woman says. You poor thing.

The girl dry-heaves and the woman throws down her heavy backpack, extracts a pack of wet wipes from a side pocket. As Rosa slowly rights herself, the woman goes over and gently, maternally, removes the gastric juices from her lips and chin.

There, she says. Feel better now?

Rosa's eyes are sore and reddened. Exertion beads her brow and her complexion's a sickly yellow – though that could just be the sulphurous quality of the light before the coming storm, the tumescence of rain clouds smothering the sun, still low in the desert sky. It's quarter to eight in the morning and they've been hiking for over an hour to get to the trailhead, half a mile from the parking lot. They could hide out in the wilderness until Venus – invisible now in daylight – slips below the Earth in the pre-dusk and the offering can be completed. But the woman knows confrontation will come for them wherever they are, and given a choice between hiding or fighting, she will fight. Even though she's weak and yet to recover from the internal rot. Until he's been eliminated there won't be any possibility of rest.

She drinks from the water flask then holds it out to the girl.

Rinse and spit, she says. Your tooth enamel will thank you.

The girl doesn't take the flask. A blustery wind tugs at her lank and bedraggled curls as she looks back across the barrenlands at the wrinkled, fissured valley floor and the rock formations of yellow and grey, black and iron-oxide red. She stares down at her worn and dusty sneakers, then at the backs of her hands – hands she's seen every day for seventeen years, but now stares at with the intensity of someone on psychotropic drugs. What's changed? The woman knows it's the position of various moles and freckles. The forked tributaries of blue veins, the knuckle-bulges, finger-creases and tattered hangnails. Everything, yet nothing Rosa can put into words. For the first time since the Tyrant came, she speaks.

I'm all . . . fucked-up.

You were hitting the mezcal hard last night. We'll get you some Alka-Seltzer when we get back to Farmington.

The woman's half-delirious herself. The edges of the landscape flicker and blur, neurons misfiring in her visual cortex, the synapses burnt. When she stares into the distance the shale hills appear to be moving, breathing in and out like large slumbering beasts.

Back before, the girl says. Something came.

The woman detects behind Rosa's dead-eyed expression the effort to piece together what happened when the sun was beneath the horizon. But whatever memory remains is in shards, shifting about as though viewed through a kaleidoscope.

You had a nightmare, the woman responds. You woke screaming. So scared you . . . well . . . had to change out of your shorts. Please don't be embarrassed though. Accidents happen.

The woman can sense Rosa turning her words over, searching them for traces of truth.

You were there too . . . the girl murmurs. Taking photographs.

In your dream? Odd.

The woman heaves up her twenty-odd kilos of backpack again, hooks arms and shoulders through the straps. She gestures to Rosa that they should continue westwards towards the boundary fence.

C'mon. Not far to go now. How about you come back to my hotel room? I know Lissy does her camming in your trailer during the day. You can have a long soak in the tub, and I can lend you some clean pyjamas, and you can sleep in my freshly made bed. And when you wake we'll order pizza, edit your Aurora Rose videos together.

The girl doesn't respond to the woman's offer. She stumbles, one sneakered foot in front of the other, over the loose and crumbling ankle-turning rocks. How much is she taking in? Deprived of sleep, the hike back's more gruelling than the hike there. But at least, the woman thinks, the sun's not as punishing as the day before. The sky overcast and bilious as though the dust of the badlands has risen up to hang suspended in the air.

The parking lot's within sight now. Because of the storm warning, hikers have stayed away and there are only two vehicles. Other than the woman's car, a red Ford pickup truck by the wilderness boundary fence. A large four-door model, ten or fifteen years old, tarpaulin covering the truck bed, the interior shadowy and empty-seeming. The woman knows where she's seen it before. Her Toyota's on the other side of the lot, over by the gravel road leading back to the Bisti Highway. Thirty or so yards from the Ford pickup, which she suspects has been strategically parked.

A large tumbleweed rolls towards them and, though Rosa's eyes are downcast, she doesn't seem to notice the desiccated plant trundling by. Nor does she appear to care when the wind from the approaching storm parachutes out the blue of her dress, despite her lack of underwear. Only when the girl looks up and sees the Ford truck does the woman detect a change in her thousand-yard stare. A flitter of nerves and fear.

I see your friend is waiting, the woman remarks. How much is he paying you? Five hundred dollars? A thousand dollars? However much, it isn't enough.

What?

Rosa is blank, but the woman can sense the stirring of panic. She turns around so her back's to the parking lot. Takes her knife out of her shorts pocket. Springs out the steel blade.

Don't move.

They stand facing each other, Rosa staring down at the blade pointed inches from her throat, holding her breath.

How much did he tell you? That all you have to do is spend a night with me out here then run off with him? And you didn't think there might be more to it than that?

Rosa looks from the knife to the woman, too scared to deny anything.

He only told you half-truths, Rosa. And now he's destroyed you.

Destroyed?

The girl's eyes redden again with tears, but the woman has no sympathy. What instructions did he give you? she asks.

Rosa whispers the memorized lines. *Go with her to the car. When she's behind the wheel, say you need to pee. Run to the pickup. Fast as you can.*

Here are your new instructions, the woman says. Go straight to my car. Get in. Lock the door and wait.

Rosa's breathing quickens as the woman touches the tip of the knife to her throat. Gently, without breaking the skin.

Now.

The girl looks away. Helpless. Trapped.

Thunderheads are seething up overhead as they enter the parking lot, boiling in their internal chaos. The woman glances to the east and sees a rare daylight apparition of Venus between the swollen clouds. Freakish even when skies are clear, never mind with a storm coming, but she hasn't time to contemplate it. As they walk by the large Ford pickup and its New Mexico plates, the woman scans the shadowy front and back seats, and though she senses the Sculptor's son, crouched and watching out of sight, she doesn't take a closer look. They walk across the mudflats, zigzagged by tyre marks, and the woman points her keys at the Toyota. The doors clunk unlocked and the girl walks round to the passenger side as the woman heaves her backpack and DLSR camera into the trunk, slams it shut. She gets into the driver's seat and slots the Manila envelope containing the Polaroid into the sun visor above the steering wheel as Rosa stares into the side-view mirror, frowning and touching her fingers to her cheeks, to her eyebrows and lips. Disoriented by the sight of her own face.

In the rear-view the pickup is empty and still. The antagonist yet to emerge.

Buckle up, she tells the girl.

But when she puts the key in the ignition and twists, the engine sputters and turns over only once. Anger spikes the woman's blood. She reaches across the girl into the glove compartment, pulls out some metal handcuffs – a last-minute purchase from a sex shop in Albuquerque, but fit for purpose. Widening her eyes at the cuffs, the girl says, I won't run, I promise.

Wrist.

The woman snaps on a silver ring, then locks the other cuff to one of the headrest's metal poles, so the girl's left hand is up by her shoulder. She presses a button to pop the Toyota's hood and gets out to check underneath. The engine appears undisturbed, but the fuel pump's twenty-amp fuse has been removed, as well as the spare. The large pickup is parked facing them, its wide grille a grimace of steel. Leaving Rosa shackled to the headrest, the woman arms herself with a foot-long iron crowbar from the trunk and starts towards the truck, cursing herself for not bringing a gun.

Five or so yards away from the pickup, she stops. A boisterous squall tugs at her T-shirt and dark hair, swirls up a layer of dust. Under the menacing grey clouds she points the crowbar at the pickup and says, You're not the first to attempt to sabotage me.

The truck is silent. She stares through the windshield at the empty front seats. Was it her imagination, or did the purple Little Tree hanging from the rear-view ever-so-slightly sway? Eddy. A once solemn-eyed child of six or seven, like a shadow at his father's heels. Older now than his father was when he died.

You have predecessors, she warns. The Tyrant crushed each and every one.

Nothing from the pickup.

I want my fuse or the keys to your truck. You have one minute before I come and take them for myself.

She counts to sixty, then she starts towards the truck. And finally, there's movement. Someone emerges from the footwell, into the driver's seat. Not the Sculptor's son, but a white guy in a baseball cap. *Joseph*, the woman instinctively thinks. No, not Joseph. Knowing she's been had, she spins around. The Sculptor's son is meddling under the Toyota's hood, having surfaced from the desert scrub.

The woman shouts and sprints towards her car as he jumps into the driver's seat next to Rosa and the engine starts with a roar. She chases after them, waving the crowbar, but the Toyota's pulling away, up the gravel road to the Bisti Highway. Eddy opens the driver's-side window and throws something out on to the mudflats. The envelope with the Polaroid the woman took of Rosa possessed by the Tyrant at Venus rise.

The woman's so furious when she hears the pickup behind her she laughs. She turns to the truck reversing through the wire boundary fence and into the badlands, then accelerating towards her, the man gripping the wheel, pressing the pedal hard. The woman stands there, glaring at the driver. *Come on then*, she thinks. *Charge.*

Twenty miles per hour. Thirty. Forty. The woman stands firm at the entrance to the parking lot, staring him down. Two tons of truck come at her at speed, the man gritting his teeth in determination to run her down. She stands with the crowbar, holding her nerve until the pickup, a yard or two from hitting her, crashes as though into an invisible pole. The airbag explodes, the driver thrown into the billowing white as the front-end of the truck crumples, the windshield shattering into a dense web of Autoglass. The hood peels back from the internal mechanical parts – engine, carburetter, oiled pipes – with a hideous wrenching sound. The proximity of carnage exhilarates the woman as she stands there, unscathed. She's torn. There's satisfaction that the driver got what he deserved. And despair, because the Ford pickup – her one means of leaving the Bisti – has been wrecked.

The driver's-side door is hanging open, the man groaning to himself, concussed from the airbag's impact. She slashes through his seatbelt with her flick knife, then yanks the man by the arm so he tumbles out, head and shoulders first, thudding to the ground. He squints up at her, opens his mouth to speak. But she's too angry for conversation. She raises her crowbar up over her head and brings it down on his skull with a rewarding crack. As he lies unconscious, she studies his face and says, Where have I seen you before?

She remembers then a faded photograph of a boy in Spiderman pyjamas, next to a small Chinese girl in a blue gingham dress, both with paper plates of crisps and cake on their laps. The photo had been stuck with a magnet to a fridge in an IKEA fitted kitchen, at a dinner party in an East London suburb in 2011. He was thirtyish that evening. Fortyish now with grey streaks in his hair. Jonathan? Jack?

The woman turns to the mudflats behind her, to the skid marks left by the Toyota – now speeding to Highway 371 with her offering in the passenger seat. She picks up the envelope. Takes out the Polaroid of Rosa, up on the shale hill as the Tyrant moved through her, the black of her eyes portals to the immensity of that other world. The woman knows that somehow they understand the significance of the photo. They know the girl mustn't look. Not if they want to bring her offerings to an end. Perhaps they even know when the ritual's next stage – Rosa seeing herself possessed – must occur. And though Venus won't set and disappear for some hours yet, the Sculptor's son isn't taking any chances.

Lightning flashes nearby, obliterating the world in a blinding white. A rumbling and the sky begins to tentatively weep on the woman and the unconscious man with the fractured skull and blood trickling out of his nose. Cold rain drips on the totalled Ford truck and a sharp pain in the woman's gut brings her to her knees. As the rain begins to pound, harder now, she holds her side, then laughs as it comes to her.

Tell me, Jake, she says. When was the last time I was so completely fucked?

Testimony 7 – Theo

1982

June 20th

At what point do I admit I've failed, pack up & go back to New York?

One year ago today I started work in this studio, 2,000 miles from the buzz & distractions of the Lower East Side. One year of 12-hour days hammering & chiseling marble & alabaster, limestone & onyx. And it's all <u>still shit</u> & headed for the chasm.

Lancing palm blister w/ a hot pin earlier, had an epiphany: I'm <u>hiding</u> behind this geometric minimalism. This striving for the perfection & immutability of Platonic forms.

But hiding <u>what</u>? A lack of blood & guts. A dearth of fire & <u>imagination</u>.

Nothing here <u>needs</u> to exist. Nothing here fills any void of creation in the world. It's all just so limited & inhibited. Shiny exteriors & zero depth. 'Send this to the lobby of Goldman Sachs!' Prof. Hartmann would say (were he alive to survey this mediocrity).

Speaking of fucking banks, latest Citibank statement says I'm $200 in the red. My inheritance is now officially wiped out. Want to go back & shake the Theo of 18 months ago for thinking <u>this</u> was the way to artistic greatness. Living like a recluse with no electricity or running water, no lovers, no friends. Seldom bathing & shitting in a hole I dug out back.

This 'process journal' has dissolved into self-pity since my work's stopped progressing. Time to knock it off. Put away the tiny violin. Go to bed. Tomorrow, start over. Or burn everything to the ground for the insurance & buy a ticket to JFK.

June 22nd

Too hungover & disheartened to work today. Larry's visit has completely derailed me.

I thought I was hallucinating when his mustard-yellow Buick showed up last night. Then I remembered the Basquiat postcard that landed in my Questa P. O. box last month – he was coming to Santa Fe for an opening & threatening to visit. I didn't reply & reassured myself Larry hadn't the nous or sobriety to figure out where I lived. Yet there he was. Coming at me w/ the eagerness of a Labrador that hadn't been trained not to leap up at people. Floppy hair. Bulbous nose. Wagging his tail.

L: Theodora Waite. My hermit sculptor! Wow. You're really out in the boonies aren't you?

Larry looked gleefully around my dirt clearing, at my two mud-colored adobe buildings & outdoor tin tub & dingy graying underwear pegged to the line. He then took in my stone-dust filthy vest & dungarees (worn for God knows how many days in a row) & my dinner of BBQ beans, eaten out of the can.

Me: Larry. You didn't tell me you were coming.

L: Theo. You need a fucking phone.

Me: How did you find me?

L: Some guy in Bumblefuck Tavern said you'd hired him to help build your studio. He drew us a map.

Us? A dark-haired woman got out of the Buick. Petite. Attractive in an even-featured way. Leather cowboy boots, blouse, denim miniskirt. First thought she was Larry's girlfriend. But at 37 or 38 (I guessed) too close to him in age for that.

I'm Eva, she said, accent European.

Smiling, she held out a canvas bag, heavy with wine bottles, a baguette poking out the top. I could just about manage a gruff 'thanks'. Other than grocery store clerks & gas station attendants, I haven't been around other people for months.

L: So what's for dinner, Theo? We're starving. What're you feeding your guests?

★

I fed them spaghetti boiled in a pot of rainwater on the wood-burning stove. Served al dente, w/ a jar of out-of-date store-bought tomato sauce. No Parmesan. No side salad. No butter for the bread. But plenty of wine, <u>thank God</u>. We dined by kerosene lamplight at a wooden table in the yard as Larry filled me in on 18 months of NY art scene gossip. Max Lehrer's got in with Warhol and gone stratospheric despite being a lazy fucking hack. Maggie Prideaux ODed after the Times trashed her solo show & was last seen in Hell's Kitchen with track marks up her arms. Joel Ogden Brown's dropped his anti-capitalist posturing for the support of a 'patron of the arts' from Exxon etc. . . . etc. . . .

I didn't say much & Eva was quiet too. Shyness? Something else? Caught her staring more than once. At the long wavy hair turned white in my 26th year? At the angular face my mother once described as '<u>ruined</u> by her Roman nose'? One thing I miss about the Lower East Side is that a woman looking the way I do isn't freakish, has some cachet even. Here the locals gawp like I've escaped from a carnival sideshow cage. It made me paranoid Eva was judging me the same way.

Anyway, Larry's doing great. Group show lined up in Tribeca, a teaching gig at Parsons and a 19 y/o student he's fucking. (Eva, it turned out, was just an acquaintance. A German photographer recently met at a party in Taos.)

L: Cynthia's from Iowa. Blonde. <u>Corn fed</u>. She kept calling me Professor Erskine, so I told her to call me Larry. So now she calls me Professor Larry. <u>Professor Larry</u>. I know, I shouldn't . . . But oh sweet Jesus, those <u>tits</u> . . .

I rolled my eyes & Larry's grin turned lupine.

L: And what about you, Theo? Everyone wants to know what the hell you've been up to.

He waved a hand at my adobe studio.

L: Well? Do we get a tour?

I admitted I hadn't anything to show yet & Larry widened his eyes.

L: Why don't you come back to New York then? Crazy fucking idea coming out here in the first place. I mean, do you even have any friends? You're what? 32? You should be having fun. Not living out in the desert, carving monoliths like some Old Testament hermit. When was the last time you got <u>laid</u>?

I flushed & was about to tell Larry to mind his own fucking business when the German photographer spoke up.

<u>Perseverance is where the gods dwell.</u>

We turned to her & she smiled.

E: It's a Peruvian saying. You don't have any sculptures yet, Theo. But you will. And not the work you'd produce if you were in New York. They will be original. Extraordinary.

I nodded, grateful for her words, even if she was only being kind.

L: That's all very well. But there's no need for the vow of abstinence.

E: Ignore him. How glorious it must be waking everyday to all this land and sky and the mountain range. I could move out here myself.

After dinner I'd hoped they'd go, but Larry put a mix tape on in the Buick and they danced in the headlights, spinning around to new bands I didn't recognize since the radio out here's mostly static. I stayed at the table, drinking the 4th bottle of wine. Larry kept thrusting his hips over to me, grinning and beckoning with a curling finger, but I resolutely shook my head. The German photographer kept glancing over too, but more furtive & contemplative than Larry. More complex. They didn't leave 'til midnight, Eva behind the wheel, Larry slumped in the passenger seat, too wasted to drive. Though I'd been willing them to go, as the Buick LeSabre's headlights were swallowed up by dark I was overcome by a crushing loneliness. The empty miles of Taos County night suddenly a landslide I was buried beneath with no way of digging myself out.

June 23rd

The day got off to a lousy start. Uninspired in the studio, in the afternoon I abandoned my work & hiked w/ shotgun to the Sangre de Cristo to shoot a wild rabbit. Stalking the low hills where the cottontail burrows are, I ranted at Erskine in my head. ('Carving monoliths? Fuck you, Larry. Like your Plexiglas boxes of used syringes or whatever crap you've picked up on East 2nd are any good . . .')

Shot & killed 2 rabbits. 3rd got away, trailing blood. Walked home carrying them by the hind legs. Felt good to swing that deadweight in my hand.

When I got back Eva was prowling in front of my casita. Red head-scarf over dark hair. Cowboy boots & denim cut-offs & white shirt knotted at the waist. She smiled at me, unperturbed by my Remington, dead rabbits or tribal streaks of zinc oxide on my cheeks. I looked around warily. Larry's Buick was nowhere in sight.

T: You walked here?

E: I hitched partway.

T: It's rude to just show up.

I was being a churl myself. But I'd had enough of these ambushes.

E: You don't have a telephone and I wanted to apologize. Last night, Larry gave the impression you were expecting us. I had no idea we were intruding.

Then she laughed.

E: And here I am intruding again. But I have offerings at least.

She unzipped a backpack. Inside: crusty bread, blue cheese, dried herbs, two bottles of wine, jars of artichokes, olives, sun-dried tomatoes . . . Gourmet luxuries I'd covet but never buy myself.

T: I don't need you to go grocery shopping for me.

She nodded at the limp & bloodied rabbits.

E: I can see. Need a hand skinning those? I know a great recipe for stew.

We sat outdoors at dusk to dine on rabbit casserole with bread & a bottle of red wine. Preparing the meal, I'd been chilly toward E, but seated across the table from her, drinking her expensive Merlot, it seemed mean-spirited to keep that up. So I let my defences down & was pleasantly surprised.

We didn't swap life stories or slide into the sloppy emotional incontinence of women when the wine & estrogen flow. Nor did we gossip about other artists – the cliques & feuds & screwing of each other's wives. Instead we spoke of Walter De Maria's Lightning Field: the scintillation of electricity across the hundreds of stainless-steel poles during summer storms. Robert Smithson's Spiral Jetty & his technique of constructing coils of mud & stone in Utah's Great Salt Lake. Richard Serra's Tilted Arc. Sol LeWitt's Untitled Cube. Eva Hesse's Hang Up. Brancusi's Bird in Space. We spoke (admiringly) of modernism & minimalism, suprematism & constructivism & De Stijl. We spoke (disparagingly) of graffiti art & pop art & op art & neo-expressionism & art brut. We spoke color, shape & material. Dimensions, texture & tensile strength. The Dionysian & Apollonian. The neurotic & transcendent & sublime.

I was uplifted. Elated, even. Finally – conversations worth having.

In the Taos County darkness, orange kerosene flame glinted in E's slanted feline eyes, her dark widow's peak visible under her red headscarf. As a rule, I dislike femininity. It's so simpering, even just the <u>appearance</u> of it, striving to be pleasing to the eye. But I get the feeling E's femininity's a mask she wears to move through the world with innocuous ease. That beneath the mask's a strength of will that goes its own way and tramples society's expectations into the ground.

Halfway through the 2nd bottle of wine:

T: You hiked 4 miles from the highway just to see me? Why?

E: It's been a long time since I met someone I feel such a connection with. Another woman in exile.

T: Exile? Don't you live in Greenwich Village?

E: Not anymore. I gave up my sublet today. I never stay in one place for too long. Like you I make sacrifices for my art.

T: For your photography?

E: Living is my art. Photography's just a means to sustain it.

I frowned at this, and E laughed & shook her head at herself.

E: I get pretentious after too much wine . . . and overheated & faint. Is there <u>any</u> way to cool down out here?

★

We entered the adobe studio & I turned everything on. The generator rumbled & the electric fan blades whirred & the fluorescent light buzzed, the glare bouncing off the walls. I wasn't expecting a visitor so it was a mess. But E ignored the dust & debris all over the floor, and the workbench heaped with chisels & mallets, apple cores & mold-furred coffee cups. She went straight to my most recent crap pushed up against the back wall. Geometric forms, several feet high. Hexahedrons. Octahedrons. Tesseracts of 4th dimensional cubes. E moved between them, cowboy boots trampling fragments of stone. She stroked the alabaster & marble that I'd smoothed with sandpaper and boric acid, exploring the surfaces through touch.

Interesting, she said.

I was grateful she hadn't pretended to find the sculptures exceptional or even good. The dishonesty would've rankled after the rapport we'd struck. I said they were headed for the chasm. She glanced over her shoulder at me. The fan billowed her white shirt in its breeze.

E: The chasm?

T: It's a ravine a 20-minute drive from here. I load my pickup truck every few months, back up to the edge and push them off the hundred-foot drop. It's where all my failures end up.

E: Such theatricality. You ought to film it as performance art.

She moved to a shelving unit of experiments in soapstone and beeswax less than a foot tall. She crouched, her frayed denim cut-offs on cowboy boots, tugging at the corner of a white cloth covering a life-size bust.

E: May I?

I nodded and she unveiled a woman's head, neck and bare shoulders. She gazed at it, rapt.

E: This is good. Very good. Who is it?

T: Someone I knew in New York.

E: Close friend?

T: No.

She stroked the alabaster, tracing the slope of nose and lips, the clavicles and suprasternal notch. She caressed the short curls, the delicate ears.

E: I can't speak for the likeness to the subject. But this thing's <u>alive</u>.

I wished she'd leave it alone. I haven't spoken to Lillian since I propositioned her after my father died & left me the inheritance. It had been her dream to leave New York and disappear into the landscape like Agnes Martin or Georgia O'Keeffe and now we had the money to do so. But when it came down to it she hadn't the stomach or nerve for 'that kind of life'. So now she's married to a dental surgeon on Staten Island, and I keep the statue covered because I can't bear to be reminded of the sessions I'd spent lost in the geometries of Lillian's face. But I can't bear to throw it away, b/c it's the best work I've ever done.

Straightening up, E turned away from Lillian's bust.

E: Do you do commissions?

T: No one's ever asked.

She tilted her head w/ a thoughtful look.

E: Could I persuade you to take a break from your own projects to make a sculpture for me? I will pay you well. Several hundred dollars. A thousand dollars. Name your price.

T: What do you want me to sculpt?

Dark glossy hair spilled from E's red scarf as she tugged it off. The fan rotated toward her, her white shirt rippling in the fullness of the breeze. She stood before me, shoulders back, as though presenting herself.

<u>Me</u>, she said.

Process Journal for E's Statue

June 24th

Oaxaca granite. Dark gray, but speckled with feldspar, mica and quartz. Mohs scale: 8. Dimensions: h. 167 cm, w. 50 cm, d. 50 cm. Density: 2691 kg per m³ (or 175 lbs per cu ft, but I prefer metric, always have). Drove with E to Albuquerque to purchase from stone yard there. According to the Stetson-hatted trader the granite's '430

million years old' (<u>phooey!</u> as my Great-Aunt Millicent would say).
Right now, over <u>one tonne</u> flattening tires and straining payload of
my pickup truck.

Granite was E's choice. I objected. Not only near-impossible to
carve but a graveyard rock, for tombstones, sarcophaguses etc.
Carrera marble <u>much better</u> (softer, translucent, scatters light).
But E insisted. The statue is for a 'special project' (won't say
what). Granite 'everlasting'. She then bought me $800 of expen-
sive new toys: diamond-tipped drills, rotary saws and grinders
etc. The Oaxaca granite purchased for an undisclosed sum, but
at least <u>triple</u> the tools. Her work as commercial photographer
(Ray-Bans, Calvin Klein, Benetton etc.) must have her rolling in
dough.

7 hours driving there and back. Stopped for tacos in Santa Fe.
Now writing this in hole-in-the-wall Questa bar with mosaic-tiled
floor. Don't usually come here – local men hostile (recognize one
who'd called me 'bruja' in the hardware store). But E drinking
tequila and joking fluently with them (E lived in Mexico City for a
few years, she said, whereas I flunked Spanish senior year). No
tequila for me & will stop after this beer. Today's the 2nd day this
week with hangover. Want to avoid a 3rd.

June 25th

Hoisted granite from truck with pulley and sling. Moved to studio
on pallet with E's help (for a woman so slight, she's v. strong). E
posing in muslin shift that falls to knees. Barefoot. Dark hair loose
about shoulders. Chin up & back straight. An average 6.5 Hu. 163
cm tall. Bust 86, waist 66, hips 91.

Tape measure, calipers, protractor, T-square. Took as many pre-
liminary measurements as I could, jotting them down on diagrams
scaled to life. Surface anatomy charted to the millimeter, every
slope and angle to the degree. 5 hours in this topographical survey
of E, then 2 hours on charcoal sketches – not from digits and coord-
inates, but instinct and sight. Need spontaneity, not technicality, to

215

capture her sinuosity of form. Need to focus on the flesh: the tense and slack, the wrinkles, creases and folds.

E the perfect model. Freakishly so. Posed for 7 continuous hours in 95-degree heat. Didn't sweat much or ask for the fan to be cranked up. I need to work in silence – no music, no conversation. Can't concentrate otherwise. But E didn't seem bored.

Productive day. Have I ever been so finicky in my caliper measurements before? Iris diameters, nostril holes, and don't get me started on the cartilaginous structure of the ears! But despite my exactitude there's something slippery and evasive about E, beyond the tape measure's reach. It intrigues me. Sculpting will find a way in.

June 26th

Quarrel with E today. She won't let me work from a clay scale model. Doesn't want statue to be 'a copy of a copy' and wants me to sculpt granite 'from life and inner eye'. <u>Absurd!</u> Explained she'd have to pose for 12 hours a day for weeks. Explained the dangers of granite dust (silica, lung damage etc.) & that I can't well sculpt her with a respirator clamped to her face! E's response: I have stamina to stand for 12 hours. And the dust won't harm my lungs. <u>Nothing</u> <u>can</u>(!)

Horseshit. But let her be stubborn. Wreck her lungs. For 1,500 bucks, I can acquiesce. Half a day of the ear-splitting aggression of drills breaking rock, she'll change her mind.

More measurements today. Plus study of the muslin shift – how it hangs from shoulders, breasts, buttocks and skims the knees. Spent about 10 hours sketching E and have to concede she <u>does</u> have stamina. Seldom needs the toilet or a sip of water. Stomach doesn't growl. Not so much as a cough or sneeze.

Will spend 3 more days on sketching (since clay model prohibited) to build confidence before I start on that 430 million y/o rock. Will refer to Eugene F. Fairbanks Anatomy for Sculptors from SUNY days. Perhaps a study of underlying musculoskeletal structure too.

July 2nd

Sweating in heavy respirator, sound-muffling headphones and safety visor. But how satisfying to be breaking stone! The diamond-tipped drills and circular saw E bought for me are <u>outstanding</u>. Powerful & precise. Using them to remove the larger areas first.

I need to find the prominences, the absolute prominences (apex of head, base of chin, tip of nose etc.) before the gradients and lower points. V. absorbing and I entered into the 'flow' with ease, hours passing quickly in hypnotic trance. Didn't even notice blister in right palm until it burst. Should have E's statue roughed-out by the end of the week. Completed in six.

Turns out I underestimated E. Stood for 10 hours, did not flinch at the excruciating high-decibel drills. I've positioned the electric fan between us, to divert the dust from her airways. Power usage <u>high</u>. The generator already half out of fuel, but E driving to town later to buy some more oil plus groceries, bandages and Epsom salts (powerful as the drills are, drilling still demands strength, and back and upper arms ache). While E's running errands, a soak in the outdoor tub. Cold water. This 430 million y/o granite an absolute bitch.

Torso tomorrow. Blister weeping. Sure hand will be mummified by time the sculpture's done.

July 8th

Process journal neglected for 6 days. Can feel Prof. Hartmann's disapproval from beyond the grave ('An unexamined process is a <u>mindless</u> process!'). But I'm just <u>too exhausted</u> by the day's end. After work I soak in an Epsom salt bath, then dinner: E's stove-top risottos, pasta dishes or casseroles. Glass of wine, hand-rolled cigarette, and some conversation. By 9 or 10, can barely keep eyes open, so bed – a blessed relief. Is there <u>any</u> muscle that doesn't ache? Upper & lower back, shoulders, arms. Lumbar spine out of whack & legs sore from standing all day. This blistered hand barely has strength to move this pen . . .

Anyway, perseverance. Out of respect for the late Prof. H, brief notes.

Blocking out of E completed from head to toes. Drills put aside and now using 2–4 lb mallets and carbide-tipped chisels, edged pitches and points. Something timeless about the sound of chipping stone – like sculpting in antiquity, in Imperial Rome. But this is the laborious part, demanding even more focus & concentration. How much force is needed to strike the chisel with 3lb mallet? How to angle the chisel edge? Important to look, measure and translate to the hands. Must strike judiciously, remove precise quantities of stone.

This is why confidence wavers. Why I resent E's 'no clay model' stipulation. Have to keep referring to scale diagrams and charts, which met with E's censure today. Look at me, she said. Put down the calipers. Use your eyes. Imagination. <u>Trust yourself</u>. Those numbers won't help.

I begged to differ. Wanted to rip off visor & suffocating respiratory mask and shout: You do it! It's harder than it looks! How else to get the nasal-labial creases exactly right? The indentation above the chin? E then promised to pay me even if I mess up. So grudgingly I switched to working from sight. Grudgingly concede it worked. Feel a kind of breakthrough actually. Like I've caught something unique about her; a rare butterfly in my swooping net. Still very rough though. Have to move onto limbs, hands and feet before I return to the minor details of face. Nervous. The smallest miscalculation could damage E's statue beyond repair.

E continues to pose as though suspended in time, without even the appearance of daydreaming. I've ceased to be troubled by it. Take it for granted now that ordinary human limits don't apply where E's concerned.

July 14th

Had a nightmare I was entombed in a sarcophagus. Oaxaca granite, of course. Utter darkness. Immovable lid. But in each hand a chisel and 2 lb mallet to chip my way out. Had the realization I would rather just lie there and die. Then woke up.

Told E about it over morning coffee and eggs. She laughed.

Since I last wrote (10 days ago) there have been good and bad days.

Good days: Intense focus. Satisfying weight of the mallet on sharpened point. Falling into the hypnotic rhythm of pounding on igneous rock. Accuracy of calculations of speed, force and slant of chisel-edge, removing perfect amounts of stone. Carving through the pain barrier until it all ceases to hurt. Successes: the sui generis (how else to describe it?) of her eyes, her widow's peak, her up-tilt of nose. Her muslin shift, how it ripples and falls.

Bad days: Headache days. Slow-going days. Stone-callused finger-cracking days. That day (Thursday? the 9th?) where I spent 10 hours on her left foot (phalanges! metatarsals!) and chipped the big toe. Then the next day when I spent another 10 on the right and botched the heel. E assured me it didn't matter, no one would notice such minor dents. But I was so pissed I wanted to take a sledgehammer to them both.

Today was sufferable. The studio thermometer was 97 degrees. I'm working in vest and shorts. Soaking towels with my sweat. E (who fares much better than I in sweltering heat) drives twice a day to fill jerry cans from the stream. Electric fan runs continuously. Generator needs refueling every three days.

Generally, progress satisfactory. E is emerging, liberated from the stone, but some part of her still evades. Hope work with 2 mm chisel on the finer details of her face will bring it out. (Caught the rare butterfly, now like any lepidopterist must pin it down.)

Taking codeine for the pain – for the spasms of lower back, the stigmata wounds in my hands. 4 tablets every 3 hours. Hour-long soaks with Epsom salts (bathwater granite-dust gray, re-used 2 days in a row). It nags E's conscience that my body's a wreck. Before bed last night she massaged my shoulders and back and it was so much pleasure I could have wept. Going to need a chiropractor once the sculpture's complete. A prescription for something stronger than codeine. For now holding off – can't work with opioid-fogged thoughts.

There've been omissions from this journal. A lack of disclosure about certain feelings I have. Staring at the heat-shimmering mirage of E day after day has fevered my brain. Led to an infatuation. Concealed & irrelevant to the sculptor / subject dynamic, I thought. But now there's something I ought to reveal.

Last night at dinner. Darkness. Kerosene lamps. Half a bottle of red.

E: Someone should sculpt you, Theo. You're striking.

T: Ah, striking. A euphemism for 'ugly'.

E: That's what you think?

T: My mother was always blunt about my looks. She used to say: 'I botched you, Theodora. But your sisters have my genes, thank God.'

E: Your mother despises herself.

Then she reached and stroked my cheek, my Roman nose.

E: I don't speak euphemistically. Theodora means God's gift in Greek. That's how I think of you, you know.

The tenderness in her eyes struck me as – what? Patronizing. I pulled away.

I got up, went & brushed teeth, scooping a cup of water from the barrel around the back. As I called goodnight and entered house for bed, E came to me. Stood in front of me. Barefoot. One of my long shirts hanging over her denim shorts. Dark hair tucked behind ears, gleam of curiosity in her eyes. She asked, Have I done something wrong?

Had she done something wrong? Had Meredith at Groton? Had Edie in junior year at Pratt? Had Lillian? Had any of these women who liked to flirt, to string along? Who craved the attention & validation of a lovelorn woman? I had been professional with E. I had suppressed my feelings (though still she could tell). So I told her: If you want to fuck me, be straight about it. Don't play games.

E reached for me, kissed me. All my senses blazed with her – her lips, her tongue, her soft hair, her flushed & sweaty skin. She pressed herself against me with explicit need, her mouth against mine, on my cheek, my neck, my quickening pulse. Then she reached down, unbuttoned my shorts and began to touch me where no one else has in 2 years. Slid her fingers half inside me as she brought her mouth to my ear. I want to fuck you, she said.

Today, 10 hours working on E's sculpture, both of us hazy from no sleep. Focused on E's dark hair. The descending waves are so hard to get right. Once or twice, I stopped and went over & ran my hard-callused fingers through E's tresses as she remained in her pose, staring through the dusty opacity of air.

Now writing this by kerosene lamp at the table. E's finished washing dishes and I can see her through the doorway, kneeling by the mattress. She lights a candle, places it on the stool for the night ahead, and my heart's an animal hurling itself at its cage.

July 24th

1st day off in a month today. Out of fear of losing momentum the long 10-hour days have gone on, despite only getting 3 or 4 hours sleep per night. Astonishingly, despite being 1/2 delirious, I can still concentrate in the studio, still enter the zone. It's compartmentalized – the sculpting, the sex. By day, I consider E with the intellect, the sculptor's eye and mental processes. By night, I consider her in more carnal & reciprocal ways. And when I sleep E enters my dreams: metaphysical, yet somehow more substantial than life. One way or another she's always in my head. Idée fixe.

Picnic by the lake today. Tomatoes, olives, feta, crusty bread and lemonade. Swimming and lazing on a blanket in the shade of a tree. E is a strong swimmer, can hold her breath for a very long time. I watched her dive from a boulder, waited for her to emerge. She didn't and panic clamored in my chest. Had she drowned? She then surfaced on the other side of the lake, dark slick hair, pale gleaming limbs. No lung-gasping breaths. Completely serene. As though underwater for seconds, not a minute & a half.

She approached, naked, dripping wet. On the blanket I opened my mouth to comment on the strangeness of what I'd just seen, but she sank to her knees. Crawled over to me, pushing me down. Lie back, she said. Close your eyes.

The more time I spend with her, the more unreal she is. Even at night, as her body twists and contorts against my own. Even as I feel the thrum of her blood, her beating heart. Even as I taste her, bite her, fuck her. She's hallucinatory. Only half-corporeal.

Not that this dampens how I feel when I'm with her. The jittering excitement. The old insecurities coming back. 'Cunt-struck' was Larry's diagnosis when I came undone over Lillian. But she's so unlike Lillian. So unlike anyone I've ever known.

Despite all the hours we spend together, I don't know her. Tacit between us: no personal conversations. No backstory, no past. Speak only of art & history & ideas. Only of geology & astronomy & Greek myth & Los Alamos & 20th-century man's capacity to destroy. Only of our days in the studio, sculpting in the here & now. But now my desire to know her has grown to be all-consuming. Where do you come from? Why do you keep moving from place to place? I've heard you speak fluent sentences of Russian and Japanese. Where did you pick these languages up? Do you have friends? A family? How many times have you been in love? Are you in love now?

Who are you? I want to ask.

But I daren't. If I ask, she just won't hear. Or she'll leave. The last thing I want is to drive her away.

July 30th

E cut her left hand yesterday. Sharpening the ax blade on the whetstone to chop wood when it slipped. She cried out & I ran. The dishrag she'd wrapped around it was soaked red & E's face was disfigured with pain. When she showed me the hatchet wound, how bloody, how deep, I sucked air through teeth. I'll drive you to the

Taos Medical Center, I said. You need stitches right away. But E refused. Made me fetch the first-aid kit & pour iodine over it. Wrap her hand in gauze & bandage-roll & safety-pin it up.

E: It's not as bad as it looks. It'll stop bleeding soon.

She swallowed 2 of my codeine & went back to chopping for the wood-burning stove.

Unconvinced, I skipped wine with dinner to be clear-headed in case the bleeding <u>didn't</u> stop & I had to drive her to the ER. But E didn't mention it, and I sort of forgot until hours later, making love on the mattress by candlelight. E on knees, lips grazing my navel, dark hair obscuring her face, hands reaching up for my breasts. The safety pin had come undone and the bandage unraveled. The cut on the right hand wasn't there. No trace of injury at all. Just smooth pale skin. I sat up and E did too. She didn't pretend (Oh, but it was just a scratch!). Didn't attempt to re-bandage the 'wound'. Our eyes met (mine shocked, hers flat & resigned) and E said, There's half a bottle of whiskey in my backpack. Tobacco too.

We drank and smoked and fucked, and I had the sense I was falling throughout. Falling deeper into the terrifying vortex of her, too infatuated & cunt-struck to get out.

As we lay down to sleep, E held me from behind. Whispered: I thought the Tyrant had neutered my ability to love. But I was wrong.

The Tyrant? I asked.

No reply.

August 2nd

Does it matter who or what she is? When the fear of her leaving is stronger? E just walked into my life one day and one day could walk out. The sculpture is a week or two from completion. When it's finished, she will go. How to make her stay? Perhaps I could push the statue into the chasm? Buy another granite block & carve her all over again?

Rogue thought: What would Prof. H make of my 'process jour-nal' these days? ('<u>Drivel!</u>' he'd scrawl in the margins. '<u>Do not</u> taint the process with the personal!' Grade it an F.)

This morning, I woke before dawn & E's side of the mattress was bare. I got up and found her outside in the half-light staring at the Sangre de Cristo mountain range, just like the morning before. E was naked on the bench but appeared as immune to the chill as to the simmering heat of the studio. I stood behind her & she spoke.

E: Do you know of the Transit of Venus?

T: Vaguely. You mean when it crosses the sun?

E: The next one is in 2004.

T: In 22 years? I'll watch out for it.

E: After that, 2012. Then 2117.

T: We won't see the one in 2117, I guess.

E: I'm optimistic of my chances.

I went & sat beside her on the rough wooden bench. I gazed with her across the shadowed plains of yellow grass to the mountainous ridge extending from Colorado, the low peaks silhouetted against the mauvish sky.

E: I was born during the Transit of Venus.

T: Oh?

I kept my tone blasé. Concealed my hunger for these scattered crumbs of her.

T: What year?

E: 1761.

I laughed.

T: You're 200 years old?

E: Closer to 260.

I said nothing. For weeks I had waited for E to reveal something of herself, and even in fiction there might be truth.

E: Reborn during the Transit of Venus, I should say. Rebirth's more accurate.

T: Like a resurrection?

E: Yes.

Again, I said nothing. 1761. Rebirth. Resurrection. I didn't know what to think. But for some reason, I didn't entirely disbelieve her. We sat in silence for a while, watching the dip in the mountainous horizon from which Venus would ascend into the crepuscular sky of night's end. I was thinking of another question to ask about E's mysterious past. But E spoke first.

E: You think you're in love with me, don't you?

T: I don't think. I know.

E: First listen to what I have to say, then let me ask you again.

I looked sideways at her. And staring at a point beyond the Sangre de Cristo, waiting for the second planet in orbit of our sun, E spoke more than I'd ever known her to & what I can remember I put down here:

In 18th-century Russia, E told me, there lived a woman who'd married into a minor family of the Tsar. Let's call her Katerina. An elegant but conventional woman, known in St Petersburg society for her charm & refinement & devotion to family. On June 5th in 1761 a stranger came to her residence, claiming to have fought with Katerina's late brother in eastern Prussia. She was still grieving Aleksander (who'd died in battle in '57), so she invited the stranger into her parlor and they sat drinking tea as the man – a Muscovite – shared stories of Aleksander's valor & heroics in the Russian cavalry.

As Katerina wiped her tears, the Muscovite, apropos of nothing, said he'd heard she was an extraordinary artist. That her parlor trick was to sketch any guest in (he extracted a silver pocket watch from his vest dangled it by its chain) five minutes or less. That she had produced many vivid & lifelike portraits of her Tsarist milieu. That she was said to capture a person's essence. Katerina stirred her tea.

Oh, people are too kind.

I don't believe so, the man replied. Would you sketch me?

Anything for Aleksander's comrade-in-arms.

A servant brought her her easel and she sketched the dome of the Muscovite's head, his rapacious eyes, sharp nose & half-smirking mouth. A rara avis he was, but she depicted him well. The

Muscovite grinned at the portrait. Impressive, he said. His pocket watch spun lazily on its chain. Three minutes forty-six.

He confided in Katerina. He was a man of esoteric beliefs. A Luciferian. Would she like to learn about his theosophy? By this point Katerina was frightened and wanted him to leave. During her sketching, she'd detected a strange energy about him. A malevolent thrum unlike the creaturely hum of other human beings. So she said no. She was Eastern Orthodox. She had her own God. And a prior engagement to get ready for, so if he didn't mind . . .

The Luciferian interjected, Your God abandoned you, Katerina. Married you to that brute of a 2nd cousin who beats you and takes you by force at night. And your three sons have grown up as vicious & wicked as their father, haven't they? You wear the finest dresses, corsets and petticoats, but I know they hide bruises & burns from tongs, poker & flat-iron. Scars from the chamber pot shattered over your back. You have every appearance of a respectable family, but much depravity goes on behind these closed doors. Depravity visited upon <u>you</u>.

Katerina stood and ordered the man to leave. How dare he slander her husband and sons? But she was trembling. Aleksander had been completely ignorant of the abuse of his sister 'behind closed doors'. So how did the Luciferian know? Had the maidservants who helped dress her each morning betrayed her trust? The man saw her shaking hands and smiled.

Worship my God, he said. Make Him offerings and He will offer in return. Rid you of your sadistic husband for a start.

This gave Katerina pause.

How? she asked.

The man told her. One could become a Luciferian during the Transit of Venus. Only during this twice-a-century astronomical event, when Venus is a black dot traversing the sun, could one deviate to the 'left-hand path'. As luck would have it, there was a Transit of Venus the very next day – beginning at five o'clock on the morning of June 6th. At that precise time, Katerina should rouse her husband & sketch him, taking care to capture the expression in his eyes. Then she should show him the portrait <u>after</u> Venus had descended from the sky, but <u>before</u> the planet rose again on June 7th. Only in this 10-hour passage of time when Venus was absent could the ritual be completed. When Venus began to rise again, it would be too late.

Katerina asked, Why these rules?

Must our Venusian god explain Himself? the Luciferian replied.

And how long will it take for my husband to be . . . got rid of?

That depends on his fortitude of mind. On how many days or weeks he can stand the affliction before, well . . . either it kills him or he kills himself.

The <u>affliction</u>? exclaimed Katerina. I don't want Nikolai to <u>suffer</u> . . .

The Luciferian smiled. Do you not? The path to freedom is yours to take. I have told you how.

He rose to see himself to the door and Katerina realized, You never fought alongside my brother. You've never even met Aleksander, have you?

I wish you a long life, the man said.

Then he left.

So early the next morning, Katerina gritted her teeth, reached down between her husband's legs and roused him in the only manner she knew wouldn't send him into a rage. Afterwards Nikolai appeared stunned – but by something other than his wife's pleasuring. He did not object as she sketched him, and after Venus set (an astronomer was consulted for the exact time), Katerina showed him the portrait & completed her offering.

Six weeks later her husband shot himself in the head.

But as one oppressor departed, another came to stay.

The entity the Luciferian had brought into her parlor had now attached itself to Katerina – the incorporeal being casting its sinister shadow over her existence. The veils of reality shifted and rippled around it like the illusion they were and Katerina soon became cognizant of the underlying nature of things. Even the hierarchy in her family was inverted. When Katerina's firstborn son confronted her, accusing her of inadequate grief for his father, and reached to pull her hair, it was he who had his hair pulled by some unseen force. Wrenched so hard, follicles & scalp were detached from head & hurled like a wig against the chamber wall. He didn't howl or cry out. Only stumbled away in shock, bloody cranium now visible where once were chestnut locks.

Some months passed and just as Katerina was becoming used to life with the Venusian entity (whose baleful presence kept her sons at a distance), her health deteriorated. The illness was rapid, turning her sallow and causing her to bleed from every orifice and be incapacitated by stabbing pains in her internal parts. The doctor couldn't diagnose or cure her wasting disease. Only offered the prognosis that in a matter of days she'd be dead.

Such was her fate. Until a servant brought her a letter that a courier from Moscow had delivered by hand.

'Now is not your time to die, Katerina. Look to Venus as it rises. Phosphorus, bringer of light, will tell you what to do. Continue the propitiations – the Tyrant will choose who – and you will thrive. Perhaps even for as long as I have . . . Though after a thousand years this Luciferian has grown weary. The Transit of Venus is when a successor can be chosen. I chose you, Katerina. I bequeath my duties to you. And now I've departed the left-hand path without suffering for it, I live out my last days.'

So Katerina staggered from her bed, watched the Morning Star rise and understood what she had to do to survive. Her secondborn was the one the Tyrant wanted. She summoned him to her 'deathbed' before Venus rise (promising to leave him all her jewels if she could sketch him), then showed him the portrait once Venus had set and disappeared from the sky. And after Secondborn ran amok through the streets and got himself trampled to death beneath horses and carriage, Firstborn and Lastborn confronted Katerina with pistols and matricidal intent (though it was they who ended up massacred before any shot was fired – E did not elaborate).

And the woman lived on. Agonizingly lonely and struggling at first to survive, but stronger with each passing year. Cleverer and more resourceful. Near-clairvoyant in her insight into other minds. Her passion for life deepened and she traveled out of Russia and all over Europe and every continent of the world, unencumbered by any human bonds. Her weaknesses – her guilt and shame and moral superstitions – faded away. Venus traversed the sun three more times – in 1769, 1874 and 1882 – but she did not choose a successor. Not when life is so glorious. Victorious. Eudemonic. She never, ever wants it to end.

When E finished her story Venus had risen. Lucifer, son of the morning, outshining the few remaining stars. My heart beat erratically & my mouth was dry. What was she saying? That she was Katerina? That 220 years ago she'd made some Faustian pact?

E: So, let me ask you again. Do you still think you're in love with me?

Pinyon jays were raucous in the trees by the adobe studio. The sun was rising over the Sangre de Cristo and any minute the alarm clock would ring from inside the house. The story was impossible. Ludicrous. She was bullshitting or insane.

I said what I knew to be true.

T: It doesn't change how I feel.

Staring at Venus, fading like a ghost as the sun appeared in the sky, E moved her hand from her lap to the bench. Hooked her little finger over mine. I looked at the profile I knew intimately from weeks of carving it into granite & I recognized her pain.

August 8th

We drove to a diner in Questa this morning. Sat in the leatherette booth by the window as a waitress with a glass-domed pot sloshed coffee into our cups. Around us were locals; blue-collar men hunched over bacon and eggs at the counter. Families in church-going clothes having pancakes & maple syrup & French toast. I jangled my keys at E and said: I'm going to check my mailbox.

Something flickered across her face.

E: Our food will be here soon.

T: I'll be five minutes. I better do it now. Or I'll forget.

I leant across the Formica table & kissed her as though we were in the West Village and not some rural Catholic town with a population of 800. (Amazing how E makes me not give a fuck about 'public decency' or the angry dyke-hating stares.)

There were a couple of Citibank statements, in the black since E's cheque cleared. A letter from my mother (Cousin Harper's wedding this fall – I ought to attend <u>or it will look bad!</u>). A postcard of the Statue of Liberty. On the reverse: <u>It's about Larry. Please call me, urgently.</u> The postcard was signed by a Cynthia Nelson and the number underneath had a 212 dialling code.

The phone kiosk was over the road from the diner and I could see E drinking coffee in the leatherette booth as I dropped quarters in the slot & dialed. As Cynthia picked up and began to speak in anguished tones, I watched a white-aproned high-school-aged boy serve our breakfasts. Cynthia broke down into sobs nearly 2000 miles away, and E slathered butter on toast, squeezed ketchup on eggs, & tore into everything on her plate.

When I returned to the diner, E had finished eating & was smoking a Parliament. I slid into the booth, pushed my plate of waffles and bacon away. E frowned at me.

E: Everything okay?

T: Larry's dead. Jumped off the platform at Broadway-Lafayette as the F-train was pulling in.

E: <u>Oh.</u> I'm sorry, Theo. I know you go way back.

In her eyes, sympathy for my loss, but something hard & obdurate too. She ground her cigarette out on her plate.

T: Cynthia says Larry was acting weird when he got back from New Mexico. Jumpy. Paranoid. He was a lapsed Catholic but started praying & going to church for confession. Begged a priest for absolution – thought his soul was damned. He mentioned you to Cynthia. Several times.

She was quiet, E. Didn't ask in what context Larry had mentioned her.

T: What happened that night you drove him back to Taos?

E: I dropped him off at his hotel. Left the Buick & walked the two blocks back to mine.

I couldn't bear to look at her then. Out the window the sky gleamed blue & sunlight glared off the pale adobe buildings. I haven't cried since I was a small child, but I choked up then, realizing what was lost. I'd known Larry for 15 years – we'd met on Intro to Metalwork at Pratt and were room-mates in '72 on East 9th. He was a bon vivant. Could turn the dullest party into the wildest, most unforgettable night. We got drunk and slept together once. It was disastrous but brought us closer together somehow. I could tell Larry anything. Larry was the first person who knew I loved women more than men.

I looked back at E and for the first time, instead of lust & attraction, felt a skin-crawling aversion and guilt, as though I was somehow complicit in – <u>what</u>?

T: The funeral's on Wednesday and I want to fly out from Albuquerque tonight.

I started trembling. The signals between mind & body distorted, jumbled up.

E: I'll drive you back so you can pack.

She waved to the waitress, gestured for the check.

T: Larry went mad & killed himself. Like Katerina's husband.

E: In my story?

T: The coincidence is chilling.

E: Yes. But that's all it is – coincidence.

Perhaps then I should have interrogated her more. But my rational mind intervened: <u>coincidence</u>. How could it be other than that? We settled the bill, left the diner, & I made some calls from the kiosk over the road. Reserved a $150 ticket for the red-eye to JFK. We got to Albuquerque late afternoon after driving in silence nearly the whole way. Near the airport, without speaking, E pulled into a cheap motel and booked us a room for a couple of hours. Inside we stripped off our T-shirts & jeans and lay down together on the double bed. Blinds lowered. Fan rattling, blades whirling overhead.

She has a way of fucking me that makes me forget everything.

She unhooks my bra, peels down my underwear and gazes at me, her eyes dark and intent. Reads my body, knows what it wants. She touches me, kisses me, and I liquefy beneath her. She runs her tongue along the cleft of me & I dissolve, incapable of thought.

I make love to her with the same intensity, but she's always frustratingly out of reach. Always only half there. But today in the motel room something changed. The final time she came she shuddered against me, let out a cry. Then she clung to me on the stale & cigarette-burnt sheets as though something had broken inside her. As though she knew, like I did, it was the last time.

I can't explain it. Paradoxical in my head: devastation over Larry and what I suspect she did. Devastation that I won't see her again.

Above us, blades spin & clatter. The ceiling pulses with their shadow.

E: I have to go back to Berlin for a while.

T: Oh. Why?

E: For work.

I said nothing to this.

E: Do you still think you're in love with me, Theo?

T: Yes.

E: Don't worry. That will change.

Anger flared up in me then. I asked the question that had been on my mind since Questa.

T: If the Tyrant wanted me, what then?

From E, a pause. Then a slow, dark laugh.

E: I'll have to give that some thought.

She dropped me off at the airport terminal at eight thirty.

E: You're back next Saturday, right?

T: Yes. I'll finish the statue then. Ship it to you, if you forward me your address.

I'm in the final stages, refining the details with rifflers & tiny chisels & rasps. The statue's mimesis is outstanding. Somehow the enigma of E has been chiseled into stone. Her preternaturalness. Her separateness from others. Her life in extremis. And beneath it all, repressed in the core of her – a vulnerability, a need for connection, for love. It's my finest work. Yet I'm overcome by the conviction it shouldn't exist. That it belongs in the chasm, smashed up on the rocks.

I dragged my suitcase out the back. I said goodbye and walked resolutely toward the airport entrance before a pang of missing her had me turning back one last time to say please, stay in touch.

But E had driven away.

1985

April 6th

Here I am, back for the first time in 5 years.

My sublet's on East 6th near Avenue C, in a building overlooking a vacant lot of junk & the carcasses of burnt-out cars. Couldn't sleep after I arrived last night, so went out on the fire escape and smoked a cigarette, watching the dealers and dope fiends making their transactions amongst the smashed-up TVs. Eventually drifted off at 3 a.m. to the lullaby of distant sirens and a man shouting over & over, 'you don't got to fuck other people over to survive, mother-fucker' (wished he would shut up; he's preaching to the converted here).

Strolled around Bowery, St Marks Place & Tompkins Sq. Park this morning, taking in all that's changed. All the new galleries & bars, thrift stores & boutiques. All the hip new 23-year-olds with their Cyndi Lauper make-up, tulle skirts & fingerless leather gloves. Had a slice of Stromboli's pizza for lunch, then sat on the terrace outside Cafe Orlin, where I used to drink tea for hours w/ my sketchbook back before I left. Barbara Tait (the performance artist, '12 Proposals to Strangers' etc.) was walking by with her poodle Snooki and came and sat with me. Surprised by how happy I was to see her again, how happy I am to be back in general . . . I was so frustrated & bitter when I left. So cynical about the mechanisms by which NY artists ascend (nepotism, cult of personality, coke-snorting party cliques etc.). Nothing's changed, of course. But I have commercial representation now, so it bothers me less. I no longer feel as though I'm simmering on the sidelines, curdling at others' undeserved success . . .

Anyway, enough griping. Meeting w/ Magenta tomorrow (Semaphore East closed today). On Thurs, interview with East Village

Eye, then a reunion in Chinatown with classmates from Pratt. On Friday driving upstate to Buffalo w/ David to visit Professor Carey. Then, next Wednesday, the opening (yikes!).

As for tonight, my only plans are a beer & cigarette out on the fire escape. Some of the 'anarcho-artist collective' squatting in the adjoining tenement are in the lot, scavenging for scraps (for sculptures? furnishings?). They make me wonder why I'm spending $500 to sublet a lousy studio w/ intermittent hot water in a building just as graffitied, dilapidated and structurally unsound as theirs. Then I remember my 3 months in the Rivington commune in '77 – the rotas & despotic 'democratic' meetings, the pervasive odor of lentil stew & BO – and I shudder & decide it's $500 well spent.

April 7th

Got to the Semaphore East at noon today and Magenta pounced as I walked through the door, waving a copy of Artforum magazine.

Theodora! she shrieked. Have you seen your interview?

She opened the latest issue to a full-page photograph of me in my Taos County studio. White tresses flowing over my shoulders. Wielding a circular saw in my dusty dungarees with Phosphorus & Herosphorus in the shot behind me. I skimmed the accompanying text: 'Carved out of black basalt and white, blue-veined marble, the statues in Waite's "Everlasting" series are both neoclassical and ultrafuturistic . . . A dazzling feat of craftsmanship . . . The sculptural equivalent of long-exposure photographs . . . The distorted blur of human heads and bodies an attempt to convey our temporal persistence . . . Avant-garde & neo-Renaissance . . . Kinetic & multidimensional' etc.

More baloney than a Newark diner, but feeling my ego inflating, I shut the magazine.

Fabulous, isn't it? Magenta beamed. They gave you 4 pages! And you look like a fucking goddess, Theo. Maybe we can nudge your prices up?

Dollar signs were practically flashing in her eyes & dismayed by the vulgarity I changed the subject to the installation as a fame-struck (by me?) gallery assistant brought me an espresso.

Hard to believe that it was just 6 months ago I mailed my query letter and some Polaroids to Semaphore East. Or that just two weeks after that Magenta descended on my studio like an alien from outer space with her purple asymmetric haircut and silver lamé dress. Took one look at the sculptures in the Everlasting series, lifted her wraparound shades and exclaimed: Theodora Waite. You are the real fucking deal.

This afternoon, Magenta, the technicians & I got to work, unpacking the sculptures from the wooden crates, then walking around Semaphore's vast white spaces, discussing the exhibition design. Hours of standing & looking, bending & lifting, drilling & climbing ladders & me and Magenta butting heads. Around 5 o'clock Magenta ordered in sushi from a Japanese restaurant, then we went to Ben Ari for the Kiki Álvarez opening. I usually hate openings. All the small talk with people trying to figure out how successful you are while indiscreetly scanning over your shoulder for someone more important to network with. All the pretending not to notice the famous artists and socialites whilst secretly jock-eying to talk to them. But the Álvarez show was different – people now recognized me from the Artforum piece (Magenta: You stand out like Warhol with that white hair) and came up to congratulate me on my show. Even the biggest celebrity at the opening, Sybil Jackman (whose Guggenheim exhibition I skipped class & took the Amtrak 4 hours to see in high school), shuffled up to me in her Goodwill rummage-bin clothes. Squinted at me from behind cat-eye glasses as she said, Say, aren't you . . . ?

Theodora Waite, Magenta burst in. A sensational new sculptor, with her show opening at Semaphore East next week. She's phe-nomenal. Truly the next big thing.

Sybil glanced at Magenta – at her purple hair, her leather bond-age dress, her too-bright eyes & the traces of white residue around her nose. Then she leant in closer to me.

That so, sweetie? Well, just make sure you don't go ruining your-self by believing all the hype.

April 14th

E is here in New York.

I was on East 8th tonight, walking home from dinner, slightly fuzzy with wine, when there was a shriek of laughter across the street. The shrieker was a peroxide blonde in a ripped polyester negligee & fishnets, standing with two punks loading guitars and an amp into a hatchback outside 8BC. The blonde was so eye-catching with her flamboyant make-up & bangles jangling up tattooed arms, it took me a second to notice E next to her, androgynous-looking with a shaven head & baggy shirt and jeans. Shocked, I stared at her under the yellow streetlight. Was I mistaken? No, I was not. There was no mistaking the imposing presence of her. Those dark eyes.

I yelled her name and began to dash across East 8th but had to leap back from a honking yellow cab & rumbling truck. By the time I got to the other side, E and the punks were in the hatchback, pulling away from the curb. I yelled after them, but they didn't stop.

The black doors to 8BC vibrated with the shouted vocals and high-speed drumming of a live hardcore band. A green-mohawked punk was smoking outside, and I asked if he knew the band that had just driven away.

Yeah, The Fallopian Tubes, he said. They were just onstage. Fucking diabolical.

Do you know where they went?

He looked me up and down. I was in a Burberry trench (a hand-me-down from Aunt Cicely), Milanese leather boots (ditto), and my white hair was in a French twist. Not 8BC's usual clientele.

I need to speak to the woman they're with, I said. With the shaven head. Do you know her?

Nah. But she should watch out for Deedee. That's the singer. One of those kamikaze bitches, y'know?

I stared up 8th Street, in the direction they'd disappeared, knowing Deedee was the one who ought to watch out.

★

I keep in the back of my journal the pencil sketch E did of me – the one I found in my studio when I got back from Larry's funeral. Me in the summer of '82, standing in my yard with a long-barreled shotgun in one hand and a clutch of dead rabbits in the other. Tall and rangy in shorts and vest over unharnessed breasts. Zinc-oxide stripes on my cheeks and my hair standing out like a mane around my head. It's unnerving, her portrait. E knows her subject well – the fierce independence & the aching loneliness within. It's truer than any photograph. Truer than any reflection in the mirror. She's captured my <u>essence</u>, you could say.

Since that summer, I think of her every single day. Several times a day.

I think of her smile, her laughter, her words & idiosyncrasy of mind. When I masturbate I conjure her and only her to mind, and in the 2½ years since she drove away from Albuquerque Airport there's been no one else.

But she's more than an ex-lover whose hooks are still sunk in my heart. I think of her as I work in the studio. The destabilizing effect she had on me & my reality is all I want to express. She's the dark muse behind every sculpture in the Everlasting series. Behind every sculpture I've yet to make.

Then I think of Larry & the agony he went through losing his mind. I think of the F-train slamming into him as he leapt from the platform, mangling him against the tracks.

It's 4 a.m. The opening's tomorrow & I really should get some sleep. But the pendulum of my mind won't stop swinging back & forth.

<u>You don't got to fuck people over to survive, motherfucker</u>, yelled the man on Avenue C.

E would disagree, perhaps.

April 15th

3 a.m. & I just got back to my sublet. My head is spinning from all the booze and coke (yes, Magenta got me) and all the names and faces and flattery and dancing at the Aztec Lounge.

The opening <u>went well</u>. Magenta's hard work w/ press releases & promotion meant a great turnout, w/ people spilling out into the street. Three of my sculptures (Phosphorus, Ishtar Terra & Aphrodite Terra) sold and Hugo the gallery manager tells me buyers are interested in the rest. Before the show, I let Magenta talk me into borrowing her black YSL jumpsuit w/ shoulder pads and getting my white hair 'blown out' at a West Village salon – and I was glad I did. It was the high-fashion armor I needed to get through the nerve-jittering first half of the opening. The second half just <u>soared</u>.

I ought to be unconscious right now, collapsed on my futon. But I'm wide awake, and not just because of Magenta's coke.

I was distracted by thoughts of E all night. I'd got it into my head that E <u>must</u> know about the show – must have read the preview in the Village Voice or seen one of the flyers pasted about, and I was on tenterhooks that she'd show up. I kept twisting my neck to check out everyone coming through the door, scanning the gallery crowd for her shaven head & dark eyes (which would shine with amusement at the loud & phony scene, and with approval – I hoped – at my work).

Anyway, she didn't stop by. Naive of me to think she would. That she'd compromise herself in that way.

Do I want to see her again? Yes and no. The pendulum swings back and forth.

But perhaps there's a way I can get closer to the truth of what happened to Larry. The latest East Village Eye came out tonight & I picked one up on the stumble home. Tore through the listings in the back pages, until I found what I was looking for, 4th on the line-up of 6 bands at CBGB's in 2 nights' time.

April 18th

The mohawked punk outside 8BC wasn't wrong about The Fallopian Tubes being diabolical. The guitar, bass & drums were shambolic in the manner a punk band can get away with, but Deedee fell way beneath the standards of even the most anarchic of singers. Chaotically drunk or high, she staggered about in a leopard-print fur coat & heels and shrieked tunelessly into her mic. She forgot the words to entire verses and instead rambled about an uncle whose hearing aid picks up signals from space and a neighborhood kid who tortures frogs. The audience of 12 jeered or clapped sarcastically between songs, and when Deedee tripped and landed on her hands and knees near the end, her bandmates looked on in disgust, as laughing, she rolled about on the scuffed & duct-tape-covered stage.

After the set, I followed Deedee to the women's bathroom. Waited outside the decrepit stalls, staring at the claustrophobic wall-to-wall graffiti & peeling flyers for bygone shows as Deedee snorted up long lines of powder inside. When she reappeared, she went straight to the broken shard of mirror screwed into the tiles above the sink, flaring her nostrils and staring at herself with a maniacal coked-up intensity. How old was she? 25? 26? She took a tube of lipstick out of a leopard-print pocket and smeared it all over her mouth, and I admit, I wanted to shake her then. I'm so sick of these messy damaged women acting out their psychodramas all over the East Village. Get your act together, I wanted to say. Find some mode or setting other than self-destruct. But instead I politely asked if she had a minute to speak with me.

Deedee turned to me with dilated eyes.

You a narc?

I told her I wasn't. That I saw her outside 8BC with E the other night. I asked if they were friends.

Who are you talking about? she asked.

The woman with the shaven head? I said. German. Or Russian . . . ?

Deedee blinked at me.

Olga? From Belarus?

For a second I was confounded. But it made sense. Perhaps E was an alias too.

Do you know how I can reach her?

She's gone to Tokyo. To learn rope bondage or some shit. For her performance art.

She's a performance artist?

Deedee shrugged. Then she moved her face closer to mine, her eyes fervid & intense beneath her peroxide hair with its dark & greasy inches of roots. Her skin was grimy as though she hadn't washed in days and erupting with pimples and a nasty-looking staph infection on her left cheek. Mascara flaked from her lashes and when she spoke her breath reeked as though something had crawled into her throat to die.

You been to the higher place?

The higher place?

I have. Olga turned me into an angel and I flew up into the face of God with the rising sun, and God got a hard-on and fucked me so hard and deep He turned me inside out. And when I was inside out I could see everything. Snakes were coming out of my eyes and those snakes had more snakes coming out of their eyes and every eye was a moment. Baby Dee-dums in the crib. Deirdre in 4th grade. Deedee on the Greyhound, from Lincoln, Nebraska to NYC. I was living every moment of my life and dying every moment of my death. And I saw you too, Theodora, speaking to me now, like Detective fucking Columbo in your fucking narc coat.

How do you know my name?

Up until that moment she'd sounded like someone on angel dust or LSD. Drug-addled & easy to dismiss. But her knowledge of my name made me lurch & I stared into Deedee's eyes for an explanation and her eyes stared back; black and enormous with immeasurable depths. For a moment I was so convinced someone other than Deedee was staring out at me, a sound nearly escaped my mouth.

My name, I repeated. How do you know it?

Perhaps she'd seen the Village Voice preview? Perhaps E had told her? But instead of answering, Deedee opened her leopard-print coat, holding it wide like a flasher to expose her scrawny body in her black negligee and fishnets.

See that rose? On my right tit? Used to be on the left. All my tattoos have flipped. That's what happens in the higher place. You get flipped.

Deedee let go of her coat and put a finger to her lips.

Shhh . . . Don't tell on me though. I don't wanna be in no freak-show. I don't wanna be on T.V.

She turned and walked out, just as a flock of crucifix & bustier-wearing Madonna clones walked in, blocking my way. I pushed past them, then past the crowd gathered for the next band, catching sight of Deedee's peroxide head leaving through CBGB's main doors.

When I got out onto Bowery, she was gone.

The other members of The Fallopian Tubes had packed up and left also, so I went to the bar and asked to speak to the booker. He came out of the back, and when I told him I thought Deedee was in trouble, he laughed.

Yeah, no shit.

Do you have a number for her? I asked.

Seeing my distress, he went through a ledger under the bar and scribbled something down.

That's for the guitarist, he said. Though Donnie looked <u>pissed</u> when they were leaving tonight. Gonna give Deedee the heave-ho, I reckon.

Then he laughed again, showing metal fillings in back teeth.

They should re-form as The Testicles. Now <u>that's</u> a band I'll put on my bill.

I don't scare easy. I've lived on my own for 4½ years in the back of beyond with only a shotgun to defend myself from potential rapists & murderers. I walk about my property without a flashlight in the night & I don't believe in ghosts. But the encounter with Deedee has shaken me up. The liquor store whiskey I bought on the walk home tonight is already 1/3rd gone.

Linda, a classmate from SUNY, has offered to sublet her Bleecker Street apartment to me while she goes to an ashram in India. It's rent controlled, $400 a month, and Prof. Carey has offered me a part-time teaching gig at Parsons and some studio space. New York is welcoming me back with open arms, but I find myself pulling away.

Staying here will be to the detriment of my work. My creative energy's frittered away on openings & parties & other distractions. But that's only part of it. I can feel the disturbance of E here, somewhere in this crowded metropolis, the ripples of her destruction radiating out through the sidewalks & city blocks.

I dialed The Fallopian Tubes guitarist from a vandalized, piss-stinking phone booth outside, but the line was disconnected. I've gone through all the listings in the Village Voice, but they have no other shows lined up. Perhaps I could use some of the money coming in from the Semaphore East show to hire a PI to track Deedee down? Or stake out the Lower East Side drug dens until I run into her, speak to her & offer some help?

But _what_ help? I get the feeling that whatever happens to Deedee is _fait accompli_.

Why am I so shaken up? It was what I saw in her eyes, I think. The black whorling possibility of a 'higher place' where Venus is God and the devout can breathe underwater and heal their own wounds and live for 260 years.

I want nothing to do with it. All of my instincts tell me to book a one-way ticket back to NM, to get the fuck out.

I need to go back, to focus on my work. All that matters now is the art.

1988

October 16th

At quarter past 7 – knocking.

I paused feeding Shilah, and Wolf and Eddy looked up from their bowls of green chile stew. Wolf frowned at me. We hadn't heard any car approach.

You expecting anyone? he asked.

I shook my head & looked at Shilah, wriggling in his highchair, toothlessly grinning and reaching for the spoon of mushy carrots & peas I held suspended halfway to his mouth. Who would walk through all the miles of Taos County emptiness to our door? I thought about the shotgun locked away in the bedroom cabinet. Should I get it?

Knock knock.

Wolf rose up.

Stay there, he said to Eddy and me.

At the door, Wolf's 6 ft 3 frame blocked the view of the yard. But her voice – European, with polished vowels – a voice I hadn't heard in 6 years – drifted in, and my panic was as though I was behind the wheel of a car skidding suddenly on black ice. Watch your brother, I told Eddy, and rushed to throw myself in front of my husband like a human shield.

Out in the yard, E was thinner. A heavy coat hung from her gauntness & through her sunken cheeks & recessed eyes, her skull made its presence known. Her hair was longer but sparser and frayed at the ends. AIDS, I thought, because she reminded me of all the men I'd known in NYC, wasting away as their immune systems failed. But her eyes still had some of their dark mesmeric power and I knew she wasn't any less dangerous.

She says she's a friend of yours, Wolf said.

He frowned at me. Suspicious but unthreatened by this strung-out junkie-looking woman who'd come crawling out of the backcountry darkness. Looking for a handout, he no doubt thought. E's eyes flickered from me to Wolf's rough-hewn face, leathery from two decades of working in construction under the New Mexico sun, his nose broken by a tire iron in a bar fight in '72. Sensing her interest, I didn't introduce them. I turned and pushed him indoors.

Leave this with me. Go and watch the boys.

Keep the door open, he murmured. Shout if you need me.

He shot E a warning look, then retreated inside.

The October night was chilly and I shivered as I stepped out into the yard. I could feel E taking in my milk-stained blouse, buttoned up wrong after feeding Shilah. My babyfood-splattered hair and the exhaustion in and around my eyes.

Theo, E said. What's it been? 6 years?

Her voice was weaker, hoarser. But retained some of its power, like her gaze.

Much has changed, she said, nodding at the kitchen window, bright with lights powered by the solar panels Wolf had installed & Eddy's colorful paintings on the walls. Wolf was pacing, bouncing Shilah against his plaid-shirted chest, and casting wary glances at E & I in the yard. Eddy was in the doorway, scowling as he ran a toy car up and down the door jamb.

Eddy, I said sharply. Go back inside.

My stepson slunk away. How long had E been standing outside in the dark, watching our family dinner? I'd never thought to get blinds or curtains before, but now it seemed a terrible oversight.

Your husband's Navajo, E remarked. Your pearls-clutching mother must be thrilled.

Remembering her covetous look at Wolf, I gestured to my adobe studio.

Let's speak in there.

Under the fluorescent strip lighting, E looked even more wretched. I watched the pale haunt of her moving around, casting the dark wounds of her eyes over all that had changed. Over Shilah's playpen of cuddly toys and mobile of sun, moon & stars. Over Eddy's home-schooling table, covered in plasticine models of dinosaurs, wooden abacus and assorted children's books. There wasn't much evidence left of my stone carving. Any sculptures and marble and alabaster blocks that could topple and crush a child had been put in storage. The sharp chisels and diamond-tipped drills and saws had been locked away. I could feel E's judgment of my child-safe studio. Well, let her fucking judge.

What do you want? I asked.

She turned to me and the stark push of bones in her face shocked me again. A cold sore blistered on her lip & I realized I'd never known the fortress of her body to show signs of invasion before. The only time I'd seen her bleed, the wound was gone in hours. Something I have trouble these days believing ever really happened.

I wanted to see you, E said. The summer I spent here . . . has stayed with me.

She gazed at me, inappropriately intense. As though we were still on fucking terms and it hadn't been 6 years. I wasn't sure how to respond. The summer of '82 has stayed with me too, but the state of enchantment I was in then frightens me now. The constant flow of my energy into the dual rivers of creativity & sex, and the way I remained undepleted, as though the unnatural forces that sustained E were sustaining me too.

I saw you, I said, on the Lower East Side. In April '85.

You're mistaken.

You were with Deedee, the punk singer.

Who?

She was as poker-faced as the time I questioned her about Larry. But my conviction didn't waver as it had done then.

I can't talk to you if you're just going to lie to me, I said.

E shivered then – a shudder moving through her weak & feverish body. All at once her defenses seemed to fall.

I'm dying, she said.

I could see how badly she was suffering. But I couldn't go to her, extend any part of myself to her. Not when my husband and sons were only 30 yards away.

I can't live the way I live anymore, she went on. I can't keep doing what I do to survive.

What you did to Larry? To Deedee? I asked.

Her eyes met mine.

Yes. So I'm ending things.

My first attempt to speak caught in my throat. On the second, I asked, How many others . . . ? If you've . . . lived as long as you say?

I honestly don't know.

Another shiver and E swayed on her feet. She looked frail but she was monstrous. A <u>monster</u>. I didn't believe for a second she'd changed her mind about how she kept herself alive. The love of her life is life itself and I doubted that had changed.

All I wanted was for her to be gone, but E said, I don't want to die alone. So I came here, Theo, to die with you.

My heart slammed & my response had the force of repulsion.

You <u>can't</u> stay here.

E's face twisted with momentary pain. But then she hardened. Laughed a short, bitter laugh which turned into a hacking cough. She shook, coughing into her hand, before wiping a dark & bloody smear onto her coat.

I can drive you back to where you're staying, I offered.

E suppressed another shiver & lifted her chin, as though to regain some dignity & pride.

I don't need a ride. I'll walk.

I nodded & did not insist the dying woman accept my offer of a ride.

But before I go, I need painkillers, E said. Strongest you've got. And liquor, for the road . . .

I turned to run to the house, to get her what she wanted. But not before catching sight of E's hurt at my desperation for her to be gone.

In the kitchen, Shilah was squirming on the changing mat, kicking his plump legs as Wolf leant over him, sleeves rolled up, pinning him into a diaper. Eddy was at the window, rolling his toy car on the ledge and glowering through the darkness to the studio.

Eddy, I said. Go get the pills for Daddy's back pain from the bathroom cabinet.

I went to the cupboard where the whiskey was kept on a high shelf. Wolf lifted Shilah, freshly changed, into his arms.

What's going on? Is your friend in some kind of trouble?

I grabbed the Wild Turkey. I hadn't touched it in months and Wolf (12 years sober) had never touched it. I was relieved there was still 2/3rds left.

She's not well. She just wants painkillers and liquor and then she'll go.

I can drive her back to wherever she's going, Wolf said.

<u>No</u>. Please, stay away from her. She'll walk.

My vehemence took Wolf aback. He dropped his voice.

Look, is she using? Heroin? Meth?

No. She . . . she's promised to leave if I give her something for the pain, so that's what I'm doing.

<u>Theo</u>.

Swamped by my faded high-school lacrosse team sweater, Eddy stood behind me with the plastic container of pills. His scruffy hair needed a cut, but he refused, wanting to grow it long and wear it in a ponytail like Wolf.

That lady's not a regular person, he said. She's a skinwalker.

I swallowed back my unease.

Skinwalkers don't exist, Eddy, Wolf said patiently. You've got to stop believing Grandma Ann's stories.

<u>Please, Theo</u>. Don't go out there.

My stepson tugged at my shirt, his eyes pleading. I took the codeine from him.

10 minutes. Then she'll be gone.

When I re-entered the studio, E was seated in her coat at the home-schooling table. She glanced up from the pages of the exercise book she was flipping through – pages of Eddy's compositions of talking animals and Diné myth.

How old's your stepson? she asked.

7, I said.

Where's his mother?

Dead.

How? E asked.

I put the pills and whiskey down on the table. That's all we have.

And the little half-Navajo, he's 18 months?

I didn't say anything.

And a third boy on the way. Congratulations.

My shock & anger must've shown in my face. I'm still in the first trimester and not at all showing. I've no idea of the gender yet. I folded my arms low over my stomach, as though to protect my gestating baby from E's penetrating gaze. But she'd turned her attention to the codeine, unscrewing the child-proof cap and shaking half a dozen out. She threw them into her mouth, washed them down with a long swallow of whiskey, then closed her eyes.

Ah, she said. Small pleasures.

I willed her to go.

Dying feels awful, said E. Every minute, I want to change my mind . . . There's the possibility that death will be worse. That the Tyrant's waiting for me on the other side. I'm meant to choose a successor to serve him, but Venus won't transit for another 16 years.

Suddenly my perspective shifted. I could sense the malign shadow the Tyrant cast from the 'higher place', seeping over E and me and my unborn child. A stampede of terror in my chest, I said, I want you to go. <u>Now</u>.

Slowly, E stood up. Wild Turkey swilled as she drank again. One of Eddy's toy trucks was on the rug by her shoe. She kicked it out of the way and cast her gaze again around my studio.

I barely recognize this place.

It's temporary, I replied. My husband's building an extension for the kids. Then he's quitting his job to look after them full-time.

I stopped myself. <u>So what</u> if she thinks I've turned my back on sculpting to be a housewife?

He's a good man, E said. I can see that. But I have to say, I'm surprised.

This time I didn't take the bait. I wasn't going to defend loving who I love to E.

E started toward the door, then turned to me with her dark & devastated eyes.

When you've lived as long as I have. When you've encountered as many people. Only then do you realize how <u>rare</u> the connection we had was.

She stared at me & I could feel something weakening & buckling within. The truth of what she said was drawing me back. Our bond had once been powerful & intoxicating. But too destructive to sustain.

It wasn't real, I said. But my husband, my children, they are.

<u>Theo.</u>

We both turned. Wolf was in the doorway. The calm interrogation of his eyes & broad-shouldered presence didn't reassure me as they usually did. Only sharpened my fear and awareness of what I had to lose.

Everything okay?

I was just leaving, E said quietly.

Wolf entered the studio as E drifted out, gripping the bottle of Wild Turkey by the neck, without a backward glance or word of farewell. Wolf placed his hand on my shoulder and we watched as E was swallowed up by the darkness of the trail leading 4 miles back to the highway. I didn't allow myself to feel relief. Not yet.

Eddy wanted me to bring the shotgun, Wolf said. To scare 'the skinwalker' away. <u>But man</u>, she looks <u>weak</u>. She really okay to walk by herself?

She's fine, I said.

Sensing the subject was closed, Wolf asked nothing more about her, and made no attempt to pry into my past.

Well, he said. Let's get back to the boys.

5.30 a.m. and I'm at the kitchen table as my husband and sons sleep. Inside me, my unborn child is sleeping too and to combat my nausea I sip black tea. My levels of HCG usually rise about this time, waking me up. Though tonight (or today, now) there's been no sleep for my hormones to disrupt.

We went to bed at 11 and made love, the passion and urgency I brought to the act surprising then pleasing Wolf. A hunger that I haven't felt since before Shilah was born overtook me as I moved with my husband, pressing him into me as though to keep us from ever coming apart. Grateful for his solidity, his body muscled from years of hauling timber and bricks. Grateful for the fact he never pretends to be someone he's not. For all the ways he isn't E.

Afterward, he slept and I've been up since. Writing in this journal, then pacing with the lights out. Gazing out the kitchen window at the yard in the moonlight, the breeze rustling the ponderosa tree. Listening out for Eddy's cries of night terrors or Shilah's whimperings for attention or milk, though for once, neither of them has needed me, leaving me alone with my obsessive fears.

Just 20 minutes ago I was sitting at the table when some compulsion made me stand up, walk across the kitchen, open the back door and step outside. In the clearing, I turned to the dark craggy mountains and there it was. Venus. Appearing on the horizon, having summoned me to watch its ascent. Standing in the yard I could feel the pull of the Morning Star on me, just as the oceans and seas feel the pull of the moon. A shining influence that wasn't gravity, but some other force emanating from this planet of volcanoes and solar winds, spinning backwards so slowly that a Venusian day is longer than a year. Watching Lucifer rise, I knew that somewhere out there E was watching too. That she was powerless to defy or oppose its command.

Soon Wolf's alarm clock will sound and he'll rise and turn on the bathroom faucet to wash and shave, the plumbing he installed two summers ago shuddering with the exertion of drawing water from the nearby creek. Then he'll go to the stove and make skillet eggs and bacon for himself, and oatmeal with cinnamon and raisins for me and our sons. And over breakfast, all the noise & demands of the kids will distract me from my fears. But when Wolf gets up to leave I'll see him to the door. 'That woman who came last night . . .' I'll say, 'if you see her today, stay away from her. Promise me you'll <u>stay</u>

away.' Wolf will be confused, but nod and promise. I'll kiss him goodbye and watch him get in the pickup and drive away, certain that Wolf has never broken a single promise to me yet.

October 17th

I don't know what to do.

Why didn't I <u>fucking strangle her</u> when I had the chance?

Wolf finished work at 5 today and should've been home at 6. But at 6.30 p.m. we were still waiting for him, the macaroni & cheese drying out in the oven, the boys fractious & fed up in front of the TV.

At 8 p.m. I put the boys to bed. Two hours later I was hustling them up and into the Chevy in their PJs to drive to use the pay-phone on Hwy 522 (cursing AT&T for refusing to extend the telegraph wires to our house). I dialled Wolf's co-worker who said he'd clocked out at 5 p.m., just as Wolf always did.

I drove next to the police station in Questa, leaving the boys locked in the Chevrolet outside. The officer on duty called around the hospitals to check if Wolf had been brought into the ER. He had not. No serious accidents tonight, vehicular or otherwise.

He probably went for a beer with his buddies, the officer said. It's only 11. He's probably driving home right now.

I told the officer Wolf's a recovering alcoholic and hasn't been to a bar since '76. I told the officer about E. That I suspected she'd harmed him in some way. He opened his notepad to take down some details. 5 ft 4. Terminally ill . . .

He lowered his pen and looked at me. You sure this lady's a threat?

We got home around midnight. Shilah was asleep as I carried him from the car to the house, but Eddy wide awake, his 7 y/o judgment boring into me. Even as he obeyed my instructions to get into bed, his eyes were mutinous.

That skinwalker lady's got him, he said.

Go to sleep now, Eddy.

The skinwalker's got him and it's <u>your</u> fault.

I wanted to yell at him to shut up, this obstreperous child. But keeping my voice steady, I said, Your father will be back in the morning.

I left the bedroom & stood outside the door, shaking with the certainty that what Eddy had said was true.

October 20th

Wolf came back and I am broken.

1 a.m. the night before last I was woken by someone moving around the darkness of our bedroom, pulling things out of drawers and stuffing them into a bag.

I clicked on the bedside light. I cried out, <u>Wolf</u>. Where have you been?

I sprang out of bed, flew at him. Low and growling, he said, <u>Don't</u>, Theo. Don't touch me.

Where have you been? I reported you missing.

He jerked away from me and fiercely whispered, Keep your voice down, I don't want to wake the boys.

In the unzipped bag: some clothes & our emergency cash & credit cards.

What's going on? I asked.

I can't be around you and the kids.

<u>Why?</u> Where are you going?

I don't know. Motel maybe.

He zipped the bag & slung it over his shoulder.

I stared into my husband's face for answers and a half-stranger stared back. Wolf's tire-iron broken nose and crooked teeth were angled wrong. The scar dissecting his left eyebrow now dissected the right. But it was Wolf's eyes that made the scream rise in my throat. Or the other consciousness staring out of their dark centers, now cohabiting his skull. The same one I'd encountered in the bathroom of CBGB's in '85, in a woman I suspect to be long dead. (<u>That's what happens in the higher place. You get flipped</u>.)

What did she do to you? I whispered.

Not here. We can talk in the truck.

I followed him outside in my nightdress, too shocked to feel the cold or stabbing of stones against my bare soles. He led me in silence five minutes down the moonlit trail to where he'd left the pickup, far enough away so the engine rumble wouldn't wake us.

In the darkness of the truck, I looked at my husband, fighting back tears.

Wolf. Please talk to me.

Staring straight ahead, he did.

2 miles from home the previous evening, Wolf saw someone collapsed up ahead on the trail. He slammed on the brakes, jumped out of the truck & ran over. It was E. Barely conscious. He lifted her in his arms (she weighed nothing), strapped her in the passenger seat & drove her to the Taos Medical Center, where hospital staff wheeled her away on a gurney. He remembered his promise to <u>stay away</u> & was anxious to return to me & the kids. But a sense of responsibility kept him in the ER. He had to make sure E was okay.

An hour later E appeared before him in her heavy coat, startling Wolf. She glanced nervously at the empty ER reception desk. She had no insurance, she whispered. Could Wolf just drive her away? Though Wolf doubted she was well enough to leave the hospital, he was sympathetic to her predicament. 5 years ago he'd injured his back onsite & his insurance wouldn't cover the surgery or rehab, burdening him with debt he was still paying off. So they left.

Driving up Hwy 522, Wolf asked E where she'd been headed when she collapsed.

To the chasm, E replied. Where all Theo's failures end up.

Wolf didn't know what the chasm was but didn't ask. Only followed her directions to a rust-corroded trailer on cinder blocks on a lonely tract of wasteland off Hwy 378. E was still trembling and pale, so Wolf got out of the truck and helped her to the trailer and up the steps.

The single-wide was similar to the one he'd rented back when he was a twenty-something alcoholic, subsisting on paychecks from his

Walgreens security guard job. Everything inside it from the worn linoleum to the roach traps reminded Wolf of the squalor of his past, back when he'd needed liquor upon waking to steady his shaking hands.

E gestured to a folding chair at a folding card table and Wolf sat, even as a voice in his head urged him, get the fuck out. E went to the kitchenette. She returned with two tumblers of whiskey – deep measures without ice, just the way he likes it – and put one down on the card table in front of him.

I don't drink, Wolf said.

But E smiled & replied, You look like you could use one, though.

Then she turned and put a cassette into the tape deck. Returned to the table, drinking her neat whiskey as Jimi Hendrix played.

My husband said, That'll only make you feel worse.

Worse than dying?

Wolf was silent. If a terminally ill woman wanted to spend what remained of her life drinking, that was her own business. He was about to push his folding chair back and leave, when E added, Dying's what I want. My husband shot himself in the head. Then I lost my sons, one after the other. I don't know why I held on so long.

I'm sorry, Wolf said.

Leaving E right then seemed as wrong as abandoning her in the hospital would've been, and Wolf found he couldn't rise from his chair. E drank some more whiskey, and continued, Theo mentioned you lost your wife too. It must be hard for Eddy, losing his mother so young. Hard for you both. How did she die?

Wolf wasn't going to say anything at first, but he looked into the depths of understanding in E's eyes, and heard himself telling her about how he came back from 3 days away on a construction site to find Stephanie dead, their 2-year-old son clinging to her ODed corpse.

You were angry, E said. Very angry.

I hated her for a while.

I bet you did.

But Steffy wasn't a bad person. It wasn't her fault; she just came from a very damaged place. Something Theo doesn't get.

E smiled. It exasperates Theo that we all aren't the same as her. She doesn't get how easy resilience and strength of character are when generational wealth and entitlement flow through your veins. She doesn't know what it is to come from poverty. <u>Suffering.</u>

Wolf didn't defend me – he didn't disagree with what E had said. They sat without speaking for a while, then Me & Bobby McGee came on the tape deck and Wolf said, Steffy loved this song. Loved singing along.

What was her voice like?

Beautiful. Husky. She sang in a community choir on the rez.

What other singers did Steffy like?

As E asked more questions about Stephanie, and as Wolf answered them – briefly at first, then at length – he realized how seldom he got to talk about his first wife in this way. That her death – abhorrently selfish and irresponsible to most – had overshadowed her life. And he realized he loved her still. That the grief and pain were still there, the tourniquet keeping it all inside so tight and constricting around his chest he suddenly couldn't breathe. Somehow the glass of whiskey was in his hand; he was drinking from it. And as he ended 12 years of sobriety, nothing had ever tasted so sublime.

On the 2nd or 3rd whiskey Wolf stopped making up excuses to tell me about where he'd been. He stopped trying to leave and settled in for the night. He knew I'd be worried, but the warmth of the liquor spread through him, and as he answered E's questions about Steffy and his family, unburdening himself of all the shameful things he usually kept inside, he could almost hear the clink of heavy chains unshackling from his psyche.

E listened with compassion, without judgment. She poured him another drink.

At what hour did his perception begin to change? The trailer's blinds were lowered but Wolf could see the gray light before day bleeding in around their edges when everything surrounding him became brighter and began to pulsate. It wasn't like LSD or mescaline, drugs he'd taken many years before. It was more expansive than that. The words to describe it just didn't exist.

What's going on? he asked.

E only smiled and closed her eyes. Beautiful, isn't it?

Wolf closed his eyes too while the expansion continued – his heart expanding beyond his ribs and his mind beyond his skull and out into the trailer and beyond. But what was most extraordinary about this expansiveness of being was how ordinary it felt. It just was as it was.

How long did he spend like this? Minutes? Hours? How long before the dark smudge appeared in the corner of the trailer and began to grow larger, more threatening, until his perception was dominated by it. Until Wolf's expansion began to collapse, and the evil invaded him from the inside out until he was suffocating, until his mind went blank.

Wolf.

His eyes sprang open. E was calling his name. He was naked, standing on the desolate tract of wasteland outside the trailer. Shivering in the October cold before dawn. Disoriented. Confused.

Wolf. Look at me.

He turned to E who was holding a camera up in front of her face.

And the eye of death blinked and captured him.

Beside me in the truck, Wolf hung his head. I put my hand on his shoulder, moved to embrace him, and in a strangled voice he said, Don't touch me, Theo. Don't.

I flinched & said, Wolf, whatever's happened to you, we'll get through this. We'll figure out a way.

His strange eyes, hard and set with determination, met mine. You don't understand. There's something bad inside me. I can't be near you & the boys until it's gone.

I thought of Larry and Deedee, and realizing I might never see him again, that he might be going away to die, I started to beg.

Please don't go. We'll figure out a way to fix whatever she's done to you . . .

It was then we heard Eddy in the distance, up the trail. Wolf leant across me and opened the passenger-side door.

Get out, he said. Out!

He shoved me. Shoved forcefully again. Shocked by the aggression of it, the disregard for me & our unborn child, I tumbled out. He slammed the door, started the engine and the headlights flashed on, capturing Eddy in their glare. Eddy running toward us in his pajamas, in his bare feet, waving his small hands at the truck.

Dad . . . Wait!

Wolf sharply turned the truck around, veering onto the dry grassy plain as Eddy ran past me, chasing the pickup & yelling at his dad to wait. But Wolf did not wait. The truck rattled & rumbled up the trail to the highway until the headlights disappeared from our sight.

2022

August 17th

I can't stand the smell of palliative care, the medications & disin-
fectants & lingering vomit & that tumorous malodor coming up
through my skin (that Kyla insists I'm imagining). Every morning
after my 7 a.m. pharmacopeia I ask my daughter-in-law to open
the bedroom window <u>wide</u>, then help me to shuffle to the walk-in
shower. I shoo her out, then slowly undress and lower myself, diz-
zied & weak, onto the plastic chair and go through my ablutions.
Kyla's offered her assistance – she worked in a old folks home
when she and Eddy lived in Albuquerque. But I need my privacy,
to keep my 72-year-old body, battle-scarred from all the failed
medical warfare against stage IV cancer, to myself. The shower
chair's where I clean my teeth too. I haven't strength to stand at
the sink, nor can I stomach the bald-head & beak-nose & jaundiced face the cabinet reflects. To whom does it belong? Not me.

After showering, I change into a kaftan (I absolutely <u>refuse</u> to
wear a nightdress in the day) and Kyla helps me shuffle painfully
back to bed. It takes 45 minutes, this ritual, and exhausts me. But
God, anything to make me feel halfway human again.

I also stay on top of the showering out of consideration for our
house guest. Jake's been here for 8 days now, conducting his bedside
interviews & recording my answers into his phone. There's a British
earnestness about him, and an awkwardness too – his discomfort in
the presence of my dying shows. Not that I take offense. It makes
me warm to him even, his transparency a welcome change from
Eddy, whose feelings are anyone's guess.

We usually speak for 2 hours in the morning and 2 hours in the
afternoon, until Kyla bursts in and insists I need to rest & orders

Jake to leave. (Whispers to Jake in the hall: Don't <u>retraumatize</u> her. She's very frail.)

'Retraumatize'. Fucking spare me.

I shouldn't be harsh. Kyla only has my best interests at heart. Has given up months of her life so I can die where I've lived for 42 years and not among strangers in a hospice. When Eddy & Kyla married last year, I admit, I was dubious (the 40-year-old man and his 27-year-old bride). But they're very much in love and Kyla's an angel with a thermometer, an efficient bedside manner & clipboard for recording the dispensing of my meds.

And she's usually right. As soon as Jake's gone, I conk out for 2 or 3 hours straight. Yesterday, I felt so guilty about lacking the stamina for his interviews (he flew all the way from London, after all), I gave him my journals to read. What's in them I only half-remember, but I have no intention of rereading them myself. I can't bear the thought of revisiting all that blazing youth & passion & ambition.

I ought to be more gracious. I ought to look around my bedroom at the photos of my 3 adult sons and 7 grandchildren and feel content. I ought not to dwell on my losses. I may not have become the sculptor I wanted to become, but without turning this into one of those loathsome 'gratitude journals', I've much to be thankful for.

Jake offered me the 'testimonies' he'd written in exchange for my diaries. But I know what E does and how she does it and I don't need anymore horror in my last weeks. It's the same reason I can't look at what Jake and the Hungarian computer whiz have called 'The Dark Web Archive'. The mere name's enough to put icicles in the blood.

Luddite that I am, Jake had to explain to me what the dark web was. An internet beneath the internet where traffic is untraceable and all sorts of illegal activity occurs.

Which I suppose is what the Dark Web Archive is. A record of illegality. 686 scanned photographs Jake suspects span 150 years, ordered in 343 pairs.

On the left, a Venus rise, sometimes obscured by clouds. On the right, a victim, some naked, some clothed, some indoors, some outside. But all with the Tyrant staring out of their eyes.

The photos, left & right, aren't taken at the same time or location. The differing landscapes & meteorological conditions make this clear. So why the pairings? Perhaps the 1st image is when E is called to make an offering (<u>Look to Venus as it rises</u> . . . the Luciferian said) & the 2nd image – the victim – her response to the call. We can only speculate.

Wolf's in the Dark Web Archive. Standing in the desert. Naked, with furred chest and genitals. Long black hair gusted across his face by the wind. (Eddy was fuming when he told me about his father's photograph. Spitting in his rage.)

I am in there too. Or at least my photograph clipped from the April '85 issue of Artforum magazine. Me in my sculptor's studio, with my circular drill and long white hair. The only image not paired with a Venus rise. The only image that Jake was able to reverse-image search on the 'surface web', which was how he tracked me down and got talking to Eddy (who not only invited him to stay, but offered to pay 1/2 his flight).

Why did E put me in there? I wonder. Out of sentimentality? Nostalgia? Or am I just another scalp?

One night when they thought I was sleeping, I heard Eddy and Jake trading theories about the Dark Web Archive at the kitchen table. Was it an aide memoire? Because when you've lived for 300 years, you start to forget? Or is she involved in some underground ring of Luciferians? <u>Dear God</u>, were there more of her out there, and this was how they exhibit their human sacrifices to one another?

But I personally think the reason for E's Archive is simpler than that. That it's the same reason she wanted me to carve that granite statue of her. Because whatever else she might be, she's human and craves a record of herself. To leave some monument behind.

Jake's been attempting to catalog the Archive, working systematically through each photograph, and noting down clues to the identity of the victim, as well as the year and location in the world. Over dinner on the evening of Jake's arrival, I suggested they take the catalog to the police, tell them about Wolf.

Eddy flashed impatience at me. Sure. They'll reopen the file of a

Navajo man who went missing 34 years ago. The FBI and Interpol'll coordinate some international effort to track this voodoo lady down.

Ed, Kyla said in a warning tone.

Sorry, Theo, he said.

But I can see his point & understand his anger. My stepson wants revenge.

What could Eddy have become if Wolf had been around? Perhaps he would've been happier & more open as a child, instead of retreating behind a wall where no one – not me, not his brothers – could reach him. Perhaps he would've got on better at school instead of the constant detentions for fighting & absences from class. Perhaps Wolf could have persuaded Eddy not to drop out at 17, and he would have gone to college instead of becoming a long-distance truck driver – a job suited to his solitary nature, giving him reason to be always on the move, driving 1000s of miles across America, outrunning all emotions but anger, and all relationships & love & anything that could be taken from him . . .

(Praise be, Kyla came along.)

Another question that keeps me awake at night: To what extent does Eddy blame me for what happened to Wolf? For leading Eva to our door? I don't know, though sometimes I blame myself.

And now he and Jake are in my adobe studio 'til the small hours, monitoring the Archive, searching for a route back to that woman. As they plot & hatch their plans, I cannot help but blame myself for that too, because I know nothing good will come of it.

August 18th

Jake's flight to Heathrow leaves from Albuquerque Sunport at 14:00 hours. But I know he won't be on it. I may be dying and stoned out of my gourd with opioids and marijuana gummies, but I'm no fool.

He came early this morning to say goodbye. In the bedside chair, he thanked me for my generosity in letting him stay & interview me in spite of my 'ill health' & for my private journals and so on. What an earnest and respectful man he was, speaking of 'insight into what happened to Lena' and 'closure'. But I wasn't deceived, not least by this 'closure' BS. I could see the nervous twitch & the guilt in his eyes. I could see in him, as in Eddy, the thirst for revenge.

Against my pillows, I opened up my arms for a farewell hug. We embraced and he kissed my cheek and as he pulled away, I grabbed both his hands and looked him fiercely in the eye. I may be weak, but the old Bostonian blue-blood still flows imperiously through my veins.

Make a dying woman a promise, Jake, I said. Promise me this ends here. No more 'testimonies'. No more dark web. I've grown fond of you. I don't want to see you dead.

Jake swallowed. Unlike Eddy, he's not much of a liar. I squeezed his hands with all my strength.

Do you promise?

I promise, Theo.

Eddy was in the doorway. He's the same age now as Wolf when he disappeared and looks so much like his father it quails the heart. Same build, same long thick black hair and crooked teeth (oh I fought with Eddy as a teenager, but he <u>refused</u> to see an orthodontist and 'fix' what he'd inherited from his dad).

You too, Eddy. You <u>promise</u> your stepmother.

Sure, Theo.

Then he jerked his chin at the Brit.

C'mon, Jake. You don't want to miss your flight.

And what I would've given, watching them leave, for just 10 minutes back in my old body. To be able to leap up & run after them & make them both stay.

Because not only does the Tyrant see them coming. The Tyrant's luring them to meet their ends.

Farmington, New Mexico

The night before I was due to fly back to London, Zóltan informed us another photograph – no. 688 – had been uploaded to the Dark Web Archive. Another Venus rise in a photo that was mostly early morning sky and flat barren landscape reminiscent of the South West. Scenery that gave Eddy, a long-distance truck driver of twenty-two years, déjà vu. Far in the background was a road sign, too blurry to make out. Zóltan got to work, and in three hours had geolocated it.

The sign, for Highway 371, was in Farmington in San Juan County. A small town with a population of forty-seven thousand in the north-west of New Mexico. A hundred and fifty miles from Theo's home.

That she would be in the same state as those who are tracking her is a staggering coincidence. But I've come so far. I couldn't not go and find out.

We checked into a motel when we got to Farmington and Eddy opened Google Maps on his laptop on one of the twin beds. An avenue running north to south divides the town in half and Eddy suggested we split up – one taking the east, the other the west – and systematically walk every street and search every restaurant and diner and shop and hotel we pass. When we'd completed searching our half of the town, we'd reverse our steps back to the very beginning, searching all over again.

For two days, in a baseball cap and sunglasses, I walked the streets of the west of Farmington under the hot August sun. Broadway and Apache Street and Main Street and Butler Avenue, all the way up to Pinon Hills Boulevard in the north. The streets were wide and mostly pedestrianless, the citizens of Farmington preferring to shuttle about in the air-conditioned convenience of their cars, and as I searched every church and pizzeria and civic centre and residential street, I half-hoped not to find her. That she was only passing through Farmington when she photographed Venus's ascent. That she was miles and miles away.

But today, late afternoon, Eddy called.

Fuck. I saw her. In TJ's Downtown Diner with a teenage girl. I hung around down the street and followed her when they left. They drove to Aztec, to a trailer park. I parked round the corner. She drove out on her own again after ten minutes.

She didn't know you were following her?

I don't think so. I kept way, way back. Listen, Jake. The girl was in some kind of housekeeping uniform. I think she works in her hotel and she's the next offering.

Do you know where she lives?

Not exactly. But we can figure it out.

It was the fifteenth trailer we knocked on and as soon as the curly-haired girl answered the door we knew we could drop our Mormon double-act (it had been Eddy's idea: 'You're the Mormonest-looking motherfucker there is'). The girl was alarmingly young – seventeen at the most. She'd changed out of the housekeeping uniform into a white *Friends* T-shirt and blue drawstring sweat shorts and held a glazed ring doughnut in her hand. She stared at us both with the widest, most ingénue grey eyes as Eddy cleared his throat.

We've come to speak to you about the woman you were with earlier.

Therese?

Eddy and I exchanged looks.

Yes.

She was home alone ('my sister's on a Hinge date') but invited us into her tiny two-room trailer and gestured to the sofa where Eddy and I sat after moving some blankets and heaped laundry aside. The girl – 'Rosy-Lee, but call me Rosa' – perched on the coffee table, put her half-eaten doughnut back in a crumpled Dunkin' Donuts bag and turned off the TikTok of a girl clamping her eyelashes with metal curlers playing on her cracked iPhone. She offered us some of the Lay's potato chips and Mountain Dew out on the table (we declined) and something about her ease and openness in inviting two strange men into her home struck me as off. It reminded me of a radio show I'd listened to once about a woman who was biologically incapable of fear, and all the dangerous situations she'd cheerfully waltzed into in her life.

We introduced ourselves, using fake names, then Eddy asked if she had plans to meet up with 'Therese' again. Rosa said they'd planned a trip to the Bisti Wilderness the next afternoon. Therese had offered to be her videographer, helping to make content for her TikTok and YouTube channels, and then they were going to camp overnight. Though she'd only known her a few hours, Rosa said they'd 'connected . . . like, on a spiritual level'.

Why d'you want to talk to me about her?

We've come to make you an offer, Eddy said. Money in exchange for you doing something for us. The morning after the camping trip, when you get back to the parking lot, we want you to ditch Therese and run over to our truck. See that Ford pickup parked outside? Jump in and drive away with us from the badlands.

Eddy left out the part about hiding out overnight – in a motel or on the road – until Venus rise the following morning. I suppose he was planning to break that to her in the truck, when she was too messed up and scared of 'Therese' to not go along with it.

Rosa laughed. *Why?*

It's to pay her back for something she did to my sister, Eddy said. She had an affair with her wife, who left her and their kid. Our plan's to mess with her car so she's stranded out there for a few hours. Therese hates to be alone.

Eddy had come up with this motive on the drive to Aztec. I thought he sounded convincing enough, but would she buy it? Apparently not. Rosa laughed again.

Are you guys for real? You expect me to believe that?

I waited for her to ask what the actual reason was. But instead she asked, So how much?

A grand, Eddy said.

Rosa put on an offended look. Really? That's all? Only a thousand dollars to ditch my new friend – who's only been nice to me – and run away with you guys? What if you're, like, *rapists*?

A grand and a half, Eddy said. And we're not rapists.

Rosa eyed us with the gleam of a hustler. I'm gonna lose all that content Therese's helping me make to launch my career. If I'm starting over on my own without her, I'll need a laptop and camera equipment. And my own place – you ever seen an influencer in a shithole like this?

Rosa gestured around the trailer – at the tobacco-stained particle-board and the battered second-hand furniture.

I need a place to shoot videos – a studio apartment with white walls, wooden floorboards and lots of green plants in pots . . . y'know, like peace lilies and palms. I'll need a security deposit, plus six months' rent up-front. I'll need, like . . .

She screwed up her brow in her mental arithmetic.

Six thousand. That's what I need to do your crazy-assed plan.

Three thousand, Eddy countered. That's the highest I can go.

Rosa's curls trembled as she shook her head. She retrieved her glazed doughnut from the crumpled Dunkin' Donuts bag. Took a large bite out of it and chewed. Deadpan. Unimpressed.

Five thousand, I said. Half now, half after.

Despite her attempt to look bored, Rosa couldn't suppress her delight. Three now, she said. Two after.

Deal, I said.

Rosa put her doughnut on her knees. Licked the glaze and sprinkles off her fingers one by one, before reaching for a handshake.

As we shook, I said, But we need you to promise you won't back out.

I promise, she said.

Resisting the urge to wipe my sticky hand on my jeans, I remarked, You seem so . . . *unfazed* by this.

Oh, I was thinking how I could really use five grand earlier. So I manifested you both.

Manifested?

Rosa smiled and pointed upwards.

Ask the universe and the universe will give. The Law of Attraction's totally changed my life.

It's now two a.m. in our motel room. Eddy's sleeping in the other twin bed as I sit and type up the day on my lap. The guilt started as soon as we drove away from Aztec, after the hour we spent in Rosa's trailer. Instead of talking her through what to do in the Bisti parking lot, we should have warned Rosa of how dangerous 'Therese' is. We should have given her that money so she could get as far away from Farmington as possible. But instead we're using her as bait.

Back in the pickup, Eddy read my silence for what it was. So the kid's gonna be messed up for a while.

Messed up for a while? Eddy, she's going to look in the mirror and not recognize herself. Her insides are going to be *permanently reversed* . . .

But she'll live. She's not gonna be tortured to death like Lena or my *dad*.

Eddy's voice cracked in his anger. Don't tell me you came all this way to let her escape. Think of what that Hungarian woman said. We destroy the photo, fuck up this cunt's offering to the Tyrant or whatever, strand her in the desert, and it'll be too late for her to make another. She'll die. And all the murdering will end. Think of how many lives will be saved.

I thought of the Dark Web Archive. Of Hiroji and Ceridwen and Ursula and Klára and Larry and Deedee and Wolf.

I thought of Lena.

Lena aged eleven, Blu-tacking posters of New Kids on the Block to the wall. Lena at sixteen, in the pub in a vintage dress and DMs, laughing with lipstick on her teeth. Lena at twenty, posing drunkenly in front of the drawings she was proudest of at her first group show. Lena aged thirty, hungover and remorseful, swearing to quit drinking as we walked along Regent's Canal.

If she hadn't met 'Marion' she would've stayed sober, gone back to making art, perhaps even met someone and started a family. She might've always been medicated, slightly fucked-up. But she would've been living. Alive.

I knew Eddy was right – not that it made it any easier.

Tomorrow we go to the badlands. The day after that, our sabotage. I'm beyond nervous. So much could go wrong. But I owe it to Lena to try.

Taos County, 2022

The red Jeep Cherokee rolls towards the parking lot under a sky battered into haematomas, the clouds swelling up mauve, black, blue. The rain-drenched woman staggers, waving her arms towards the SUV, and the fiftyish driver brakes and jumps out, gaping at the smashed Ford truck: the crumpled hood and windshield shattered opaque; the unconscious man lying by the driver's-side door, bleeding from his temple on to the mudflats. The woman is hysterical, screaming about another truck crashing into them, masked men dragging her husband out and beating him. The SUV driver, a grey-bearded hippy in T-shirt, batik pants and sandals, looks between the wrecked pickup and injured man as though on a bad trip.

Nasal, high-pitched, he says, You called 911?

No signal out here, the woman cries. *Please*, drive my husband to the hospital.

The SUV driver shakes his head. We shouldn't move him until the paramedics get here.

The woman lets out a shrill, panicked cry. *What* paramedics? We have to get him to the ER *now*.

The hippy kneels by the unconscious man, wincing at his wounded temple. He reaches for his wrist, for the weak beating pulse.

I'm trained in first aid. I'm telling you, move someone with a head injury, it could kill them.

And I'm telling *you*, there's no reception out here. If he dies, it's *your fault*.

The Jeep Cherokee driver glances again at this woman, suddenly noticing her hideously ill appearance. Something doesn't add up. The pickup doesn't look like it's been front-ended by another truck, but as though it rammed into a utility pole at eighty miles an hour. The rain's slowed to a drizzle but the wind's gained strength around them, whistling through the jagged crash wreckage as the unconscious man's hair and clothes remain slicked against him with rain and blood.

The hippy takes an iPhone out of his pants pocket. Let me try. Look, I've got bars.

He unlocks the phone to dial 911 and the woman removes the crowbar tucked in the back waistband of her shorts and raises it over her head with both hands. The hippy looks up in time to see the blood-stained iron bar coming down with all the woman's strength, and his astonishment before it knocks him out is almost comical. He slumps to the ground next to Jake.

Hello? What's your emergency?

You wouldn't believe me if I told you, the woman thinks as she hangs up his phone. Feverish and bone-tired, she could do without a second unconscious body to drag out of sight, but what fucking choice did she have? She kneels and reaches into the SUV driver's pocket for his wallet. The driver's licence belongs to Joel Matheson. A senior software engineer, his business card informs her, at a Denver investment bank. So the hippy works for The Man, which explains the thirty-thousand-dollar SUV. In his other pocket she finds the car keys on a Buddhist keyring: a Hamsa Palm with a third eye that saw none of this coming for Joel.

Ten minutes later she starts the ignition of the Jeep Cherokee and a strange moaning fills the car. On the passenger seat, next to the CD case for *Song of the Humpback Whale: Volume 5*, is a large vacuum flask. She unscrews the lid and swigs, expecting coffee, but grimaces. Kombucha. She opens the glove compartment and rifles through the clutter. CDs of Tibetan monk chanting and The Grateful Dead. Peanut M&Ms. Desiccated mushrooms in a Ziploc bag. No Tylenol or first-aid kit or liquor. She slams it shut.

There's a steady drumbeat of pain in her temples as she drives down the bumpy gravel road to the highway. As she grips the steering wheel, she can feel her fingernails detaching from their nail beds, taste the bleeding gums and suppurating ulcers in her mouth. The feverish ache has sunk deep into her viscera and exhaustion tempts her to park the SUV somewhere and lie down in the back seat – just for half an hour or so. But she looks in the rear-view, fixes herself in her bloodshot eyes. *Lie down and you won't get back up*, she hisses. She twists the air conditioner to the lowest setting, hoping the icy blast will keep her alert enough to catch them up.

But catch them up where? She'd used Jake's fingerprint earlier to access his Android and Gmail account and saw he'd been billed $207 by the Best Western Hi-Desert Inn in Tonopah, Nevada – pre-payment for a room for three nights from tonight. Should she go? Does she have any other choice?

The whales drone lugubriously on. Pink chakra crystals and a silver pendant of St Christopher sway from the rear-view as she approaches the highway east of Navajo land. Her nerves are frayed and the stabbing pain's returned to her guts. Her bowels heave and she clenches, loath to start dribbling her own putrefaction on to the seat. The Tyrant's bearing down on her too, menacing the edges of her perception for letting the one he's staked his claim on be stolen away. For now she shuts him out.

Tonopah's an eleven- or twelve-hour drive. West on to the I-40 through Arizona's deserts of red rock and saguaro, then north-west into Nevada and through Las Vegas to the Great Basin Desert. It's a risk. What if the Sculptor's stepson knows she'll look in Jake's phone? And takes Rosa to another state entirely? What if the reservation itself's a trick? What if she drives seven hundred miles into the Nevada desert only to meet with her own end?

Humpback whales lament in the ocean depths and she's seized by a hacking cough. Despairing, she wipes the blood and mucus splattered in her palm into Joel's upholstery, and the obvious occurs to her. Suddenly there's a chink of light in the darkness of her predicament. For the first time since the Sculptor's stepson drove Rosa away, there's hope.

Half an hour later, when she reaches the interstate, she doesn't turn west towards Arizona, but east to Albuquerque instead.

*

Two p.m. in a truck stop outside Las Cruces, Eddy brakes in an empty parking spot. The rental car came with a full tank of gas and he's too wired for hunger or thirst, but figures they should eat and it's OK to stop for ten minutes. He looks at Rosa who's barely spoken since they left the Bisti Wilderness. Only stumbled along with him like a sleepwalker as they abandoned the Toyota in a Walmart parking lot (taking the woman's backpack and digital camera out first), then picked up the economy Mitsubishi from Enterprise. On the interstate she's stared out the window for hours – at the empty Chihuahuan Desert and distant mesas under the glowering New Mexico skies. Or stared in the side-view mirror – frowning at her reflection like someone she bumped into once, someone she can't quite place. On her left wrist is the handcuff the woman attached to her, the dangling chain and second broken cuff on her lap. Eddy had used a screwdriver to free her from the Toyota's headrest. A method of brute force too dangerous to use with the cuff on Rosa's wrist. Later, he'll attempt to pick it or buy some bolt-cutters. Until then she can wear his jacket outside the car, hide her right hand and the cuffs in the pocket.

You hungry? he asks Rosa. Need the bathroom or anything?

Her gaze doesn't shift from the car parked in front of them (Texas plate, bumper decal: *I lubricate my guns with liberal tears*).

That crash . . . Rosa says. It hit . . . nothing?

I don't know.

Is he dead?

I'm sure he's OK, Eddy says. The truck has an airbag . . .

But he's called Jake about twenty times, and he hasn't picked up. He knows even if Jake survived the crash, he won't have survived her.

I want to go home.

Rosa's voice is whiny, like the child that she is, and Eddy pushes back his guilt.

We need to lay low tonight to make sure you're safe. Maybe in Mexico, maybe Texas. We can decide when we get to El Paso, which'll be soon.

Rosa turns towards the driver's seat, looks Eddy straight in the eyes. She's coming back to herself now, returning from her dissociative state.

You lied to me, she says. You didn't tell me Therese was going to . . . to . . .

But she can't remember what happened in the badlands – what to accuse Therese of. The metal of the handcuff clinks as she palms the tears running down her cheeks.

Do I look different to you? Like, from yesterday?

No, Eddy said. You had a rough night last night. That's all.

Something else was out there . . . in the desert. Some . . . I don't know what. But *you* do.

In his pocket his cell starts to buzz and vibrate. He takes it out and he and Rosa see the caller ID: Jake. Firecrackers going off in his chest, Eddy answers.

Jake?

Silence. A low static fuzz. Then her voice – quiet, barely audible.

Eddy. Is Rosa with you? Answer only yes or no.

The seven-year-old inside Eddy shrinks against the driver's seat. The skinwalker knows his name. He wants to hang up, but thinks of Jake and forces himself to comply.

Yes.

Are you in the car?

Yes.

Tell her the signal's bad. You have to step out.

And Eddy says, *Jake*, I can't hear you. You're breaking up. Lemme try and find a better signal.

He glances at Rosa. I won't be long.

He jumps out, slams the driver's-side door. Turns his back on the car and the skinwalker says, I'm calling to offer you an exchange . . .

Eddy knows he's trapped. That the voice messages he left Kyla after abandoning Jake didn't get through. He can't breathe, his lungs ripped out of his chest. Yet when he turns to Rosa, watching him through the windshield, he manages to speak in a loud, bright voice.

We're in Las Cruces. I'll come up the I-25. Four, five hours tops.

He turns away again. *Don't hurt them*, he's about to whisper, but the line goes dead.

On the interstate vehicles speed north and south. Eddy sees

drainage ditches, warehouses and the desert plains beyond, studded with saguaro and stretching to low plateaus. He takes a deep breath. Then another. He gets back into the driver's seat and turns to Rosa.

Jake says he's OK. But Therese . . . died.

Fuck, Rosa gasps. How?

She collapsed after we left. Jake called an ambulance and they were both taken to the hospital. He's OK – he just has a concussion. But Therese had pneumonia and didn't make it.

Eddy's usually a confident liar, could pass any lie detector test. But the stakes are so high this time he's sure Rosa can detect the desperation beneath his calm.

You sure Therese's dead? I don't know. She's not like us somehow.

Jake was there. They put her on a ventilator, but the pneumonia congested her lungs or something. Anyway, this means we don't have to hide out any more.

We can go home?

Sure. Jake's got your two thousand dollars. He's at my stepmom's house, on the way to Aztec. We can stop there and get your money. And you can keep her digital camera and the content you made too. Win win.

But the girl has no lottery winner's demeanour. She's mistrustful. Scared. But doesn't protest as Eddy starts the rental car and prepares to drive as fast as he can back upstate.

*

It's horrifying how you haven't aged, the Sculptor remarks.

Her bony legs are stretched out on the adobe studio's pull-down Murphy bed and she shivers in her kaftan, despite the ninety-degree heat. The woman's in a wooden chair opposite her, the loaded shotgun – the same Remington Theo'd used to kill rabbits back in '82 – crowbarred out of the bedroom cabinet and resting diagonally on her lap.

Decrepit old age is more horrifying, the woman says. If you ask me.

Yet she stares at her former lover – bald, emaciated, the

seventy-two-year-old body under her kaftan now arousing the opposite of lust – and there's still a yearning, a nostalgic ache. Though that could just be the Zomorph from the Sculptor's medical supplies kicking in.

But you're dying, aren't you, Eva? Just like I am. I can smell it.

The woman says, You shouldn't antagonize me. Not when I have this gun.

You'd be doing me a favour, the Sculptor replies. I have terminal cancer.

The woman points the muzzle of the shotgun at Kyla, lying bound and gagged in the corner of the studio. Her back turned against them, tense with listening.

This one doesn't, she says.

The Sculptor heeds the warning, holds her tongue. The sun's descending and the light coming through the studio's vast skylight is becoming deeper, more coppery, gleaming from the mosaic tiles on Theo's pottery-firing kiln and the metal edges of the sculpting tools which hang on the walls. In the tides of her blood, the woman can sense Venus in the descendent too – due to set at 18:57, Mountain Standard Time. Just before Eddy should reach the end of his three-hundred-mile journey back, delivering Rosa to see the Polaroid.

The Sculptor breaks the silence between them. There's something I've always wanted to know, Eva.

Yes?

What did you do with the statue? When I came back from Larry's funeral, it was gone. Where is it?

The chasm, the woman says. Where all your failures end up.

Her bitterness takes them both aback.

No, Theo says. You've put it somewhere.

The woman half-smiles. What does it matter? I paid you, right?

It was never about the money, Theo says. You know that.

They regard each other across the studio and the woman remembers how after they'd said goodbye at the airport, she'd spent months – years – with a rupture in her. But that was four decades ago and now she's astonished that she ever doubted her path. The

Sculptor's imminent death only makes her more determined to avoid the same fate.

I saw your archive on the dark web, Theo says.

The woman starts. How did they find the URL? When did she fuck up? At least now she knows how they tracked her down in Farmington. Serves her right for, out of some vain compulsion, cataloguing her work. As soon as she can, she'll take the site down.

Has it been worth it? the Sculptor continues. All those lives in exchange for your own?

The woman doesn't need to think about her response. Yes. Whatever it takes to stay alive.

But you're *not* alive, the Sculptor says. That's the truth of it.

The woman sighs, points the Remington at Kyla. You know I won't hesitate to blow off her foot.

Kyla squirms in her bondage, bends her knees to chest.

But whilst we're on the subject of truth, the woman continues, has it been worth it for *you*, Theodora? Sacrificing your sculpting for your sons? You were once so set on artistic greatness. But now all I see are plant pots and tableware. Bourgeoisie crap.

The woman gestures with the shotgun muzzle at the heavy industrial shelving units, stacked with glazed ceramic plates and bowls that Theo has made over the years. The Sculptor lifts her chin, indignant.

You took away my husband. I had three fatherless boys to raise on my own. I had to be practical.

I had sons too, but I chose my freedom. What stopped you from doing the same?

The Sculptor laughs. *My God*, what stopped me from abandoning my children? Love. Conscience. Humanity. The list is endless.

Is cowardice on there?

The woman rises from the chair, walks over to the block of granite Theo had been working on: a column in the first stages of carving, with angular sections hacked out.

You left it late to start sculpting again. It must be frustrating knowing you'll never finish it.

Theo shrugs. No, actually. I don't care.

I don't believe you.

The woman turns to Theo's industrial workbench. Lowers the shotgun and picks up the circular saw with the diamond-edged blade – the one she'd bought Theo at the Albuquerque stone yard back in '82. The one Theo had posed with for Artforum magazine.

Sculpting was your calling. You loved it more than anything.

I found other things to love.

The woman turns on the rotary saw and Theo shrinks back on the Murphy bed as the gasoline motor rumbles and the blade spins at four thousand sharp, serrated rpms. When the forty-year-old motor sputters and cuts out, Theo is visibly relieved. The woman puts it back on the bench.

I came here that night in '88, the woman says, because I'd had enough and just wanted a quiet place to die. To be with someone at the end.

I don't believe you ever wanted to die.

I did. For the reason I told you then. But you sent me away.

So you just changed your mind?

Anger's . . . *invigorating*. It can give someone who wants to die something to live for again.

The Sculptor can't conceal her disgust. You died long ago, Eva. And for all your talk about freedom . . . well, you're nothing but a slave. All your choices in '88: wanting to defy the Tyrant and die, then wanting to live and take my husband in revenge. None of that was you. Don't you think it a coincidence that the Tyrant wanted Wolf that night? Ever crossed your mind that the only reason you came here was because Wolf had *already been chosen*?

The shotgun blasts, a glazed vase on the shelf behind the daughter-in-law exploding into fragments which tinkle on to the cement floor. Kyla screams into her gag and twists in her corner. Theo jolts in shock, before her relief that the bullet missed.

Last warning, the woman says. I don't want to hear another word.

They are both silent. The Sculptor hating her from her bed. A hatred the woman, back in the wooden chair, doesn't reciprocate; it's beneath her, a waste of psychic energy. She's only impatient. She can sense the boundaries of reality buckling and contorting around the dark matter gathering in the studio, seeping in through the tiny spatial tears as they expand into the aperture between worlds. Through the Tyrant she feels the girl coming up the highway, nearer with every beat of her right-sided heart. In one hour it will be time to show Rosa the photograph, and then the woman will be free from the ignominy of her decay.

18:57. Venus exits a Taos County sky of low stratas of clouds glowing orange and blushed pink as the sun continues its descent. A quarter of an hour later there's a car engine and tyres rolling into the clearing outside. Screeching brakes and the slam of two doors.

The woman jerks the gun at Kyla and speaks to the Sculptor. Not one word.

Footsteps. A jiggle of the door handle. The woman opens the door, points the shotgun at Rosa, who lets out a cry of disbelief, spins around in her crumpled blue sundress and runs smack into Eddy, who wrestles her by the arms and drags her into the studio. The woman relocks the door behind them, pockets the key, then she steps towards them both, shotgun aimed between Theo's stepson's eyes. Struggling against Eddy, Rosa yells, You said she was *dead*!

Seeing Kyla lying by the far wall of the studio, Eddy lets go of Rosa, who stumbles to the side, the metal handcuff dangling from her left wrist.

She OK? Eddy calls to Theo in her bed.

I think so, the Sculptor replies.

Eddy moves to go to his wife, but the woman jabs the Remington at him. Stay there.

Rosa's gaze darts wildly between the four people in the studio. What the fuck's going on?

The Tyrant's gathering around Rosa, moving through her limp curls, winding around her throat and agitating the molecules surrounding her until they vibrate at insurrectionary frequencies. The woman lowers the hunting gun, removes the Polaroid from the back pocket of her shorts.

I want to show you this.

She holds the photograph up. Just one glance. Then you're free to go.

Why? What's going to happen to me?

Nothing.

Why would he drive me five hours for *nothing*?

Come here, Rosa.

No. That thing from the Bisti's here.

The woman aims the Remington again at the girl. That wasn't a request.

Rosa drops to the floor, crosses her legs in her blue sundress. Loose handcuffs jangling, she presses fingers over her ears. Squeezes her eyes shut tight.

I am not a victim. The universe will protect me and I will overcome this situation. I am not a victim. The universe will protect me and I will over-come this situation . . .

The woman sighs. Swivels the gun over to Kyla in the corner.

Eddy, she says.

He goes reluctantly to Rosa. Hoists her by her armpits from behind and drags her nearer to the woman as the girl continues to chant, fingers clamped to ears, her sneaker toes dragging on the floor.

I am not a victim. The universe will protect me and I will overcome this situation. I am not a victim. The universe will protect me and I will over-come this situation . . .

Eddy lets her go and she sinks back into her sit-down protest. The woman watches Rosa's lips move as she chants her mantra over and over, and she's almost impressed by the girl's blind faith – by her astounding stupidity.

Eddy, the woman says again. Hold Rosa's head still for me.

Don't.

The woman turns. The Sculptor's out of bed and by the work-bench, her weakened arms struggling with the circular saw which rattles as she turns it on and steps towards them. But as the woman aims her shotgun at her, the whirring of the motor stutters then stops. The Sculptor turns the switch on and off, on and off, but the

280

serrated blade doesn't restart. Shotgun still raised, the woman says impatiently, Get back in b—

As she speaks, Eddy lunges sideways, grabs the gun's long barrel and the woman pulls the trigger, shattering the skylight which rains down broken glass. Eddy wrestles the gun from her, but doesn't get to use it because the Tyrant snaps his neck in the same instant the Sculptor comes straight at the woman's head with the saw, the motor roaring back to life. The woman instinctively raises her hands to shield herself and all is lost in a red splattering blur as the Tyrant – surging over from Eddy – slams the spinning diamond-edged blade back into Theo's throat in a spray of arterial blood. The Sculptor falls, near-decapitated, the saw rattling beside her at several thousand rpm. The woman stares grimly at Theo's slashed wide throat, the blood soaking the scattered fragments of skylight glass around her on the cement floor. And as though it knows its job is done, the rotary saw cuts out.

By the wall, Kyla's screaming and screaming into her gag, twisting against the ropes binding her ankles and wrists.

Shut up, the woman says. Unless you want to end up like your husband.

The screaming stops and in the silence the woman hears a strange *pitter patter pitter patter* beside her. Blood is dripping from stumps where fingers are missing from her hand. The woman gasps – more in shock than pain, which the Zomorph has dulled – and drops to her knees, staring at the mutilated fingers in disbelief. Fore, middle and ring – missing near the knuckle. The right hand – *fuck*. Where are they? She crawls about on the floor and, instead of amputated fingers of flesh and bone, she finds shrivelled-up, tannin-coloured things. Embalmed digits snapped off a mummified cadaver in a glass museum case, which she can't bring herself to touch. But she hasn't time for fury or remorse. She has other concerns.

Rosa's in the corner of the studio, wedged in the gap between the wall and one of the high industrial shelving units. Knees hugged to her chest. Curly head buried in knees. Her mantra to the universe has stopped. Perhaps she's realized the universe isn't coming to rescue her anytime soon. Maimed hand wrapped in a dusty cloth, the woman goes over. Kneels in front of the girl. Though the stumps are hurting now, and her rage at Rosa close to murderous, the woman struggles to keep her voice steady as she solicitously asks, Rosa. Are you OK?

Hugging her knees tighter, the girl inches back against the wall. The woman gently says, I know, I know . . . it's been a rough day . . . But don't worry. It's nearly over. All you have to do is open your eyes.

The woman softly touches Rosa's cheek with her uninjured left hand. Lifts her chin with a finger, raising Rosa's head a little.

You wouldn't want anyone else to die, would you?

Tears leak out of the girl's screwed-tight eyes.

Not Eddy's wife over there? Not yourself?

Rosa sniffs. Tears drip from her chin as she shakes her head. Whispers, No.

Please don't cry, the woman says. You're going to be OK. Open your eyes. Look.

Left-handed, she takes the Polaroid out of her pocket. Holds it up to Rosa.

See?

Rosa opens her eyes and sees the Tyrant staring out of the photograph at her, out of the black centres of her own smoke-grey eyes. *No*, she says, twisting her head away. But it's too late. The woman drops the Polaroid in relief.

The Sculptor's severed throat has stopped bleeding. The woman stares at the pink flesh, white cartilage and bone, now exposed in cross section. The Sculptor's eyes are open as though she's staring through the gap in the studio roof where the skylight had been, up at the first stars appearing in the dusk. Avoiding the slick red puddle, the woman bends down and touches Theo's cheek with something close to a grudging respect. Since she became what she became the Sculptor's the first person to wound her, emotionally, physically. And the last person – perhaps the *only* person – to have known her in any meaningful way. The woman stays with her for a while, keeping her hand on the Sculptor's cheek as the final warmth departs, though she knows there isn't time.

★

On the highway, driving at eighty mph in Eddy's rental car, bandaged-up hand on the steering wheel, backpack and digital camera on the back seat, the woman runs through all her options. She hasn't slept for over forty hours but can't stop now. She needs to get to another town, another city, dump the car, rent another with a fake ID and then keep on driving. Or dump the car and hide in the wilderness for a few days or weeks. How long before they start looking for her? The woman doubts Rosa's made it back to civilization yet, she was in such a traumatized state. Killing her would've made things easier, but Rosa belongs to the Tyrant now, so the woman pointed the Remington at her and sent her stumbling towards the Sangre de Cristo, in the opposite direction to the highway.

Once the girl was out of sight, the woman opened the trunk of the Jeep Cherokee. In the Bisti parking lot Jake and the hippy had been unconscious but breathing, so she'd struck them each with the tyre iron until they were dead. The corpses, legs bent to fit in the trunk, were stiffened and pale, blood sunk to the lower parts. Jake looked serene. If not for the nasty head wounds, he could've been drowsing and yet to wake. The woman stared at him, this man who'd pursued her halfway around the world, determined to bring her down.

Why? she said. Lena was already dead.

A blowfly landed on Jake's cheek, crawled over his eyelid.

You must've known how it would end.

She heaved both men out of the SUV and dragged them one by one into the Sculptor's studio. She made a pyre of logs and wooden furniture and corpses around the fifteen-gallon propane tanks for Theo's ceramics firing kiln. The explosion happened when she was half a mile down the trail, and as the inferno turned the sky orange in her rear-view the woman lamented the waste. The last thing she had wanted was to leave so many dead. But really, had she any other choice?

Driving into the night, the woman is missing three fingers. She is splattered with Theo's blood and there's glass in her hair. But she's survived. And the more distance she puts between herself and Theo's burning property, the more strength and vitality she feels returning to her.

You died long ago, Eva. And for all your talk about freedom . . . well, you're nothing but a slave.

But the Sculptor's wrong. The woman feels her heart beating powerfully in her chest – beating with its determination to be in the world for as long as it can – and knows she's more alive than anyone. And if she's a slave then she's only swapped the tyranny of other people for another kind of tyranny. She knows which one she prefers.

What it all comes down to is this: in a few weeks the Sculptor's remains will be placed in an urn or interred in the ground. And the woman will live on; thinking, sensing, seeking out and experiencing all the pleasures of the flesh. She will bear witness to all the terrible beauty of the world, and the spectacle of humanity going up in flames. And throughout it all Venus will rise and set, rise and set, spinning slowly backwards in elliptical orbits of the sun.

She will live on.

And on.

Yet, as the woman turns on to a desolate backcountry road heading north-west into Colorado, passing through the empty, empty windswept plains, she doesn't feel victorious. No exultation at all the decades – perhaps even centuries – ahead. Instead, in her headlight beams, the road ahead blurs and her cheeks become wet as she realizes that she's crying for the first time in two hundred and sixty years.

Epilogue

Imagine the carved likeness of a once living woman. Now queen of perpetual darkness in a cave deep under a mountain range once called the House of the Gods.

She reigns over a palace of metamorphosized quartz, over subterranean streams of cavefish, scaleless and pale and spawning in the pitch-black. Over blind salamanders stalking eyeless insects and translucent leaping frogs. Over cyanobacteria. Speleothems. Slowly the teeth of the cave close around her; a grimace of stalactites and stalagmites, caging her in.

During her rule in the interminable dark, cataclysmic events on the surface of the Earth register only as the merest of tremors and quakes. Meteors strike and volcanoes erupt. The magnetic poles flip and reverse. The skies blacken and rain ash for thousands of years and the species of her origins become extinct. Deep in her quartzite labyrinth of caves she encounters none of the new creatures that evolve to roam the Earth in their place.

How long does her reign last? A hundred million years? Two hundred million? Above the House of the Gods her Venusian god shines on. The sun blazes larger and brighter than ever before over land now mostly desert, scuttling with strange new invertebrates.

Near the end our queen's unrecognizable. Stromatoliths have bloomed all over her. Million-year-old mushroom-like growths that make her animate again as they breathe into the dark. She's carbuncled into grotesquery, mineralized into the cave morphology. Instead of degenerating she's continued to grow, which is a deathlessness of sorts.

But mountains don't last forever. As the continents of Earth drift into one landmass again, the caves under the House of the Gods will fissure and crack. The mountains will fall upon the granite queen of the underworld, crushing and entombing her in their collapse.

And somewhere, in the darkness, the Tyrant will be watching still.

Acknowledgements

Thank you to my incredible agent, Emma Paterson, for the incisive feedback that made *Old Soul* a stronger book and for the seemingly boundless guidance and support. My immense gratitude also to Clare Alexander, Lesley Thorne, Monica MacSwan, Lisa Baker, Anna Hall, Laura Otal and everyone at Aitken Alexander Associates.

Thank you to my brilliant editors, Helen Garnons-Williams at Fig Tree and Sally Kim at Putnam, for the enthusiasm, editorial wisdom and advice. Thank you to Daphne Ming Durham for generously stepping in at Putnam to help send *Old Soul* out into the world.

I am indebted to the amazing teams behind *Old Soul* at Fig Tree / Penguin UK: Ella Harold, Anna Ridley, Micheal Bedo, Rosamund Hutchison, Juliet Dudley, Zoe Coxon, Sam Fanaken, Autumn Evans, Ruth Johnstone, Eleanor Rhodes Davies and Elspeth Dougall. And at Putnam / Penguin US: Aranya Jain, Ivan Held, Nicole Biton, Alexis Welby, Ashley McClay and Andy Dudley.

Old Soul was supported by grants from Arts Council England and the Society of Authors, and a Northern Writers Award from New Writing North. Thank you to these organizations for all the amazing work they do in sustaining writers' projects and careers. Many thanks to the Royal Literary Fund, especially Steve Cook and David Swinburne, for the fellowship at Manchester University, the RLF Consultant Fellow role and the countless other ways the RLF has supported me over the years.

Thank you to Sandra Palmer for the wonderful friendship and the place to stay during my first Manchester visits. Thank you to Gladstone's Library for the month-long residency during *Old Soul*'s earliest stages.

Many thanks to friends and colleagues at the Manchester Writing School and the Department of English at Manchester Metropolitan

University. I am very fortunate to have a job that I love and for the generous sabbatical during which I finished the book.

Thank you, as always, to my parents and sister, and to Reuben and Chris. Thank you to John and Jacqueline Brown and Lauren Rich.

Most of all, thank you to Glen James Brown, for the endless conversations about *Old Soul* and your generous notes on draft after draft. Thank you for making the years of working on this book such happy ones. I am extraordinarily lucky to have you in my life.